The Shadow Murders

The Shadow Murders

JUSSI ADLER OLSEN

The Shadow Murders

A DEPARTMENT Q THRILLER

Translated by William Frost

QUERCUS

First published in Danish as *Natrium Chlorid* by Politikens Forlag in 2021
First published in the USA in 2022 by Dutton, Penguin Random House, New York
First published in Great Britain in 2022 by

QUERCUS

Quercus Editions Ltd
Carmelite House
50 Victoria Embankment
London EC4Y 0DZ

An Hachette UK company

A CIP catalogue record for this book is available
from the British Library

HB ISBN 978 1 78648 623 3
TPB ISBN 978 1 78648 624 0

10 9 8 7 6 5 4 3 2 1

Printed and bound in Great Britain by Clays Ltd, Elcograf S.p.A

MIX
Paper from
responsible sources
FSC® C104740

Papers used by Quercus are from well-managed forests and other responsible sources.

Dedicated to Ellie,

our beautiful and intelligent grandchild

PROLOGUE

1982

It only took five minutes after the emergency call before the ambulance turned across the lawn toward a chaotic scene that would forever haunt those who saw it.

Around a steaming hole lay six lifeless bodies, and the rancid smell of burned flesh mingled with the stench of ozone still lingering in the air from the lightning strikes.

"Move back!" shouted one of the paramedics to a group of students who had come running from the university on the other side of the road and who now stood as if nailed to the spot by the sight.

His colleague took him by the arm. "There's nothing we can do here, Martin, but look over there!"

He pointed at an elderly man whose knees were slowly sinking into the soaked grass.

"Why were they standing so close together, and why didn't the lightning strike the trees?" sobbed the man when they approached. And even though it was pouring rain, and the man's jacket clung to him like a wet rag, he cared about nothing except what had just happened.

Martin turned toward the university buildings, where sirens and flashing blue lights signaled that more ambulances and patrol cars were on their way.

"We'll give him something to calm him down before he ends up having a stroke," said his partner.

Martin nodded. Through the downpour, he could just make out two women crouching down by a growing pool of water close to the wind-break.

"Come quickly!" they shouted, and Martin grabbed his bag and started running.

"I think she's breathing," panted one of the women while cradling the back of the neck of a seventh victim.

Apart from the unconscious young woman's heavily blackened clothes, she didn't appear to be seriously burned like the other victims.

"I think she was thrown over here by the lightning strike," said the woman in a faltering voice. "Can't you save her?"

Martin pulled the frail body away from the pool of water, which was still growing deeper, as the shouts rose behind him. His colleagues, who had just arrived, concluded that there was nothing they could do about the others. The lightning had killed all six who had been huddled to-gether in the rain.

Martin put the injured woman in the recovery position and checked her pulse, which was slow and weak but seemed stable. Just as he stood up and gestured to his colleagues to come over with a stretcher, her body twitched. A couple of short, deep inhalations caused her chest to tighten, and with a sudden jerk she rose up to rest on her elbows.

"Where am I?" she asked, looking around with bloodshot eyes.

"You're in Fælledparken in Copenhagen," answered Martin. "You were all struck by lightning."

"Lightning?"

He nodded.

"And the others?" She looked over toward the hectic scene.

"You knew them?" he asked.

She nodded. "Yes, we were together. Are they dead?"

Martin hesitated for a moment, but then confirmed.

"All of them?"

He nodded again and observed her face. He expected to see shock or grief, but her insidious expression told another story.

"Right, then," she said, completely composed. And despite evident pain, a devilish smile spread across her face.

"You know what?" Without waiting for an answer, she continued, "If I can survive this, then with God's help I can survive anything."

1

MAJA

Tuesday, January 26, 1988

Twenty-six days into the new year, a harsh winter unexpectedly hit the country with biting winds and unusually low temperatures below zero. When Maja saw the blanket of ice spreading across the backyard of her residential complex, she sighed deeply. This was the third year in a row she would have to change to winter tires, but, because it was just after Christmas this time, there was no way she could afford to have her usual mechanic change them. Luckily, an auto-repair shop had placed attention-grabbing ads in the local newspaper for a lightning-fast, effective, and super-cheap tire service—and as the shop was even closer to her son's nursery in Sydhavnen, she decided to give them a try.

This was the reality of being a single mother. You had to make money stretch.

The owner of the combined auto-body-finish and repair shop, Ove Wilder's Auto, was masculine and trustworthy, an archetype of the sort of man who has grown up with his strong arms buried deep in a car engine. Maja gave a sigh of relief. Everything would be okay.

"We'll just check that all is in order," he said, and nodded to a couple of mechanics who were pointing a flashlight underneath a car raised on a lift.

"It should be ready in a couple of hours. We're a bit busy, as you can see."

No more than forty-five minutes later, she received a call at work.

That was nice and quick, she thought happily when she heard the voice of the man from the repair shop. But then her smile faded.

"I'm afraid this will be complicated," he said. "We noticed that the rear summer tires are worn unevenly, so we thought something was wrong with the wheel suspension. But the problem is actually with your rear-axle housing, or rear shaft, as some people call it. And that's a whole different story."

Maja clenched the receiver. "Rear shaft? But you can weld it, right?"

He sounded serious. "Let's see, but I'm afraid you shouldn't get your hopes up because it's very corroded. It probably needs to be changed."

Maja took a deep breath. She did not even dare think how expensive that would be.

"I'll pop by after I pick up my son from nursery," she said, and noted how her hand on the desk had started shaking. How was she supposed to pay? And how was she supposed to do without the car if . . . ?

"You'll pop by, you said? Okay, then. We close at five," he replied dryly.

Children in snowsuits are time-consuming, so Maja had her heart in her throat as she finally rushed off with Max in his stroller to the repair shop just after five. She let out a sigh of relief when she saw the open gate at the end of the street and her car protruding slightly from the shop with snow up to the hubcaps.

She had made it. "My car!" said Max. He loved that car.

When they passed the fence, she could see a man's legs sticking out from behind the vehicle.

Strange! Why is he lying on the ground in the snow in this weather? she just managed to think before a blast caused the windows of the building to blow up in a blizzard of glass. A moment later, a second explosion detonated in a wave that ripped the stroller with Max out of her hands and threw her several meters back.

When she finally managed to get to her feet, surrounded by flames and smoke, she saw that the repair shop in front of her had collapsed and that her car was lying upside down a few meters away from her.

With her heart racing, she spun around in all directions.

"Maaax!" she screamed, unable to hear her own voice.

Then there was yet another explosion.

2

MARCUS

Monday, November 30, 2020

Not a pretty sight, thought Chief of Homicide Marcus Jacobsen when he discovered his chief inspector slouched behind his desk with his eyes closed and mouth open.

He gently nudged the feet behind the table.

"I hope I'm not interrupting anything important, Carl," he said with a wry smile.

Carl seemed to be too drowsy to react to irony.

"Well, that's a question of definition, Marcus." He yawned. "I was just testing whether the distance from the edge of the desk to my feet was perfect."

Marcus nodded. The renovation of the basement under police headquarters had forced out his colleagues in Department Q, the cold cases division, and it was no exaggeration to say that he was not pleased to have the country's most anarchistic department moved so close to him out here in the new facility on Teglholmen in Sydhavnen where the Copenhagen Police investigation unit was now located. The combination of Carl Mørck's grumpy face and Rose Knudsen's incessant ranting could drive anyone crazy. He wished that Carl and Co. could be sent back to the dungeon at police HQ, especially during this horrible year of the coronavirus, but Marcus knew that was not going to happen.

"Take a look at this, Carl." He opened a case file and pointed at an obituary ripped from the newspaper. "What do you make of this?"

Carl rubbed his eyes and read.

Maja Petersen,

November 11, 1960–November 11, 2020.

Sadly missed.

The Family

He looked up. "Well, the woman died on her sixtieth birthday but, apart from that, it doesn't mean anything to me. What's the deal?"

Marcus gave him a serious look. "I'll tell you what. It reminds me more than a little of the first time you and I saw each other."

"Really? That's an unfortunate association. The first time, you say? When was that?"

"January 1988. You were a sergeant at Store Kongensgade police station. I was an inspector in homicide."

Carl straightened up a little. "How the hell can you remember that? You didn't even know me in 1988."

"I remember because you and your colleague were the first to arrive at a burning auto-repair shop that had just been blown up, and I remember how you took care of a half-conscious woman whose child had been killed in the explosion."

Marcus's best investigator sat for a moment staring blankly. Then he picked up the newspaper ad and looked it over. Were his eyes welling up? It was hard to believe.

"Maja Petersen," he said slowly. "Is this *the* Maja Petersen?"

Marcus nodded. "Yes, it is. Two weeks ago, Terje Ploug and I were called out to her flat, where she had already been hanging in the hallway for a few days. We didn't have to investigate much to establish that she'd taken her own life. There was a photo of a small boy on the floor underneath her, which she'd probably held in her hand until the moment she died." He shook his head. "In the sitting room, there was a moldy layer cake on the table, completely untouched. Neatly written on top of it with light blue icing was "Maja 60 Max 3." And, slightly oddly, the cake was decorated with two crosses instead of flags and candles. One after each name."

"Okay." Carl put down the obituary and leaned back heavily. "Sounds depressing. Suicide, you say. And you're sure about that?"

"Yes, I am. Her funeral was yesterday, and I attended. And apart from the vicar, myself, and an elderly lady, the chapel was completely empty. It doesn't get much more depressing than that. I spoke with the lady afterward, and she was a cousin of the deceased. She turned out to be the one who had ended the obituary with 'The Family.'"

Carl looked at him pensively. "And back then you were also present at the explosion site, you say? That's one detail I can't remember. I remember the snow and the biting cold and many other things, but not you."

Marcus shrugged. It was more than thirty years ago, so why should he remember?

"The fire was extremely violent and the fire brigade couldn't establish unequivocally how the explosions had happened," said Marcus. "However, it turned out that the repair shop also had a completely unauthorized body-finish shop, so there had been plenty of combustibles in the building, certainly more than enough for things to go wrong. And, yes, I also arrived on the scene shortly after the accident, which was more of a coincidence because I was on an assignment in the neighborhood."

Carl nodded to himself. "I remember that the little boy was dead—I could see that straightaway. His tiny body lay over the curb with his head thrust into the snow. That isn't a sight you forget in a hurry. I had to hold his mother tightly to stop her from getting too close to him and seeing the terrible state he was in."

He looked up. "Why did you go to Maja Petersen's funeral, Marcus?"

"Why?" He sighed. "I've just never been able to let that case go. Even then, I got the sense that something wasn't right about it." He tapped the case file on the desk. "Now I've had a few days to reread and consider it."

"And what's your conclusion? That the explosion wasn't an accident?"

"I guess I never really believed that, but here on page two in the technical summary, I stumbled across a sentence that I didn't notice back then. And maybe there wasn't much reason to notice it more than thirty years ago."

He pulled the paper out of the file and pushed it over to Carl.

"I've highlighted the sentence."

Carl Mørck leaned forward in his office chair. He read the sentence marked with yellow a few times before looking up at Marcus with an expression that made his eyes appear darker.

"Salt?" was all he said, repeating it a few times.

Marcus nodded. "You have the same suspicion as me, I can tell."

"The thing about the salt, yes. But when was that? Give me a hint."

"I don't know exactly which case you had, but there was another one involving salt. You're with me, right?"

"Yes, I think there was."

Carl appeared to be racking his brain, but in vain.

"Maybe Rose or Assad remembers," said Carl finally.

Marcus shook his head. "I don't think so because it must have been before their time. But what about Hardy?"

"Hardy is having treatment again in Switzerland just now, Marcus."

"I know, but you've heard about a smart invention called the phone, right, Carl?"

"Sure, okay, I'll call him." He frowned. "You've had some time to think about it, Marcus. How about letting me in on what happened back then in Sydhavnen?"

He nodded. It would almost be a relief.

Marcus told him that when the second blast sounded, all the windows in the apartment they were searching close to the repair shop imploded so violently that the pieces of glass penetrated deeply into the woodwork and furniture. Thankfully, Marcus and his colleagues were in the bedroom facing the backyard, so nothing happened to them. However, the inhabitant, a miserable junkie who was hiding weapons for some of the hard-core criminals in Vesterbro, broke down completely and started rambling on about back when he was a boy and the gasworks in Valby had exploded.

Marcus tiptoed to the kitchen, out to the Siberian cold coming in from the smashed window, and immediately saw the jet-black clouds of smoke and the flames rising at least twenty-five meters up in the air above the roofs a few streets away.

Two minutes later, Marcus and his sergeant entered the street where a patrol car with flashing lights was already parked, blocking the entrance. Just inside the courtyard sat a young colleague with his arms tightly wrapped around a woman. Everything was utter chaos, and burning wreckage and the asphalt emitted yet more black plumes of smoke. A child on Marcus's left had undoubtedly died on the scene, given that the small body was lying lifeless with his face pressed down into the snow.

Now the flames rose at least forty meters in the air from the middle of the building, and the heat almost knocked them over. A Citroën Dyane had been thrown upside down, wreckage and car parts were scattered in the meltwater that was fast covering most of the area, and a few cars that had been displayed for sale on the left side had been compressed like discarded vehicles in a junkyard.

A van lay crushed underneath the rubble a bit farther along, and from behind it protruded a pair of naked charred legs—the only indication that there had been any life in the building.

It was a few hours before the fire brigade brought the flames under control, but Marcus stayed on-site and followed the discoveries of his colleagues and the fire brigade.

Before midnight, they had found another four bodies farther inside the building, which were so charred that it was almost impossible to determine their sex. And even though all four heads had very similar lesions, they could not immediately establish if they were caused by the violent explosion and subsequent tumult of projectiles from the shelves of metal objects in the shop.

While it was highly probable that they were dealing with an accident, Marcus spent the next few days routinely investigating a number of possible motives someone might have had. They had to reject all suspicions of insurance fraud because the repair shop, in spite of all regulations, had no insurance policies, and on top of that, the owner died in the explosion, so what could he have gained by starting a fire? Any connection to gangs was also unlikely because none of the deceased, who were subsequently identified as mechanics, had criminal records.

With support from the owner's distressed widow, Marcus went over the few available records on the repair shop.

"Did your husband or family have unsettled business with anyone?" he asked. "What about any outstanding debts? Enemies? Had they been threatened by competitors?"

The wife just shook her head every time. She was at a loss. Her husband was a skilled mechanic, she said. He might not have been much for paperwork, but then who was, in that line of employment?

Marcus had to face the fact that this small business certainly lived up to that reputation, having neither an accountant nor a bookkeeper. And everything that resembled correspondence, client records, or financial statements had gone up in smoke—if they had ever existed in the first place.

The woman knew that there would be plenty to do when the tax returns were due, but the repair shop had only existed for a few months, so no doubt it would be fine.

When the site was cleared a few weeks later, they were still clueless. Only one apparently insignificant fact, which an alert technician had nevertheless noted in the report, stuck out from the rest, and Marcus had only just noticed it now, many years after his latest scrutiny of it.

It read:

A few meters outside the entrance gate, right up against the metal railings, there was a nine-centimeter-tall pile of salt.

And then a brief added note that should probably have raised alarm bells:

And it was kitchen salt, not road salt.

3

CARL

Tuesday, December 1, 2020

"**There was a** copy of the case in the archive, Carl." Rose threw it on the desk in front of him. "Gordon and I read it this morning. It says that you were the first to arrive at the scene?"

"Yes, apparently." He nodded and pointed at Marcus's copy. "This report has been gathering dust in Marcus's various offices for all these years. You probably know what that means?"

"Yes, he hasn't been able to let it go," answered Gordon unnecessarily. "And now he wants us to take it off his shoulders."

Carl gave him a thumbs-up. "Spot on. And that's why we're taking over, putting everything else to one side, and solving it. And there you have it."

"Put everything else to one side? Isn't that a bit drastic, Carl?" mumbled Rose. "Don't you think we've got our hands full as it is just now?"

Carl shrugged slightly. She might be right but it was the chief of homicide who called the shots, and the case had also struck a surprisingly sensitive chord in Carl. So many years later, and it was still immensely painful to think about the little boy and his mother, who had lost what she held dearest. He could not shut his eyes and think about the terrible accident for very long before he felt her shivering as vividly as if it were yesterday. Was it because he was now a father himself?

"I suppose you've seen what Marcus has highlighted at the bottom of the fire incident report, so no need to explain the priority of this aspect of the case. And not only for Marcus's sake, but just as much for us and Department Q."

"You mean the kitchen salt?" asked Gordon.

Carl nodded. "Rose, you've been here in Department Q since 2008, so it must ring a bell, doesn't it?"

"The kitchen salt?" She shook her head.

"Well, look into it, because I know for sure there was a case some years back that was shelved that had something to do with salt. Marcus also remembers it. But, as I said, it must have been ages ago because we can't quite remember when. Give the older cases a look, starting with those from 2000 to 2005, and you might hit on something."

"Something about salt?" She didn't look happy.

"Yes."

"Wow, what an amazing task to be given. Thanks a lot, Carl. And now that I think about it, there's actually a huge pile of salt in my cousin's yard. Are you going to arrest him now?"

Carl raised his eyebrows. If she was in that mood, he would just have to put his foot down.

"Thanks for the sarcasm. Just think about what Marcus has done for you, Rose. He's got you back on the job in more or less the same shape you were five years ago—back in the field and everything that goes with it. So don't you think Marcus deserves that you do everything within your power to take this case off his mind?"

She sighed. "You were easier when you were a bitter old asshole instead of a sanctimonious bitter old asshole. But, yes, if you want to torment me by making me review old cases while Assad solves the ones on our desks, I'll oblige."

She turned on her heel before he could retort. Bloody annoying.

He turned to Gordon, who looked like he expected to take the fall for her.

"And *you*, Gordon," he said with an emphasis that made the guy jump, "you'll help me."

Gordon relaxed his shoulders.

"You need to find the widow of the guy who owned the auto-repair shop. And then you need to locate the old woman who attended the funeral the other day—Maja Petersen's cousin. And when you've done that, you'll bring them both to me. Pronto!"

Carl's new office on the first floor was identical to all the others, with standardized, wipeable furniture. He opened the window, placed Marcus's report on the windowsill, and started from the beginning. It took him almost a quarter packet of smokes to read it because it was unusually meticulous, just like all the reports Marcus Jacobsen had written during his time as criminal superintendent. Still, he seemed to have taken even more care with this one, probably because he had nearly been a firsthand witness and because he had never forgotten the despair of the young mother.

On the first page, Marcus had already expressed his dissatisfaction with the then chief of homicide stopping his investigation and having the case recorded as an accident.

The many pages that followed were excerpts of Marcus's interviews with witnesses, but objectively, there was not much meat to any of them—if any at all.

What did you see? and *What do you know?* Marcus always asked the people he interviewed. And for this case: *Do you know about anything that might have led to this violent explosion?* No one gave him any leads. The young woman who had lost her child explained why she had gone to the repair shop. It was something to do with a rear shaft on her Citroën Dyane that needed changing because it was corroded. And every time she came to the point where she had to tell him about the moment of the explosion, when the stroller with her three-year-old son was ripped out of her hands, she broke down.

This was followed by some explanations from the widows of the deceased mechanics, and all in all, there was nothing to indicate that they had been anything other than an industrious and skillful young shop.

They often worked overtime, but the wages were always paid on time, and it was not a bad wage—on the contrary, said one of the wives.

Carl underlined that fact in particular.

"It wasn't difficult to locate the widows, Carl. The one who was married to the owner of the repair shop has remarried and changed her last name, but, thankfully, she's still at the same address."

"When will she be here, Gordon?"

"She's here already. She's waiting in Rose's office."

Carl gave him an approving nod. He would soon have to admit that the youngest member of their department was no longer completely wet behind the ears.

"And the cousin who placed the obituary in the newspaper will be here within the hour. She was a bit nervous and confused about why you want to talk to her, but I told her that you normally don't bite." He grinned.

Normally don't bite? thought Carl. He smiled halfheartedly. Perhaps Gordon was still damp behind the ears after all.

"Send her in."

Carl closed the file so the widow would not see the unsettling photos of the bodies at the scene.

He had no idea what she had looked like thirty years ago, but for a sixty-something-year-old woman she was unusually youthful. *Not much of her face could have been created by God*, he thought when she removed her face mask. She did actually try to smile, but it never quite materialized.

He struggled through the usual questions for the first few minutes, but then he thought, *Nothing ventured, nothing gained*. So he asked a question that did not appear on the report. A shot in the dark.

"Your husband handled a lot of money during that time, but how did you experience it?"

She brushed her hair back behind one ear while a single wrinkle on her forehead tried to make an appearance. "But we did pay all our bills on time, if that's what you mean?"

"No, I'm thinking about all the perks. Car, dishwasher, new clothes, all that kind of stuff."

She looked relieved at the offer of concrete options.

"Well, Ove did buy the holiday home. It's the one I still have in Tisvilde."

Carl whistled. "That must have been the optimal time to buy a holiday home in Tisvilde. You can't get your hands on them for love nor money now."

She held her head high.

"How much did you pay for it? Do you remember? You bought it with cash, right?" he prompted.

She nodded, looking thoughtful. She was an easy one to lead down the path.

"Just over a hundred thousand, I think." She nodded as if to confirm the statement.

"So the repair shop was doing well?"

She nodded. "Ove worked a lot. They all did."

The rest of the interview lasted twenty minutes, and it would probably be the last with her.

"I think they were busier than most repair shops," he said to Rose when the widow had left.

She was not listening. "Do you realize what you've asked me to do, Carl?" Rose had many expressions, and the one she was wearing right now was not to his liking. And *she* was talking about grumpy assholes?

"The cases from 2000 to 2005 haven't been digitized yet, so I'm leafing through report after report. Don't think that you can get out of paying me overtime if you want me to do this quickly."

"Just let me know how many hours you spend and continue with your exquisite work."

Did she stick her tongue out at him?

4

CARL

Carl opened the file and scrutinized the many photos of the bodies from the repair shop. Neither the investigations from the site nor the findings from the autopsies made him any the wiser. The coroner who had carried out the autopsies wrote about one of the bodies:

> Since the deceased was found under a steel table and therefore had not suffered serious injury apart from the one to the back of the head, it can be concluded that the object that hit his head also killed him. Subsequently, this object most probably fell to the ground intact, given that we did not find fragments of it in the skull, which was also the case with two of the other bodies. It is conspicuous that in three of the cases, the lesions are almost identical and have only injured the back of the head, which may indicate that the explosion took place at a certain height and that all three victims were standing close to it with their backs turned.

Carl read the intricate explanation several times while studying the photographs. The last two bodies also had head wounds, but they were located closer to the temple, and, apart from these, there were numerous other lesions on their bodies. One of the victims even had so many pieces of metal lodged in his body that it resembled a nail board.

He leafed ahead to the photos of the excavation from which the victims had been recovered. That could not have been a pleasant task.

Just as he reached the photo documentation of the state of the repair shop courtyard, he heard footsteps in the hallway, so he closed the file and waited.

It was the cousin of the deceased woman, Maja, who had arrived, and she was clearly very affected by the situation.

"Oh, it's so horrid that Maja took her own life on her birthday. She'd actually invited me, but, unfortunately, I had to decline the offer at the last moment. I can hardly bear the thought. I'm a nurse and, as usual in these corona times, they needed a hand on the ward, so I had to . . ." She pursed her lips, trying to compose herself. "If only I'd gone, then maybe . . ."

She looked imploringly at Carl, as if in hope that he might let her off without further discussion.

Carl considered taking her hand in his, but the face mask hanging under her nose made him think better of it. "You can't blame yourself; it can't be your fault that things turned out the way they did. It's my experience that people who want to kill themselves usually make sure that it doesn't take long before they're found. Even in death, most people cannot bear it if the sight of them becomes too grotesque and horrible. So Maja would've done it before you arrived anyway. I'm sure of it. You would just have found her a little earlier."

She nodded. "Yes, I've thought the same, but thank you for saying it. Maja was very difficult to understand and predict. Since her little boy died, she never quite returned to her old self again. She managed, yes, was actually quite good at her work, but I could sense how life tormented her."

"You were close to her, I understand. You were the one who wrote the obituary."

"Yes, I'm the only one left who really knew her. She never really socialized with her colleagues, and she didn't have any contact with her ex-husband either, who was the father of her son, Max. That relationship was broken before the accident, and he was never there to support her in her grief. I think that also affected her deeply."

"But you and Maja saw each other?"

She nodded. "Yes, but for all these years, we've never really talked about the accident. Well, maybe to begin with, of course. That was all we talked about. But not since then. Not really."

She wiped away the clear mucus running from her nose, exuding resolve even in that.

"Oh, there was so much troubling her. She especially cursed herself for choosing that repair shop to save a few hundred kroner. And for having bought such a crap car. She blamed herself for wanting to drive it even in the winter, and being so keen to know how much a rear shaft would set her back. You should know how much her self-blame controlled her life. She couldn't talk about snowsuits, strollers, old cars, or lots of other things without breaking down in tears. They must've been very tolerant at her work to have dealt with her. They really must have."

"I can see from the coroner's report that the little boy had a splint on one of his legs. What was the problem? Do you know?"

"Yes. Max was born without a functional knee joint in his right leg, so he had to undergo a lot of surgery in his first years."

"But he could walk?"

"He made the best of it, yes, but that was all down to Maja. That was the reason why her husband left her a few months after Max was born. He couldn't live with a disabled child and a wife who couldn't think of anything else. He was just one of those weak bastards who leave their wives and start over again when the going gets tough."

He got the cousin's work number so he could call if new questions came up, but Carl sensed that he probably should not expect any vital leads from her.

His brain would have to work with multiple theories for now, the most important being the young Maja's claim that she had seen a pair of legs sticking out from the entrance to the repair shop even before the first explosion. Even though she might have been wrong and the legs could have been protruding from under the car, not behind it, he chose to believe her statement. After all, she said that she had noticed that in particular, so why shouldn't it be right? And if it was right, then why was the man lying there? Was it possible that he was already dead before the explosions?

Carl pondered the scene. If the man was already dead, then the natural next assumption would be that a crime had been committed, which led to several new questions.

What had caused the head and neck lesions on the bodies? Did the man in the entrance to the repair shop try to get away? Why had none of them managed to get out—was it because they had already been killed before the explosions? According to the floor plan of the shop, four of the bodies were positioned in close proximity to the changing room in the middle of the building. But then how had someone managed to kill them all without them putting up a fight? Or had there been fighting? And what caused the explosion? There were theories that the first explosion came from tanks of toluene, a strong solvent, but was that the case? And why was there a small pile of salt outside the building? Had it been left there on purpose or had someone walked past with a bag with a hole in it—and why on earth would anyone walk past this godforsaken place with a bag of salt? Most of these questions would probably never be answered, but Carl could already understand why Marcus did not want to stop his investigation and why he had never managed to get the case out of his system.

For Carl and the other investigators, there was just one significant question left if they were dealing with a crime: What was the motive?

Apparently, Ove Wilder's Auto brought in more than the usual. But how? Was it drugs, money laundering, or some kind of scam?

Carl shook his head and looked at the photos in the file once more. It had been more than thirty years, so how were they supposed to make progress on the case?

————

"Did you manage to get anything out of the ladies I brought in for you?" asked Gordon eagerly. "Did they bring anything new to the table?"

Carl's head moved from side to side. "Well . . . at least now I know a good deal more about the woman who lost her child in the . . . explosion," he said, his voice faltering. He would have said "the accident," but he could not bring himself to.

"Cases like that can really get you down. Imagine how an entire life can be ruined by something like that. Just a spark and then . . . Booooom!" Gordon shook his head but then suddenly frowned at the sight of the top photo in the file. He dragged the chair by the wall over and sat down slowly, with his eyes fixed on the photo.

"That's Maja's upturned Citroën Dyane lying there, isn't it?"

Carl nodded. It was clearly written on the bottom of the photo.

"That photo was not in our copy file!" said Gordon in a suspicious voice.

"I see. You seem to think there's something special about it."

"Do you have a magnifying glass in your drawer?"

Carl rummaged around and handed it to him.

Gordon moved the magnifying glass over the photo a couple of times. "Well, I'll be damned," he said.

He grabbed the file and leafed systematically through the pages until he found what he was looking for.

Then he read the passage a couple of times to be entirely sure, put it down, shook his head in disbelief, and pushed the page over to Carl.

"Look at this, Carl. This is from when Marcus questioned Maja about a month after the incident." He tapped the text.

"Yes, I've just read it. She was told by the foreman of Wilder's that her rear shaft needed changing because it was corroded."

"Exactly. And now look at the photo of her upturned car. What do you see?"

Carl moved the magnifying glass back and forth a few times.

"I see that they've changed the rear shaft like they said they would.

Not that it looks brand-new, but at least it isn't corroded. They probably used a spare part they already had."

"Okay. But then allow me to refresh your memory. The repair shop calls this Maja only forty-five minutes after she dropped the car off, telling her that they'll probably have to change the rear shaft."

"Yes."

"Excuse me for saying so, but you don't know much about cars if you think that a rear shaft can be changed so quickly."

"So, you think that they'd already done it before they called. So what's the problem?"

"It's not a new rear shaft. Take a look again. It looks like the original. So, if you ask me, it didn't need changing at all."

"I hear what you're saying," said Carl, glancing at his cigarettes. Why the hell could a man not just have a smoke inside if it helped him think?

He sighed and looked at Gordon. "They lied to her and wanted to make a repair that wasn't necessary. Is that what you're thinking?"

"Yes. Or they didn't want to make the repair at all—just take the money for it. And regardless of whether they did one or the other, they very consciously wanted to con the woman out of a lot of money."

Carl nodded and looked at the photo again.

"So, you're telling me that Ove Wilder's Auto conned their customers?"

"Hell yes. Do you have any idea what kind of money they could earn like that if they had enough customers? And I think they did, given the cheap prices they advertised. I bet they always invented some kind of problem with the cars that were brought in, which the customers didn't question and had fixed. Can you imagine it?"

Carl frowned. Maybe they needed to get an overview of the finances of all the mechanics.

Had they also had so much cash in their hands that they bought holiday homes and the like?

5

NORTH OF COPENHAGEN

Tuesday, December 1, 2020

On the table next to the Advent candle that was burning its way doggedly down lay papers with the details of the two most recent candidates for the next liquidation. Both xeroxed faces beamed with complacent smiles and steely gazes, and both of their résumés oozed with sickening, selfish career choices. They were two cynical and powerful people who would never shy away from anything to succeed in their endeavors. So, the question was, which of them should be first?

It was a difficult choice. One of them had been on the waiting list for some years, while the other had only just made the list within the last few months. Why not just take the one who caused most damage? Or would it make more sense to take the one whose life was easier to terminate, where the risk of being discovered was smallest? This was the dilemma that had to be seriously considered every time.

The fact that the first candidate lived alone naturally spoke for them being the first choice. Extroverted people like him, who live alone, often do unpredictable things. They constantly make new acquaintances so that their social circles are continuously updated, and the image of their current personal contacts becomes more blurred. Any possible investigation would easily end up pointing in myriad directions at the same time, which would drag it out and divert the police work, and that was never a bad thing. The second candidate, on the other hand, lived with their almost dysfunctional and slightly meddlesome family—a second marriage—and who could predict with any certainty where the members would be and what they would be doing when the abduction took place? The first candidate was reaching an age at which the liquidation might be prompted by their natural death, and that was not very desirable in any context. But surely he would last another couple of years—he seemed strong and healthy. The other candidate, however, had this very recent controversial newspaper interview which was lying on the table speaking against him. So who was it to be? There was still a week left before the abduction, but the preparations would take some time.

A strong light shone through the window and across the two photos. Someone had stepped onto the paving stones and was heading for the front door.

The doorbell rang. It was twenty to midnight, so who could it be?

A green desk pad was placed over the photocopies and a double-edged, pointed paperknife was produced from the drawer. Precautions of that sort had been compulsory at this time of night for many years.

The approaching figure was observed closely on the security monitor. The light above the door was flashing, so the view was not entirely clear, but there was only one person and they were standing very still. No sudden movements, no stepping back and forth. So the front door was slowly opened a little while the knife was carefully concealed behind the back.

The figure who approached the light from the vestibule was known.

"Oh, it's just you, Debora. Why didn't you call?"

"You know I don't when it's about someone who has been excommunicated."

"Excommunicated? But it's been a long time since Eva was excommunicated. Has it been two months?"

"Yes, and she'd been an aspirant for quite some time."

"Will we get in trouble?"

"The thing is, I'm just not sure about her. You hear things."

"I trust she understands the full consequence if she breaks the silence."

"I hope so, but I understand your concern."

She stepped through the opening in the door with a calm expression to emphasize her words.

"That's good, Debora. Very good. And her replacement, is it working out?"

"Yes, she's a gem. I call her Ruth. A good biblical name, I think. But her name is Ragnhild. Ragnhild Bengtsen."

6

RAGNHILD

1993

Ragnhild was sitting on an old duvet on top of cardboard boxes filled with "old crap," as her father always said, and he was a real tough nut, which was something she had heard on the television that you could be. But it was not a good thing to be a tough nut because people like that could be difficult to crack and so you had to be very cautious.

Ragnhild almost always sat alone on the duvet on top of the cardboard boxes in the sitting room. It was actually the only place to sit because the sofa and armchair were covered in old, disgusting things, and she did not want to be on the floor because there were all manner of small bugs crawling about and the thought gave her the creeps.

If she accidentally said something about it not being like this at her friends' houses, her mother became really furious and shook her, which often left her with a lot of pain in her head and neck. So Ragnhild was careful and kept to herself if she could.

Her mother and father argued every single day. Her father shouted that her mother was a pig, and she answered even louder that he was one himself, just in a different way.

Ragnhild did not understand what they meant, but it made her sad.

Her father was never home in the evenings, and her mother sat in the storage room behind the bedroom moving things from one side to the other, back and forth. On nights like these, Ragnhild sat happily watching their small black-and-white television without the grown-ups shooing her away.

And Ragnhild loved many things on that television. It didn't matter at all that there were no colors like in all her friends' homes because it was almost as if Ragnhild had her very own television. None of the other children saw what she saw. Shows with wild animals, and late at night when the other children had gone to bed, Ragnhild might even stay up after midnight if there was a good movie.

The good movies were the ones with a man her dad's age who was nice to those who were good and beat up those who were not. Her favorite was John Wayne. He had a wry smile, walked proudly and slowly, and had big hands and guns so everyone was afraid of him. And if they were not, they were in for it because he would give them a good beating, and then John Wayne would flash his wry smile again. John Wayne, Arnold Schwarzenegger, and Sylvester Stallone were the best, and she had practiced pronouncing their names many times. Sometimes she talked so much about them at school that the others stopped listening. One of them said that she did not think they were anything special—if they even existed. That in particular made Ragnhild sad and angry.

Sometimes, when it was hot outside, the house would smell terrible and her dad would not come home during the day either. When he was extra grumpy and mad, he kept saying words that the teachers at her school did not like, which they told her if she accidentally used one of them. Ragnhild's dad also shouted bad words right to her face, sometimes in a way that really scared her. Last summer, when she had just turned six and the sun had shone wonderfully, she got a lot of freckles that made other people smile at her. But not her dad. He said that they came from being a bad person like her mother, and that the badness was trying to get out through her skin. Then he tried to scrub them off with a cloth and grabbed her thigh and between her legs, saying that this was where the freckles came from. But they did not go away.

She did not have so many freckles this year, but he did the same thing, and Ragnhild did not like it. But if she complained, it only got worse.

Ragnhild wanted a cat because that would give her something to play and talk with, but her mother became furious and shouted that cats stink with all their pee and fishy food and she certainly was not going to put up with that, so Ragnhild had better not dare to drag one into the house.

But Ragnhild did not care because the whole house smelled so horrible anyway. And when the neighbor's cat had kittens, they gave her one with brown stripes that she could keep.

When her dad heard it meowing, he turned bright red and kicked at it with his big shoes and Ragnhild started crying and pulled the kitten into her arms. That did not stop her dad from being furious, and he hit her instead.

In the middle of the commotion, her mum came into the sitting room and shouted that she deserved no better when she had refused to listen. That was when Ragnhild became really scared.

It was the first time in Ragnhild's seven years that her dad and mum had agreed on anything. And it was in that exact moment that Ragnhild thought for the first time that she might be better off without them.

7

MARCUS

Wednesday, December 2, 2020

It was one of those sorts of calls that Marcus did not need on a busy day, and the narcotics superintendent, Leif Lassen, aka "Sniffer Dog," also sounded hesitant passing on what he had just learned.

"There isn't much to say about it just now, Marcus. I just wanted to give you a heads-up. But the thing is that the Dutch police, the police in Slagelse, and our department here in Copenhagen are putting together an indictment against Carl Mørck, possibly Hardy Henningsen, and post-humously the deceased Anker Høyer, who as a group are believed to have encouraged a large-scale cocaine trade up until Anker's death in 2007. I'm talking about the case that we've all been referring to for years as the nail gun case—a very serious case. I'm sorry, Marcus. I have a suspicion that Carl means a lot to you and your department."

Marcus took a deep breath.

"Did you hear me, Marcus?"

Marcus gulped and exhaled. "Bloody hell, that's bad news. Did you say cocaine? And Hardy and Carl are supposed to have been mixed up in something like that? I find it hard to believe. What did you say they're claiming? I mean, how are Carl and Hardy supposed to have been involved? Do you have any solid evidence? You'd better, because you're talking about a couple of highly esteemed colleagues."

"I know. This is very serious, and apparently enough to warrant a minimum of a six-year unconditional sentence in Carl's case. Hardy's role is still unclear, whereas we have watertight evidence of Anker Høyer's guilt. If he was still alive, I believe he'd be facing twelve years at least!"

"You say 'apparently,' but that won't hold in my department, Leif. Anyway, thanks for the heads-up. It was very thoughtful of you. I'll keep it to myself for now. And I'm relying on you to inform me about any developments."

Marcus was genuinely shocked. It was not unthinkable that Hardy and Carl's colleague Anker Høyer might be guilty of something like this. The fact alone that cocaine was discovered in his body at his autopsy spoke volumes. But Carl? He could not and would not believe it. But he knew Sniffer Dog. Once he picked up the scent of something, he followed his nose.

He got up and stepped out into the long hallway. Just now he could not stand sitting alone in his office with these thoughts.

"Er, Lis," he said to the ever-present department secretary. "Would you do me a favor and find everything on the so-called nail gun case and make me copies? Just take your time, there's no rush."

He glanced at the two separate offices of Department Q when he said the words "nail gun." He would have to be more careful, because people on this floor specialized in reading faces.

As usual, the door to Carl's office was ajar, while the door to Gordon, Assad, and Rose's office was wide open. As far as he could see, only Gordon was there, and he was wearing a headset and glued to his notepad.

Was he smiling?

Energetic footsteps approached from the end of the hallway, and as there was only one person in the department who could exude that level of energy, Marcus waited.

"Hi, Assad. Pop into my office for a moment, would you?" he said as the guy came striding toward him.

Marcus knew he had to catch him before he disappeared into the strange and private world of Department Q. Assad's curly hair was graying by now, which was not strange considering the last two strenuous years.

"Been out on an assignment?"

Assad nodded and yawned at the same time as they sat down in the office. "Sorry, excuse me, but I've been ringing doorbells since seven this morning."

"The old case out in Hedehusene, I imagine."

Assad yawned again. "Yes. I'm afraid we're not going to get anywhere with that one anytime soon, Marcus. The case has just gone too cold."

Marcus frowned. When Assad said something like that, there was not much hope of solving the case, but accepting that was completely against Marcus's instincts and upbringing. No murder case could ever be allowed to fade into oblivion, especially not this one, if he had anything to do with it.

He looked empathetically at Assad. "How are things at home? Are you doing okay?"

Assad tried to muster a smile. "You know, when the camel at the zoo is about to be slaughtered, it puts on a spotted skin and hides with the giraffes."

Marcus gave him a knowing smile. Was that really how Assad was feeling?

"But I take it your wife is okay?"

"Yes, Marwa is doing better than anyone else, which is no wonder. She feels Danish and is very grateful to be back. Nella is also doing okay—after all, she had her mother's support in the many years in Iraq, and she has always spoken Danish with Marwa. But they'll never be the same again after the sexual assault, the killings of her and Ronia's newborn babies, and the many threats to their lives." He paused for a moment to hold back his tears. "I'm doing what I can, but it'll be a long, long time before they can sleep soundly at night. It's even harder for Ronia. The time in Iraq and Syria broke and changed her completely.

Even though she's been treated absolutely abominably for years, she still speaks almost only Arabic. And, unfortunately, it seems the longer we stay here, the more radicalized she's becoming. She's not as Danish as the other two. That much is clear."

"Okay, I'm sorry to hear that, Assad. I think it might be a case of Stockholm syndrome. Ronia became attached to the people who hurt her—it's hard to believe but it happens very often. But I assume she is getting support and is in therapy?"

"We all are, yes. We've been going for over a year. In that respect, Denmark is a wonderful place. My family is luckier than most others in our position."

Marcus nodded. "And your son?"

"Yes, thank you for asking, but it's a bit different with him. The biggest problem is that Afif was born in Iraq and isn't a Danish citizen. We're lucky that he can stay with us while his asylum case is being processed. But what are we supposed to do if they demand that he's sent back to Iraq? Should we all move down there then?"

Marcus knew the rigid rules and shook his head. "We can't do without you here, Assad, so I'll make sure to get that message through and sort it."

Assad gave him a tentative smile that seemed to convey that no one had that kind of power. And, unfortunately, he was probably right.

"If that were to happen, it would tear us apart. And Afif will never live up to the tests and requirements to stay in Denmark. He can barely speak Danish and will probably never learn. We actually don't know why he's so far behind, because Marwa says that the birth was totally normal. He's still being examined and observed closely. But even though he's now a young man of almost nineteen, he still has the mind of a young boy."

"Yes, it's very understandable, Assad. After all, he grew up under very different circumstances and without anything to ground him."

"To be honest, I don't know how he grew up." Assad glanced down at the table with tears in his eyes before straightening up. "The relationship between him and his captor, Ghaalib, may the bastard rot in hell, was most like owner and dog. I'm sure Afif was isolated and understimulated for years, and now Marwa and I have unfortunately had to face that he'll never be normal, even though we try to guide him in all sorts of ways. Before he came to Denmark, for example, he had never used a mobile phone, an iPad, a computer, streaming TV—any kind of electronic device—so we've had to teach him to press buttons and look at a screen. The first time he watched football on TV, he screamed as if he was in the stands. It's better now. He loves playing computer games and watching TV all day long, taking everything in. We've heard him lately trying to use more words, so he is learning after all. But with Marwa and the three children, isolated for months now in the apartment because of corona, things are getting . . ." He sighed. There was no need to say more.

Assad looked at Marcus. "I've said it before, Marcus, but I can't thank you enough for cutting me and my family so much slack. There is no doubt in my mind that the six months I spent with my family after what happened in Berlin are what saved our lives. So, let me know if there is anything I can do for you in return. No matter what, just say the word and I'll be there. If you want us to mow your lawn, we'll do it. Anything."

Marcus laughed and waved it off. "Stop, stop, Assad. I don't even have a lawn."

"All right. But if you get constipated, I'll make you a cup of real Iraqi coffee, and then you'll see."

He laughed at that. Thank god they still had him.

"Well, thanks. I guess I'll look forward to that. But speaking of favors, you can tell Carl that from now on, you're helping them solve the new case they're on. I've recently discovered that it means more to me than I realized."

Assad nodded and left.

Marcus pondered for a minute. If Sniffer Dog's warning materialized, he would damn well have to face the opposition. Carl Mørck might be hard to read, and no doubt something had happened to him during the shooting out on Amager where Anker was killed, but suspecting that his best investigator was a drug criminal? Not Carl, the man who had founded an entire department, solved so many cases with his brilliant team, and who stood head and shoulders above his colleagues.

8

CARL

Wednesday, December 2, 2020

"**You should open** your window and air it out in here before Rose comes storming in," said Assad. Carl looked at him wearily and waved his hand in the air to clear the smoke. That would have to suffice. Now that Assad had been put on the case, Carl proceeded to fill him in.

"I've asked Gordon to make calls to the mechanics' widows and ask whether their husbands spent significant amounts of money before they died. I've told him to say that they can come clean if anything illegal has taken place, since the deadline for prosecuting that has expired. We're only asking them so we can establish a possible cause for the repair shop explosion and the death of their husbands."

Assad shook his head. "Don't we know that already, Carl?"

"No. Back when the investigation took place, they searched intensely for a motive for the killings—if they even were killings. They investigated whether there was a gang-related motive or something drug related, and they also investigated fraud with number plates and trading of stolen cars with Eastern Europeans. But everything led to a dead end. The company only existed for six, seven months, and, apart from the first two VAT returns, which showed significant deficits, we found nothing about their income because they weren't in business long enough to file tax returns. And because everything had gone up in flames—computers, customer records, order sheets, records of spare-part purchases, et cetera—it was another dead end. Some people at police headquarters were willing to believe that if it wasn't an accident, the actual target could've been somewhere else and it was all a mistake. But that was as far as they got."

Assad scratched his stubble. "You told me Gordon discovered this morning that they swindled their customers, so there must've been someone fishing. And so the question is whether it was with a rod or a net."

"You mean there must have been something fishy, Assad." Carl smiled. Assad often misunderstood idioms and created new ones. "But even if the shop conned their customers into paying for repairs that they didn't do or that were unnecessary, they may have done much worse things too," said Carl. "Do you have any suggestions?"

"Have we asked the boss's widow if they also bought and sold cars?"

"We know they did. There were several adverts in the free ads and local newspapers."

"Stolen cars with their vehicle identification numbers changed and a spray job, that can easily lead to trouble. For example, Eastern Europeans get very cross if you cheat them. We're talking mileage counters that are turned back, false service books, stuff like that. Were there traces of explosives?"

"No."

"Why is this case troubling Marcus so much, Carl? Do you know?"

Carl looked away for a second. He knew all too well.

"It's probably a combination of many things. The dead boy, the boy's mother who took her own life, and all the questions that were left unanswered."

"If you ask me, I think Marcus promised the mother of the dead child that he'd find those responsible for the explosions."

Carl nodded. That was highly likely. It wasn't the first time that a police officer had had to go back on their word. In a case like that, you were willing to promise anything if it offered solace. But you can never walk away from a broken promise. That was a fact.

"You were right, Carl," sounded a loud voice from the hallway. Why could the guy not just wait until he was in the office so they could keep their business from all the busybodies on the floor?

Gordon's milky-white baby cheeks still sported neat red spots. He was all worked up.

"Yes, you heard me right. All the mechanics had made large investments in the time leading up to the accident. A hell of a lot of money exchanged hands in that small business."

"Okay. Good, Gordon. Like what?"

"Cars, electronics, travel. And to top it off, the widows told me that they always paid cash."

"Under the table," mumbled Assad.

"Sure. And the mechanics all knew one another from college, and they were all lads up to no good when they were together. Scoundrels, the lot of them, one of the wives told me. But she didn't care because she had left her husband before he died. She was very candid and said that they never missed an opportunity to cook the books at the repair shop. The cars they sold were old junk they had given a superficial make-over. She knew for a fact that they always went to used-car auctions and bought cars that no one else would touch with a ten-foot pole. She reckoned that they probably sold four, five of these painted carcasses a week."

"Christ, that's more than a hundred cars in the brief time the shop existed. Did she also know who they sold them to?"

"To everyone who was gullible enough, she said. A lot of immigrants."

Assad and Carl looked at each other. They were thinking the same thing.

"She said that they never said anything about how things were going, and if she asked her husband, he always told her to shut up and mind her own business."

"And she didn't report it to the police?"

"By the time of the explosions, she'd already left him and had been living with a Swedish restaurateur on the Costa del Sol for three months.

She only heard about the accident when she returned home. So, no, she didn't talk to the police."

"Did she mention any of the other scams they had?"

The red spots on Gordon's cheeks became even more visible. They were about to hear his big finale.

"She told me that she heard from one of the other wives that they cheated with the repair bills—and they didn't hold back. So I was right, Carl. Every bill had a couple of thousand kroner added for repairs of so-called very serious faults that they found on the cars." He was bursting with pride and almost hopping up and down on the spot.

"Good, Gordon. A picture of vengeful customers is starting to emerge. Now we're just waiting for Rose to see if she can locate some of the cases where a pile of salt has been found close to the crime scene."

"A pile of salt?" Assad looked puzzled.

Carl pushed the file over to him. "Bring yourself up to speed. You can read this yourself because I have to pick up Lucia from the nursery today."

He felt a tinge of tenderness.

If Carl was honest, this was the best time of his life despite the corona pandemic. Everything had come up roses. He and Mona had the sweetest little daughter. They lived together and spoke about getting married. For the last few weeks, Ludwig had been staying with a friend every other week and was currently staying with Carl until Christmas. When it sometimes became difficult to coordinate picking up Lucia after Mona had started working again, there was a young girl in the apartment next to them who was keen to earn a little extra. The only snake in paradise was that Mona's oldest daughter had turned her back on them entirely after Lucia was born, and that Assad's work was clearly affected by his new home life. In fact, Carl had several times seen the otherwise robust and strong man with tears in his eyes when he thought he was alone.

"Assad has been assigned to the case," he told Mona after having related the details of the case over their post-dinner coffee. "You had a session with him last week. How is he doing?"

She shook her head and concentrated on getting their daughter to take the spoon of baby food in her mouth.

"Ah, I see. A psychologist has to respect patient confidentiality. So let me ask you in a different way. Am I wrong in thinking that he can manage a normal investigation now? I think this will be a complicated one because Marcus and I suspect that there's a connection with other unsolved cases, so I have to delegate the tasks. Assad can't continue ringing doorbells and doing routine tasks when we have a case like this on our hands."

She still just smiled as if she were wearing earplugs and could not think beyond the next spoonful of banana purée.

Carl sighed. "Mona, I need to know if I risk harming him by expecting too much."

She looked at him. "You'll work it out, don't you think, Carl?"

9

ROSE

Only a single task lamp was on that evening in the investigation unit, where Rose was picking at a packet of stale crisps she had found in a drawer. After five hours of overtime, she was done in and felt sick at the smell of musty paper. But then she stumbled across something.

The meager report from 2002 was easy to miss in the large piles of files, given that it only consisted of a cover, some photos, and two sheets of paper. The conclusion in the case was that it was a suicide, but the final flourish, which was typical of Hardy Henningsen, indicated that he suspected something was awry: "Shelved under mild protest."

The case was about a middle-aged man who had been found with carbon monoxide poisoning in his garage a few days after Whitsun. The body was discovered by accident when his cleaning lady went into the garage to collect supplies. The coroner's inquest established beyond reasonable doubt that he had been there for three days and that his Volvo, which he had just filled up, had been running idle for the same amount of time. Despite the fact that he was an MP and publicly known for his radical views, such as forced sterilization of women on social benefits who had had more than two children, the death did not make headlines. The attitude seemed to be that this end to his political career served both the world and himself well.

The reason why this rather straightforward suicide in 2002 had still made the pile of possible crimes was that the coroner noted two shallow indentations around the wrists of the deceased, which the blushing cleaning lady associated with the man having certain sexual tendencies that she and her husband certainly did not entertain in their home. Marcus Jacobsen assigned Carl Mørck and Hardy Henningsen to the task of locating one or more of the man's possible sexual partners, and, when they failed, the case was shelved with Hardy Henningsen's final remark.

Halfway through the report, there were a few descriptions of what had been observed in the garage: the usual shelves with heaps of kitchen towels, tinned tomatoes, and toilet paper. In addition, there was painting equipment, dried-up cans of paint, oil spills and salt on the floor, and a bike that had not been used for years, if ever. Finally, a ceiling rack had been hung under the roof together with a broom and a bucket.

By the time Rose read the report, her stomach had already been rumbling impatiently for an hour despite the crisps. Had she given in to the hunger and raced through the report so she could get home quickly, she probably would not have noticed the small, and anything but insignificant, fact that there was salt on the floor.

She quickly went over the photo evidence.

The body sat leaning slightly forward in the driver's seat. His hands were placed on his lap, and he was dressed smartly in a tweed jacket, which was his trademark. Apart from that, there was nothing unusual. The photo from the autopsy table clearly showed the pink blemishes that were characteristic of carbon monoxide poisoning. Not a pretty sight. Rose remembered the plump idiot of a politician all too well—he was a horrible person.

For a completely ordinary house in Rødovre, the garage was huge. If the man had been married and had teenage children, they would have used it for wild parties. But instead, it was just a neatly kept outbuilding with an entrance to the rest of the house and an electric door, which, incidentally, was unlocked.

It was only when they removed his car from the garage that the small pile of salt showed in the photo evidence. A white pile six or seven centimeters in height—nothing anyone would find unusual in a place where groceries were carried back and forth every day.

Rose forgot all about being hungry.

"You should have called me last night, Rose," said Carl the following morning.

"No, I didn't want to wake up Lucia, and I just wanted to get home. I didn't get back to Værløse until ten thirty, Carl."

Her boss nodded. Her efforts were appreciated.

"Follow me," he said, pulling her along behind him with the file in his hand. Was he smiling at their colleagues on the way to the chief of homicide's office, and was there a sparkle of schadenfreude in the corner of his eye?

Marcus Jacobsen could see the triumph in their eyes straightaway and cut his phone call short. "What do you have for me?" he asked when Carl put the file down in front of him.

"This is the case you were thinking about, and it's down to Rose that it's been excavated from the archives," he said, beaming at her. "And now that I've read the report, I also remember the case clearly. You were right that I should've called Hardy, because with his help I would've remembered it immediately."

He pointed at Hardy's protest in the final sentence.

"He definitely would've remembered this conclusion to the report, and maybe also this."

He placed the photo of the empty garage in front of his boss and tapped the spot with the salt.

Marcus looked over his half-moon spectacles.

"I'll be damned, there it is!" He turned to Rose. "Do you realize what you might have started?"

"I think so, because that pile of salt looks exactly like the one outside the repair shop that blew up in 1988. Maybe there's a connection with that and possibly also other cases." She frowned. "But just now, I'm worried because if that *is* the case, we'll be insanely busy going over all cases from 1988 up until today. I hope you realize that, boss. Maybe we won't even find any similar cases with piles of salt, or maybe we'll have to go further back than 1988. But I bloody well hope not."

"I know it's a huge task, but why do you think we're doing it anyway, Rose?"

"Because we have two crimes where the perpetrator has clearly made sure that they appear as something they aren't."

"So, you think it's premeditated murder in both cases?"

Marcus observed Rose carefully.

"We both do, and so do you, Marcus," interrupted Carl. "That's why you couldn't let the repair shop case go."

"Yes, but listen, you two. Let's stay objective. Intuition is one thing, but it's quite another to engage in a wild goose chase because of coincidences. Until you find one or two more cases with a pile of salt next to a victim, let's assume that it's all just coincidence. If you find another case, we can talk again."

"As you wish," said Rose. "But *if* there is a crime behind these cases, we should assume that the cause of death has been concealed so effectively that the cases maybe never reached homicide, and so won't be in our archive. For instance, cases that were filed as 'lethal accident,' 'suicide,' or so-called natural causes, and then we're talking thousands of cases. Apart from that, we should also assume that geographically they could've happened anywhere in Denmark."

Marcus placed his hands on the desk and leaned toward her. "Yes, Rose. I agree with the latter. But tell me, when did that MP die? I don't quite remember—was it ten years ago?"

"Almost twice as long. The time of death was established to be Whitsunday, May nineteenth, 2002, in the evening, and his name was Palle Rasmussen," said Rose.

"Oh yes, that's a very long time ago!" Marcus whistled and leaned back in his chair. Was he trying to leaf back in his mental calendar to that day?

"Honestly, Marcus, isn't Department Q too small to handle this case all on its own? I think we are," said Carl.

Marcus stuck his index finger in the air. He was not finished thinking.

Rose looked at the photo on the desk and interrupted his train of thought. "I think we should copy this and the pile of salt from 1988 and send them to all police districts in the country. All we need is just one investigator or forensic technician who has a similar pile of salt stuck in their memory."

The look she gave them left them in no doubt that she was serious about the idea.

"Dare we say out loud that we think there are more of these salt cases?" asked Marcus.

"Do you mean if we have a serial killer?" said Carl.

"If there are more than the two cases with piles of salt close to the crime scene, then yes."

"Which would mean that we roll out the big guns: profile analyses, MOs, hundreds of interviews, interrogations, forensic reviews, and comparisons of all manner of reports et cetera, et cetera. It could take months." Carl's pessimism was hard to miss.

"Yes, that's true, Carl. But imagine if more cases point in the same direction. Don't you want to solve a series of them so you can clear them from your backlog? Imagine if we solve the explosion at Wilder's Auto and end up solving lots of other cases along with it."

Carl's face cracked into a network of wrinkles, revealing mixed emotions. He looked like something an architect could have drawn while tripping on LSD.

10

CARL

Thursday, December 3, 2020

"**As long as** our offices are only five meters away from our colleagues down the hall, you must promise me to be discreet about the work ahead of us. You can't avoid talking with the other heads of investigation, I know that, but don't tell them how we do things in our department. If we do well, two thirds of our colleagues hate us, and if we struggle, they laugh, and I can't be bothered with either. We need to keep things under wraps as long as we're close to the other investigators. Understood?"

Carl pointed at the row of whiteboards stretching all the way along the wall of Assad, Rose, and Gordon's office.

"From now on, this is our situation room, okay? I've drawn five columns, which I expect to be filled out ASAP. The first column is self-evident: 'Date/Crime Scene.' The second column named 'Victim' is a little more complicated. If many years have passed after the assumed murder, it'll be very difficult to create a victim profile and uncover that person's activities and habits. The third column is for 'Murder Method,' and I expect that one will also be difficult to establish. The fourth column is one I don't expect us to be able to fill out before we've identified a possible perpetrator. I've called it 'Motive.' Can we assume that the two current cases share the common denominator that the victims were in some way pacified before the actual murder took place?"

Carl nodded to Rose. "What do you think points in that direction?"

"Well, the mechanics were certainly pacified before the shop blew up, and the MP, Palle Rasmussen, had presumably already been neutralized behind the wheel before the carbon monoxide finished the job," she said.

"Do we know how old the Volvo was?"

"Old enough not to have a catalytic convertor."

Carl nodded. That was too bad for Palle Rasmussen, as it explained why it emitted so much carbon monoxide. He turned to Assad. "You look like you've got something on your mind. Care to share it with us?"

"Uhh, it's a bit difficult the way things are spinning around in my head just now. But I'm wondering how you make five mechanics drop to the ground. How did someone manage to bash all their skulls in without any of them putting up a fight?"

Gordon politely stuck a finger in the air. He would have to drop that habit. "I was thinking the same. I think the cause of death was actually the blow to the head, and the explosion was set off to cover it all up so no traces of DNA, surveillance, or anything else would be discovered."

He couldn't think of other examples, but the others got the idea.

"I think so too," said Rose.

"But then they must've been sedated somehow before the blows," said Assad. "The man lying in the entrance may have tried to get out into the fresh air, but didn't quite make it. That's kind of where I was going with that."

"Well, spit it out, then. How were they sedated? Any suggestions?"

"Maybe with some sort of gas?" suggested Gordon.

"Yes, but they did auto-body finishing in the building, so we can almost guarantee there would have been good ventilation. Doesn't that point in a different direction?"

"Can't you reverse a ventilation system like that, just like an old vacuum cleaner, so that it blows air into the room instead?" asked Rose.

Carl shrugged. "No idea. Maybe. But it sounds a bit complicated, doesn't it?" They all appeared to share his opinion.

"But what about the MP? What could have happened there?"

"The same, I think," said Assad. "First he was sedated so he couldn't escape from the car while he was slowly poisoned with carbon monoxide."

"That could have been done with either ether or chloroform, right?" asked Gordon.

"Yeah, I guess that's a possibility." Obviously Carl had thought of that explanation. "Both chemicals are quite difficult to trace in a body, and they certainly wouldn't be able to smell them three days later, especially considering the fumes from the exhaust. Should we write it as a possibility on the board?"

Everyone nodded.

Carl wrote it. "Could this method also have been used for the repair shop killings?"

"Yes, possibly," said Gordon.

"What does that tell us about the perpetrator in that case?"

"That he knew a lot about the crime scenes and the victims. When the MP returned home. The layout of the shop and so forth," continued Gordon.

"Yeah, and that he or she knew about the right chemicals, and finally that the killings were carefully planned. That much is evident from the complicated crime in the shop. But what indicates that was also the case with the garage killing?"

He looked around, and Assad was the first to reply.

"The salt was found under the vehicle. It was placed there in a pile before the car was parked in the garage."

Carl gave him a thumbs-up and looked around at them all again.

"Rose, send out a memo to ask for information about salt in connection with deaths. Send it to all police districts and, of course, also everyone in house. You know what to do. This makes you their contact person. If they don't react immediately, call the police districts and put the pressure on." He smiled at her, but apparently to no avail. She hated this sort of assignment.

"Do any of you actually recall a single case in which there has been a pile of salt close to the victim?" he continued.

They shook their heads.

"Well, that's too bad, because neither do I. This means that we'll keep our focus on cases from the period between 1988 and 2010 that Rose has already started on, and you'll take over that assignment for now, Gordon. Based on Rose's experience, you should start by reviewing all the photo evidence from the cases to save time. If you find salt in any of them, read the case in question closely and report back to us. Be careful not to miss anything."

"Why don't I just inform the chief superintendents that if the different departments and crime investigators don't remember any cases involving salt, they can start with the photo evidence?" suggested Rose.

Carl nodded. "Of course. And now to you, Assad. I want you to investigate any possible motive for the two killings here on the board because I think they share one similarity. The mechanics' car sales scam and the MP Palle Rasmussen's pigheaded and very radical views, in my opinion, point to the possibility that one or more immigrants could be behind this. I know it's not much to go on, but the wife who left her husband did mention that immigrants were good customers for the cheap cars that the repair shop sold. If you go through the vehicle registration records from the time before the explosion, you'll find a list of the buyers' names. If one of them turns out to be someone Palle Rasmussen harassed, there might be a shared motive, even though I'm aware it would be a long shot."

"I don't think that'll work, Carl," said Assad.

"Okay. And why's that, Assad?"

"Because I'm pretty sure that those car sales were done under the table, so the name of the shop won't appear on the sales records."

Carl frowned. "Sure, but someone had to be responsible for the sale, right? So I suggest that instead you just look for the mechanics' names in the records because they were the ones responsible for selling the cars. And see if you can also find out a little bit more about the mechanics."

Assad shrugged. He was not convinced. Unfortunate, but Carl didn't care as long as he did his work.

"And what will you be doing, Carl?" Rose gave him a bitter glance. What was it now? "Smoking your stinking coffin nails while you wait for us to find something for you?"

Carl frowned. "Hmm, that too, yes. But first and foremost, I need to secure us a huge amount of extra funding to cover all your overtime. I don't expect you want to take time off in lieu over the next ten years, right?"

"Great, Carl, you do that." Gordon looked ecstatic because he loved working overtime as long as he was paid. After all, he did not have much of a life outside HQ.

"And I'll also compare the findings of the two cases to try to discover the potential perpetrator's psychological profile," Carl added.

"Ohh, I'm sure you'll make Mona do it, you cheat. Then you can sit back and play with your daughter while the rest of us work away." Rose really was in an antagonistic mood.

Carl chose to smile. "Brilliant idea. Thanks for that."

"Just one small problem, Carl," she continued. "If the salt was placed there on purpose, we're dealing with a perpetrator who is playing a dangerous game and risks being exposed, or someone who at least wants to make their mark. I'm thinking a very systematic serial killer who we should be very keen to put behind bars. But what if the thing with the salt is just coincidence?"

"That's one of the reasons why you all have to keep quiet about our progress or setbacks. But if what you're saying turns out to be the case, our story is that we're merely trying to solve two old cases. And isn't that what we're doing?"

When they were finished, Carl sat down in his office and smoked a cigarette with his head halfway out the window. Seeing the bluish-white smoke swirl up to the sky helped him think.

What to do next?

Marcus would fight tooth and nail for the funding, so that would almost take care of itself. In terms of the victims' psychological profiles, he would have to start with the career of the MP, his public persona, and any possible slander or other police cases. Carl remembered him well from back then, when he and Hardy were on the assignment. But there was one thing he was sure of: Hardy no doubt remembered the case better than he did.

11

CARL

Thursday, December 3, 2020

"I'm waiting in an outpatient clinic—there's a lot of noise, so speak clearly, Carl."

Carl listened. He could not hear any noise. "Morten says that you're making progress in Switzerland. Are you feeling optimistic, Hardy?"

"Optimistic? Are you asking me if I'll walk again?"

"Do you think you will?"

"If the last few operations on my spine work, and if they can make an exoskeleton with loads of stabilizers for a man of my height, and at the same time manage to reactivate my nonexistent muscles, I'll be able to stand, but you shouldn't hold your breath that I'll be doing the hundred-meter sprint."

"Hardy, I haven't thought that far ahead. I hope you understand. But what about the mobility in your arms? Is there any chance you'll be able to use them again?"

The long pause was answer enough. Hardy had been paralyzed almost a hundred percent from the neck down for more than ten years, so why would he even bother considering such a stupid question? He couldn't even take this call if not for Morten holding the phone to his ear.

"I think so, yes," he said, nevertheless.

Carl gasped. If Hardy regained just a fraction of his mobility, it would change everything. It was almost too good to be true.

Apart from that, Hardy did not want to talk more about his treatment. As long as Morten and Mika gave him his daily pep talk, there was no need to make any more fuss about it. It was all still an experiment for which no one knew the outcome. He was a cautious man.

"And while we're on the subject of Morten, Carl, he mentioned that you're working on the suicide of the MP Palle Rasmussen. I assume that's why you're calling?"

"No, I . . ."

"There was something rotten about that case. Why the hell would a public figure who loved being in the limelight suddenly put it out? No explanation, no suicide note, no indication that he suffered from depression. Yes, I remember that case clearly. He was one of the most despised politicians in the country and seemingly thrived on hatred, regardless of whether it was directed at himself or others. Why would he suddenly question his miserable life?"

"Yes, it doesn't make sense. But, Hardy, do you remember that there was a pile of salt on the garage floor?"

"Did you say a pile of salt?"

"Yeah. We found a similar pile of salt in another case from years before."

"No, I don't remember that particular detail. Why is it important?"

Carl told him about the similarities between the cases.

"I'll be damned. But it could be coincidence—what do you think?"

"I don't know. I'll look into Palle Rasmussen again. Back then we checked whether he had had sex with someone who might have tied him up. Don't you remember that forensics found indentations on his wrists?"

"Yeah, but like I said at the time, which was also confirmed by the coroner, indentations like those don't remain on the skin for very long if the person is still alive. So either he had some kind of sadomasochistic sex on his way home from parliament, which I remember us establishing that he could have had time for, or someone tied him to the wheel. Don't you remember his cleaning lady saying that there used to be a kind of artificial fabric on his wheel—plush or something—and that it wasn't there when they found him?"

"I'm afraid not, Hardy, I don't. Do you mean that if it had still been there, forensics would have been able to find traces of whatever was used to tie him on the plush?"

"I just meant that it was weird that the wheel cover wasn't there anymore."

"Why did they shelve the case? I can't remember. Of course, I could talk to Marcus about it, but if you—"

"I think they'll be here to pick me up in a second, Carl, so I'll be brief." He considered for a moment. "The case was shelved because something came to light about a family dinner Palle Rasmussen attended before Whitsun, just a couple of days before his death."

"Okay, I must have missed that."

"But you weren't on the case for the last few days. You were on another case with Anker."

"Was I? Well, okay, what's the deal with that dinner?"

"The family claimed that Palle Rasmussen, in his usual drunken stupor later that night, joked about a TV hostess who had shot herself in front of a live camera, and that it was the most insane suicide anyone could imagine. 'If you plan to take your own life, in my opinion you should make sure that you leave a beautiful corpse when you do it,' he had said. '*When* you do it' were his exact words, which in the family's opinion was a sign that he might do it himself. We had a lot of cases that month, so I reckon Marcus simply deprioritized it. And, to be honest, it pissed me off when he did."

Carl could hear a bit of a commotion in the background and some French phrases, which Hardy answered in English.

"Shouldn't all that stuff about the wheel cover and the dinner with the family have been in the report, Hardy?"

"Well, isn't it?" There was more noise. "Oh, this is me, Carl. I hope it was of some help."

It certainly was, but it also gave rise to lots of new questions.

"We'll be in touch, Hardy, all right?"

"*Ciao, ciao,*" Hardy replied before ending the call.

"Hi, Rose, sorry to disturb your work."

With her mobile still pressed to her ear, she gave him a surly look.

"Is it possible that there could be other appendices or pages in the file re: the MP's suicide?"

She reluctantly ended her call. "What do you mean?"

Carl told her about his chat with Hardy.

"God, is he doing okay?"

"Yes, he's making progress. He doesn't know much yet, but he sounded optimistic. But back to my question: Is it possible that one or more sheets from that file have been misplaced?"

"No idea. But if they have, Gordon might come across them as he goes through the pile of files. Ask him yourself." She pointed back toward the pale, skinny man sitting surrounded by paper cutout Christmas elves and a tower-high stack of files on one side and a very small one on the other.

"How are you doing, Gordon? Making any progress?"

Gordon looked up at him in a daze. He had clearly been miles away.

"You're almost done, I see," joked Carl, pointing at the tall stack that Gordon still hadn't worked his way through.

"What do you mean? This is nothing. There are still lots of unsolved cases of violent crime with fatal outcomes down in the archives."

Carl gave him a comforting pat on the shoulder, glancing at a pale elf on the top of his computer screen. "Someone's been decorating for Christmas. It looks very festive," he lied. He quickly brought Gordon up to speed to help him with his search and then disappeared into the hallway before the lad had time to vent his frustration.

It was not difficult for him to decide which of Palle Rasmussen's next of kin to call on because he could only locate the person who, as his closest family member, had been called in to identify the body.

A man in a lumberjack shirt, a loose brown corduroy jacket, comfortable shoes, and baggy jeans opened the front door. He probably used to have a full red beard but now was left with just a gray straggly mass with only hints of its former color. This prototypical hipster, a shabby schoolteacher from the seventies, was not a welcome sight—just like his modern hipster counterparts.

Carl took out his ID and pulled down his face mask. "I'm under the impression that you're the cousin of the deceased MP Palle Rasmussen. Is that correct?"

"I can't deny it, so yeah," he said, without any sign that he intended to invite Carl in. "He isn't the sort of man one remembers fondly, to put it mildly."

"Do you remember if you attended a family dinner with Palle a few days before he died?"

"May I ask why you've turned up here out of the blue digging all this up again? It's been more than fifteen years."

"It's in connection with another case we're investigating at the moment. It shares some similarities with Palle's, but that's all I can say."

"Okay . . ." That sort of answer was clearly insufficient for a former schoolteacher.

"I was on the team that investigated his death back then. That's why I'm the one following up."

"But he killed himself, the idiot, and good riddance."

"What makes you so sure?"

"You got me there." He laughed, revealing teeth that were aged by many layers of red wine and pipe tobacco. "But yes, I did attend that dinner party. It's a family tradition just before Whitsun, and as we explained to your incredibly tall colleague back then, Palle made some remarks about suicide, which were particularly inappropriate given recent events in the family."

"I see. What events?"

"Just after our cousin Laurits had told us he had cancer. He was very distressed."

"No sense of timing, I gather."

The schoolteacher gave him a reproachful look as if he had not done his homework. "No sense of timing? That is one thing Palle definitely did have. He was very consciously trying to shock and scare our cousin by poking at his grief. That's the way he was: malicious and entirely devoid of empathy. A bastard to the core."

"Do *you* believe that Palle killed himself?"

"Me? To put it bluntly, I didn't give a damn back then and I still don't."

"Do you think that's the general consensus in the family?"

"If you want to talk to someone who didn't believe it," he said, stepping down onto the doorstep, "you should talk to Palle's niece. She was infatuated with him and his sick ideas."

"His niece?"

"Yes, they were almost the same age. She was the daughter of Palle's oldest brother—Palle was the youngest of his siblings."

"Do you know where she lives?"

"Oh, don't pretend you don't know. Pauline Rasmussen. You know her."

"Okay, we're talking about *the* Pauline Rasmussen? But she can't possibly be—"

"A fascist, is that what you were going to say? No, not at all. Nowadays, she is as blue as a robin's egg."

12

PAULINE

1993

Pauline was no regular teenager. While her friends were dreaming about what they wanted to be when they grew up, whom they would marry, Pauline's dreams were much more personal.

Pauline only dreamed about being seen. Standing in a room or on a stage and being looked at. Stretching her arms out toward the spotlight with hundreds of pairs of eyes following them. Not being ignored, not being looked down on, not feeling isolated. This dream made her hands sweaty and her skin flush.

And then one warm summer, when Pauline was sixteen, her small family was invited to a holiday home with a couple of her dad's brothers and their respective families.

Almost a week of boredom had passed when a young man with a cheeky expression suddenly arrived to join them. From the moment he first looked at her, his eyes made her skin tingle.

Palle Rasmussen was not one of the brothers the others spoke well of. They thought he was too much, too uncompromising when he raised his voice and started arguing, causing cozy afternoons to suddenly feel uncomfortable.

Pauline knew from her dad that Palle was embarking on a career in politics, and that was far more interesting than being a shopkeeper, accountant, or anything else that the Rasmussen family had produced.

The first time Pauline was alone with this uncle, he put a ping-pong paddle in her hand and told her to slap him across the face with it.

She hesitated, but when he grabbed her crotch and said that if she didn't oblige right away he would punch her in the stomach, she swung the paddle at his face so hard that it broke.

He stumbled backward and looked at her with surprise. She was also shocked that she had actually done it, but then he grabbed another paddle and asked her to do it again.

Another member of the family might have noticed his red cheeks when they sat down at the dinner table, but Palle was unfazed. And by then, Pauline had already fallen in love with him.

It was not long before Pauline had a key to Palle's apartment, and the things they did to each other could never be done better by anyone else. For the first time, she felt the power of her sexuality and desire, and she realized that this was the way to get what she wanted in life.

Palle praised her and listened to her in a way no one else did, which turned her on almost as much as turning him on did. Everything about those two when they were together was uniquely intimate and exhilarating in a way she could never have imagined, and the feeling gave her a high. A high from knowing that she had power over someone else's body. From hearing and feeling the pleasure of another person's moans of pain, from seeing that pain materialize in red marks and sores.

13

CARL

Friday, December 4, 2020

It was true that the comedian and cabaret actress Pauline Rasmussen was not happy to be reminded of her old affection for her uncle. So when Carl turned up the following morning during the rehearsal for her forthcoming show, publicly stating his business, she quickly pulled him backstage and asked him to lower his voice.

Carl nodded. "I think you should tell the others onstage that you're taking a break. Then we can walk over to the other side of the canal, sit on a bench, and have a quiet talk."

She shuddered and wrapped her coat tightly around her as they sat down, which was understandable. The last time Carl had checked the weather, the temperature was only just above freezing.

"I'll get straight to the point, Pauline. You and your uncle got along back in the day, but you have changed since then, so don't worry." He pulled an imaginary zipper across his lips. "I've heard from someone in your family that you were the only one who was close to Palle, and that nothing in the world could convince you that he killed himself. Do you remember why you felt that way?"

"Can you guarantee me that this will remain between us?" She looked at him nervously.

"Yes, I promise. Confidentiality, you know."

Carl knew her from TV. She was an experienced actress with a talent for comedy and a very pleasant singing voice. But sitting here on the bench, she came across as neither funny nor poised. Her voice trembled slightly and her eyes looked sad.

"I was infatuated with him, even though that must be hard to believe now. I know people judge me, especially given how we met. But his devil-may-care attitude gave him a unique charisma, which also explains why he received so many personal votes in the general election. I fell in love with him and we were in a secret relationship for almost nine and a half years. He broke up with me a couple of months before he died, saying that he had fallen in love with someone else. What hurt most was that he was positively glowing with this newfound love right up until his death. So why would he kill himself? He was an extremely strong person who could overcome anything."

Carl was careful to hide his dismay at the news of Pauline and Palle's indecent relationship. "Even if the woman he was in love with rejected him?"

She nodded. "Even then."

Carl closed the door to his office. His next interview was not suited for open doors.

Kurt Hansen, former politician and retired police superintendent, had given Carl useful advice on several occasions. It had been quite a few years since he had been politically active, but he definitely must have worked alongside Palle Rasmussen at some point. That much was certain.

When Kurt answered the call, he let out a grunt of pleasure upon hearing it was Carl on the other end. Very odd. Maybe he was losing his marbles from the idleness of retirement, not to mention the numbing lack of contact in these corona times.

"Palle Rasmussen! Yeah, you'd be hard-pressed to find a bigger bastard. Imagine that I had to sit in the same room as him during negotiations. He was everywhere in Christiansborg—there was just no avoiding him in parliament. Even worked holidays, the bloody atheist. Just the thought of the man!"

"Kurt, hold your horses! I'm investigating his suicide and need to know immediately about any enemies he had."

"Haha! You don't know if it was actually suicide, is that what you're telling me? I damn well hope it was because if it was murder the murderer should get a medal instead of time. Don't quote me on that." He laughed. "Yes, that man had enemies galore. Are you sure you have enough time to hear about it?"

"I've read quite a few hateful readers' letters addressed to him and also some of his statements and interviews, so I'm well aware of the scale. I also assume that he received threatening letters at his parliamentary office in Christiansborg?"

"If I received a few over the years, he must have received hundreds more."

"Do they keep things like that?"

"Keep them? No, I seriously doubt it." He cleared his throat and thought. "But you know what, try talking to Vera Petersen. She was the secretary of his tiny political group, poor thing. Vera was all right, she just had a shitty job, but today she works as a secretary for Danish Industry. Give her a call and have a chat. I'm sure she must've read most of that shit."

It was a useful tip because Vera Petersen turned out to be a fount of knowledge, a treasure trove of solutions, and an endless source of memories. She was one of those secretaries who almost render their bosses obsolete.

Yes, it was true that she once worked for Palle Rasmussen's party as a secretary and coordinator, she freely admitted that. Carl could sense that it had not been a walk in the park.

"I can tell you that almost all the threatening letters were anonymous, and they all contained the same filth. That he should just lay down and die, that he was an idiot who ought to jump off a bridge, that he

was ugly and disgusting, and that his breath smelled rotten each time
he opened his mouth."

Every other moment, she broke off their conversation to pass on a
message to someone in the room before returning to the matter at hand.
She was a very busy woman.

"Do you think there's any chance that those letters still exist?"

"Not at Christiansborg, as far as I'm aware, but he had a tendency to
take things like that home. I think the harsher the letters, the more they
amused him. They were almost like trophies for him. I wouldn't be surprised if he'd been planning to sue the senders at some point to tie in
with his next election campaign. He loved it when the media wallowed
in that sort of thing because it ensured him publicity. He was, generally,
an amazing strategist when it came to promoting himself. There is no
bad publicity, as they say. That's rubbish, of course, but not in his case.
Just a second!"

She disappeared again, but Carl was finished anyway. He just needed
to thank her and move on to the next person on his list.

Pauline Rasmussen sounded somewhat uneasy when she heard his voice
again on the telephone.

"Just a quick question, Pauline. Who inherited Palle Rasmussen's
estate?"

"Er, I did. But surely you don't think—"

"I just need to know what happened with his possessions and personal effects."

"It all came to me, but there wasn't much of any value, I can tell you
that. Just his computer and some furniture—and we're not talking Danish designer furniture like Hans Wegner or Poul Kjærholm and those
guys. And anyway, I already had all I needed."

"His computer? Do you still have it?"

"Yes . . . maybe . . . actually, I'm not sure. But if I do, it'll be in the
attic. I couldn't open it because it was a Mac and I couldn't log in."

"Can I ask you to look for it?"

"I'm a bit stressed out at the moment."

"Surely it won't take very long? Perhaps we can give you a hand?"

"Er, no thanks. I'll do it myself. But not until after our opening night."

"Okay, I understand. And when is that?"

"Tomorrow."

Carl nodded to himself. A computer! It was doubtful that anyone in the police had checked its contents, given that the man had allegedly died by suicide, so they would have to take a look now.

"I think there might also be a box of various papers."

"There was more than one box!" She laughed mockingly. "There were at least fifty boxes bursting at the seams. I sent them straight to the incinerator. Palle kept all that crap at home, but it didn't interest me. What was I supposed to do with it?"

Did she sound a little rehearsed?

"Thanks, Pauline. Still, check to see if there are any boxes left. I assume you'll get in touch once you've checked the attic. And break a leg tomorrow night. Isn't that what you lot say?"

The conversation was over.

"May I come in?" Marcus Jacobsen had opened the door silently and was standing in the doorway, looking like a man who needed someone to confer with.

Carl pushed his office chair back and pointed to the chair at the end of the table.

"Look at this," said Marcus, handing his mobile to Carl. "What do you see?"

"A coffin in a church. Is it Maja's?"

"Yes. And on top of it?"

"A few bouquets?"

"Yes, three in total. One from Maja's cousin, and one from me . . ."

"And the third one?"

"That's what I wondered. So when the funeral was over, I went up and checked. And there was no card or ribbon on it."

"That's not so strange, is it?"

"Well, that depends on how many people attended the service. In this case, we were only two."

"An anonymous mourner?"

"I asked the church warden and he said that the bouquet was already lying on the lid when the undertaker brought in the coffin."

"Then it must be the undertaker who put it there."

Marcus nodded. "Yes, it was. I called him and he said that the bouquet was outside the door when he opened up for the day. There was a small note attached to the bouquet with a pin simply reading 'Maja's coffin.' He thought it was strange, and it certainly was out of the ordinary, but he still placed it on the coffin."

"And did you ask him if he still had the note?"

"He dug it up from the wastepaper bin."

"Spit it out, Marcus. What's nagging you about the note?"

"I had it checked and there were no fingerprints or DNA traces. It was printed in Times New Roman and cut from a piece of ordinary eighty-gram photocopy paper."

"I assume you took the bouquet with you back to HQ?"

"Yes, and I contacted all the florists, supermarkets, gas stations, and kiosks within a reasonable radius from the undertaker's. There was no paper or foil wrapped around the bouquet, and, even though many of them sell bunches of tulips like that, no one could give me any information except that type of flower doesn't grow in people's gardens at this time of year. And now it's bothering me that there were no traces of DNA of any kind on the note."

"I'm with you on that, Marcus. That is suspicious. So the person who left it was keen to stay anonymous."

"Yeah, right? I've been working nonstop all day checking up on Maja's comings and goings over the last couple of months, hoping that the person in question would pop up somewhere or other. But no such luck."

"Are you thinking that Maja was murdered?"

"No, not really. But as you know, I feel our fates are tied together somehow. I also checked through many of her things in my search for this person, and do you know what I found?"

"Tell me."

"All Maja's personal finances neatly and chronologically arranged in files according to year, all the way back to 1980, when she got her first job. So now we have a complete overview of her finances."

"I see. You've been busy, Marcus."

"Mhmm. Every month since March 1988, I found substantial incoming payments that had been marked with a highlighter. And they weren't wages."

"March 1988. So a good month after the explosion."

"Yes, and we aren't talking about small amounts here. From 1988 to 1998, she received five thousand kroner a month. From 1999 to 2009, it went up to ten thousand, and from 2010 until her death, it's been twenty thousand a month."

Carl did the math—not his strong point, but then again, his math teacher in Brønderslev hadn't been the brightest mind either.

"Almost five hundred thousand kroner. That's a lot of money, Marcus. Do you think it's her ex-husband trying to make up for a bad conscience? He must've made good money if he could spare that sort of cash."

"If you ask me, anyone who can spare that much without being able to deduct it must make good money, Carl. But it wasn't the ex-husband because he died of cancer in 2008."

Carl took another look at Marcus's photo of the coffin.

"Have you talked with the cousin about it?"

"Yes. She was aware that Maja sometimes received money, but she had no idea how much it was or that it was an ongoing thing."

"I assume you've spoken to the bank about the transfers?"

Marcus gave Carl an incredulous look.

"So there were no transfers, I gather?"

Marcus sighed. "The cousin thought that the money must've been sent to her anonymously somehow. That perhaps it was put in an envelope and left in her mailbox. But that's just guesswork. According to the bank, Maja came to her local branch every month with an envelope of cash that she deposited. I think she knew how to manage money, because she never used any of it. Combined with her regular savings, there was almost three quarters of a million in the account when she died."

"She never spent it. Bloody hell. Maybe she was just as puzzled about it as we are."

"Probably. But she must have known that the money had something to do with the explosion. She probably thought it was blood money, and so do I. My conclusion is that it was never the intention that anyone other than those from the repair shop should die. But Maja's little boy did die."

Carl nodded. He had heard the expression "collateral damage" many times in recent years in relation to American drone attacks. Unintended killings of innocent people in connection with a targeted attack. If the theory about blood money held water, Maja's son had been one such victim.

"Who pays blood money, Marcus?"

"Someone with a bad conscience, or someone whose culture demands it."

"The amount in question might indicate that a group was behind the attack on the repair shop and the explosion. That could also explain why the mechanics were so defenseless."

Marcus took a deep breath. "I don't know, Carl. Would a gang anonymously leave a small bunch of tulips in front of an undertaker's door? Something doesn't add up about that theory."

Carl agreed. "So you think we might be dealing with the premeditated killing of five people and an explosion that was carefully controlled and planned?"

"Yes. The evidence is pointing in that direction, Carl. Premeditated killings galore."

14

CARL/ASSAD

Monday, December 7, 2020

There were uncharacteristic stacks of paper waiting to be photocopied on Lis's desk when Carl walked past. Lis looked tired in spite of the festive decorations with "Merry Christmas" written in five languages and just as many colors that livened up her desk. Since Mrs. Sørensen, alias Ilse the She-Wolf, had retired, no replacement secretary had been found. Another effect of the cutbacks.

Stupid mistake, he just managed to think before Rose came barging out of her office, almost knocking over one of the newly trained investigators from the office opposite. He didn't smile at them, but then who did, on their floor?

"We need you in here right now, Carl," she commanded so loudly that even people at the other end of the hallway could hear it.

"Would you mind keeping your voice down, Rose?" admonished Carl when he was in their office. "We're not isolated in the basement of police HQ anymore, and I don't want to—"

"Give it a rest, Carl. Assad and I have been in here for two hours already, in case you hadn't noticed, and we have something exciting."

Assad still looked the worse for wear, but his usual smile was on its way back. "Look at this, Carl. We've found the nail in the haystack."

"Come on, Assad, it's called the needle in the——" Carl was cut short by Assad's insistent index finger pointing at the whiteboard: "4:28:1998" and "Vordingborg" were written under the column with the heading "Date/Crime Scene."

"What is that?" he asked, stepping closer.

"As you can see, this case is from over twenty years ago," said Rose. "But not so long ago that it could have disappeared into oblivion."

"There are no other details here. Is it a killing?"

They both shrugged.

Assad swiveled around in his office chair, activated his screen, and a horrible image appeared. Carl had not seen so much blood in years. A middle-aged man was sitting on the floor with his legs crossed and his forehead resting against the front of a machine. He was very pale and very dead. Completely drained of blood. On the other side of him, there was a large industrial room devoid of people, lit with neon lights and full of large machinery.

"Where is the blood from?" he asked.

Assad clicked the mouse and the next image appeared. It was a close-up of the man's arms, torso, and crossed legs.

"He placed his arms on his lap," said Rose. "Presumably he went into immediate shock when his hands were chopped off."

"What the . . . ! Chopped off?"

"Yes. He's leaning against a stamping machine that can cut five-millimeter-thick iron sheets. It made light work of him."

"Who is he?"

"He's the owner of the company Oleg Dudek Metalworks PLC."

"Oleg Dudek. Is he Russian?"

"No, Polish," said Assad. "He came to Denmark immediately after the fall of the Iron Curtain and settled down in Herning. Later on, he relocated his factory to Vordingborg and initiated a large-scale expansion."

"He hired almost only foreign labor—unorganized and underpaid, of course—so he was a controversial figure," added Rose. "I think his budget included hefty daily fines because of his hiring policy. And on top of that, there was a grave lack of safety at the workplace—hence the frequent accidents. By the end, he was close to having his business shut down."

"Hi," came a voice from the doorway. It was Gordon with a big smile, which froze when he caught sight of the image on Assad's screen.

"*Mein Gottes!*" For a second, he looked like he was going to vomit on the desk, and he gulped a couple of times.

"Take a deep breath, Gordon," said Carl. It was about time that the boy attended a coroners' course at the university so he could toughen up a little.

"What happened there?" he stuttered between his pale lips.

"The man cut off his hands in the stamping machine. Chop, chop!" said Assad dryly. As if that would improve Gordon's state of mind.

Carl turned to Rose. "But why have you written him on the board? Wasn't it just one of many accidents because he was a jerk who didn't follow safety procedures?" He thought about it for a moment. "Or if he was really under pressure and the safety standards authority or the tax office was closing down his factory, it could be suicide, couldn't it?"

"Oh my god, that's no way to go. Too gory!" exclaimed Gordon as he slouched down on his chair.

"It's been filed as a work accident, yes, and the factory was shut down afterward. *But . . .*" Róse nodded to Assad, who clicked to the next picture. It was a close-up of the two chopped-off hands lying on some sawdust just in back of the machine.

There was a crash behind them. Gordon had passed out and banged his head on the desk. He was out cold but breathing normally, so at least they would not have to worry about him for a while.

"You said 'but,' but does it change anything? Is it the angle of the hands? Do you think they've been moved?"

"No, Carl. Forensics established beyond reasonable doubt that they hadn't. The angle and the violent manner in which it happened makes it likely that they fell on the floor exactly in that spot. But what looks at first sight like sawdust is actually cooking salt."

Salt! Carl felt a shiver down his spine.

"Get Marcus in here immediately," he said to Assad. "And you can start filling in the remaining columns, Rose."

He stroked his chin: 1988, 1998, 2002. If this was not the work of a serial killer, then he was a monkey's uncle.

Assad checked the house number and parked his car in the driveway in front of a small, square house built with light concrete blocks. This type of house would have been erected within a fortnight back in the sixties, when even the man on the factory floor could afford to move to the suburbs. He took a photo because this was the type of house he would like to build himself. *I wonder how much it costs?* he thought as a man with bright red hair opened the door.

A tray of incredibly sweet cakes that made Assad's heart melt with pure nostalgia was placed on the table, and then Jurek Jasinski, former foreman of Oleg Dudek's company, was ready to talk.

"I warned Dudek many times and told him I'd go back home if he didn't get everything sorted," he said in fluent Danish but with a heavy Polish accent.

"But he wouldn't listen. And do you know what 'Dudek' means?"

Assad shook his head. Did he think all immigrants spoke Polish?

"Ironically, 'Dudek' means 'protector of the people,' which he bloody well wasn't." He laughed so explosively that Assad almost choked on one of the sticky cakes.

"I have some questions that I need you to answer briefly. Is that okay with you?"

"Fire away," answered the guy, drawing an imaginary gun from his hip and firing it. He blew the muzzle and smiled. Assad was impressed by his high spirits.

"What type of guy was Dudek?" was Assad's first question.

"Type?" He thought for a moment. "Maybe he was like a block of granite. No humor, no empathy, but just as powerful and strong. Does that help?"

"I was thinking more along the lines of why and how his death happened. Is it possible that someone forced him to do what he did?"

He laughed. "If so, the other guy would've had to be a hulk."

"He could've been threatened. A bullet to the head?"

"I can't answer that, can I? I wasn't there, if that's what you're suggesting."

Assad shook his head. "No, but was Oleg Dudek the type to kill himself?" Leading questions seldom held up in court, but they could be useful in real life.

He shrugged. "It's what he did, wasn't it? You never know what a guy like him is capable of. If Dudek didn't get his way, he could be rather dramatic."

"I see. But the way he did it—chopping off his hands. Was that something he would do?"

Surprisingly, Jasinski started laughing again.

"Dudek was fairly tough and violent. A former military man and boxer. Unfortunately, that also sometimes showed on his wife's face."

"So, you think he would?"

He shrugged again.

"How could it even happen?" continued Assad. "Had he removed something from the machine that could have prevented the accident?"

Jurek leaned forward toward Assad. "You have to understand one thing, Detective. The machines were all old junk from the Baltic countries. If they broke down, that was that. And that stamping machine was lethal. One of the boys from Pakistan lost all his fingers on one hand on that machine." He illustrated by drawing the edge of his hand across his fingers close to the knuckles.

"That accident cost Dudek a huge fine. But luckily, the floor manager was quick to put the fingers in his mouth to maintain their temperature and kept them there until he could make it to the hospital with the poor guy. He never regained full mobility in his fingers, but at least he kept them."

"So the machine was faulty?"

"Yes, I banned my team from using it. That almost got me fired."

"How long before Dudek's death was this?"

"About a year, I think."

"If it wasn't an accident, why would he have done it?"

"I suppose he couldn't be bothered anymore with the authorities and unions. That must've been it. The factory would've been shut down anyway."

"I don't quite get that because they found out afterward that he had loads of cash lying around and deposited in Polish bank accounts. He could've just paid his fines and toed the line with the authorities."

"Yes, but Dudek was a bit of a mystery."

"Why was he alone in the factory when he died?"

"He went in half an hour before the rest of us. Always did."

Assad sighed. How would he get the man to tell him what he needed to know if he could not be bothered to reflect a little more on any of it?

"When you look back on it, don't you think it all seems a bit suspicious?"

"Listen here, Detective. All of us at the factory lost our jobs that very day, so we had more than enough on our plates. Personally, I couldn't give a shit about why Dudek died. I have two kids I needed to take care of. I couldn't leave it all to my wife, could I? 'Jurek, Jurek, how will we get by?' she complained from the minute it happened. So just like everyone else at the factory, I was already rushing around looking for work in the local area the day after, but there was no work for people like us in southern Zealand. That's why I ended up so close to Copenhagen."

"You've never considered that he could've been murdered? That someone simply wanted him dead? Did Dudek have many enemies?"

A roar of laughter made the coffee table shake. "You'd be better off asking me if he had any friends. That would be easier because he didn't have any. Everyone he came in contact with thought he was a prick. Even the customers. But he was inexpensive and that counts more than personality."

"Do you think there was anyone who particularly hated him?"

He shrugged again.

"Just one more thing. There was salt on the ground behind the stamping machine, and I find that odd. Do you know anything about that?"

He frowned. "Salt? I don't know why there was salt—there was usually sand. But Dudek was full of surprises. If he didn't have any sand, he would've used whatever was available. It was probably a sack of road salt left from the winter that he wanted to get rid of."

"It wasn't road salt. It was ordinary coarse salt—the sort used in cooking."

"Then he probably stole it from his wife." This time his laughter was not quite so annoying. You got used to it.

"Why was there sand or salt in the first place?"

"There was a lathe on the other side of the stamping machine, and the sand helped to absorb the iron chips and oil that came from it."

When Assad returned, the chief of homicide was in the Department Q office and all four of them were staring at some new questions written along the edge of the whiteboard.

Assad looked them over.

"I can answer one of the questions straightaway," he said. "The salt was in the spot where there would normally be sand. The foreman, Jurek Jasinski, thought it was just a replacement. But I'm surprised forensics didn't check if there was sand underneath the salt. They could have checked if the pile of metal chips was so oily that they'd had to pour something else over it to absorb the debris from the lathe."

"Did you get anything else out of the foreman? Did he have any theories about the owner's death?" asked Carl.

Assad shook his head. "But I managed to confirm that no one at his work or anywhere else liked him."

Marcus Jacobsen leaned forward toward Assad.

"For your information, I've spoken with the head of investigation at the time," he said, "and he definitely remembers that the tip of one of the victim's shoes was lodged in the lever on the pedal that released the stamp. That alone was reason enough to deem it an accident. He also added other facts to back that up. So it is understandable that they stopped any further investigation."

"Okay, I don't remember that being in the report," said Carl.

"Here!" Marcus leafed and pointed at the passage.

"'The victim was slumped in a seated position with legs crossed and one shoe lodged in the release pedal,'" growled Carl. "Whoever wrote this should definitely be reprimanded for sloppy vocabulary like that."

Marcus Jacobsen looked at each of them with a stern expression.

"Yes, and now this death is also noted on the whiteboard. But unfortunately, I'd be surprised if we manage to draw any real conclusions about this case other than that there appears to be a murderer, without a clear motive, who has managed to kill people in ways that leaves us investigators questioning whether they were accidents or suicides. Do we all agree?"

"Not quite." Rose pursed her lips. "The motive is still unclear. However, looking at the victims, we know that none of them were saints. So there is a common denominator that these people were not the sort that would be missed. But apart from that, you're right."

Assad sat down. "Saints." Who was? Was he? He doubted it.

"What next?" he asked.

"Yes, what next?" Carl looked up at the whiteboard. "We'd better see if we can get some more cases on the board and hope that our killer has slipped up with one of them."

"And if there aren't any more?" asked Gordon.

Marcus Jacobsen placed a hand over his and patted it a couple of times.

"Believe me, Gordon," he said, tapping the tip of his nose. "There are!"

15

CARL

Monday, December 7, 2020

"**Congratulations**" **was the** first thing he said when Pauline Rasmussen answered the phone. "I read the reviews in the Sunday papers and they were great. And booked for every day up until Christmas. That's a good sign. I just hope you don't run into trouble with corona and the prime minister's restrictions."

Carl looked down at the newspaper in front of him. "*Politiken* writes that 'the cabaret was a sublime satire masterfully led by Pauline Rasmussen's distinct singing and perfect comedic timing,' and so on. Five hearts and great publicity. You must be very pleased and relieved."

Carl waited for her to thank him and express her joy. But he could not have been more wrong.

"I've changed my mind, Carl Mørck. I don't want to go rummaging in the attic. There's nothing there of interest for you anyway, and, if there had been, your colleagues would've found it."

"Okay. But if it's so uninteresting, there's no reason for you to withhold it."

"No. Maybe not. But I've got other things on my mind, so you can forget about it. Anyway, I'm not even sure I didn't get rid of the computer and everything else in one go, come to think about it. Have a nice day now." She hung up.

Carl frowned and stood up. It was a mystery to him how adults could lie so blatantly.

"Assad, come on. We're going for a drive!" he said, dragging him by the sleeve to the parking lot.

"What's up?" asked Assad as he rested his feet on the dashboard above the glove compartment.

"What's up? My sixth sense tells me that this Pauline woman was a good deal closer to the deceased Palle Rasmussen than she's willing to admit."

They reached her terraced house in Herlev at the very moment she emerged from her front door carrying a heavy-looking cardboard box.

Her hair was disheveled, just like the tracksuit she was wearing.

"She's been busy," said Carl as he drove halfway up onto the pavement to block her car, which was parked with the trunk already open.

She froze at the sight of Carl and Assad.

"Hello, Pauline," he said, smiling and nodding to Assad, who was gently prying the box out of her hands. She could have demanded her rights and protested Carl Mørck's lack of a warrant, but instead she stayed frozen on the spot, speechless.

"Why don't we take these off your hands as well," he asked, pointing at the packed back seat. "Then you can get on with your day."

She nodded silently. "I haven't done anything wrong," she said, her voice quivering. "You might find something I'm not very proud of, but I was just being jealous."

"We've got something. There's a computer in this one, Carl," said Gordon as he opened the third and largest box on the desk. "It's an Apple iMac G4. It must be old enough by now to fetch a good price."

Carl smiled. "Ask the people on the fourth floor to help us log in to it, Gordon. Tell them that we'll owe them a favor."

"Shouldn't I just try to open it myself?" he asked cockily.

"You can try, but don't forget these cases," Carl said, pointing at the stacks of files.

"And, Assad, what is that smell? Are you opening a kebab shop?" He laughed but stopped when Assad pointed at a pot on a hot plate over in the corner behind Gordon's growing collection of Christmas knick-knacks and elves.

"We can't go to the cafeteria during corona, remember? So today Rose has ordered homemade risotto with lamb."

Carl's stomach churned. Lamb and risotto was like boiling fish with Jell-O powder. Disgusting!

"Please put the lid on, Assad. Otherwise they'll come running in from the offices across the hall."

"Oh, so next time I should make a bigger portion, you think?"

Carl brought his hand to his head in exasperation. Years in the HQ basement had left them with absolutely no sense of decorum.

"Just remember the lid, Assad. And then go through the boxes of papers. It looks like printouts of something like a thousand emails and who knows what else. Throw away everything that looks official—we're looking for personal emails. Perhaps you'll find threats in some of them."

He turned to Rose. "And what about you? Have any of our colleagues elsewhere in Denmark sniffed out cases involving salt at the crime scene?"

"Not yet. But I'm still waiting for answers from most districts. Just now I'm researching the cultural history and symbolism of salt. I've read in a book by Mark Kurlansky that salt was a currency for many years. Did you know that? They called it 'white gold.' The word 'salary' actually comes from the word 'salt.'"

"I know that in the old days it was extracted from peat and sea-weed," said Gordon. Had he already forgotten about his task of crack-ing the password for the computer?

Rose gave him a look that made him blush. "The deeper I delve into the topic, the more surprised I am at how much salt has influenced the history of the world and how cynically those in power through the ages have exploited the salt that was essential for common people who didn't have access to it themselves. Salt smuggling was once punishable by death, as crazy as that sounds. By the end of the seventeen hundreds, the monopoly on salt in France was a contributing factor to the revolution, and the same goes for America, when the Americans rebelled against the English. In India, Gandhi opposed the salt monopoly of the British Empire with his long peace march in 1930, where he and his followers collected the salt from evaporated seawater, in breach of the British salt laws. When Gandhi was arrested, the rebellion exploded in India, and England lost its power. Again, because of salt. And salt also has a specific meaning in the Bible."

Carl looked at Rose. "I'm sorry, Rose, can you repeat that last bit? I was thinking about something else."

Why the hell did her face suddenly change color from porridge to purple?

Carl looked up at the whiteboard with the three cases from 1988, 1998, and 2002. They were all from quite some time ago, so the person or people who had committed the killings could not be young anymore. If they were even still alive. The oldest case, if it *was* the oldest, was already thirty-two years old, so the perpetrator would probably be close to sixty or even older. How old would you likely be to be able to commit such a complicated crime as the attack at the repair shop? Twenty, thirty, or forty years old?

Someone knocked on the doorframe, and they all looked over.

"Hello," said a woman tentatively in a slightly husky voice as she removed her green face mask. Her shiny black hair poured out from under her scarf. She looked refreshed and her smile was genuine and warm. It was Marwa, Assad's wife, completely changed from back when she had been in a wheelchair at Kaiser Wilhelm Memorial Church in Berlin with enough explosives underneath her to demolish everything in a hundred-meter radius.

"Marwa, what are you doing here?" asked Assad, giving her a hug.

"Oh, it smells wonderful in here." She blinked at her husband. Apparently, the risotto dish was one she recognized. "I just walked inside the office to Marcus. I wanted to because you say you thank him for helping us find ourselves."

Carl smiled. It was like hearing Assad ten years ago. Full of mistakes but charming.

She turned to Carl. "And also to you, Carl. It is a long time ago, but you do not even know . . ." She was momentarily overcome by the images flashing before her eyes. "When we were in Berlin. Thank you, Carl. Thank you, thank you, thank you," she said, just like she did every time the opportunity presented itself.

She plucked up her courage and gave him as big a hug as she dared.

"Thank you to all of you. You are just so clever, yes!"

She shook everyone's hand, and Assad looked at her with a tenderness that felt almost physical. Then she turned and looked around the room. "I can understand why you like it, Assad. This place is nice and big."

She looked up at the whiteboard and read the notes. It was a little unusual, but Carl assumed that they discussed work freely, just as he and Mona did.

Then she stopped reading and became serious.

"What is it, Marwa?" asked Assad.

She pointed at the board with an expression of disgust. "I do not know what happened with Oleg Dudek, but I know the date all too well."

"I don't understand. The twenty-eighth of April. What about it, Marwa?" asked Assad.

She turned to him, surprised. "But you know what. It was the day the devil Saddam Hussein was born!"

"Weren't you surprised by how affected Marwa was, Assad?"

"She's easily affected by many things, Carl. When we receive a letter from the authorities, she sits down in the corner of the bedroom. When I come home very late, she cries. When Ronia shouts or Nella cries, she always distances herself from the rest of us."

"What does the psychologist say about that?"

"He says that it will get better but that it'll still take some time. And, in a way, I can understand her reaction to the date because we all hated

Saddam Hussein. I just didn't realize that date had anything to do with him."

Carl nodded. "How are you getting on with those boxes, Assad? Is there anything interesting?"

"If there are threats in those emails, I haven't found any. But I have come across many of these." He handed Carl a piece of paper, and Carl read:

I saw you on the TV yesterday and you turned me on for a moment. I'll be home tomorrow at four. Do you have time to pop by? Xxx.

"Well, the man was certainly popular. I'll give him that much. You said there are many of them. Who are they from?"

"They're from Pauline Rasmussen. You can see it at the top. That's probably why she wouldn't let you rummage through her boxes, don't you think?"

"Hey, give me a couple of those, Assad. I need a break. Enough salt for one day," said Rose.

He placed an entire box in front of her and laughed.

"Do we know what Palle Rasmussen's new girlfriend was called? Are there emails from her too?" asked Carl.

They both looked back blankly.

Carl counted the boxes—six in total. They were sure to find something.

16

RAGNHILD

Monday, December 7, 2020

Ragnhild felt a special rush in her stomach every time she took the first steps up the green-speckled marble staircase. In the gloomy rooms of this mansion, she had felt for the first time that life could be more than just routines and trivialities. When she and the other women reported what they had been up to every few weeks, she felt a rush even more intense than being in love.

This time, Ragnhild had experienced several things that she wanted to share with the others. This is what drove her. She had gone to university, had good jobs and a few superficial relationships. But nothing compared to this small group and what they had decided to accomplish.

"Welcome, Sara, Martha, and Ruth," said Debora as she pulled out chairs and indicated where they should sit.

Ragnhild loved the names Debora had given them, especially her own. Ruth. They were sisters now who serendipitously had found one another in a common cause that allowed them to be exactly the women they were. Free of labels, personal information, and expectations.

And they were destined to come down hard on the decay of society.

"Shall we begin with you, Ruth?" asked Debora.

Ragnhild took a deep breath at the sound of her sisterhood name. Was it really her turn to start them off today? How nice. She took a couple of sips from her teacup and then she was ready.

"Three things since last time," she said, looking at the others. Martha, who was sitting next to her, let out a slight sigh. Apparently, she had not accomplished quite as much, whereas Sara did not raise an eyebrow. She never did.

Ragnhild started with the credo that introduced all their sessions.

"You could call it taking the law into your own hands, but you could also call it due diligence because it makes the world a little better every time."

The three others applauded her quietly. And then she had the floor.

"When I think about how resolute I've learned to be, I shake all over with joy because I'm certain that this will not be forgotten."

No one interrupted her for the next ten minutes, and, when she had finished, Debora stood up and embraced her.

"I don't know what to say, Ruth," said Martha. "You're a hard act to follow."

The round continued to Martha, and you could always expect a bit of everything from her. But Martha was also the most open among them. And if she was displeased with herself, she did not try to hide it.

"These weeks have been quiet. Maybe I haven't really been in the mood to challenge myself, or maybe the chance hasn't presented itself. I must say that you've become extremely good at administering the right punishment at the right time, Ruth. Maybe I'm just not as lucky or skilled as you."

Ragnhild protested slightly, but her alter ego, Ruth, lapped it up.

"The old trick of using an umbrella as a weapon never fails," started Martha. "And this time, I decided to devote an entire day to knocking down all the bicyclists who had no respect for pedestrians and the highway code. My strategy was always the same: I'd ride the bus, exiting at the stops in the city center that let out directly onto the bicycle lane."

Ragnhild was struggling to hide her excitement, but a look from Debora told her to allow Martha to continue her account without interruption.

"Of course, not all bicyclists refused to stop for exiting passengers, but most did. I could gauge the type through the rear window of the bus, a couple of idiots approaching too quickly, clearly without any intention whatsoever of stopping. Then I would quickly get off with my umbrella positioned forward to stick right into their wheels. If I succeeded in causing one bicyclist to crash, more followed. And even though they were hurt, their wheels buckled and their handlebars twisted, I never apologized." She looked directly at Ragnhild. "On the contrary, I gave them a good scolding. Told them next time they better think twice and follow the rules."

At this point, Ragnhild could not hold back some discreet applause.

"Over the course of the day, I succeeded in breaking six umbrellas and taking down at least twenty of the totally irresponsible, stupid bicyclists who put the lives of pedestrians at risk." She smiled. "And believe me, *they* will certainly never drive past a bus again before making sure all the passengers are safely off."

She stopped and a vexed expression spread across her face. "There was just one issue."

"Tell us, Martha," said Debora.

"I stayed in the city center the whole time, and I think I managed to stop at the right moment. But still someone must have reported one of the episodes because, at the last stop, I saw a police car racing up the street with sirens blaring."

The room fell quiet, and Debora put down her cup.

"Did they file a report, Martha?" she asked.

"Yes, but without me because I was already several hundred meters away. But that's the last time I'll pull that trick."

"Good!" Debora turned to Ragnhild and Sara. "Mark my words. If any of you are ever confronted by the police, whether you are detained, caught on camera, described in detail and have a warrant put out for you, recognized—god forbid—or anything of that nature, you will no longer have a place at this table."

Martha lowered her head. "It was impossible to recognize me even if someone had seen the events unfold. I'd bought my clothes in a second-hand shop and threw them in a charity container afterward. I was wearing a scarf, face mask, and wig, which I only use every tenth time."

"Good. But if it were to happen anyway, you will take your punishment and forget all about this group for eternity. Are we agreed? You've acted on your own initiative and the rest of us don't exist. Remember that!"

They all agreed. These were the conditions. Ragnhild was the last to have joined the group, and she knew full well that she had replaced someone called Eva, who had been excommunicated because a report had been filed on her. She knew none of the details.

"And just one more thing, which I cannot stress enough. Your actions are intended to change the world for the better. So you must never cause anyone irreparable damage. Understood? You were very close this time to crossing the line, Martha. You have to remain critical of your own ideas."

When Debora's gaze was stern like this, Ragnhild avoided her eyes.

"Now it's your turn, Sara," she said in a gentler voice.

"Nothing substantial, I'm afraid. I've had the flu for most of the month, so I haven't been out much."

"That's how it is sometimes. We understand. As long as it isn't corona."

She shook her head. "But I did go to a private performance at the theater last night. The cast wasn't the best but that's just par for the course these days." She laughed dryly. "Yeah, I know it isn't much, but I did trip a few people who were inconsiderately pushing their way to their seats because they didn't have the courtesy to arrive on time or consider me as they passed. Of course, they didn't know what happened because they had their rear ends in my face. Maybe they just thought they tripped accidentally. But let me tell you, the people in the rows in front of us let them have it."

Debora smiled. "Yes, it's a small thing, but we all know the feeling when our fellow human beings show no consideration. I think we've all felt the urge to trip up idiots like that."

Ragnhild could not hold herself back. "Yes, or push them hard. Especially if they're in the first tier of the balcony."

17

CARL

Tuesday, December 8, 2020

"I've now got the vehicle registration details on the cars that were sold from the repair shop in the two months leading up to the explosion, Carl."

Gordon pushed the list over. "There aren't quite as many cars as I initially thought. In fact, they only sold half as many cars in January 1988 as in December 1987, so January ended up being only four. And none of them were sold to immigrants."

"Have you called the people who purchased the cars and asked them which ones they bought and whether there were any problems with them?"

He looked confused. "Am I supposed to do that? I'm also trying to open Palle Rasmussen's computer."

"Trying? Have you even made any progress?"

"Er, no. I've tried loads of times with different passwords, but it didn't like that and froze."

"Just get the computer up to IT, Gordon. After all, they're the ones here who know most about this stuff. Go and find the phone numbers of the four people who bought the cars and give them a call. And then continue with the cars that were sold in December 1987, and only then continue with these old case files. I can see that the stack hasn't shrunk much since yesterday."

The poor guy looked like he was about to cry.

Carl turned to Rose, who was standing firmly with her arms crossed and sporting a tired expression. "And you, Rose. Please give Gordon a hand with the files. At the moment, it seems that you're keen to just wait around for other departments to respond to your request."

She let out a sigh that could have blown down anything. "Listen, Mr. Mørck, if you opened your eyes, you'd see that I'm already busy going over Palle Rasmussen's emails. I read and read. And so far, I haven't come across anything significant. Don't you bloody insinuate that any of us here are wasting time. Right, Gordon?"

The pale guy gave her a grateful look and put on his headset.

"And what about you, Your Highness?" she asked. "What are you doing? Why don't *you* get going with Gordon's musty files?"

Carl had been staring at his packet of cigarettes for fifteen minutes. There was a biting wind outside, so he did not want to open the window.

Never mind, he thought. *I'll just smoke one and then open the window and go to the loo while the smoke disappears. No one will notice.*

He took a deep puff and thought things through.

Rose's lecture on the meaning of salt through the ages was on his mind. Politically, religiously, economically, and culturally, this simple mineral NaCl, sodium chloride, could control or conquer continents— and now it was controlling him.

Why had it been poured out close to the victims? Was it symbolic or was it a direct invitation from the killer to follow this lead? But how were they supposed to trace the purchase of something so utterly banal as cooking salt, which cost nothing and could be found anywhere?

He wondered how many times this sick individual had acted on their murderous tendencies. And when.

At the very least in 1988, 1998, and 2002. What if the intervals between the crimes were specific—a couple of years, for example? Then there would be similar cases in 1990, 2000, and 2004. If that was the case, they could refine their search. And if they did not find anything in those years, they could always review cases from the intervening or following years.

And then there was another thing that was troubling him. What was the significance of the indentations on the dead Palle Rasmussen's wrists? The most likely explanation was that he had been tied to the steering wheel of the car, which could also explain why the wheel cover had been removed. Another possibility was that he and Hardy had not been thorough enough when they searched for Palle Rasmussen's possible sex partners. Hadn't the cleaning lady said that she thought the man had "certain sexual tendencies that she and her husband certainly did not entertain in their home"?

Someone must have asked the cleaning lady how she knew that, so why was that not in the report? Were there really pages missing? Several factors certainly indicated as much.

He dialed Hardy's mobile number.

The voice that answered sounded very weary. It was Morten.

"Hi, Morten. What's going on? Why are you answering the phone?"

"Hi, Carl. Hardy has just had a minor seizure. The Swiss did something to his back that caused him pain everywhere—places he hasn't been able to feel for years."

"Okay. But isn't that a good thing?"

"We don't know. It might just be phantom pain from body parts that the brain remembers, causing sensations that aren't real. He's in a bad way."

"Can I speak to him? Two very brief questions?"

"Why do you think I sound like this? We're all totally exhausted. I've been by his bedside for hours. If you can manage to get a few words out of him, then . . ."

There was a moment's silence. "What do you think, Hardy? Is it okay?" sounded Morten's voice in the background.

Morten sighed deeply when he came back. "I'll pass you over, Carl. But just for a second, okay?"

"Hello," came the feeble voice.

"Hello, Hardy. I'm sorry you're feeling bad. I hope they know what they're doing down there."

"They do," he said, out of breath.

"Hardy, just a quick question. The Palle Rasmussen case: Do you remember why the cleaning lady insinuated that he played sadomasochistic games?"

"Because of his porno magazines," he replied promptly. Good old Hardy, encyclopedic as ever. "Sometimes blood on his bedsheets . . . when she came in to do the cleaning . . . and red stripes on his back . . . on the back of his T-shirts . . . when she washed his clothes in the morning."

"I see. But you and I did search for his sex partners, didn't we?"

"Yes, but we . . . didn't find any. Checked his mobile and computer"—he sighed audibly—"but . . . there were . . . no contacts."

"Checked his computer? Do you remember what type of computer it was?"

"It was a Mac, but nothing pointed . . . in that direction. Only politics."

"And that was noted in the report?"

"Yes! Ouch, damn it . . . yes, of course it was."

"Thanks, Hardy. Put Morten back on."

"That was out of line, Carl," Morten said angrily. "I said a second and that was almost a minute. You should see Hardy now. He's as white as a sheet." There was a slight pause, and Carl heard Morten in the background: "I'm just telling it like it is, Hardy. Carl doesn't get what's going on down here."

"You're right, Morten," said Carl. "But then you don't get what's going on up here, do you? We're talking murder, Morten. I hope Hardy feels better soon. How long will you stay down there, do you know?"

"As long as we want, thank you. At the moment, we can't get home anyway. I suppose you've heard about COVID-19, haven't you? Anyway, bye!"

That was one way to say goodbye—just hanging up.

Carl threw his cigarette butt out of the window and waved the smoke out with it as best he could.

So his colleagues had not managed to locate Palle Rasmussen's sex partners, but why not? Had they presumed they could only be prostitutes? He could not remember.

Carl took another cigarette. If he was going to smoke anyway, he might as well do it long before he went home. He did not want Mona to be able to smell that he was at it again.

He leaned halfway out the window and looked down on the street. The cigarette butt he had just thrown out was still down there smoldering on the wet asphalt. Damn it. Next time he would have to make sure he put it out first.

Anyway, they had not been able to identify any prostitutes. But who else had they asked back then? Had they, for instance, asked his new girlfriend if she knew anything about Palle Rasmussen's wrists? He simply could not remember. And what the hell was her name again?

"Excuse me, but what *are* you doing, Carl?"

He got such a shock that his mouth dropped open, sending his cigarette down toward the butt below.

He turned around to face a very indignant Rose.

"Mona says you aren't allowed to smoke. You can't smoke here on Teglholmen, and definitely not in here. I've also said you shouldn't smoke and *still* you do it. Do you want me to rat you out to Mona? Do you want her to tell you that if you keep it up, Lucia will grow up without you? Do you? You're not a young dad, to put it bluntly. You're *old*, Carl, and you won't get much older if you don't muster up some willpower."

She blurted everything out at the speed of an automatic rifle, and with more or less the same effect and precision.

"No, thank you very much. I don't think you should."

"*What?*"

"Rat me out!"

"Then you damn well better stop this crap. Don't tell me you're also throwing your butts down on the street."

He did not answer that. "Do you have something for me? What's that in your hand?"

"We've found two emails that are pretty interesting in my opinion. Especially this one. Notice the date."

Carl took it and read.

Dated May 17, 2002, two days before Palle Rasmussen's possible suicide and sent from a Hotmail address under the name "Wildling." It would be difficult if not impossible to find out who had sent it.

It read:

Palle. Your political meeting in Nørrebro Sports Hall the other day made an impression on me. I don't know how to express it, but I would, as you know, love to meet you again. You probably noticed that I sat down in the third row just in front of you and asked someone to move so that I could make eye contact with you. I will contact you ASAP.

"Was that all?"

Rose nodded. "It says it all, I think. The person uses flattery, and it seems that this was what turned on Palle Rasmussen more than anything else. And the person doesn't reveal their identity in the email, but sometimes neither do I. I also have a couple of aliases. I suppose she's just being cautious on the internet—you had to be, even back then. She doesn't write any name or give any suggestion about how the meeting will happen."

"Yes, that is striking. I agree. Do you detect an erotic undertone here?"

She shrugged. "Maybe. But in that case, it's not very obvious. It could just as well be from a fan who was fascinated by his charisma and opinions."

"'Eye contact,' it says."

"Yes, you never know."

"And the other email, Rose?"

"I have it here. It's from Sisle Park—Palle's last girlfriend, or whatever she was."

That was right, she was called Sisle. He remembered the strange name now.

"Look at the date again. I'm sure you'll find it interesting."

This one was dated the day before the one he had just read: May 16, 2002.

Dear Palle. I hope you don't feel this is an imposition, but I don't feel like we finished our chat last time. We can meet at Café Sommersko the day after tomorrow, on Saturday, around four, when I'll be in Copenhagen. What do you say? Do you have time? Sisle.

"So she suggests that they meet the day before he kills himself. That brings me to the question of whether he also printed his replies, including the one to her."

"We're well through the first boxes, Carl, and there's no indication that he printed his replies. So far, we've only found incoming emails. I assume the sent emails will be on his computer."

Carl sighed. "Has Gordon sent the Mac up to the IT geeks on the fourth floor?"

"Yes, he has. And just now, he's sweating over your next task. And he's struggling, I can tell you that much. Out of the four people who bought used cars from the repair shop, two have died in the meantime and he's trying to track down the last two. But remember, Carl, Gordon is a people pleaser. Go easy on him. He's a bit vulnerable at the moment."

"Vulnerable? Why's that?"

"He's started internet dating and isn't having much luck with it. In fact, no luck at all. And who's to tell if it's his pale face or corona scaring them off."

Carl hiked up his trousers as he scanned the several hundred brightly lit windows of the Copenhagen suburb. The company that Sisle Park owned was a place that demanded a neat appearance. He looked at the sign, which, given its size and the thickness of the brass, could have been on the front of an embassy.

The directory next to it simply read "Park Optimizing," and underneath, it listed the different sections of the company distributed over four floors. It was a rather extensive enterprise with all kinds of departments, each with their own purpose: export/import, fair trade, development, consultancy, print, chemical behavior, and at least twenty others, some of which required more explanation if Carl was to make any sense out of them.

He was welcomed by Sisle Park herself on the second floor.

Even though Carl was fairly tall, she towered above him. It certainly was not something you saw every day.

Carl gauged her high heels and found comfort in the fact that without them they would be of equal height.

Once they were inside her office, she asked her secretary to leave them alone. Her masculine clothes and far too direct gaze hinted that their conversation would be brief and that she would be in charge of how it went.

He looked at the sharp creases in her trousers and reflected that Palle Rasmussen had been a gentleman of versatile taste in women.

"I understand that this is about Palle," she said coolly.

"About Palle, yes. And about you."

"I only knew him superficially. You do know that this is almost twenty years back?"

Stupid question.

"You don't have to tell me that." He smiled at her. "The reason I'm here is this," he said, passing her the email she had sent back then. "I don't think this email comes across very superficial," he said while she read.

She looked up, unfazed. "And what of it? The man was very pushy. Isn't it obvious I wanted to meet him to break up with him?"

"Break up? I see. So you do admit that you were in a relationship?"

She looked annoyed at her slip. "I was in my thirties then and did so many silly things that didn't really mean anything."

"We have a suspicion that Palle Rasmussen didn't kill himself. So his whereabouts in the days immediately before he died are obviously of interest to us. Did the meeting happen?"

Small nerves started twitching behind her perfect skin. "I don't think I'm obligated to say anything about that here," she said, stretching a red nail toward an intercom.

"No, not here if you don't want to. So how would you like for us to take a drive down to the station?"

She frowned. "This is absurd. I think you should leave now."

"I'd like to, but first a couple of quick questions and then I'll let you off. I think."

She pushed the intercom button. "Would you mind coming in here. I think Chief Inspector Mørck is about to leave."

Carl nodded at the secretary when she opened the door from the front office. Then he turned back toward her boss.

"Sisle Park, I would like to know if you had a sexual relationship with Palle Rasmussen. Did you?" he asked, reveling in the glare she sent her secretary. A gaze that sent a clear signal for her to get lost.

"I'd be happy to repeat the question," he said when the door slammed shut behind the secretary.

"How bloody dare you—and while my secretary is listening!"

"I'm pleased to hear that we can drop the pretense. But still, isn't it better that you answer here than in a public courtroom?"

"Fine. No, we didn't have a sexual relationship by any stretch of the imagination. And where on earth did you even get that idea from?"

"A hint from his niece, Pauline Rasmussen."

She threw back her head as if someone had tried to spit in her face.

"What would she know about it? Such a vulgar woman!"

"Vulgar? In what way? Because she used to be in a relationship with her uncle or because she's a cabaret actress?"

"Oh, cut it out, you silly man. Because she was still seeing Palle when he tried his luck with me."

"Tried?"

"Can't you read what the email says?"

"You write that you don't want to be an imposition. That is what I see. An unequal relationship where he was the one in control and maybe didn't want to see you."

"He was controlling, yes. Too much so. I didn't have a sexual relationship with him because he was still seeing Pauline. But he tried. He also had some tendencies that I neither could nor would give in to."

"Like what?"

She wrung her hands and pressed her red lips together. Whatever it was, she didn't want to say it.

Carl understood. He had to tread carefully now.

"This is all confidential. So whatever you say won't go any further. I need to ask you to tell me what you're keeping from me. It might be important."

"He wanted me to do something that I loathe."

"Sexually?"

"Yes. He wanted to play sadomasochistic games with me. He came straight out with it. He wanted me to dominate him."

"I see. Ropes, spanking, things like that?"

"Something along those lines, yes."

He held her gaze for a while before looking away. It worked.

Then he stood up and stuck out his hand. "Thanks, Sisle Park. You've been a great help."

She looked awkwardly at the floor like someone who had lost all their power and wasn't sure what to do with themselves.

On his way out, he looked around at the highly efficient departments that ran Sisle Park's many lines of business. Everywhere you turned, there were women in tailored suits, all of which individually cost more than his entire wardrobe put together.

Why the hell would a woman like Sisle Park, who could achieve such a level of success in business and apparently only employed women, have anything to do with an ugly, fat, manipulative bastard like Palle Rasmussen?

Carl smiled. When he thought about Vigga, his quirky, colorful hippie ex-wife, he realized that even the strangest of opposites can attract.

18

ASSAD/CARL

Tuesday, December 8, 2020

When Rose and Assad had reached the fourth cardboard box out of six, they had found three very unmistakably threatening letters. In addition, there were ten more comical in nature, which Palle Rasmussen had commented on in the margin, and at least thirty emails from Pauline.

"You wouldn't catch me writing things like this email from Pauline Rasmussen to a well-known politician at their work. She must've known that his secretary would learn about the intimate details of their affair," he said.

"Some of them are racy enough to make even me blush," answered Rose.

Gordon looked up from his case files. "Why? You've got nothing to be embarrassed about, Rose."

Assad smiled. These Danes were so candid when the subject turned to sex. Candid and liberated. But when it came to everything else, that attitude vanished.

Especially in his experience.

That morning, there had been a crisis at home, and a big crisis at that. Since November last year, the national police force had increased security and ordered PET—the national security and intelligence service— to carry out checks on all police personnel's partners, as well as children over eighteen still living at home. They claimed that this was intended to enhance security in the Danish police force, and the close family members of the 16,900 police employees needed a security clearance at the level of "confidential" or even higher. But why had they *really* done it? What were they afraid of?

When these measures were first announced, Assad had immediately voiced his concerns to Marcus Jacobsen, who had assured him that his family would be spared from the checks. After all, Assad was a real hero and also a trusted employee, and his family's past was known by anyone who had followed the news in the slightest. If his family were sent questionnaires or anything of that sort, Marcus told Assad to come to him immediately. They could rest assured that it would not go any further. And then things went quiet for a long time.

But this morning, Assad found Marwa holding a letter from PET requesting an interview with her, their two adult daughters, and their son. And the letter stated that after the interview, there would be paperwork to complete and sign. They were all in a state of panic. First, Marwa yelled that Assad had promised her this would not happen. Then Nella started crying, and Ronia blurted out things that could never reach the ears of the officials from PET. Only Afif remained silent.

Assad needed help to put a stop to this charade. It was one concern that they could fire him, but it was a far more serious threat that Afif might be deported to Iraq and that Ronia might be confronted with her close connection to a known terrorist, and in response blurt out radical attacks on everything Danish society stood for.

"We have a number of specific matters we need to discuss with you, Carl," said Rose when he returned from interviewing Sisle Park. "We've found some emails from Pauline Rasmussen to Palle Rasmussen from the four months before his death. And it's glaringly obvious that they had a sexual relationship—and one of a very unusual nature at that."

"I know. Sisle Park just told me."

"The last email we found while you were gone was sent the day before Palle Rasmussen died. I'm guessing that the anonymous sender is Pauline Rasmussen. And the sender asks him to pop by her place the next day on his way home—where he can look forward to a special surprise. One that will hurt in the best possible way."

"I see." Carl smiled. "This might explain the indentations on his wrists. Maybe things got out of hand."

"He died from carbon monoxide poisoning, Carl. Not from his sexual activities."

"Not directly, I know. But maybe the idiot told Pauline that she was on her way out."

"So you think she drugged him to make him pass out? And you really think she could have dragged a man who weighed over a hundred kilos? How much do you think Pauline weighs?" asked Rose.

He got the point. Denmark's cabaret darling was a pixie compared to most women.

"And then there are the threatening letters," continued Rose. "These three cut right to the chase, and all date back from Christmas 2001. One is from a political opponent demanding that Palle Rasmussen disappear from Danish politics—and if he won't do it voluntarily, he'll have to be sacrificed."

Carl frowned. "Is there a name or an email account we can check?"

"Yeah, we have an email account."

"Get the person in here. And the next one?"

"We're not sure who it's from, but we think it's from the same person. It's another death threat, and the choice of words and syntax are almost identical."

"We'll check if it's the same person when we have them here. And the third one?"

"It's a very meticulous description of what awaits him. There is not a body part that won't be slowly cut from him with a blunt knife. He will burn in hell, be thrown from the town hall tower, castrated, decapitated, and on it goes."

"Let's archive that one for now. The sender is clearly a fanatic and is probably quite unstructured and confused. If someone liquidated Palle

Rasmussen, it's not him. But do make a report on him if you have time, even though there isn't much point, as the deadline for prosecuting has expired. It would do him good to be confronted with his shit email because he's probably continued sending them to all sorts and there might be a punishable offense to pin on him."

"And then there are the funny threatening letters. Like this one: 'I will collect all my shit for an entire month and shove it in your face and mix it with all the other shit that you spurt from your mouth.' Shit seems to be a recurring theme in many of them."

"I have the funniest one here," said Assad. "Listen: 'Sweet little podgy Palle, I'm standing here missing a little idiot-fat for my suckling roast. Will you deliver the fat or would you rather hang on the spit? A nice Palle roast with roasted onions and scratchings would probably strengthen our immune defenses against all that stupid nonsense you vomit. We're still considering what we can use your brain for, but we're at a loss on that score. Waste like that will just have to go in the trash, right?'"

Carl shook his head. If only God had protested when digital communication was invented.

"Palle Rasmussen has made a comment at the bottom of the email. With a fountain pen no less. He writes: 'Palle roast with roasted onions! Stupid nonsense—ha ha. Good descriptions I can use about my political opponents and make sure the voters get a good laugh.'"

Carl shook his head again. Not only was Palle Rasmussen an idiot, he was also vapid and childish.

"Listen up. I want you to keep searching until the bitter end. Put all of Pauline's emails to one side and give them to me. I think she should be allowed to see them again. And by the way, what is that smell in the office today?"

They pointed over at the simmering pot behind Gordon's ever-growing collection of Christmas ornaments. A Christmas decoration on a lump of clay, more cardboard cutout elves, tinsel hanging from the lamps, Christmas hearts on the task lamp, and a miniature Christmas tree leaning up against his keyboard.

"It's ragout á la Marwa, Carl," Assad responded. "Leftovers from last night."

"It doesn't smell of lamb," he said, relieved.

"No, it's hare ragout. One of our friends butchered it the day before yesterday."

Carl gulped. With friends like that, who needed enemies?

"The first of the car buyers is ready for you now," said Gordon over the intercom. "But I think he'll prove to be a dead end."

Carl was despondent when a man of around eighty years old came waddling into his office and looked around curiously. It was thirty-two years since the repair shop had blown up. What the hell had he expected?

"Interesting," said the old man with a shaky voice muffled by a face mask as he soaked up the atmosphere of the homicide unit. They did not get much further than that. He had been pleased with his small Peugeot but had given it to his daughter, who had then exchanged it for a package holiday to Portugal. "Dead end" had turned out to be an understatement.

"What about the other one, Gordon?" he asked over the intercom.

"He can't make it until tomorrow. But he's even older."

"Thanks, Gordon. Just drop him and go back to your case files."

There was a deep sigh. "I'm already on it, Carl."

"Try to sort the cases chronologically first."

"I already have."

"Then start with 2000 and 2004. Just look at the photos to start with, okay?"

"Why those years specifically?"

"Call it male intuition."

There was a sudden raucous laughter on the other end of the intercom, which echoed through the walls. It was Rose, of course.

Carl sat down by the window and considered another cigarette while he tried to imagine Palle Rasmussen's last day. First work on a quiet

Whitsunday at Christiansborg and then sex of a more savage nature, probably tied up in his apartment. Just how savage had it been? And then finally the suicide.

He dug out the autopsy report, and it was written with no holds barred: No fresh wounds or lesions on Rasmussen's body. There were old scratches on his back, traces of a deep lesion close to the anus. But after several days' exposure to the carbon monoxide in the garage, the report focused on that as the cause of death. He would just have to ask Pauline Rasmussen directly how the last sex game of Palle's life had ended.

After the presumed erotic encounter with Pauline, the remaining time of Palle Rasmussen's short life was still a mystery. Had he left Pauline's in his own car? Had he seriously ended their relationship that day, and, if he did, why? Was it normal for them to rumble in the sheets on his way home from work?

A roar came from the other office. It would not be long before someone down the hall would lose their temper about the commotion that their arrival had caused on Teglholmen. Poor Marcus when the complaints started rolling in.

"Carl, come in here," shouted Rose. Did she have no concept of discretion? She sounded like a foghorn.

"This had better be important. With those lungs, you'll soon have everyone in here. Haven't I told you—"

He stopped when he saw their faces.

"You look like you've seen a ghost. What the hell is going on?"

Assad's expression was one of disbelief. "We've hit the crackpot, Carl." Assad sounded like a crackpot with his newly invented idioms. "Look at the whiteboard," he said eagerly.

On the whiteboard was written:

Date/Crime Scene: May 17, 2000, Søllerød
Victim: Carl-Henrik Skov Jespersen
Murder Method: Shot to temple
Motive: Unknown

"Let me see the report. Did you find it, Gordon?" asked Carl.

"Yeah."

"But then where's the salt? Show me." He followed Gordon's index finger downward on a very blurry photo that looked like it should have been discarded. Had the photographer been too lazy to go back to the crime scene and reshoot it?

"What are we looking at?" He bent over the photo.

"Turn it around, Carl. It's upside down. Are you going blind, old man?" said Rose.

He gave her a murderous look and turned the photo.

"What do you want me to look at?"

Assad pushed a magnifying glass over to him.

He slid the glass across the photo to the desk where the body lay sprawled.

An index finger entered his field of vision and pointed at a bowl on a shelf.

Carl squinted. "Is it Asian? The symbols on it look like it, don't they?"

"Look at the whole shelving unit," Assad suggested. "There's a plate on the other shelf with a fork and knife protruding over the edge, and next to it a set of salt and pepper mills. So, we assume that the man just had his lunch. But the bowl, Carl. Look at it. It's not empty."

"So am I to understand that you all think that it's salt sticking up over the brim? I'm not sure you can come to that conclusion from this terrible photo."

"No, you're right. But now look at this photo," said Assad, putting a new one down in front of Carl. "Gordon's really kept his eyes peeled."

This photo showed the victim from another angle. The body was lying nose down on the desk atop a large pool of blood and brains on the writing mat underneath the exit hole.

"I can see that he shot himself in the right temple." Carl shook his head. "He's lying in a strange position. With that nasty exit wound, he must've used a high-caliber weapon. His head should at least have smashed down onto the desk on the left side angled away from the shot."

They nodded. "We'll get to that, Carl. But first look at the floor between him and the shelving unit."

He grabbed the magnifying glass for the second time and slid it across the photo. Sure enough, there was something there.

"Well spotted, Gordon. How have forensics described it?"

"They didn't consider it significant. They mention it as ordinary coarse salt that fell out of the bowl."

Carl nodded.

"And the position of the head? He must have died on the spot, given the huge wound. What kind of weapon was it?"

They showed him the next photo.

"What the . . . You don't see a whopper like that every day." He pointed at the engraving—"Desert Eagle, Israel Military Industries." "What caliber, Assad? Forty-four Magnum?"

"Three fifty-seven."

"Ouch! Dead on the spot! He should at least have been blown off the chair, right?"

"Are you sure you don't need glasses, Carl?" teased Rose again. "It's very clear to see here."

"What is?"

"The reason why the case ended up in the homicide archive. It's murder, not suicide."

"Notice the pool of blood in front of the table leg. That's where his head hit the floor, which tells us that the body was dragged back up into the chair. So, either the killer was a stupid moron, which we don't think, or they wanted to let the investigators know that they had their work cut out for them."

"Sorry," said Carl, looking down at the floor. When you considered how many murder cases he had worked on personally, not to mention those his colleagues had worked on, it was not strange that some of them slipped his mind. The problem was that this was a case one wouldn't forget because it had so many memorable elements. The victim was very controversial, the investigation was unsuccessful, and the aftermath generated big newspaper headlines. Was he getting too old for this game?

And was Rose right that he needed to get his eyes checked? The situation was not easy to accept.

"Yes, I do remember the case now. He dealt in weapons, didn't he?"

Rose gave him the thumbs-up as if he were a student who had finally caught on. "Yes, exactly. And the murder was interpreted as a straightforward execution where everything seemed to point toward his incredibly disreputable profession as the cause. Shortly after, a Belarusian citizen living in Denmark was arrested on the basis of his name appearing frequently in the victim's order book for owing a lot of money. He pled innocent to the murder, but after a plea bargain with the prosecutor, he admitted to significant arms trading with countries subject to trade embargoes."

"What about the victim's criminal record?"

"He didn't have one." Gordon shrugged as if it were nothing.

"An arms dealer in Denmark without a record. He must have been good at his job," mumbled Carl.

19

TABITHA

Tuesday, December 8, 2020

Tabitha had taken her exclusion from Debora's group of vengeful women as the beginning of a new era. All the rules had held her back, and all the secrecy about their real names and identities had seemed childish. Eva was a ridiculous name. Her own name, Tabitha, was also from the Bible anyway.

She was a grown woman, and she was intelligent, so why the hell should their preaching restrict her?

Oh, so you want me to stop hurting people, Debora, she had thought when she had left the house. Who was she to decide that?

It took her a few days to think about how far she wanted to go. She naturally did not want to be caught by the police again, but, if it happened, she would tell them that she had been brainwashed by Debora. She could deal with a few months of so-called deprogramming in a psychiatric ward if it meant that Debora would be the one going to prison. Tabitha would relish seeing her being picked up from her fancy house, with all the delicate china cups and cake forks and all that kind of shit, and dragged off to the slammer. The word made Tabitha laugh.

She was ready to kick things off.

It all began quite innocently. Debora had been sitting in the corner of a café writing notes at a table already bursting with croissants, cakes, and coffee. Tabitha had sat down at the next table and smiled at Debora's excess as she complained about the waitress being slow. And before long, they were sitting at the same table talking about the world and Denmark and the people they came across, and about how everything and everyone in the country was going to the dogs.

Tabitha later realized that it was a carefully rehearsed process that Debora used to recruit suitable members for her group. She praised Tabitha, called her classy and clever, and listened to her like no one else; it put Tabitha in a euphoric state where she not only felt special but also chosen.

She did not fully realize that she had been handpicked for a crusade against immorality until the day when she stood smiling after having given a tourist a slap across the face for spitting on the floor in a McDonald's.

Tabitha loved her new role, and no one who challenged her ethical worldview escaped. She was ever-vigilant and came down hard on the perpetrators with tirades, slaps, and sometimes worse. Her enemies were pickpockets, petty officials, shop assistants who left their customers waiting, cranky bus drivers, people shouting in the streets, people who pushed by when they went past or just pushed to the front of the queue, and people who gossiped or bad-mouthed others. It later became lecturers who canceled lectures and know-it-alls who said "obviously" in every sentence and manipulated others. These people were everywhere when she looked around, and she learned to despise what she called "societal decay."

At the monthly group meetings when Tabitha gave an account of her activities, Debora was over the moon, and she felt like a warrior fighting for her country. She had not felt the long arm of the law until she was arrested on the street for smashing an empty champagne bottle on a man's head because he was kicking a homeless person's dog. The arrest in the middle of the pedestrian shopping area caused quite a commotion. While people slipped in the blood of the unconscious dog abuser, they shouted and screamed that the bastard had deserved it and that the police should just get the dog to safety or go to hell. The support was all fuel to her fire but did not help her with the authorities.

Her case was still pending, and it would probably remain that way due to the extensive backlog in the courts. But she did not get off so lightly with Debora. At their first meeting after the episode, Tabitha was told to get up and leave and never return. And to top it off, she was sent off with a torrent of words threatening that if she told anyone about their group activities, she would come to regret it.

Tabitha was as cold as ice and left a note in Debora's mailbox stating that this was the death blow for the group, because once the court case came up, she would sing like a canary.

They're hardly going to kill me, she thought.

The very next day, Tabitha continued her private crusade by striking hard wherever she found someone to be lacking in her world.

She had been cruising around Copenhagen when three guys with their caps on back to front swerved their BMW in front of her, causing her to brake hard. She just managed to catch a glimpse of a couple of middle fingers through their rear window and was swearing to herself when she saw cigarette butts and paper cups thrown from one of their side windows onto the road in a cloud of ash. That was when she decided to repay their provocation in hard currency.

She followed them from a distance and soon saw that it had not been an isolated act of littering. They finally ended up on Sønder Boulevard and parked in a disabled parking spot.

Tabitha parked her car on the other side of the road and took out her knife from the glove compartment. Twenty seconds later, she had slashed all the tires of the BMW. Then she strolled over to the lawn that separated the two lanes and collected an entire bag of rubbish and dog shit. She waited patiently until they returned in high spirits, each with a cigarette in their mouths and a rehearsed and slightly too laid-back gait.

As soon as they had eased themselves into the car, she calmly stepped across the lane and knocked on the driver's window.

He rolled down the window and his contemptuous expression signaled that he was more than ready to let rip his usual threats of a beating and much worse.

"You dropped something on the road, you damn bastards. Next time remember to take it home with you, okay?" She then emptied the entire bag of filth on his head.

With a torrent of curses, the driver lunged toward his wingman, trying to avoid the stinking mess, while Tabitha ran over to her car and started it, pulling out with the tires screeching.

"You won't make it far, you idiots!" she shouted out her window and reciprocated their earlier fuck finger. Even the most arrogant guys could not get far in a car with four slashed tires.

And so Tabitha went to work every morning as Dr. Jekyll and returned home as Mr. Hyde. People who were not nice to their children or animals received such a beating with her cane that they could hardly get up, and she did not give a damn whether they were homeless or just imbeciles. Children and animals deserved to be treated right.

Unfortunately, things went wrong for Tabitha just a few months after she had been excommunicated.

Like so many times before, she took the train to Østerport Station, which was a good starting point for her reconnaissance through the broad streets toward Kongens Nytorv. She was standing in front of the rain-soaked newly renovated façade of the train station when she spotted a couple who were walking along Dag Hammarskjölds Allé and videoing everything including a sea of umbrellas, railway tracks, and the Den Frie Center of Contemporary Art. *Ahh, Americans*, she thought when she heard their boisterous excitement from a hundred meters away. They must be heading toward the Museum of Danish Resistance and on to their beloved embassy.

She shook her head, hoping that at least they were not friends with the ambassador, because you would be hard-pressed to find a bigger fool.

Tabitha looked around and was about to approach the couple when she spotted an old woman on the other side of the busy road who looked despondent at the sight of the occupied bus shelter benches. Her thread-bare vinyl bag was weighing down her arm, revealing that she had just done her shopping and that her crooked back was hurting. She seemed to have carried her share of life's burdens.

Tabitha fixed her eyes on a strong young guy in the bus shelter whose empathy was so lacking that he could not be bothered to stand up for the woman. Tabitha decided to give him a nudge. She crossed at the pedestrian crossing, but in the very moment that she was about to tell him off, the guy stood up voluntarily and offered his seat to the old woman. He also offered to hold her bag until the bus arrived because there was no room on the bench, and the pale woman smiled at him as if he was the first helpful person she had met in a very long time.

Tabitha also smiled but then noticed that the guy was looking in any other direction than Lille Triangel, where the bus would be arriving from.

What is he up to? she wondered and stood near him on the other side of the glass partition so she could stop him if he suddenly made a run for it.

"No, it's not that bus," said the old woman when the first bus arrived and passengers started getting on.

The guy nodded. "Good. I'm also waiting for the next one." He noticed with a quick glance that there were no people waiting with them on the bench anymore.

"Now I can take my bag back and put it next to me. Thanks for the help," said the old woman, moving over a little and patting the empty seat next to her.

"I'll carry it on for you when the bus arrives," said the guy with an emphasis that did not invite protest. And just as the bus pulled away, he took a step sideways and was about to make a run for it.

He had only just managed to take one long leap when Tabitha grabbed hold of the bag strap and pulled hard. But that did not stop the thief—he must have tried this before. He pulled the bag in toward him with a hard tug and heaved, but Tabitha was not letting go either. Then he kicked out at her to make her let go, but Tabitha did not. She only let go when he had pulled her across the bus lane and out toward the road. For a moment, he seemed genuinely shocked as the lack of resistance made him stumble backward out onto the road, only to be crushed against the asphalt with a terrible sound by a truck so big that it should be barred from driving in a built-up area like Copenhagen.

People cried out while Tabitha serenely soaked in the scene. It was at that moment she realized that the couple from earlier were standing in front of the station building, recording with their camera pointing directly at her.

"It was an accident!" she shouted loudly and tried to look horrified as the truck driver leaped out of the cabin and vomited next to what had once been the thief.

Within seconds she was surrounded by people shouting that she had let go of the bag on purpose and that it was her fault he had ended up on the road.

Some people were making phone calls, so Tabitha decided that she had better make herself scarce, and quickly.

But Tabitha was not the only person present who could read the mood, and out of nowhere a strong hand appeared and grabbed hold of her upper arm.

Before long, the area was filled with paramedics and crisis psychologists as well as a group of police officers reading her rights. And so Tabitha's career as the street avenger was history.

20

RAGNHILD

Tuesday, December 8, 2020

Debora had a stern expression on her face when they sat down. She always did, but this time the horizontal furrows on her brow were accompanied by two vertical ones that cut deep through the normal layer of worry with new emphasis.

"I've summoned you to go over what happened earlier today," she said.

They all nodded.

"About the corona lockdown?" asked Martha.

Debora shook her head. "That too, of course. It doesn't make the conditions for our mission easier. But it's a far more serious matter: Eva has been arrested again, and this time it puts us in real danger."

"Arrested?" Ragnhild shook her head. She had never met Eva, as she was the one who had replaced Eva in the group. "What for?" she asked.

"We don't know exactly at this point, Ruth, but as far as I know, she was arrested today and charged with causing the death of a young man."

Ragnhild looked at the other two. It was obvious that they were thinking the same. This did not bode well.

Debora nodded. "This means that from today on, we'll have to cease our activities completely, and we can't meet again before I summon you.

We need to prepare ourselves for the eventuality that Eva might sell us out. We need to make sure the police won't find anything here or at your own homes."

"She won't sell us out," protested Sara.

"No, I don't think so either, but *if* you have anything incriminating lying around that might reveal what you've been up to or intend to do in the future, you need to get rid of it immediately. I'm going to go over this place, destroy all possible evidence, and get rid of all fingerprints that might link any of you or Eva to this location. And most importantly"— she pointed her index finger in the air—"your lips are henceforth sealed! And if you feel the urge to start your own little crusades—think twice! It just cannot happen. Do you understand?"

They nodded, but Ragnhild was livid. Everything she was passionate about, everything that gave her life meaning had been made impossible now: the way she was with other people, the way she spent her free time, and, not least, her vigilante activities.

"You have to understand that Eva could convince the prosecutor to doubt her mental state. When they question her, she might claim to have been turned into a remote-controlled zombie by me and the two of you, Martha and Sara. Obviously this doesn't affect you, Ruth, because you two have never met."

Debora sat for a moment nodding to herself as she tried to grasp the entirety of the situation. Then she turned to them with a menacing expression.

"Not only is Eva probably the smartest among us, she is definitely the most cunning. So we have to be on our guard. Understood?"

"I think we need to know her real name so we can follow the press coverage on her," said Martha. "Because her real name isn't Eva, is it?"

Debora shook her head. "No, her name's Tabitha Engstrøm."

"You mentioned that things will end badly for those who can't keep their mouths shut," said Sara. "But what do you plan to do to Tabitha if it happens?"

"Have her neutralized if we can get to her. What choice do we have?"

———

Ragnhild was glued to her TV, but there was nothing about Tabitha Engström because the COVID-19 restrictions and the steep increase in the number of infections was the only topic in the media. And while she was watching this endless stream of deliberations and debates regarding COVID, Ragnhild realized that this unusual situation might be the best protection Tabitha could have wished for. As long as the fear of a second wave made it impossible to get close to her in prison, they had to accept the risk that she might at some point see the benefit of informing on them and subsequently bringing down their group and activities.

That simply cannot happen, she thought. Ragnhild had never tried to kill anyone, but she was probably capable of it. She had certainly seen many pigs being slaughtered at her grandparents' farm. The human aorta was just beneath the skin, and many objects were sharp enough to sever it. So that was no problem. The problem was getting close to this Tabitha Engström while she was in custody and making an escape after the deed. And it was this last part that was the very essence of the perfect crime.

If she did go through with it, would her star not shine even brighter with Debora regardless of her warning about what they could or could not do? And if there was something Ragnhild longed for more than anything else, it was Debora's acceptance and respect. On several nights after the meetings, she had stood outside Debora's house waiting for the lights to go out in all the windows. Her imagination was piqued by what was going on in the darkness inside. She was not in love with Debora, as far as she knew, but Debora was their leader. She was the one who recruited them, the one who gathered knowledge about their activities, and the one who encouraged them to refine and expand their moral crusade of vengeance.

The one who had raised Ragnhild's otherwise sad life to a state of euphoria.

Ragnhild stared at the TV screen, where the prime minister was sporting one of her usual smart jackets that she always wore during press conferences to project strength during times of crisis.

With her resolve to put the country on lockdown, how on earth were they supposed to stop Tabitha?

Ragnhild did not sleep much that night.

21

RAGNHILD

Wednesday, December 9, 2020

The various health measures affected all layers of society, and a case such as Tabitha Engstrøm's required interrogations, presentation of evidence, hours spent in witness stands, and summoning people who could all be infectious. Given that these difficult circumstances made it impossible to carry out normal legal procedures that might lead to incarceration, Tabitha was released after the preliminary hearing as prescribed by law. She was told not to leave the country and to inform the court if her circumstances changed significantly. They would return to her case when it was due and the state of affairs was back to some sense of normalcy.

Ragnhild thought this might present an opportunity, so she was waiting fifty meters from the court when Tabitha stepped out into freedom wearing a loose-fitting coat and a broad smile on her bloodred lips.

So that was what she looked like. Carefree and dolled up.

She's got no reason to smile, thought Ragnhild. *Her lips should be zipped shut so they don't give anything away about our little group. Tabitha Engstrøm is pleased with herself just now, but when they drag her back in, she will squeal. I can see it on her face.*

On their way through the busiest streets of Copenhagen, Ragnhild kept a firm grip around the sharp fish knife in her coat pocket. Her goal was to stop Tabitha, but it was not important if it happened now or later. Ragnhild would make sure she was ready when the opportunity presented itself.

Where are you going, Tabitha? she thought. Ragnhild kept following her until they reached the almost empty streets of Amager without finding the answer to her question.

If she leaves Amagerbrogade to walk down a side street, I can run up to her within a few seconds, she thought. But how hard should she stab her, and where? Maybe it would be better to just slit her throat. But, on the other hand, that would result in a lot of blood, and Ragnhild would risk getting some on her. Of course, she could grab Tabitha and push her away in the moment she attacked her. But that would mean she had to cut deep and very precisely, and many things might make that difficult. What if Tabitha heard her, for example, just before she attacked, or if a sound made her turn her head? Many things could go wrong.

Ragnhild felt uneasy, but she could not afford to hesitate. Tabitha had violated the strict code of the group, and Debora herself had said that she would pay dearly for it. And even though Debora had warned them against acting on their own impulses, it was a warning Ragnhild did not intend to heed. She was sure that Debora would approve of her action in the end. Was she not the one who had said that if Tabitha sold them out, they would have to neutralize her?

The solution to Ragnhild's problem appeared a few hundred meters farther ahead, where someone had crashed into a parking sign so violently that it had buckled in the middle and now lay lopsided, with the end of the frayed metal pole sticking out horizontally a meter above-ground.

Come on, Tabitha, please don't walk down the side street, thought Ragnhild. *Please don't cross the road. Please don't walk along the side of the shop. Keep walking next to the cycle lane.*

She picked up her pace. Fifty meters from the broken pole, she had almost reached her target. She took her hands out of her pockets and started imagining the push that would make Tabitha fall down onto the frayed metal edge of the broken sign.

Twenty meters from the sign, there were only a few meters between them. When Tabitha was only three quarters of a meter from the lethal iron pole, Ragnhild jumped forward and thrust her left leg in front of Tabitha while pushing her in the back with all her might. Defenseless, Tabitha fell, and the pole went directly through her coat, penetrating her torso just beneath the heart.

Her scream was cut short when Ragnhild slammed both her fists against her spine, making the pole penetrate her even deeper.

Ragnhild immediately backed away down the side street before Tabitha had even stopped breathing.

Ragnhild's heart was racing so fast that she almost fainted. And in a paradoxical state of pride and nausea, she threw up several times on the sidewalk until she regained control of her body.

Never before, not even when she used to smoke pot as a younger woman, had Ragnhild felt as exhilarated as when she was standing on the green marble staircase in front of Debora's house, pressing their usual signal on the doorbell.

It was a few minutes before the door was opened, and her euphoria vanished as quickly as it had appeared.

"Who are you?" she asked the man who opened the door. He was huge and savage looking—nothing she could associate with the delicate and beautiful Debora. They locked eyes for a moment, which was definitely not a pleasant experience, considering his strange appearance. His head did not look right, and it did not fit his body.

"Who am I? Don't you think I should be asking you that question? Why are you ringing my doorbell?"

Did he say *his* door? Did Debora have a husband? And one as repulsive as he was? This definitely did not seem right.

"I need to talk to Debora. Tell her Ruth is here."

He looked at her quizzically. "Debora? And who's that?"

Ragnhild took a step backward and looked up at the façade of the house. She definitely did not have the wrong place.

"I don't know who you are, but Debora is the owner of this house." Ragnhild was now seriously worried.

He frowned and stepped forward toward her. "I have no idea what you're talking about. I think you should leave now."

Ragnhild backed away. "Have you hurt her? Have you broken into the house?"

She took another step backward and looked around her, ready to make a run for it and jump over the neighbor's hedge if he made a move.

"Deeeebora!" she shouted as loudly as she could, keeping an eye on the curtains of the first-floor windows.

"You're out of your mind, young lady. What's so important about this Debora woman?"

"I have something I need to tell her about someone that she doesn't need to fear anymore."

Did she detect movement behind the curtain up there?

Ragnhild flashed a smile that disappeared as soon as the man in front of her punched her in the face, disrupting everything that kept her on her feet: her balance, her nervous system, her will, and her tensed muscles.

22

CARL

Thursday, December 10, 2020

The government press conference was no more uplifting than usual. And even though the vaccine was on the way, it was already clear that the infection rate in connection with Christmas and New Year's Eve might quickly turn bad.

The participants at the press conference appeared on the screen like an execution squad with enough ammunition to take down half the country. First, the minister of health and then all the others. Nine hundred and eighteen dead, they said, continuing to explain that the second corona wave was approaching and that restrictions would come into effect starting the following day at four p.m. It was nothing new: lockdown, corona tests, hand disinfecting, face masks, coughing in your sleeve, deprivation, and economic decline.

The whole thing was becoming really tiring and annoying.

"Well," said Carl. "What do you think? I for one don't intend to sit back and wait. If we have to take rapid tests all the time, we can just show our ID cards and skip the queue."

The others were clearly at a loss. Assad was obviously thinking about his family—what would they do if he became ill? Rose, for her part, had no intention of being isolated again in her apartment. She had had enough of that last time. Gordon was evidently sad because he had only just started getting into the dating game—and how the hell were you supposed to date if you could not meet anyone?

"I'm heading out to Pauline Rasmussen to confront her with the emails we found before the entire country goes crazy," said Carl. "Meanwhile, you lot keep at it. Rose, I want you and Assad to focus on the arms dealer. Gordon, you can continue with the old case files. And you can help each other finish going over Palle Rasmussen's old emails."

Was that a sigh he heard?

He had barely left the parking lot before his phone rang. It was Gordon.

"The department has just received a summons from the national police, Carl. We all have to meet in the canteen in twenty minutes."

"I see. Good luck with that," said Carl with a cheeky smile. He was not going to let the whims of the national police get in the way of his investigation.

Around a kilometer outside the city, the traffic started to ease. Several cars were pulled over with their radios blaring out regulations and warnings.

The sidewalks were littered with discarded face masks. Not exactly an uplifting sight.

Carl shook his head. Coronavirus? People did not seem to give a damn as long as their own needs were covered. But that was human nature—he had realized that a long time ago.

Carl sighed.

How long would they have to put up with all this shit?

A woman's bike was lying on the garden path in front of Pauline Rasmussen's terraced house. The front door was wide open, and from inside the hall came an agitated woman's voice complaining: "You've got to be kidding" and "Not again!"

Carl had an inkling what the problem was.

When Pauline saw Carl standing in the doorway, she put her phone in her pocket and directed her frustration at him.

"All our shows are canceled indefinitely," she spat. "Canceled, canceled, canceled! Is that all they've got to say?"

He used words like "unfortunate" and "insane" and continued without further ado to tell her what they had found among Palle Rasmussen's belongings. All the color drained from her face. Carl did not care whether it was due to tonight's show being the last for a long time or the prospect of being presented with her checkered past. When people were as unhinged as Pauline, his questioning was so much more effective. As his shady cousin always said, "Don't turn up your nose at a blessing in disguise."

"You were with Palle the day he died, and now we know for sure that he visited you on his way home and that you had the kind of sex that entails submission and physical pain. So, I'm asking you, Pauline, did you go too far? Did you end up killing him? Did he ask you to go home with him and tie him to the steering wheel of the car so he couldn't turn off his engine?"

She seemed tongue-tied.

"Let me tell you what I think. Palle came home to you that afternoon. Can you confirm that?"

She sighed.

"You tied his hands tightly and gave him a good spanking, didn't you?"

She shook her head. "I didn't tie him up. It was never necessary."

"You could inflict pain on him without tying him up? How would that work? We found lesions close to his rectum. That must have been very painful."

She turned to face him with a contemptuous look. "Palle could take it. He was a real man."

"But what I don't understand is why there were deep indentations on his wrists much like you'd expect from cable ties."

"That's got nothing to do with me. I didn't do it."

"But you did drive home with him afterward, didn't you?"

"I believe I've answered that already."

Her eyes grew colder, and Carl could sense that he was losing his advantage.

"But no, I didn't. When he had satisfied himself, he just wanted to go home. He *only* thought about himself."

"And yet you were with him for nine and a half years. I find that hard to believe."

"Believe what you want. However he got those marks on his wrists, it had nothing to do with me. I'm not proud of my relationship with him, but I can't change that."

"Was he depressed that day?"

"He was always a bit low after being humiliated and reaching his climax, but there was nothing unusual about it that day."

"Why did you try to stop me from getting my hands on Palle's boxes and computer? If there's anything that my colleagues and I have missed, I need you to tell me now. It won't help your case if we have to find out for ourselves."

"My case?" Now she was as cold as ice. "The only thing I'm worried about at the moment is how the hell I'm going to manage now that the prime minister has pulled the rug from under my feet. Do you think she's going to pay for all the canceled shows? Or maybe the minister for culture?"

Carl shrugged. It was no concern of his.

"What are we going to find on the computer, Pauline? Are you going to tell us while you have the chance?"

She shook her head. "I think you should leave now."

Rose was sitting in the very spot where he had left her, in front of some photos and a large stack of case files.

"Where are Assad and Gordon?" he asked.

She sighed. "This time the superintendent has sent quite a few of us home. From now on, everyone—including our department—must keep a distance of at least two meters. It's completely over the top. Just like

back in the spring, we're not supposed to conduct physical interrogations. We have to do them over the phone."

Carl's jaw dropped. "Didn't they learn the lesson in the spring? You
can't conduct a bloody interrogation over the phone. We've learned that
the hard way. People lie through their teeth, especially when you can't
see them. They just sit there on the other end of the line laughing at us."

He turned on the spot and stormed down the corridor. Luckily, Marcus was in his office. He did not look too happy either.

"Is it true that you've decided once again that we have to conduct
interrogations over the phone?"

"Yes, those are the superintendent's guidelines." He looked wearily
up at Carl.

"Does that also apply for indictments?" he asked almost just in jest.
Marcus nodded.

"And if I choose not to give a shit, what are they going to do about it?"

"I don't know. But if you end up with corona as a result, I'm sure
you will give a shit."

"And where do you stand?"

"I'm staying put in my office, so I won't know much about what you
all get up to."

Carl nodded. That was exactly what he wanted to hear.

"Gordon and Assad have been told to work from home for the time
being. And that won't be of much use to our investigation, Marcus. Don't
you want Maja Petersen's case to be solved?"

He nodded. "It'll just have to wait until the corona situation is under
control."

"I hear you, Marcus. Look after yourself until then."

"Assad, do you have the address for the man who sent those hate emails
stating that he would sacrifice Palle Rasmussen if he didn't leave politics?"

Assad cleared his throat a couple of times. It sounded like he was
holding his phone at a distance. Was he catching a cold?

"I've already talked to him, Carl," said Assad before speaking in Arabic to someone in the room. There was someone crying in the background.

"What's going on, Assad?"

"What's going on? What's going on is that it isn't easy to work in a two-bedroom apartment with all the wailing in the background."

Carl frowned. "Can't you work somewhere else?"

Assad shouted something out in Arabic. Apparently, he had not heard the question.

"What did that shit stirrer have to say for himself?"

"That all politicians who read the constitution according to their own interpretation should be stopped with violence. That they deserved to know how much he hated them."

"Does he know that he can be punished for violent threats?"

"I think he said that he didn't give two hoots. Such a strange expression."

Carl smiled. "Two hoots? I imagine he must be an older man."

"Carl, we won't get anything out of him. He lives in Nakskov and always has. He has muscular dystrophy and is stuck in a wheelchair."

"Okay."

"The cases we've found so far are simply too old, Carl. The leads have gone cold. But Rose and I both think that there are more cases than the ones we've already found. Lots more. If we find a more recent case involving salt, hopefully there will also be some fresh and clear leads on the perpetrator."

"I agree. We already have four crime scenes where salt has been ritually placed, so there's a good chance there'll be more. But, Assad, without a motive, we don't know what direction to look in."

"True, but now we know there have been murders in 1988, 1998, 2000, and 2002. If the interval of two years between murders means anything, I think we should start with the most recent murders first."

"Er, the most recent? But what are the most recent? The perpetrator may have stopped years back—or be dead, for that matter," said Carl.

"We only have murders in even years, so what if we start investigating murders and suspicious deaths in, say, 2010?"

"In 2010? Why not later? 2012, 2014, 2016 . . ."

"You said it yourself, Carl. The perpetrator may have started in 1988 or before, so there has to be a reasonable chance that he's still active in the year we're investigating. And I think 2010 makes sense."

"I can hear that you're already working on it."

"Yes, I'm logged onto PED Point."

"You do know that you can't search for everything in the electronic archive?"

"I know, but if I have to work from home, I have to start somewhere, right?"

23

CARL

Thursday, December 10, 2020

"**I can see** that Gordon has already returned. So according to the corona police and His Holiness the superintendent, there are too many of us present in the department. Why are you back, Gordon? Did you miss your Christmas elves?"

"I couldn't work from home because I only have one screen there and the internet is terrible. It's just too slow. It was driving me crazy."

Carl nodded and looked at Rose. "Listen up, Rose. You need to make a schedule for Department Q. Marcus has given the go-ahead to do as we please as long as we don't involve him or get him into trouble. We'll conduct interrogations out of house and make sure, at least officially, that there are never more than two of us here at a time. And we'll continue like this as long as management tries to meddle with the business of those of us in the police doing the work. Agreed? Assad isn't doing well at home, so keep him in mind."

She nodded. "This is getting complicated. Not only because of corona, but also because if we're honest with one another, we could use another five people. At least!"

Carl looked over at Gordon, who was agreeing like the nodding dog in the rear window of his ex-wife Vigga's heap of junk.

Carl stood up and walked over toward the window. He took a red whiteboard pen and wrote directly on the window.

THE CASE OF THE EVEN YEARS

"We can all write here what we're doing, and every time you catch yourself staring vacantly out the window, you'll be reminded that we have other, more important things to do. Are you with me?"

He passed the pen to Gordon. "So what do you think we should write?"

The pale guy thought for a moment.

"I think we should list all the questions and loose ends in connection with these cases."

Carl nodded and Gordon wrote.

G1: Missing pages from Palle Rasmussen's case file. Where are they?

G2: Look for salt in old cases. Are there others?

G3: Open Palle Rasmussen's PC. Any leads re: his death?

"Good. And where is the computer now, Gordon?"

"It's up with IT. And they're short-staffed at the moment, obviously. But they said they'd make it a priority."

"Okay, but chase them down. We can't wait forever. Over to you, Rose."

She sighed when Gordon passed her the pen.

"Is there anything other than questions and loose ends in this mess?" She hesitated for a moment before adding to the list.

R4: Who killed the arms dealer Carl-Henrik Jespersen?

R5: Who killed the factory owner Oleg Dudek?

R6: Who killed the repair shop owner Ove Wilder and the four mechanics?

R7: Why the hell did someone leave salt at the crime scenes?

Carl raised his hand. "I'll write Assad's question, and it's very simple."

A8: Murders and mysterious deaths in 2010. Anything relevant?

"And that is actually Assad's suggestion—that we check the year 2010 first. Am I right in thinking that we can establish at this point that all the deaths are connected and that we only check cases from even years for now?"

They nodded.

"Good. Time will tell if we're right and if there are more cases."

Gordon stuck his finger in the air.

"And what does the student in the back row have to say?" asked Carl.

"I've noticed that the more recent the murder, the later in the year it happened."

Rose nodded. "So have I. In 1988, it was on January twenty-sixth. In 1998, it was on April twenty-eighth. In 2000, it was on May seventeenth. And in 2002, it was two days later, Whitsunday, May nineteenth. Maybe it's not a coincidence but actually a deliberate pattern."

Carl stood still for a moment and looked out onto the muddy parking lot through the red letters on the window. Then he turned toward them with a shiver running down his spine. That was how he felt when Mona rested one of her legs against his stomach. And he always felt like this when he sensed the beginning of a breakthrough in a case.

He grinned before raising the pen up to the window.

C9: The significance of the dates?

"Well spotted, both of you. I'll look into that aspect."

Did they look disappointed?

Now Carl had two main possibilities. He could sort the cases according to date so that within the period from 1988 to 2000, he only searched for cases in the years 1990, 1992, 1994, and 1996 and dates between January twenty-sixth and April twenty-eighth. This might prove to be a lot of work, but he could easily delegate it to one of the others.

Alternatively, he could concentrate solely on the dates they already knew about. If the salt at the crime scenes was of a ritual nature, maybe the dates were too.

He nodded to Gordon. "Gordon, could you limit your search to the dates between Max Petersen's death and Oleg Dudek's death and only search for even years from 1988 to 1996?"

Gordon looked confused. He was probably wondering if it was a request or an order.

"And when you've done that, we'll talk. Okay?"

He lowered his head.

"And what are you going to do, Carl?" asked Rose. Her sour expression had a way of changing the mood in any room.

"I'll tell you when I've made some progress."

No breath of fresh air is better than when it has passed through a cigarette with the filter broken off. Carl scanned the cars in the parking lot, looking toward a chaotic assembly of buildings in the background that were probably meant to accentuate Teglholmen as one of the new wonders of the city. What the hell were the city planners thinking? Were they giving drugs to the architects?

Carl took one last puff and stubbed out the butt on the asphalt.

The parking lot was the place where he least missed his basement office at police HQ. No footsteps in the corridor. No polite greetings. No handshakes. Here he could be himself and try to gather his muddled thoughts.

He brushed the back of his hand against his thinning hair. Not that it made any difference, but it was one of the few habits he had inherited from his father.

They had written nine questions on the window up there. It was daunting to think that they could add at least a hundred more. But it was only question nine on his mind just now. Maybe he had phrased it wrong. He had written, "The significance of the dates?" Maybe it should have been "Why these particular dates?" or "What the hell is it with these dates?" as Rose would have succinctly put it.

He remembered Marwa's puzzled face when she mentioned April twenty-eighth to Assad, and how strange it was to her that he had not realized that it was Saddam Hussein's birthday.

If there was a theme here, then everything might be connected to the Middle East. He would have to look into that. He had three other dates, so it should be relatively easy to google.

Only very rarely could Google searches work miracles in an investigation because there was usually far too much incorrect or imprecise information, and all too often one ended up on a wild goose chase. Carl smiled at this realization when he searched for January 26, 1988, when Ove Wilder's repair shop was destroyed, and he found that this date was Australia Day, a commemoration of the British ships that arrived in Sydney Cove, but it was also nicknamed "Invasion Day" and was defined by demonstrations because it was a symbol of the British destruction of Aboriginal culture. Not that he could use that information to bolster his Middle East theory.

A more promising fact was that the relationship between Egypt and Israel was formalized on that date. So it was in fact rather significant.

Carl sighed. *So it might be another case related to the Middle East. Assad won't be happy about that*, he thought.

He immediately googled May 17, 2000, which was the date when the arms trader Carl-Henrik Skov Jespersen was found shot in the temple. On this date, there was nothing specific connected to the Middle East. Yes, the war between Iran and Iraq was drawing to a close, and there were negotiations about Israeli withdrawal from Lebanon in those days, but nothing specific on May 17.

Carl sighed. The central finds in these sorts of cases needed to have common denominators. What else could lead them toward a motive?

Then he searched May 19—the date when Palle Rasmussen died. It was apparently the date when Egypt blocked the passage of Israeli ships through the Suez Canal, which was allegedly a contributing factor to the Suez Crisis in 1956. But he had a nagging doubt about the relevance.

I'm on a wild goose chase. This is not about the Middle East, he thought.

He took a cigarette from his packet but placed it back. He didn't even feel like smoking.

He looked at his watch, which seemed to be moving in slow motion. Was he growing tired of playing detective?

24

CARL

Friday, December 11, 2020

Despite the news that the country was once again subject to partial lock-down, and the media was in a frenzy, the case of the brutal murder of Tabitha Engstrøm in the middle of a main road in Copenhagen made equally big headlines.

It had now been two days since her impaled body had been freed from a broken parking sign, two days since the road directorate and the office for technical and environmental services started fighting over who was responsible for neglecting to remove the lethal sign, and just one day since a coughing police sergeant, Bente Hansen, stood in front of a mob of reporters trying to keep the developments in the case close to her chest.

Certain residents of Amager demanded the lord mayor's resignation. The group of disgruntled residents spanned local groups of housewives, line dancers, chess and backgammon clubs, trade associations, and many individuals, all expressing their fears that the city had become lawless.

The description of the woman who had committed the murder was soon established because an alert couple who had been filming each other with their smartphones had caught her flight down the nearest side street on camera. Not much effort was expended in explaining why no one had chased this relatively slender woman or tried to stop her. People had been in a state of shock, according to the media. A philosopher specializing in contemporary studies declared on the TV show *Aften-showet* that it was symptomatic of the times that even in a state of shock, most people are more than capable of producing their beloved phones and recording.

Bente Hansen explained that they were currently investigating the more or less legal surveillance recordings from some local shops in the area to try to uncover where the woman went after the murder. She said that one of these recordings had caught how, immediately after the deed, she had been sick in the side street.

"We are checking her vomit to establish a DNA profile and what she had eaten."

The reporters shouted over one another. What use would it be to establish what she had eaten? Had she thrown up or been sick because she was in shock herself over the murder? Did this indicate that it was an impulsive action or that the woman had never before done anything so violent?

"I would hope the latter," said Bente Hansen with a cough.

And that was the end of that day.

"Unfortunately, Bente Hansen has tested positive for corona, Carl, so now many of us have to go into quarantine," said Marcus, looking distressed. "I'll probably have to send most of you on this floor home to self-isolate."

"Really? But no one in my department has been anywhere near Bente or her team for ages. And, while we're on the subject, I haven't been around anyone from this department either. Why would I have been?" Carl suppressed the urge to gloat. There was no way he was going into quarantine.

"Are you sure you don't have a temperature?"

Carl held a hand to his forehead. It was wrinkled and greasy but not warm.

"What about the others on your team? So maybe it was for the best that I sent half of you home."

Carl shrugged. There was no reason to say that Gordon was back. And who the hell noticed if people were sweating or not?

"You are familiar with Bente Hansen's current case?" asked Marcus.

"About the woman who impaled another woman on a broken metal pole?"

Marcus nodded. "It's a strange coincidence that the victim, Tabitha Engstrøm, had just left court an hour before, following a preliminary hearing. We have surveillance video from various shops all the way from the courthouse showing that her killer followed her from a short distance to the scene of the crime."

"Has the perpetrator been identified?"

"Yes, this morning. She was recognized by the owner of a clothes shop who saw the video that a young woman from Amager had recorded and sent to TV2 and *DR News*. The shop owner had sold a coat to the perpetrator. And someone working in a bakery close to the perpetrator's home recognized her as the woman who had bought a pastry with her credit card that morning, which was confirmed by the analysis of her vomit. She had gulped it down in five bites, and it was almost undigested."

Carl nodded. He knew all about having a sweet tooth.

"Our colleagues have been searching all day for this woman, Ragnhild Bengtsen. But she seems to have vanished into thin air. Someone might have seen her heading for the residential area near the Carlsberg brewery, but it hasn't been confirmed. The woman who called to report it sounded a little unsure because she couldn't provide a description of what the woman was wearing, the time, or which direction she was heading in. And now we're short of people to follow up on the lead."

"You've got to be kidding!" exclaimed Rose indignantly as she spun around on her office chair. "Marcus wants us to stop what we're doing? But it's his case more than anything."

"Yes, but we're just putting it to one side for the time being. Bente Hansen is ill and her team has been sent home, so just now Marcus doesn't have any other team to put on the Ragnhild Bengtsen case. The press and people from Amager are demanding answers—they are up in arms over what happened—so Marcus had to put someone on it. And that's us."

"Absolutely crazy! This is not a case for Department Q."

"I agree. And I have tried to make him see sense, but he insisted." He turned to Gordon. "Can you give us a rundown?"

"Ragnhild Bengtsen is thirty-three years old, works as an office assistant for national rail, is childless, had a relationship with a colleague for a while, and has been missing since the murder. That's all I have for now."

Assad appeared in the doorway with a grunt. His clothes were unusually crumpled, his hair was sticking out in all directions, and he looked despondent.

"I couldn't stand being at home," he said.

They briefed him about the chief of homicide's latest orders and what Gordon had found out so far.

"Thanks, Gordon. Has her home been searched?" asked Carl.

"Bente Hansen's team didn't have time, but I've got the search warrant here."

"Let's get going. Rose, you stay here, and us guys from Department Q will run the full risk of being in the big wide world."

He laughed, but Rose stayed stony faced. She was obviously coming along for the ride.

"Do we know anything about her movements from the phone records, Gordon?" she asked.

"She didn't have a phone on her. Perhaps she doesn't even have one. No idea."

Carl sighed. "We have to use every available resource to track her movements. We have to find her. And our second main goal is to establish a motive so we can get back to our own work."

Rose looked at Gordon. Apparently, she had not read the newspapers in the last few days. "Who was Ragnhild Bengtsen's victim, Gordon?"

"A thirty-four-year-old woman named Tabitha Engstrøm who had just left court after a preliminary hearing. Several witnesses state that they saw her the day before, deliberately causing a thief to fall into traffic opposite Østerport Station, where he was then killed by a truck. I actually have the report here."

He showed her a photo of the accused and then a photo of the dead man. It was hard to make out the mangled body.

"Okay, I heard about the accident on the radio. It's not often you feel sorry for a thief."

It was clear from the state of Ragnhild Bengtsen's apartment why she didn't live with anyone—and definitely not a man. Who would feel at home in this tiny two-room apartment with the same pink paint on all the walls and all available surfaces covered in movie posters of half-dressed male actors in their prime?

"Lord almighty," said Rose, discreetly scanning the bulging muscles of Arnold Schwarzenegger, Sylvester Stallone, Jason Statham, Bruce Willis, Will Smith, Clint Eastwood, and at least thirty others—most of whom Carl could not name.

"Yeah, this is not what I had imagined either," grunted Carl. "What do you make of it all?"

"That she was a special case," said Assad, scratching his stubble. "None of us would have had a chance with her."

"No, these men certainly aren't weak, blushing wallflowers," said Rose excitedly. "But the selection of posters isn't coincidental. Can't you see it?"

All three men frowned. Apart from studies of what hormones and protein supplements can do for the male anatomy, what were they supposed to notice?

"Well," she continued. "The posters are obviously all from action movies. But Arnold Schwarzenegger's posters, for instance, are not from the Terminator movies, where he plays a villain. They are from *Predator*, when he's not one. So, what we're looking at is a collection of the coolest action heroes in film history. Just look at how many posters there are of Bruce Willis from the Die Hard movies." Rose smiled. "The woman from this apartment definitely celebrates men who show determination and a no-bullshit approach. She obviously isn't someone who has anything against people taking the law into their own hands. You should take some photos, Carl, and show them to Mona. I'm sure she'll agree with me."

Carl nodded. "Right. But we aren't forensic experts, so stick to the golden rules of doing a home search! Whatever you do, keep your latex gloves and shoe covers on and keep your wits about you and your eyes peeled because we don't know what we're looking for. We have to be extremely systematic to avoid ruining something that might be a lead. Let's get going."

Ragnhild Bengtsen was an extremely organized person. The things in her drawers were categorized: tax papers in one, health insurance papers in another, and bank statements in a third. Memories from her time as a girl scout and a short spell on a handball team were collected in a drawer with letters from a pen pal in Møgeltønder and a few pencil drawings from places she had visited when she was at school. There was nothing to indicate any special talents or alarming character traits. A photo on her shelf from a party certainly did not indicate anything out of the ordinary. It depicted a smiling, sweet-looking young Danish woman.

Rose was the most skeptical among them. "There must be something that can bloody well tell us what drove the crazy bitch," she said, checking to see if the windowsills were loose and might have something hidden under them.

"She obviously isn't an avid reader because there isn't a single book here." Gordon noticed things like that immediately.

"Is there anything indicating that she might have a safe deposit box somewhere?" asked Rose. Gordon waved a hand dismissively.

"Do we know if she has a storage room in the basement or the attic?" asked Assad.

"We'll have to get hold of the janitor again to find out. Can you call him, Assad?" asked Carl.

He nodded.

"Have a look in here!" shouted Rose.

Carl and Gordon walked over to the far wall of the bedroom.

"Her old flat-screen TV is conveniently mounted on the wall at the end of the bed, but it isn't connected to any streaming services or satellite. According to the janitor, she has the channels the housing association supplies, but that's only the basic national channels and a couple of others." She turned on the TV to demonstrate.

"Yes, but she does have hundreds of DVDs," said Gordon.

Rose nodded. "Yes, and look at the titles!"

Carl knew absolutely nothing about movies, so he kept an eye on TV2 News on the television screen instead. There was nothing other than updates on the COVID-19 restrictions. Things looked bleak in very many countries. The murder on Amager had taken a back seat, but it was no wonder that it could not compete with a pandemic for long.

"They're all action movies," said Gordon.

"Yeah, but the themes, Gordon," said Rose, looking triumphant. "Look again."

"Er, I haven't seen most of them. Where I'm from, those films aren't that popular."

"Okay, but we've got Charles Bronson in *Death Wish*, Bruce Willis in the remake of the same film, Liam Neeson in all three Taken movies, Viggo Mortensen in *Eastern Promises*, Michael Caine in *Harry Brown*, just to mention a few. And like I said about the posters, all the films are about revenge and taking the law into your own hands."

Carl could sense where this was going. "So, the lady has been lying in bed, having a cozy time with these types of men."

"Yes, and women." She pointed up to the shelf with Jodie Foster's *The Brave One* and Charlize Theron in *Monster*, among others.

"A few of them aren't in their boxes," said Carl. "We'll take them with us, but be careful not to leave fingerprints. Boxes like these can reveal many secrets."

"Do we know if Ragnhild Bengtsen has ever made a report that she was attacked?" asked Rose.

"Do you mean rape? No, she hasn't. The murder of Tabitha Engstrøm is the first time she's ever appeared in a police report," answered Gordon.

An hour and a half later, they were none the wiser. They had all worked hard, not least Rose, who had gone through everything in the flat. She had looked for hiding places in the mattress, turned the sofa upside down, moved rugs, patted down pillows, been on all fours under the dining table and desk, pulled out drawers, and inspected the back of all the furniture.

She was extremely frustrated and cursed to herself all the way down to Ragnhild Bengtsen's storage room in the basement, where the janitor was waiting. And just like the woman's apartment, there did not appear to be much of interest there either. In fact, Carl had never seen a storage room like this, where everything was placed neatly on shelves with stickers clearly indicating the contents of boxes and folders. It was also so spotlessly clean that you could eat your dinner off the floor.

Rose looked at the tip of her finger, having just brushed it over one of the shelves. "She must have been down here recently and used a lot of elbow grease, given how clean and tidy it is."

"Elbow grease?" Assad looked confused.

"A good going-over, Assad!" said Carl. Assad still looked confused.

The janitor nodded. "Yes, I know she was down here last week. It must have been on Tuesday, when I wheeled the waste containers up to be emptied the following morning."

Carl turned toward the badly lit basement corridor behind him, where the green waste containers were neatly lined up.

"So you're saying that they are emptied on Wednesdays. Well, then I don't think we'll find anything here, folks," continued Carl. "If there was anything compromising, she threw it in the containers and our friend here unknowingly helped her send it off to be incinerated. We'll just have to accept that we're two days late."

25

CARL

Friday, December 11, 2020

The naked body looked fresh and could not have been in the ground for more than one or two days. Based on the condition of the woman, it would be hard to establish her identity. She was badly battered, but Marcus Jacobsen and Carl Mørck still had a well-founded hunch about who she was. The height and age certainly fit the bill.

There had been a sign outside the plot for several years reading UN-AUTHORIZED ACCESS PROHIBITED, but a couple of young guys from the village south of Arresø had ignored it and eyed an opportunity to create a sanctuary where they could get high or laid.

"We're lucky that these youngsters were so curious." Marcus looked out toward the highway that meandered past in the distance. "Otherwise this would have been the perfect hiding place."

"Why did the boys start digging?" asked Carl.

"They noticed the fresh, dark soil in among the weeds and thought that it must have been dug overnight by the biker gang from the neighboring village. They planned to take whatever weapons, drugs, or money they found and move it on as quickly as possible."

"Okay. It must've been a shock for them," said Carl while photographing the body with his phone from a distance to avoid getting in the way of the glaring forensic floodlights.

It was not a pretty sight. Carl would never get used to the thought that some people could commit such atrocious acts on others. All the woman's fingertips had been chopped off just above the last joint, and all her teeth had been pulled out. Her face had been bludgeoned with a blunt object—and judging by the deep holes in her skull, they had been inflicted with a heavy instrument with a square head. Probably a sledge-hammer.

"I agree. It must've been a shock for them. The two guys are speaking with the local psychologist just now."

Marcus Jacobsen nodded to one of the forensic team who was walking toward them.

"I'm sorry, but we haven't found any intact footprints, tire tracks, or traces of someone being dragged across the ground due to the youngsters' digging and rummaging around," he said dryly. "And we haven't found anything near where the body was buried."

"Do you know who owns this plot?" Carl asked a colleague from the North Zealand police.

"Yes, it's owned by Hillerød Municipality. It was originally intended for industrial facilities, but the plans have been postponed for the last ten years. I think a few people from the town have visited it every now and then to keep down the weeds and grass. Not that you can tell in the dark, but it hasn't been done for quite some time."

"When exactly did the young guys find the body?"

"Just over an hour and a half ago, at four twenty p.m.," answered their colleague.

"And when do you think the body was buried?" Carl asked the forensic technician.

"No more than twenty-four hours ago."

"Okay. And when did the sun go down yesterday?"

"Same as today. Around twenty to four."

Carl turned to Marcus. "Unless we get any other information, my guess is that the body was buried after dark. And let's also assume that whoever tried to get rid of the body knew about the site beforehand and where to dig."

"So you think they took into account where future foundations would be laid if the site was ever developed, and that there was little risk that it would happen here so close to the fence?"

Carl nodded. "Yes, and if that is the case, I think it would make sense to continue digging. It seems likely that they might've been here before on a similar mission, doesn't it?"

Back at the office, Carl stared at the photos on his phone of what was presumably the body of Ragnhild Bengtsen. The contrast between the smiling woman in the photo they had taken from her flat and this bludgeoned, naked, dirty corpse was heart-wrenching.

Carl took a cigarette and rolled it between his fingertips. How often had he sat like this, wishing that he had chosen a different path? What had happened to the innocent, optimistic boy from a small backwater town in northern Denmark? What had happened to the hopeful young man who graduated from the police academy? And why did he have to sit here late on a Friday when everyone else was at home on the sofa having a cozy night in with their family in front of the TV?

He breathed heavily through his nose. Luckily, it would not be long before he could head home and give his little girl a big hug.

He put down the cigarette on the desk, eased himself out of his chair, and walked over to his colleagues in the other office to brief them about the day's findings. It was impressive that they had not left hours ago.

He only managed to say, "Listen up," before Gordon turned away from his computer and interrupted.

"We finally have news about Palle Rasmussen's Mac," he said. "IT didn't have time to work on it, so they sent it over to NC3. They've confirmed what we already knew—that everything has been deleted and they'll have to restore the files. They also wrote that it's very common when a computer has been used at Christiansborg for all the contents to be wiped if it's given to the next of kin. The files are work related and may be confidential. It's as simple as that."

Carl frowned. That was one thing he had not thought to ask about when he met Palle Rasmussen's secretary, Vera Petersen. Bloody hell! He looked over at Gordon. Was there a smug expression on his face due to the delay with the computer?

"IT, NC3—all those acronyms are enough to drive anyone crazy," grumbled Assad. "You need to be a walking encyclopedia. In text messages people write btw, lol, brb, and more keep coming all the time. When I call businesspeople, I always end up talking with a CEO, CCO, CPO, CIO, and all that sort of nonsense. Why the hell do we need all those abrasions in the police?"

"Abrasions? You mean abbreviations, Assad," said Gordon. "And by the way, NC3 is an abbreviation of NCCC, which stands for National Cyber Crime Center in the national police, FYI!"

"I see. But then at least they should call it NCCCNP to give us a fair chance." Assad pouted. "Anyway, from now on, I want my business card to say SAAFT3AE."

"It doesn't quite slip off the tongue, does it?" said Gordon.

Carl looked at his watch. He would be out of here in twenty minutes.

"When can we expect to have the Mac back?" he interjected.

"They'll take a look at it tomorrow. They reckon they'll have something for us just after eight."

"On a Saturday? Right. So they've be working through the night?"

"No, they'll start on it first thing tomorrow."

"Okay. And when does the weekend shift start work?"

"At eight, and they said it won't take more than ten minutes." Gordon tried to force a smile. He should not have bothered. He turned to Assad. "And what does SAAFT3AE stand for?"

"Swarthy Arab and father to three and exhausted, what else?"

Carl drew a deep breath. He could not get the cigarette on his desk out of his mind.

"Why are you smiling, Gordon?" asked Rose without waiting for an answer as she entered the room and placed a small cardboard box on her desk. "I've called the hospital and spoken with Bente Hansen."

"What about?" asked Carl.

"Shouldn't you start by asking how she's doing? Where's your empathy?"

Carl sighed. "Fine. How is she?"

"She's actually really ill. I'm afraid we won't have a chance to talk with her again before she's transferred to intensive care. She could barely breathe."

"Give it a rest, Rose. I actually like Bente and obviously I'm sorry to hear that."

Rose nodded. She got the message.

"What did you get out of her?"

"She hadn't been informed that we've been assigned the two cases involving Ragnhild Bengtsen and Tabitha Engstrøm, which I sensed annoyed her a little. But she still asked me to contact someone from her team, Manfred, who's currently in isolation and working from home."

"And did you?"

"What do you take me for? He told me that the murdered woman, Tabitha Engstrøm, often spewed hatred on various social media."

"I see. But that's generally not a crime in itself," said Carl.

"No, but in her case, she often threatened people with death and destruction if they didn't toe the line."

"Examples, please."

"Women who left their children in strollers on public streets deserved to have their children kidnapped."

"Wasn't there a case in New York years back where the mother was arrested?" asked Gordon. "And a Danish woman at that."

Rose nodded. "Yes, it was called the stroller case. The mother wrote a book about it a few years ago."

"And what else?" asked Carl.

"Everyone who spat on the street deserved to have their face rubbed in it until their skin was hanging off."

"Okay. She sounds very uncompromising. But do you think she went beyond writing about assaults and actually carried them out?"

"Yes, I do. And pretty systematically."

"And she finally overreacted in Østerbro?"

"Yes, definitely. After the murder of Tabitha Engstrøm, Bente Hansen's team got a warrant to search her apartment. Unfortunately, they didn't manage to analyze the objects that were seized before the entire team were forced into quarantine. I've heard that Bente Hansen collapsed just out there in the parking lot when they returned from the search." Rose pushed the little cardboard box over to him. "The guy from her team, Manfred, told me where to find the box in their office, so I went in to get it. Manfred told me that the first thing he would address when he returned was this, so naturally that's where I decided to start."

She produced a bound notebook from the box, opened it to the first page, and read aloud:

LOG, Tabitha Engstrøm, March 2018—

1. *Group leader: Debora, around 50*
2. *Group members: Sara, around 35; Martha, around the same. My group name is Eva.*
3. *Group objectives: "You could call it taking the law into your own hands, but you could also call it due diligence because it makes the world a little better every time."*

Rose looked up at the others. "The next three pages are a summary and documentation of sixty-five assaults in the period from 2018 to 2020 that Tabitha has committed. Quite violent activities if you ask me, so I'm sure that what she was accused of doing in Østerbro is true. She deliberately caused the death of the thief."

"We've struck gold with this," said Assad. "Does she mention Ragnhild Bengtsen anywhere? Was she one of the group members?"

"No. But Tabitha is called Eva, so we can't rely on the names. It could be one of the other two she mentions. We don't know."

"I take it the notebook wasn't presented in court, seeing as she was released," said Carl.

"No. The search of Tabitha Engstrøm's apartment didn't take place until after her death. And that was first and foremost because Bente Hansen's team wanted to see if they could establish a link to the woman who killed her."

"We obviously all need to read this notebook carefully. But let's hear one of the violations she describes in it," said Carl.

"Okay. Apart from the killing in Østerbro, the most brutal example is probably the time when she publicly punched a young man in the throat with keys sticking out between her fingers because, in her mind, he had yelled something hurtful at a disabled woman. I've checked the case and read that the guy had to undergo several operations and is now struggling with his speech."

"And she wasn't under suspicion?"

"No, she had a way of wriggling out of everything she did, except for her last deed."

"Is there any other information about the three women she mentions? Debora, Martha, and what was the last one called?"

"Sara. No, there isn't. She only mentions them on the first page."

"You get a vague idea of the group's objectives, but what was the real purpose?" asked Gordon. "They certainly weren't getting together to eat or discuss books."

"Any theories?" asked Carl.

"It definitely wasn't a club you'd want to get on the wrong side of," said Rose.

Assad frowned. "In Lithuania, we came across an extremely violent revenge group that attacked people who had worked for the Russian intelligence when the country was behind the Iron Curtain. Could it be something along those lines?"

Rose and Gordon nodded.

"Have you had a chance to look at the unmarked DVDs we found in Ragnhild Bengtsen's apartment?" asked Carl.

"Well, I'm on it at the moment," said Gordon. "I can see that there's a bit of data on all three, but I haven't been able to retrieve any of it yet.

I'm running two of the disks right now." Gordon pointed at a couple of black screens behind him that looked like they were turned off.

"Can't you fast-forward?" asked Carl.

Gordon nodded. "I'm just about to." He pushed the fast-forward button on both DVD players.

"But I was just about to tell you something," said Carl. "Marcus and I went up to Skævinge. We got a tip from the local police, and it turned out that—"

Suddenly, one of the screens flickered before a couple of brief recordings flashed past.

"Hey, rewind, Gordon," shouted Rose and Carl in unison.

There was a flicker again before a quick succession of clips from an American TV program.

"I know that program," said Gordon. "It's pretty bizarre. It only features recordings where people act stupid and often get hurt while the host and his audience laugh. It's called *Ridiculousness*."

The other screen also started flickering while the first one showed someone tripping at the side of a pool and someone else hitting land on a Jet Ski, falling off and almost breaking their neck. Then a series of recordings appeared on the second screen.

"Do you also know what that is, Gordon?" asked Carl, nodding toward the screen.

"Yes. I even know this particular episode. It's a guy called Johnny Knoxville from a famous show called *Jackass,* where the participants always hurt themselves badly. Knoxville does all sorts of idiotic and stupid things in this episode—gets pepper-sprayed in his eyes and stunned with a Taser. In the clip we're watching, his nipple is bitten by a small crocodile and then his car is rammed by another car. It's completely insane."

Carl huffed. "Why the hell was Ragnhild Bengtsen turned on by this stuff? And why would she hide it at the very end of an otherwise blank DVD? Are these not fully accessible TV programs even though they're crazy?"

Assad pushed a glass of tea over to him. "Almost no sugar in it," he promised, pointing to the screen. "I think she was trying to cover that up."

Carl took the tea and turned toward the screens again.

"That's disgusting," moaned Gordon, and Carl couldn't agree more.

On both screens, the TV shows had been replaced by recordings that were by no means innocent. One screen showed one serious accident after another, while the other showed real-life recordings of violent assault and murder. The recordings were blurry, but there was no doubt about what they depicted. Highlights from group attacks with clubs, men stabbing other men from behind, shots being fired into crowds, high-school mass murders, and police brutality.

"Turn that filth off, Gordon," exclaimed Rose.

Assad said nothing. Where was his mind these days?

"Right. Now we have proof that Ragnhild Bengtsen was a total nutcase," she continued.

"What the hell could have driven her to collect this shit?" Gordon was as pale as a sheet now.

"I'm thinking about her movie posters, where all the heroes take the law into their own hands. And even if these clips are more intense, it's basically the same thing," said Rose. "At this point, she's so far gone that she does it herself to an extreme degree, just like Tabitha did. But what is the connection between them? She'll have to answer that when we manage to track her down."

Carl nodded and took a sip of his tea. He cleared his throat and tried to avoid coughing. Then he swallowed, cleared his throat again, and then had a coughing fit. They all patted him on the back, but it only made matters worse. After a minute, he caught his breath again and looked teary-eyed at Assad.

"Urgh, Assad! I'd rather have the version with sugar. What've you done to it?"

"Just a little ginger, Carl. You take an entire ginger root, grate it into the pot, and let it infuse for an hour before reheating it. It's supposed to be good for you."

Carl nodded. "Okay. But do me a favor and warn me next time,

Assad." He turned to Rose. "Yes, we could certainly do with her answer, but Ragnhild Bengtsen isn't going to be answering any questions."

"Why?" asked Gordon.

Carl found the photo of the woman's bludgeoned body on his phone and passed it to Gordon. "This is why!" he said, and he saw the last hint of color drain from Gordon's face.

26

MAURITS

Saturday, December 12, 2020

Before he had even turned thirty, Maurits van Bierbek had built up a sizable fortune from reality TV. He started as a lowly casting agent, then he became a script writer, and, finally, when he founded his own company, Unbelievable Corporation, he became a concept developer and produced a large number of shows that could leave most people open-mouthed with indignation.

But Maurits had no moral scruples about how he made a living. As long as there were TV stations willing to invest in his ideas, what was the problem? Yes, his Catholic family in Rotterdam had raged and warned him that he would burn in hell, but he had tackled that effectively by breaking any link with them and moving to Denmark. In fact, he could not care less.

His home life did not present any problems in relation to his professional one either, because he and his second wife, Victoria, had met each other on set during the shooting of one of Maurits's early shows, *Four Rooms in a Hotel*. She certainly did not have any objections to demonstrating the effect of her sex on men. On the contrary, Victoria and the girls were happy that the money kept rolling in and that their house in Gammel Holte was located close to a riding stable. It was a life of high-class friends in cashmere, indoor swimming pools, and home cinemas in the basement. What more could they wish for?

During certain periods, Maurits had so many ideas for TV shows buzzing in his head that he almost couldn't keep up. So it was perhaps not so strange that the development of a new reality show every year simultaneously drained him of energy and gave him a boost. At any rate, there was no ignoring his success, and his endeavors paid off in abundance. And when *What to Do with a Drunken Sailorboy* hit the top of the TV ratings in twenty-five countries, Maurits decided that his company should aim to become the largest reality TV concept developer in the world. As he had not yet achieved this goal, despite popular shows such as *Reality Prison, Cougars and Youngsters, Who's Next on the Couch?, Paradise or Hell*, and, most recently, *Did She Really Say That?*, Maurits knew that he still had not developed the ultimate show.

It was not until COVID-19 seized the entire world in its merciless grip that Maurits finally came up with the idea that would most probably let him exceed the profits of any production company across the world.

It was called *Who Is Going to Die First?*, and the cast of relevant participants was endless: soldiers heading off to war, terminally ill patients on a cancer ward, an entire residential area where poor people lived too close together, giving corona a free pass. A show like this could follow groups of people up close and pit the participants or their next of kin against one another, making life difficult for those who were most vulnerable. And if the last five were promised a huge financial reward, the fight for survival would be all the more gruesome. And it would give Unbelievable Corporation the ability to keep developing new themes and featured groups where the stakes in reality only concerned who died first and the order in which the others followed.

The more Maurits thought about the concept, the more eager he became. This particular idea simply topped everything he had done before: TV shows with promiscuous, self-promoting, body-fixated men and women; shows where people were tattooed with the most outrageous designs in the most provocative places; and shows where people dated based on the criteria that only one-night stands counted.

This show was bigger, much bigger.

And Maurits bragged about his idea for an amazing new reality show and claimed in a newspaper interview that it would be the most provocative and insane show ever seen.

Just one week after the interview, he was contacted by a representative of the world's largest reality TV network, Global Rea Inc. The representative declared their interest in taking over his company if his new idea held water. Maurits mentioned the title and briefly explained the premise of the show without revealing too much, and they made him an offer so astronomical that he held his breath for half a minute after they had hung up.

On that basis, Maurits van Bierbek had no hesitation in agreeing to being picked up from his home the following Saturday at ten a.m. and driven directly to a conference room at the airport to meet the representative of Global Rea Inc. to discuss the idea in more detail.

If everything went well, they would sign a letter of intent on the spot and then the lawyers would take it from there.

An elegant woman wearing an immaculate suit was sitting behind the wheel of the Lexus that was parked outside his house with the engine running.

"Maurits van Bierbek, this time of day it'll probably take us thirty-five to forty minutes to get to the airport, so do make yourself comfortable," she said in a distinctive southern U.S. drawl. "We have some exquisite beverages for that purpose. You'll find a chilled Dom Pérignon, some Hernö gin, tonic water and still water, ice cubes, and, not least, a very decent Puligny-Montrachet white wine and a magnificent Château la Cabanne Pomerol in the refrigerator." She nodded to him in the rearview mirror. "Our representative for Global Rea Inc., Mr. Victor Page, who is also the vice president of the company, enjoys a light atmosphere during meetings, so do help yourself. I'm Victor Page's PA, and I've been tasked with procuring preliminary information about the initiatives Unbelievable Corporation is planning to introduce in the foreseeable future. Do you feel comfortable sharing information with me?"

Maurits nodded into the rearview mirror and popped the Pérignon while melting into her eyes. Could she be interested in sharing more than just information with him?

"We've been following the development of your company for some years, and we're amazed at how well you've succeeded in challenging the viewers' sexual norms in countless countries without any pushback. At Global Rea Inc., we've always sat on the fence that you jumped over a long time ago, and we've realized that we need to revolutionize our fundamental mindset before we dare take the leap. It seems that Unbelievable Corporation can provide us with the inspiration."

She turned her head and looked at him as if he had already signed his company over to them.

"But haven't you ever had any personal scruples, Mr. van Bierbek? Haven't you ever reached a point where you considered stopping while the going was good?" She smiled. "You don't have to answer, because your latest concept tells us that you've got no intention of stopping."

Maurits tried to smile, but already with the fifth sip of the Pérignon with its fragrant, almost undetectable tickling of his throat, he felt like all his senses were being challenged and his eyelids seemed to stop obeying his will.

"How on earth can a brain be as sick as yours and suggest a show like *Who Is Going to Die First?* Don't you ever choke on your own complacency?" the woman suddenly snapped.

Maurits had to let her words sink in before he realized how the mood in the car had suddenly turned sinister.

"And how can you defend your contribution to breaking down all natural human moral boundaries?" she continued, while her eyes in the rearview mirror narrowed and her tone grew more acidic.

Maurits tried to reach for the water bottle but his arm would not obey.

"Allowing young people to act like prostitutes? Encouraging men and women to be disloyal, fornicate, lie, deceive, and destroy people who were their friends only moments before? Wanting other people to die?"

Maurits was smiling now. This was no doubt just a test, and he knew exactly what to answer, if only his tongue would cooperate. He should not have hit the champagne so early in the day.

"Let me tell you what lies in wait for you, Maurits. We've decided to give you an important role in your last, ultimate concept."

Now Maurits was frowning. This was definitely not what they had agreed on the telephone. Once he had sold his company, he was supposed to come up with five new concepts and then he would be free of any further obligation. He was not supposed to participate in his own shows.

"I can tell from your face that Mr. Page failed to inform you about this part of the deal, but the situation is that we'll give you the credit for being the first contestant to die. Don't you think that'll give the concept the extra push it needs?"

He leaned his head back to loosen his jaw. Why would Mr. Page start out by making him the butt of a joke?

"In five minutes, you'll be unconscious, Maurits. And then Unbelievable Corporation will no longer have its president. You'll never, ever return to the company. And when you're dead, we'll demolish your business premises and all your equipment. We'll bring down everything. Employees, participants, and all. Everything that belongs to you will be wiped from the face of the earth."

"But Mr. Page . . . ," he stammered with difficulty, trying to force a smile. But his face was already paralyzed.

"Oh, yes. I might have mentioned a Mr. Page," she suddenly said in Danish. What was happening? "I don't actually know him, and I certainly don't wish to. In fact, it's basically just me, and you're not going to be happy about that when things go down."

His brain came to first. Not with thoughts and concepts, but only with a pounding pain that seemed to emanate from every pulsating artery. He wanted to scream, but the connection to his speech center was blocked. Then all his facial muscles began to twitch and his eyeballs rolled from side to side behind his lids. It was a long time before Maurits could open his eyes even a little and glance at his watch and then at the white walls surrounding him in all directions.

The room was the size of a small gymnasium devoid of bathroom or kitchen facilities, and there weren't even any doors. At the end of the barren room was the only thing that indicated any form of life: a stainless-steel freight elevator with a door that opened upward that seemed to be the only access to this floor. That was when he realized that not only were there no doors, but there were no windows either, so he had no idea whether it was day or night. A few dim electric bulbs glowed from the walls as if they were intended to make up for the lack of windows. That was all.

He looked down over himself and immediately realized the hopeless situation he was in. Underneath the metal armor restraining his upper body, he was wearing nothing except underwear. Even his socks had been removed.

He looked up to the side. Two eyebolts had been welded to the shoulders of the armor, from which two strong iron chains rose upward. He slowly hoisted himself up and could see that the chains were connected to two robust metal runners in the middle of the ceiling, spanning almost the entire length of the room.

I can move, he thought, and he stumbled forward a couple of steps while the chains above him slid along the runners. There were four to five meters to the wall in front of him and a bit less to the wall behind him. He pulled a little at the chains, which were so loose that he could reach the sides of the room and thereby move around almost the entire floor. He pulled hard at the chains and knew immediately that they were made to resist even the most ardent effort.

"You bitch!" he shouted loudly, sending an echo back in the sterile room that contained nothing except the chair he had just been sitting on and an industrial steel table that was bolted to the concrete floor just like the chair. If he needed to relieve himself, there was a small bucket but no sink to clean himself, no towels, not even a cup to drink from.

Everything was white and gray, and apart from damp spots near one of the side walls, there was no color to catch his eye.

Maurits van Bierbek could not believe it. On this peaceful Saturday morning, he had been sitting in his warm kitchen with a caffe latte in front of him and a skimpily clad woman parading around him, and he had just sent his youngest girl off with Roxan, their new au pair.

And now he found himself here, bursting with rage because an insane woman had made him a contestant in the most uncompromising of all his morbid games:

Only the Strongest Survives.

27

CARL

Monday, December 14, 2020

Carl went to work early Monday morning. The weekend had been a blur of unknown factors and questions that only tedious desk work would help him solve, so he would just have to get on with it.

"If you ask me, Carl, there has to be a logical connection between the murdered woman, Tabitha, and the perpetrator, Ragnhild," Mona had said to him the night before. "And if you're so sure that the body you found yesterday is Ragnhild, my guess is that there is an underlying malicious and very consistent connection between the two women. One person who takes the law into their own hands killing another. I'm not sure that I'd define the women's actions as insane on this basis, but I'm sure that they are motivated by some kind of compulsion. That said, compulsive acts are often rooted in personal defeats that bring people down. These compulsions, on the other hand, seem more like something that give the perpetrators a boost. The question remains, who, or what, led Ragnhild and Tabitha down the dangerous path that ended up being the downfall of them both. That's what you need to find out, Carl."

These thoughts were still in Carl's head as he drove to work and sat down behind his desk.

After reading for half an hour in Tabitha Engstrøm's notebook, he was none the wiser. He still had no doubt that Tabitha Engstrøm was a psychopath who loved punishing others and did not hold back when selecting her methods. In fact, four or five of the episodes she described had ended up being reported in the newspapers, and at least two of them had resulted in police investigation.

He went to Marcus's office and spent the next fifteen minutes bringing his boss up to speed on the contents of the log and his own thoughts on the matter.

Marcus turned another page in the book. "Yes, this doesn't make for pleasant reading. It almost makes you think that Ragnhild Bengtsen did society a favor by ridding the streets of Tabitha."

"Yes. And the same could be said for Ragnhild herself." Carl took back the log. "Are we totally sure that the body from Skævinge matches Ragnhild Bengtsen's profile?"

"I don't have the coroner's report yet, but he called me last night and confirmed it with ninety-nine point nine percent certainty. So we can assume it's her."

"I see. He was that sure. Why?"

"Because a wisdom tooth in the jaw had never grown out, and because you and I gave them a lead with our suspicion that Ragnhild Bengtsen might be the victim. So the coroner's office sent for X-rays directly from her dentist, and there was a match."

"The X-ray of the jaw confirmed it?"

"Exactly. Despite the lack of fingertips and her bludgeoned face, there is no doubt about the identity of the body. It *is* Ragnhild Bengtsen."

Carl nodded. "Anything else of interest from the coroner?"

"Well, maybe not in relation to the death of Ragnhild or Tabitha, but perhaps in relation to understanding who Ragnhild Bengtsen really is."

Marcus looked out the window facing the parking lot, where Gordon was parking his small sardine tin of a car. "The autopsy was thorough, and the coroner found that Ragnhild Bengtsen had suffered substantial genital trauma."

"Rape? But she didn't report anything. We've checked."

"No, I know. Nevertheless, they found some old but very substantial lesions in the genital area that undoubtedly caused her to be unable to have vaginal intercourse for quite some time after the assault. And we're certain that they can't have been self-inflicted."

Carl and Rose drew the short straw when it came to the first task of the day, and now they were standing in front of the shabby holiday home in Tikøb where Ragnhild Bengtsen's retired mother had probably been given permission by the municipality to live all year round.

Rose looked unimpressed at the dilapidated wooden house that was more suitable for demolition than restoration. Corroded guttering, clear signs of rot that revealed the sparse insulation between the outer and inner walls, windows hanging on one hinge and with broken panes—the list went on. Dilapidation that bore witness to poverty, loneliness, and a municipality that did not care.

Carl pushed aside a blackberry cane that was growing into what used to be a porch and knocked on the door.

The woman who answered did not look the least bit surprised. She tucked her gray hair behind her ears and made way for her guests to enter.

"I guess you're here to evict me," she said, unfazed, as a rank stench of rot and urine hit them. She walked in front of them past stacks of cardboard boxes and piles of trash and pointed at a sofa in the living room that was so green with mold that even an animal would not lie on it. They remained standing.

"You're Ragnhild Bengtsen's mother, is that correct?" asked Carl while pulling his face mask over his mouth and nose—and not because of corona.

She looked surprised. "What about her?"

"I take it you haven't been following the news over the last few days?"

She pointed at a stack of local newspapers that had been thrown in a corner and only half-covered a mound of empty cans of food, leftovers, and plastic packaging. It was like a scene from the tragic TV program *Hoarders*. As far from her daughter's extreme orderliness as you could get.

"We're here to inform you that your daughter is dead, Mrs. Bengtsen. We're very sorry."

There was no sign of emotion in her furrowed face.

"We think she was killed a few days ago. Her body was found Friday," said Rose insensitively. She probably just wanted to get it over with so she could get back out into the fresh air. "Am I right in assuming that you also don't know what led up to the crime?"

"I haven't spoken with her for over ten years, so how would I?" She still seemed completely unfazed.

"Ten years! May I ask why?" asked Rose.

"She killed her father, so why would I have anything to do with her?"

Suddenly, Carl did not notice the stench anymore. "That's news to me. What do you base that on? A suspicion or . . . ?"

"Suspicion? Ha! After he had his legs amputated, she gave him his insulin injections. And take it from me, she didn't hold back. She killed him."

"But then it must've been out of mercy," said Rose.

"Yes, you could say that, but you look like an idiot, if you ask me. Are you really in the police?! Jesus Christ!"

Rose tilted her head back momentarily. She was not used to insults like that. "Thanks for the compliment," she replied. "Can we go outside and finish our conversation out there? This place smells worse than death and dung."

She took a firm hold of the woman's arm and pulled her outside before Carl could object.

She let go of her in the wilderness that had probably once been a lawn. "Now, this idiot is going to ask you why Ragnhild would kill her father. And at the same time, I want to know why you failed to show any emotion even though we just informed you that your daughter has been murdered."

The woman crossed her arms and spat on the ground. "I'm sure she had it coming, the lying, evil bitch."

Carl tried to catch her eye. "Why would Ragnhild murder her father?"

"Oh, she had an obsessive personality. Crazy bitch."

"Obsessive personality?" Carl looked at Rose, who was nodding along.

"Yes, obsessive. If she didn't, she wouldn't have said that her own father abused her as a child, would she? That he stuck a coat hanger inside her when she was naughty, would she?" She turned directly to Carl and shouted so loudly that she spat all over his jacket.

"YOU WOULDN'T SAY THAT ABOUT YOUR OWN FATHER, WOULD YOU?"

It was Assad who gave them the news as they were driving back toward Teglholmen. "They've found two more bodies on that building plot up in Skævinge, Carl."

So he and Marcus were right. There was more than one body.

"Are we talking about something recent, or . . . ?"

"No. Both bodies have been there for more than a year."

"Were they disfigured like Ragnhild Bengtsen's?"

"No, there doesn't seem to be any sign of trauma. But being in the ground for so long means that it'll take a few days before we can get a report. They've actually already been taken to the coroner."

"Right! So we won't be able to drop that case anytime soon," protested Rose. She still looked like she wanted nothing more than to give a good beating to the woman who had been so rude to her.

"Maybe, maybe not. It depends whether there's anything to link those two bodies with Ragnhild Bengtsen," said Carl.

"And that's damn well why we'll be stuck with that case, Carl," said

Rose, venting her pent-up frustration. "Of course there is some link or other between these murders, and we'll have to rack our brains trying to figure it out. Can't you get Marcus to give the case to someone else so we can get on with our own investigation? And that's a complicated enough case on its own, if you need reminding. I mean, aren't we supposed to be a department dealing with old, unsolved cases? And yet here we are dealing with murder where the last body was hardly cold in the grave. It's not Department Q's responsibility, is it?"

"Put a sock in it for a minute, Rose. I'm thinking."

Carl looked out at the road. Somewhere in this gray, wintery landscape of fields and farms, there was probably a dog walker who had noticed a van winding its way up to Skævinge without realizing that it was carrying bodies to bury in the dark. Somewhere in the vicinity of Copenhagen, there must be one or more people who had wondered how women like Tabitha and others of a similar age had found out about their club. Somewhere . . .

"Before we direct all our efforts to discovering the identity of the other bodies, we might as well decide what we do or don't work on in Department Q."

He did not hear Rose sigh, but there was no doubt that she had.

"I was only informed about Palle Rasmussen's Mac by NC3 an hour ago, but I can already say that it's going to be problematic," said Gordon when they were back at the office.

"Because?"

"Because they are snowed under and because the hard drive has been very thoroughly wiped."

"Why the hell didn't you at least ask them if they thought there might be any accessible files on the drive?"

He looked disappointed in himself.

"Press them again, Gordon, and now. We need to restore those deleted files. Tell them that we understand they're under a lot of pressure but that this is a case of life and death."

Gordon looked hesitant. "Isn't that taking it a bit far, Carl? We can't—"

Carl stopped him with a wave of his hand and turned toward Assad. "You're a bit quiet today, Assad. Anything wrong?"

"I think I'm going to have to leave the police force soon, Carl."

You could have heard a pin drop in the room. The only sound was the wind from the rain-soaked parking lot.

Carl caught Assad's eye. His brown eyes were lackluster and his normally rosy cheeks behind his beard were completely gray.

"Hell no, Assad, you don't want to do that." Carl could hear that his tone was a little too commanding and firm.

Assad's pupils constricted, which was not a good sign. "PET have summoned the whole family to an interview before Christmas because we haven't filled in the form, Carl. And Ronia is threatening to go back to Iraq. It's all so hopeless. She and Marwa fight all day and cry. Nella sits in Afif's room and is totally silent, just like her brother. That's why I need to leave the force, Carl. I can't risk my family being torn apart, can I? I won't let the police intelligence service destroy us."

They did not notice that Rose had stood up until she slammed the door out to the hallway. She had left without a word, but it was no more than a few seconds before they heard her shouting out there. Their new quarters in Teglholmen might be modern and solid, but the walls could have been more soundproofed.

Three minutes later she returned.

"Marcus understands the situation," she said, her face exploding with frustration and anger. "He's going over to PET right now. He'll put a stop to this, Assad."

Carl turned to Assad, who stood as if glued to the spot, looking down at the floor.

"Shouldn't we try to get on with the job at hand and let Marcus work his magic for us?" Carl laid a hand on Assad's shoulder. "It'll all work out, so let's leave it for now, Assad." Carl ventured a small squeeze of his shoulder. "Do you have anything new for us?"

Assad took a few deep breaths and raised his head in slow motion. Carl had never seen him like this before.

"I've checked the clips that were on the end of Ragnhild Bengtsen's DVDs, and I can't see any connection between them apart from all of them being extremely violent and public." He wiped his fingertips over his eyes as if to check if he had been crying, but there were no tears. "Going through the attacks in Tabitha's notebook, the common factor seems to be that they were all done in public, just like when Ragnhild Bengtsen murdered Tabitha. I didn't get anything else out of them."

Carl nodded. Of course it could seem like Assad was wasting his time, but at the moment they just had to let him work at his own pace.

"So, as it didn't lead anywhere, I went back to the other cases and worked on finding one from 2010 where there might be salt, just like we agreed."

"And I imagine you weren't able to find one."

"No, I didn't, but I sort of did."

He pushed a copy of a newspaper clipping toward Carl.

"This clipping was on our shared drive. It was sent to us this morning from a colleague in Odense."

Carl leaned over the table, holding the copy in both hands.

"Head consultant of TaxIcon found drowned in swimming pool," he read aloud. "Was it one of the cases our colleague in Odense had worked on?" he asked.

"No, but when he saw Rose's request about cases involving salt, he recalled this case immediately. It was big news in Odense back then."

"TaxIcon. I've never heard of the company."

Rose smiled impishly. "That's because you don't read the papers and because it's more than a little above our pay grade to know a company like that, Carl. TaxIcon is a tax consultancy for very rich people."

"Yes, and Pia Laugesen, the woman who drowned, owned the company," added Assad. "She was sixty-four and lived alone, so it was hours before her employees found her floating in the swimming pool in the garden."

"Yeah, you hear those stories from time to time. Brian Jones from the Rolling Stones, for example."

Carl did not exactly feel young when he saw their blank expressions. They had no idea who Brian Jones was. But then, neither did he before his cousin Ronny, who died in Thailand, told him.

"I just mean that a swimming pool and a bad turn make a dangerous cocktail. So just as well none of us have one." Still no reaction. "Well, what is it about this case?"

"It was a big deal because Pia Laugesen wasn't just anyone. She was a huge blow."

Carl was confused.

"She was a very important person for many people because her company turned over around one hundred million euros every six months."

"Oh! You mean she was a big shot, Assad."

Assad shook his head. He thought that was what he had just said.

"Laugesen's grown-up daughter stated back then in a crime report in one of the local newspapers that her mother knew how to swim but never used the pool. So she found the whole thing both strange and suspicious. In fact, it was the only time she had ever seen her mother close to the pool, and the gardener confirmed that she hated it so much that she had told him to get rid of it. He just hadn't gotten around to it yet."

"How did the police record the death?"

Assad took out the print of the police report. "Well, what do you think? She allegedly tripped on a bag lying close to the pool, hit her head on the edge, and fell unconscious into the water. Completely accidentally, of course."

"But then why do you think the case is of interest to us?"

Assad pointed at a sentence in the report. "Because the bag she tripped over was full of salt."

"Salt for the pool? Don't you use chlorine?"

"Yes, and sometimes a mix of salt and chlorine. But this seems to have been a pool with only chlorine."

"Well, I'll be damned! So it was table salt?"

"According to the report, it wasn't analyzed. But why would forensics think to do that?"

Carl looked at the copy of the newspaper clipping again. It was dated August 20, 2010.

All four of them turned to the timeline on the whiteboard. Carl was the first to speak.

"Okay. Let's try to sum this up. We already have several murders involving salt. But let's look at May nineteenth, 2002, when Palle Rasmussen died. If we assume that Pia Laugesen's death was also a murder, and if we still think that our killer works their way through the specific dates, and if we go with the theory that a crime takes place every two years involving salt—I think murders must've been committed in 2004, 2006, and 2008 on consecutive dates between May nineteenth and August twentieth. This should be our focus."

"Jesus," said Gordon.

They spent most of the day locating the coroner's report for Pia Laugesen.

"Don't you think there's something cryptic about it?" asked Gordon. "The report describes her as an unusually strong and physically fit woman for her age. Yet, as expected, it concludes that she drowned but that she was still alive when she fell into the water because she had chlorine in her lungs. So we're supposed to believe that she was still breathing when she hit the water. Then you have to ask yourself if it could have been suicide. But why would she have been suicidal? She was a healthy, successful woman with a great career, lots of money, a large social network, and a good relationship with her daughter. It makes me wonder why she didn't just get out of the pool." Gordon scratched his cheek. "The report states that she might have hit her head on the edge, but the autopsy found no trauma to the head or body, just like forensics didn't find blood, hair, or skin cells at the scene. There was no alcohol or drugs in her blood. She knew how to swim but hated water. It just doesn't add up. The report doesn't even directly address whether she was unconscious when she fell in."

"No, it's strangely nondescript." Carl ignored his phone vibrating in his pocket. "But that's the way it is sometimes with accidents. They're never fully accounted for. What do you think happened?"

"Maybe it *was* an accident. She simply had a dizzy spell and fell in." That was Gordon's guess.

"Yes, but what about the salt? Why was it there? Isn't it strange when you look at our timeline how salt is part of one case after the other where we can't know for sure whether we're dealing with murder and we have no motive or suspect? The police have been clueless every time, but yet every time there's the salt."

The phone was buzzing in his pocket again.

"Yes, it is strange," said Rose. "My guess is that it's a fair assumption that we're dealing with murder. A woman in her position can make lots of enemies. Just one case of bad advice where someone loses their fortune could be fatal."

"But what about the method, Rose?"

Assad shrugged, walked over to the whiteboard, and slowly started to fill in some of the gaps.

Date/Crime Scene: August 20, 2010, Odense
Victim: Pia Laugesen
Murder Method: Victim's head held under the water

Then he put down the pen. "This is my guess."

Carl nodded. "So you reckon that the person who killed her was very strong?"

"No, not necessarily. But have you ever tried to sit on a camel that didn't want you on its back? Suddenly you find yourself lying there with your nose buried in the sand and with no idea what just happened. All I'm saying is that the person who drowned her knew exactly how it should be done and acted without hesitation. And then it's actually not that hard."

"Okay. Sounds like you've tried to drown someone yourself, Assad." Rose flashed a broad smile that soon froze when he did not reply.

"Do we have a photo of the deceased apart from the blurry one from the newspaper?" asked Carl. "Can you check on Google, Gordon?"

A moment later, they were all staring at photos on the screen of Pia Laugesen through the years. No matter how her weight fluctuated, how old she was, or how her appearance changed, her fur coat, broad shoulders, and ponytail gave her an air of nobility.

"These photos tell me that she was a unique and dedicated woman who put her work before everything else," said Rose.

"Unique? You can say that again. Fur coat all year round, loads of jewelry, and a good thick mane of hair to hold on to after giving her a karate chop to the throat," said Assad sardonically.

Carl's phone was buzzing again.

"Yes," answered Carl, sounding annoyed when he finally managed to fish it out of his pocket and take the call. He did not recognize the number.

"Am I speaking with Carl Mørck?" asked the voice. "Good. You're speaking with Laslo from North Zealand police. One of the forensic technicians asked me to let you know that while he didn't find anything where the woman was buried yesterday, he did find something in the other two graves. And it struck him as strange that he found the same thing in both of them. When he took a closer look, there were deposits of salt around the edges of the graves. It almost looked like someone had cured the bodies. Does that mean anything to you?"

28

MAURITS

Monday, December 14, 2020

It was two days since Maurits had seen the woman who kidnapped him, and he had not had anything to eat or drink. The stench from the bucket he was using as a toilet hung like a fog in the room, and his bowels were empty, just like his bladder.

I'll have to be careful not to walk around too much. It drains me, he thought. *I just have to keep myself together and they'll eventually find me. I'm sure of it. It was a good thing that I didn't give a shit that a couple of the surveillance cameras at home are recording outside our private property, even though it's illegal, because now the police will be able to see the license plate of the car that picked me up. Perhaps they've already arrested the woman and that's why she hasn't been here.*

He smiled to himself. Kidnapping was punished severely in Denmark. And it would soon be the bitch's turn to stare at bare white walls. Her time to be the star of her own grave reality.

The show could be called *It's Time for Me to Kill Myself!* He laughed. It was actually a great idea, even though a reality show like that would probably meet a lot of resistance. People were strangely sensitive when it came to suicide.

Maurits nodded and smiled, leaned his head back, and sang so loudly that the ball bearings above him started vibrating: "Oh no, not I, I will survive / Oh, as long as I—"

Then he coughed. His throat felt dry and his tongue was stuck to the roof of his mouth.

This is fucking shit, he suddenly thought, looking around him. This place could be anywhere. A basement with concrete decks separating the floors. A storage building in the middle of nowhere. A new build abandoned before it had been finished. *I could be anywhere on Zealand. So how are they going to find me if the woman keeps her mouth shut?*

When he woke up after the kidnapping, he had looked at his watch and seen the time was 11:45. If he calculated that he had been chained to the chair for ten to twenty minutes before then, they were a good hour and fifteen minutes' drive from his home.

How far could they have come from Gammel Holte? He stopped himself even before he had started calculating, because how the hell could he know? There were far too many factors in that equation. The woman could have driven round in circles. Or she could have sped down the highway with her foot on the gas. She could have crossed the Øresund Bridge for that matter.

Maurits started to sweat. If he was in Sweden now, and if the bitch did not start talking, they would never find him. He would be sitting here tomorrow foaming at the mouth and shaking. And the following day . . . How long could he hold out?

Maurits's father had died from thirst. The memory suddenly popped into his mind. It had seemed undramatic because his father was already old and decrepit, and his life was slipping away. The doctors had to find a way to let him go, and the only thing they were willing to do was to deprive him of fluids. But it had not been quick, and Maurits also recalled that it had scared his father. Before his eyes closed and he slipped into unconsciousness, his gaze had become far too intense. After all, it was his only connection with the world. The sight of those who could not help him. The sight of his only son, who just looked away and left him.

Bloody hell. Get lost, bloody memories. Get lost, old man. You were a prick anyway, so why would I care that you died of thirst?

Maurits looked at his Rolex Submariner watch. Blue face, gold casing, gold strap and buckle, date but no numbers on the face. He had paid two hundred and fifty thousand kroner for it, and he did not give a shit what other people thought about it. When he showed it at the dinner table, his oldest daughter had held up her Apple Watch in front of his face and mocked him.

"Can your watch monitor your pulse? Can you receive calls via your watch? Ha, you're really stupid, Dad. You could've gotten forty Apple Watches for the same money. Or you could have given me a horse and still bought a watch. Stupid!"

Back then, he had just smiled and served himself some food. What did a silly teenager know about what gave a grown man joy? What did she really know about the pleasure of owning something? She would replace her Apple Watch when the next model came anyway. Disloyal brat.

Maurits looked at the date. It had been almost three days since he had anything to eat or drink. How long had it taken for his father to die? Six days, a week? But then, he had been very weak already. Maurits seemed to recall that he had once read that it was possible to last three weeks without solid food or liquid as long as you were fit and healthy. And he was.

Maurits looked at his watch again. If he had taken his daughter's advice and bought an Apple Watch, he might have been able to call them.

He shook his head. The woman who was holding him captive was no fool. She would just have taken it off him. And even if he had had a watch like that, what would he have said? That he had been kidnapped? They must already know that. But who had done it? The woman's story about the possible merger of Unbelievable Corporation was pure nonsense. Global Rea Inc. and Victor Page would have no idea who the woman was. The license plate number on her Lexus was undoubtedly fake—or the car was stolen. And what could he say about the place where he was chained up? There were no distinguishing features in the room. None whatsoever! It was so anonymous that it could be anywhere.

Maurits could feel his tongue swelling a little. Bloody thirst! He leaned his head back again and stared up at the slides that held his chains in place on the runners.

Would it help if I climbed up one of the chains and grabbed hold of the slider? Would I be able to twist the slider, bend the runner out of shape, and wrench the slider loose? And could I do the same with the second chain? Could that be a solution?

There was obviously a risk that he would end up hanging on the second chain if he managed to wrench the first slider loose. Would he be able to wrench the second one out of the runner while hanging from it with his entire weight?

Maurits stood up and simulated the situation. It did not bode well.

He followed the two runners in the ceiling spanning the room from one end to the other. If there was anywhere he would be able to hold on with one hand while wrenching chain number two free with the other, that was where he should climb up.

He heard the ball bearings above him spinning as he walked back and forth the entire length of the room, searching the ceiling. The sound had a momentary calming effect. But it was an illusion—because it was really the sound of his own personal hell. The sound of a trap from which he could not escape.

That was when he saw it. Like the ceiling, it had been painted white and was almost invisible. But it was there. Up there, close to the far wall, there was a twisted eyebolt similar to the two he had attached to his son's swing set more than twenty-five years ago. And the one up there was located only around forty centimeters from one of the runners. If he could only squeeze two fingers through the eyebolt, would he be able to hold his own weight while wrestling to release the other chain from its slider? He hoped that those twenty minutes a day in the exercise room in his basement since his heart attack had paid off.

Maurits began hoisting himself up one of the chains while the other one slowly grew slack. Rope climbing had been one of his favorite disciplines in his school days, but this was different and thirty-five years later. The chain was made of steel and very hard to get a grip on. His knuckles became white with the first grip, and the ceiling was higher up than he had estimated. Possibly more than four meters.

He clamped his naked feet around the chain. If he had been wearing sneakers, it would have been easier. If he had been wearing trousers, the chain would not have chafed the skin around his groin.

"You *must* make it," he whispered to himself. He had no idea how he was going to escape the room if this failed. But perhaps the elevator worked. Perhaps he could use the chains as weapons when he had loosened them. Perhaps.

If anyone came, that was.

He had now managed to grab the top of the chain hanging next to him. The slider on the runner was imprinted with a logo for Mexita Steelware, and like the runner, it was also made from reinforced steel, so this was not going to be easy. He tried with all his might to twist the runner out of shape, but nothing happened. A crowbar might have helped—but he did not have one. All he had was his broken hopes.

He slowly slid down again, went over to the chair, and sat down. Even this relatively limited exertion had exhausted him. The skin on his naked arms had turned gray, and his veins had come up.

And was he imagining it or had the temperature gone up in the room?

Maurits looked at the elevator, which at no point had made a sound while he had been conscious.

Was he going to die in this godforsaken place?

29

CARL

Tuesday, December 15, 2020

Throughout his career as a detective, Carl had several times encountered uncanny coincidences between different cases, and this was another one of those cases that could make him and his colleagues in Department Q shudder.

Two bodies in the ground had been cured in salt like pickled herring— and very close to where they had found Ragnhild's body.

This meant that her case now had a connection with the other case on the whiteboard. There was just the small question of why.

Both the deceased were men. The best-preserved and most recent victim was estimated to have weighed more than fifty kilos and been close to two meters tall. The older body had weighed about the same but been twenty centimeters shorter.

"If we put Ragnhild's case to one side for a minute, what do the others tell us?" Carl asked them.

"We can certainly establish that *those* two murders are connected," suggested Gordon.

Carl nodded. "Yes, but there's one thing that stands out more than anything else. Do you know what it is?"

"That the perpetrator was consciously trying to tell people like us

that the deceased are connected to something up there on the whiteboard," said Assad.

"Yes, but why? Was the perpetrator trying to tease us or is he bragging? Or could it be a hint so we can stop him?"

Carl walked over to the window with the unanswered questions.
"We can begin by erasing a couple of these questions."

He pointed at the bottom two:

R7: Why the hell did someone leave salt at the crime scenes?
A8: Murders and mysterious deaths in 2010. Anything relevant?

"I think we have a partial answer to Rose's question, R7. We don't
know why it's salt in particular. But, as we discussed, the presence of
the salt means we can assume that the perpetrator consciously tried to
tell us that they committed both crimes. Do you think we can work
with that hypothesis?"

They nodded.

"And in terms of A8, Assad has found a case that could potentially
be the murder from 2010 that we're looking for." Carl gave him a nod of
recognition. "Now that you've written it on the whiteboard, Assad, let's
go on assuming that the case of the financial consultant Pia Laugesen is
the 2010 murder we're looking for. Does everyone agree with Assad?"

Rose and Gordon nodded.

Marcus Jacobsen seemed strangely unimpressed. Department Q had managed to link two older deaths, and possibly Ragnhild Bengtsen's, to the old
cases Marcus had fobbed off on them. So why was he not more pleased?

The chief of homicide tried to sigh, but it sounded more like he had
something stuck in his throat. "Ragnhild Bengtsen was buried no more
than a meter from the two other graves, which is conspicuous. But a
meticulous autopsy and investigation of the site didn't reveal any salt
in or on her."

"So?" Carl did not see the problem.

"Given that the bodies were buried so close together in such a remote place, we can assume that we're dealing with the same perpetrators or whichever people are behind it all. So now my question is, if the two older bodies are connected to your cases, then why isn't hers?"

"Maybe it just isn't a ritual murder like the others."

"What do you mean by 'ritual'?"

"She doesn't fit the bill. She wasn't killed at the right time."

Marcus looked puzzled. "You'll have to explain that."

"Okay, but we'll have to go into the other office."

Marcus stood for a long time looking at the whiteboard. He evidently found it plausible that there was a pattern in the years and dates linking the cases together.

He let out a real sigh now. "There's still quite a few holes in your timeline, folks."

Assad walked in front of him with his hands in his pockets. "When will you go to PET and help me and my family? Will you do it today?"

Marcus nodded.

"Good. Then I'm happy to tell you what I think. I think the two bodies that have just been taken to the coroner's were killed in 2016 and 2018. So if you could help me out and put the pressure on PET, and then let me know the identity of the two deceased men, I'll make sure I fill in some more of these gaps."

"Assad, what makes you think that we can establish the date of death so precisely?" retorted Marcus. "They may have been lying there for much longer. They might even have been frozen for years before they were buried."

"I know it's tricky, and especially if the bodies were preserved in salt. But do you know what I think? I actually think both bodies are stuffed with salt. I'm willing to stick my neck in on this one."

Carl imagined the scene. "Stick your neck *out*, Assad. Decapitation, you know."

Assad looked forlorn. That was enough of being corrected for one day.

———

Not ten minutes later, they received a call from the coroner explaining that the stomachs of both bodies had been filled with salt water and their trachea and esophagus stuffed with salt. Table salt, naturally.

"The salt has obviously had some effect, but nothing like real embalming. It hasn't prevented the decomposition of the organs, just like the salt in the graves didn't prevent the decomposition of the skin either. We're working with the assumption that one of the bodies has been in the ground for a couple of years and the other for up to five. But I have to stress that this is pure guesswork."

"Can you tell us anything about the cause of death?" asked Carl.

"No, it's too early. And even when we get to that stage, we might not be able to say for certain. The bodies don't appear to have been stabbed or shot, but, as I said, they are in a fairly bad state. We'll just have to wait and see."

"Any distinguishing characteristics?"

"Well, what can I say? Both men had their pubic hair shaved off, which, oddly enough, is completely normal these days for certain age groups. So let's just conclude that it emphasizes some level of sexual activity. My gut instinct is that they're both somewhere between thirty and fifty, but now we'll have to wait for the dental analysis."

"Are you telling me that their teeth are intact?" asked Carl.

"They most certainly are. And no money spared if you ask me."

"Meaning?"

"Implants, obviously. Plus the usual treatment for cavities due to braces used in childhood. And then there are a couple of crowns and a bridge. There's more than enough to go on."

The atmosphere in Department Q was almost ecstatic.

30

LOUISE/CARL

Wednesday, December 16, 2020

Louise von Brandstrup was the daughter of a failed fashion factory owner from Herning, who had married and subsequently divorced an equally failed carpet wholesaler. Things slowly went downhill for her. She had no skills worth mentioning, no education, drank a bit too much, and had no real friends to speak of. So it was more than fortunate for her when she managed to hook her second husband, Birger von Brandstrup, who made a fortune from investing in online gambling. The hopes of gullible, ordinary Danes trying to make their limited means grow without putting in any effort had made the couple sixty million kroner richer each year over the last decade. Why would they have any scruples about the fact that they and their family were ultimately the only ones taking home the winnings?

Louise's husband disappeared one gray November day in 2018. And since their fortune was solely in his name, all the pleasure, admiration, and partying to which Louise had become accustomed evaporated along with him. In fact, from one day to the next, Louise became easy prey. She was let down by everything and everyone. Von Brandstrup's first wife demanded her share of the estate, and her children demanded that their trust funds be released. The creditors for the leased cars, and the workmen who had built the stables, as well as everyone else to whom they owed money, regularly came knocking with angry expressions and demands for payment.

Louise remained hopeful for the first few months that Birger would turn up again. That his hankering for new flesh and exotic desires would wane and that he would return to make amends and resume his position in their marital bed. But Birger did not turn up, and now she had moved to their holiday home in Hornbæk, which was the only one of their possessions held in her name.

She was lying in bed watching the news when the discovery of the bodies in Skævinge was announced as breaking news. Louise loved the yellow sensationalist and macabre banners that rolled across the screen, and she felt a tingle down her spine for a few seconds before her suspicions were raised. She jumped out of bed because the banner read that one of the bodies was a tall man of at least two meters who had probably been buried for more than a year.

She should have been shocked at her suspicion, but Louise was rather relieved and sensed better times ahead. Imagine if it *was* Birger. Then she could get a death certificate and the estate could finally be settled. He had a large fortune, and she was in line for the lion's share. She was sure of it.

The police were not wearing uniforms, which took her by surprise. A very odd pair—like ebony and ivory. A man who appeared Middle Eastern with bloodshot eyes and tousled hair and, next to him, a lanky, pale-faced guy who looked like a schoolboy stood on her doormat. They introduced themselves, but she did not pay attention. She never did.

"We're here because you called the police about your suspicion that one of the two dead men might be your husband, Birger Brandstrup," said the pale one.

"Von!" she said. "Birger *von* Brandstrup."

The Middle Eastern guy looked down at his papers and mumbled to himself: "There's no 'von' on our papers."

"We're here to inform you that the dental analysis has confirmed that the deceased *is* your husband," said the schoolboy. "We're very sorry."

Yes! sounded a voice in her head. She hid her face in her hands to feign shock. In an instant, her future seemed bright and the possibilities endless.

"Do you need something to drink?" asked the young guy. "Do you need some time to compose yourself? Do you want to call someone?"

She shook her head.

"We've checked our records and can see that you reported your husband missing on November twenty-second, 2018. Is that correct?" asked the Middle Eastern guy.

She nodded from behind her hands.

"Your husband was immensely wealthy. Have you ever at any point received a ransom note, or in any way received information about why he disappeared?" asked the pale guy.

She sighed and looked up at them. Hopefully they could not read her tearless face.

"No, nothing. He just disappeared."

"Can you think of any explanation for his death?" asked the other guy. "Did he have any enemies? Did he owe any money that he refused to pay? Gambling debts, perhaps?"

She scoffed. "Birger didn't owe money to anyone, and, if he had gambling debts, he would've just paid them. Why are you asking me such a stupid question? Birger made money from *other* people's gambling habits. He would never have gambled himself. He always said it was the most stupid thing to do."

"And yet he invested in more than ten gambling platforms here in Denmark and in tax havens abroad over the last twelve to thirteen years. It's not inconceivable that he might have made enemies in that line of work," said the schoolboy.

Louise looked at him with an expression of pity. "Are you thinking about people with gambling addictions? Then let me tell you something. Birger had absolutely nothing to do with the gamblers, and I can't imagine him making himself known to any of those wretched losers." She looked at the other one with a suitably suffering expression. "Where is Birger now?"

"He's still with the coroner."

"I won't have to identify him, will I?"

"Not unless you want to. But I'd advise you not to," said the Middle Eastern guy.

Jesus Christ! As if she would.

"He called himself Birger *von* Brandstrup and disappeared November 22, 2018, after which he was killed and more or less embalmed with table salt. Assad and I agree that we can write another victim up on the whiteboard, Carl," said Gordon.

"And the wife? How did she seem?"

"Do you know the one about the camel who had big ambitions, Carl?" asked Assad.

He shook his head. Gordon did not know it either.

"Well, the camel was convinced that it could fly, so it spread its humps out to the side like wings and jumped off a tall sand dune in the middle of the desert."

"My guess is that it couldn't," said Carl.

"No. It had to perform an emergency landing."

"I don't really get the point, Assad."

"Just like with the camel, we didn't manage to take off anywhere with the wife."

"Okay, clever. So you're telling me that the wife had no information about Birger von Brandstrup's disappearance?"

"No. Nothing except the addition of the 'von,' which wasn't actually his real name."

Carl shook his head. You could fill the entire Colosseum with conceited people who thought that the addition of a "von" or "de" made them more important than others.

"I can see you're enjoying yourselves," came a voice from the door.

It was the chief of homicide. "Maybe it'll contribute to the good mood to find out that the other body was also identified this morning."

They all looked at Marcus Jacobsen.

"The man was called Frank Arnold Svendsen. He was a public figure who received numerous daily fines back in the day for breaches of environmental legislation."

Carl shrugged. "A public figure?"

"Yes. But you probably know him by his alias, Franco Svendsen. He was reported missing, and the general consensus has been that he drowned."

This rang a distant bell in Carl's mind.

"I can also inform you that the autopsy of the two bodies has established that the cause of death was the same for both victims. They died from very large amounts of potassium chloride being injected into their bodies—probably directly into the heart. Potassium chloride is one of three substances used for lethal injections, but normally the person on death row is sedated before it is administered. The interesting thing here is that the killer has made no attempt to conceal their method."

"What do you mean?" asked Carl.

"Forensics went out there again today and checked the site. And when they dug a little deeper, they found two identical syringes in the two graves. Large two-hundred-milliliter syringes that are often used with tubes for enemas. But these were equipped with needles. And damn long ones at that."

Carl shuddered. "Was there still potassium chloride left in the syringes?"

"Yes, about five milliliters."

"How much do they think there was in the syringes originally?" asked Rose.

"It's hard to say for sure, but they were probably full. At least that's what the forensic investigation indicates."

"And what is the lethal dose? I'm sure it doesn't take a hundred and fifty milliliters," said Rose.

"I've no idea how it works when it's injected directly into the heart. I believe that if it's administered intravenously, a much larger amount is needed."

"What did the coroner's office have to say?" asked Carl.

"They support the theory."

"So, they were killed with potassium chloride and embalmed with sodium chloride. It's suddenly all very chemical, isn't it?" said Rose. She shuddered as if she felt something down her spine. "The men were kidnapped and killed in the same way that people are executed on death row, but without the benefit of being sedated first," she said gloomily.

"Yes, they found no traces of other substances in the bodies. It was a quick, effective, but probably very painful death." The chief of homicide turned to the whiteboard. "Their deaths don't seem to have much in common with the others, which the police initially filed as accidents or self-inflicted. Do you still think we should put them on the whiteboard? There's certainly some very conspicuous empty spaces for the years 2016 and 2018."

Carl nodded to Assad, who stepped forward and wrote "Frank 'Franco' Svendsen" on the whiteboard under the year 2016.

They looked at the whiteboard for a moment. Then Assad wrote "Birger von Brandstrup" under the year 2018.

Carl counted the number of bodies discovered with salt in the vicinity.

Now there were seven.

31

ASSAD/CARL

Wednesday, December 16, 2020

It was truly a tale of past glory when Assad parked in a suburb of Odense and stared up at the white mansion situated on a hill at least two hundred meters up from the villa-lined street full of expensive cars bought on credit.

"I was quite baffled when you called me," said the woman who answered the door, dressed elegantly from head to toe, as was to be expected of the heir to a billion-euro fortune. "It must be almost ten years since I talked with the police about mother's death." She invited him in.

"Yes, I've lived here in Mother's house since the inheritance came through in 2012," she said. "It came as a surprise to me to find out that as a young girl, Mother had given up a baby for adoption, so things dragged out, given that she had included the child in her will."

Pia Laugesen's daughter walked ahead of Assad into a room lavishly decorated with Persian rugs that looked like they could have been taken straight out of the adventures of *One Thousand and One Nights*. He sat down on a leather couch that was bigger than his entire living room. She told him that she was in her forties, had been divorced a couple of times, and lived in the house with her fourteen-year-old daughter, who was going to attend a boarding school this summer.

Assad flashed her his brightest smile and tried to swallow the sugarless white tea steaming in the delicate cup.

"Very nice," he forced himself to say, and he continued to tell Tytte Laugesen that the case had been reopened a few days before and that they were looking into investigating further.

"I'd like to see the pool first," he said when the last sip of tea had challenged his sugar cravings.

The swimming pool was a good deal larger than he had expected—over twenty by fifty meters—and pompously designed just before World War One by a German merchant with five children whom he wanted to be more athletic than he was.

"It's covered with a tarpaulin for the winter. Well, the whole year, actually. We have no intention of bathing in corona soup with our friends."

She pointed at the place where her mother had allegedly tripped over the bag. Assad could picture the scene, but the question was whether it really had been an accident.

"Mother hated swimming. She only kept the pool because the photographs of her social gatherings and business meetings looked great with the pool as a backdrop. It certainly wasn't for my sake."

"Who looked after the pool?" asked Assad.

"Our gardener, August."

"The gardener? You wouldn't happen to know if he's still alive?"

"Oh, yes. Even though he's getting on in years, he's still alive and well."

"Maybe you can also tell us where we can get ahold of him?"

She pursed her lips and pointed down toward the bottom of the garden behind her. "At the moment, he's in the orangery tending to our camellias. We'd like them to blossom in time for Christmas."

August Nielsen was at least seventy-five years old but looked closer to eighty-five. The outdoor life had weathered his skin, and the furrows on his face spread like a cobweb from his forehead to his cheeks. There was not much left of his voice, but there was nothing wrong with his memory.

"It sure wasn't me who left the bag there because Pia couldn't stand things lying around. I've been asked many times if I might be mistaken, but do I look like someone who can't remember things?" He laughed hoarsely and almost inaudibly. "Actually, I tried to tell them several times that I didn't understand where that bag of salt had come from, and that it must've been someone else who put it there. I just couldn't tell them who, and apparently they didn't believe me. When people treat me like that, I just clam up."

"When you clean the pool, don't you just pour in chlorine directly?"

"Well, that's what I told the police—that the case was more complicated than they thought." He pointed at a small wooden shed close to the hedge. "In there, we've got special containers for the purpose and the amount has to be just right. In fact, there's quite a lot of chemistry and adjustments involved in getting the right water balance. There's also a heating unit, but Pia Laugesen never used it because she didn't like swimming."

"So was the salt in the bag something you used for other purposes?"

"Well, you certainly ask all the right questions. Can I ask how you're so good at Danish?"

"I've lived here since I was a boy."

"Ohhh," he said, walking down along the rows of flowers. "Then maybe you won't be able to cope with the heat in here?" He laughed. "But to answer your question—yes and no. It was a bag like the ones we use when we salt the driveways in winter, but the salt in this one was much finer than usual. And that also puzzled me."

"Assad, have you heard that the government has ordered another lockdown? It starts from tomorrow morning." Gordon's voice was shaking, and he sounded as if the world were coming to an end. "Everything is closing down—schools, hairdressers, shopping malls, and department stores. I haven't bought my Christmas presents yet, and who knows if I'll manage before the lockdown gets even stricter. It's a disaster!"

He looked over at Rose and Carl, who both seemed unfazed. Assad did not care either because they did not celebrate Christmas in his family.

"I feel so damn sorry for us all. It's not a real Christmas party when we can't even hold hands while we dance around the tree. And we're not supposed to sing, and no more than ten people can be together at a time. I think that . . ." Gordon sat down on the chair in the corner and looked like he was about to start crying.

"No, it sure isn't good. A genuine disaster for many people." Carl nodded and turned to Assad after a suitably dramatic pause.

"What do you make of your visit to Odense? Can we erase Pia Laugesen from the whiteboard?"

"No. I still think Pia Laugesen was killed," answered Assad. "Her daughter told me that she tried to initiate a thorough investigation but had no luck. Then she showed me a couple of scrapbooks she had made of her mother's interviews—and also in connection with her death. They're lying on my desk, and I plan to skim through them later."

Carl turned to Gordon. "I can't believe you're still here, Gordon. Why aren't you going to buy Christmas presents while you still have the chance? We can't put up with your complaining."

The pale guy breathed heavily and tried to compose himself.

"I think I've discovered something," he said. "It could be a common denominator for all the murders, and it's got nothing to do with the Middle East."

They stared at him intensely.

"I had dinner at my parents' house yesterday together with a couple of their friends. Everyone was tested for corona, so you don't have to worry about that. The husband has a business importing wine, and he had bought three bottles of Puligny-Montrachet white wine that tasted absolutely heavenly."

"That gives me a sudden thirst," said Rose.

"Yes, it was delicious. And I drank quite a lot—a whole bottle, I think. And then I ended up being a bit too chatty and mentioned the Pia Laugesen case. I said that we're investigating it and that it's tricky because the case dates back all the way to August twentieth, 2010." He looked over at Carl. "Yes, I'm sorry, Carl. I normally never talk to anyone about work outside these four walls."

Carl shrugged. Luckily, they did not know what *he* might say after an entire bottle of white wine.

"Then the wife said that it was funny because August twentieth is her birthday."

Carl attempted a smile. If funny coincidences like that could solve cases, he had a whole arsenal from his ex-mother-in-law.

"And she added that she's always been sad about the date of her birthday because she's a Bosnian Serb, and the man who started the Bosnian War, Slobodan Milošević, was born on the same day."

"And?" asked Rose.

Gordon looked directly at Assad. "I'm sure you all remember Marwa saying that the day Oleg Dudek died was the same date that Saddam Hussein was born, right?"

The room went quiet for a moment.

"Just before the prime minister gave us this shock, I checked May nineteenth, the date when Palle Rasmussen was killed." He gave them a teasing look. It seemed like he had forgotten all about Christmas being ruined.

"Spit it out," said Rose.

"May nineteenth was Pol Pot's birthday. The Cambodian who committed one of the largest and most brutal genocides in history with his group, the Khmer Rouge. So it's starting to look like a pattern, don't you think?"

They nodded. Saddam Hussein, Pol Pot, and Slobodan Milošević. Together they made it very likely that these killings were committed on dates that coincided with the birthdays of gruesome dictators and murderers.

32

PAULINE

Wednesday, December 16, 2020

It was a very tired and resigned face that stared back at Pauline in the mirror. Deep furrows were appearing on her forehead, similar to the ones that pulled down the corners of her mouth. Pauline had not smiled for days, and there was certainly no reason to smile. There was nothing in her refrigerator, and her bank account was just as empty. Her prospects of returning to work seemed hopeless now that the prime minister had put the country in lockdown for the festive season. Pauline was alternating between despair and anger.

A large proportion of the country's shops and institutions would shut down the following day at noon. What a shitty year, what a shitty Christmas. Across the country, people were rushing to the few remaining shopping malls that were open. They were losing their minds, but at least they had money to spend—unlike her. Never before had Pauline been in such dire straits, with all her expenses for the house and life in general and no income at all. She had been desperate for months, and any hope of a quick fix was becoming less likely for people like her. It was only a small comfort that her friend had supported and encouraged her and empathized with her situation.

What the hell does the minister for culture imagine that artists are going to live on? she had said. *Reciting* Hamlet *on a beer crate in the town hall square or perhaps begging for change on the church steps like in southern Europe?*

Pauline glanced over at the shoebox under her bed. It had been her secret pick-me-up for almost twenty years when she felt down and life took a turn for the worse. Passionate letters from Palle that tickled her senses and fantasies and reminded her of their rough love and twisted relationship.

And now this sanctuary was also under threat. Imagine if the policeman had managed to get hold of that box. Would it have fueled their suspicions against her? Would they have found words and descriptions of acts that sowed doubt about the sincerity of her love and affection for her uncle? That would be the last nail in her coffin.

Although she had nothing to do with Palle's death, all the thoughts about it had resurfaced, especially now that she had heard for the first time about the deep indentations on Palle's wrists. That piece of information had forced her to realize that Palle had planned to pull away from her. But what had happened? Palle *never* let her tie him up. Once in the heat of the moment, she had suggested handcuffing him because he wriggled too much when she beat him. But even then, he had said no.

Pauline had cried the last few nights because of her terrible situation and because she would never find answers to the many questions she had about the days leading up to Palle's death.

The policeman had suggested more than once that Palle had not died by suicide. And even though she had found it hard to believe back then that he had done it to himself, she had still come to terms with it many years ago. She had been told time and again that Palle was exactly the sort of person who could do something like that, considering all his dark secrets.

But what about the indentations on his wrists? Where did they come from?

Her mind led her down winding paths to places that were better left alone. Under normal circumstances, she would have been distracted by the usual chores of daily life and her busy career. But now that everything was so crazy, was she going crazy too with all the thoughts racing in her mind? Had her loved one been murdered? And, if so, who could have done it? If it wasn't the result of a robbery gone wrong, or politically motivated, it could only have been committed by someone close to him. And that someone could very well be Pauline's rival, Sisle Park. Why not?

Of course Sisle had been able to knock Pauline off her throne back then. It became more and more clear, and it haunted her. Sisle was more beautiful, wealthy, intelligent, and refined—she was in a league of her own. So it took no time at all for her to become a threat to Pauline's position. But had she also posed a threat to Palle? Had they gone too far?

Pauline smiled for a moment.

I'm going to bring her down, she thought.

Pauline took out the shoebox and put it on her lap. Somewhere among these treasures, there must be an email that was so anonymous that it might just as well have been addressed to Sisle Park as to herself. An email that hinted at a far too intimate and violent relationship. And regardless of whether Sisle was guilty or not, Pauline would make sure that she gave her such a fright that she would pay her way out of it.

Pauline laughed. It was incredibly liberating.

Yes, Sisle Park would pay big-time. And if anyone could afford it, it was her.

A few hours later, they were sitting across from each other in the heart of Park Optimizing in a cornucopia of classic furniture and rare paintings with signatures of artists Pauline could never afford.

Sisle Park was sitting behind a streamlined steel-and-glass desk, eyeing her with an inscrutable expression.

"Yes, I know who you are, Pauline Rasmussen. Your lifestyle isn't exactly discreet."

Sisle Park looked like someone who has just been served something other than what they ordered.

"You don't seem happy to see me," said Pauline, looking around at the riches she hoped to harvest.

"Why would I be? I don't know you, and we have nothing in common. And I am actually busy." She pushed a button and signed a sheet of paper. "So make this quick. What is it you want? Did you say you had a business proposition for me?"

"I certainly have something you'll want to buy." Pauline pushed out her chair and tilted back her head. It was an attitude that worked onstage, so why not here? "You say you don't know me, but that's not entirely true now, is it?"

Sisle Park turned to the door and handed the paper to the secretary who had just entered. "It's urgent, so use the courier service." Her eyelids looked heavy when she turned her gaze back to Pauline. "Well, spit it out, then. Apart from having read about you, where is it I'm supposed to know you from? And what is it you have to offer me?"

"You know full well that I'm Palle Rasmussen's niece—and that you stole him from me. That's how we know each other."

"Palle Rasmussen! Lord almighty, what are you insinuating? Stole him? I had absolutely no interest in him apart from what he could do for me politically. Jesus Christ! That fat, disgusting man. Look at me. What would a woman like me want with someone like him?"

Sisle Park's contemptuous expression made Pauline feel momentarily lost. Then she composed herself, took her lipstick out of her handbag, and painted her lips in a red color that was no less daring than the one her opponent was wearing. "Apparently enough to want to kill the fat, disgusting man I loved." She put the lipstick back and avoided Sisle Park's gaze and the anger she was expecting.

"You're out of your mind, woman," she said. "Creep back into the hole you came from."

Pauline grinned. Any second now the woman would unleash her anger.

"If you have anything to say about Palle's death that hasn't come to light yet, I'll be happy to call the police and inform them myself about your twisted theories," Sisle said.

Pauline nodded, her eyes fixed on Sisle Park's black boots. If she was not mistaken, they were Celine boots with high heels that would have put her back more than ten thousand kroner.

"Look at me, woman! Do you want me to call the police?"

Pauline raised her eyes up to Sisle's hand, which was resting on the white receiver of the landline.

"I think that would be a good idea if you want to do time for fifteen years with other murderers. On the other hand, you could also put your hand down on the table and listen to my proposal. Yes, it is going to cost you half a million—but then you can draw a line in the sand on your past. Wouldn't that be nice?"

Sisle waited a moment before slowly moving her hand away from the receiver. Then she buzzed her secretary.

Got you now, thought Pauline as she fumbled for the paper in her handbag.

She sat for an hour waiting on the ground floor. The secretary who led her down there had been friendly and assured her that Sisle Park would come as soon as she had finished her work. She pointed over at a sideboard with chocolates and urns with coffee and tea next to the obligatory bottle of water.

"Help yourself while you're waiting. Sisle Park asked me to tell you that she's looking forward to settling a few misunderstandings between you."

Pauline's state of mind had changed over the last hour. From being sure that she had gotten the better of the woman to thinking that the next people coming in through the door would be uniformed police. Had Sisle recorded their conversation? It was probably something a woman in her position would do, come to think of it.

She had demanded half a million to draw a line in the sand. Some people would call it extortion, and that was a punishable offense.

Pauline was annoyed with herself. How stupid could she be? She clenched her fists. *I'll still get in a few blows, Sisle. You can count on that,* she thought, and poured herself a cup of coffee.

She would tell the police that she had tried to lure Sisle Park into a trap, and that it was Chief Inspector Carl Mørck—if they knew him—who had brought to her attention that the Palle Rasmussen case had been reopened.

After another fifteen minutes, she considered leaving. That would teach Sisle that she was not a dog who could be dragged around on a leash. And apart from that, her eyes felt dry and she was growing tired.

She squinted up at the ceiling lights, which felt far too bright, and caught sight of something that was either an advanced projector system typical of this high-tech environment or surveillance cameras.

"Hello!" she shouted. They were bound to react soon—they would not just leave her sitting here twiddling her thumbs.

She stood up, walked unsteadily over toward the door, and tried the handle.

She yanked at it a couple of times before realizing that the door was locked.

Pauline stared at the handle, which slowly became a blur.

When someone finally came into the room, she was lying on the floor gasping for air.

33

LISBETH

1984

"**So you think** you feel ready to be discharged. What do you base that on, Lisbeth?"

She tried to infuse a little warmth into her smile. As if that had ever had any effect on someone like him.

Had this man even looked at her once? He just sat there scratching dry skin from his eyebrows while his glasses kept sliding down his nose.

And who was he anyway? Was he the consultant in charge? Was he a substitute doctor? Another registrar? She had no idea.

She took a deep breath and imagined the smell of spring out there on the other side of the windows where freedom beckoned.

Over the fourteen months that she had been committed in different wards, Lisbeth had seen a hoard of psychiatrists who probed around in her head. Some of them had taken eons of time, asking the same questions over and over, while others had emanated exhaustion, stress from overwork and all the responsibility, and just wanted to get home. They came in myriad sizes and with a kaleidoscopic spectrum of common Danish names. But they were otherwise surprisingly uniform.

She looked at the name tag on the doctor's chest, which read "Thorleif Petersen." Maybe he was the one who was really in charge. She seemed to recall coming across that name at some point, but she was unsure where just now.

She only recognized one of the people sitting next to him behind the conference desk, and that was the ward nurse. The other two doctors might just as well have been taken straight from the street. They were not even wearing lab coats.

"Yes, I want to be discharged because I'm feeling great now. The treatment has worked, and I'm ready to return to my life and go back to university."

The doctor scanned her medical record again and nodded.

"Yes, this has all been quite a traumatic experience for you, and we should all be thankful that you're still with us. But you still sometimes exhibit unprovoked outbursts of anger, which suggests that you still haven't put the past behind you. I'm sure you're aware that if we agree to discharge you, you'll have to continue taking your medication. I can't say for how long, but, in my opinion, it might have to be indefinitely."

She nodded. If that withered example of a man thought he could scare her, he was really too stupid to be in the job.

"Yes, but it was a long time ago."

"What was a long time ago?" He pushed his glasses back up and gave her a penetrating look.

"The anger. I'm not angry anymore. I told you, I'm feeling great."

"Your record states that the lightning bolt almost killed you. That your brain and your central nervous system suffered a severe shock. But I also understand that the neurological department thinks that, thankfully, you won't suffer any chronic secondary damage. But what does concern me is the severe somatic and mental impact all this has had on you."

The other two doctors nodded along authoritatively. But she doubted whether they had ever really taken the time to discuss it with her properly.

"I can see that you believe that it was God's will that you survived the lightning strike while the others died."

"God's will, yes. Who else could be behind it?"

He frowned.

"Don't you believe in God?" she asked.

He leafed through her medical records. That was more than enough of an answer in itself.

"You've had several conversations with God while you've been on this ward, I'm told. Do you hear voices, Lisbeth?"

"No!"

He looked up at her as if to say, *Are you sure?*

"You haven't been willing to tell us in detail why you believe that your fellow students deserved to be punished by God. Why is that?"

"Listen, I voluntarily agreed to be committed because my mom convinced me to. Now she's dead and I'm feeling great, so . . ."

"You don't seem to be very affected by your mother's death."

She placed her hands on her lap and leaned slightly forward toward him. "She was a disingenuous person, so no. Our love for each other was never built on anything profound or lasting."

One of the other doctors broke in.

"Lisbeth, there was a period when you didn't talk about anything except justice, God's wrath, and what Satan has done to our planet. It almost seemed like an obsession for you. Where do you stand on that now?"

She nodded. She had stopped talking about those things out loud. Who in this godforsaken place could understand the full extent of it anyway?

"It's over. It was a long time ago. I feel great now."

"So you're saying that you're no longer controlled by your extreme anger toward other people?"

She allowed herself a small chuckle. "Absolutely. By no means."

Now all three of them nodded solemnly. But, to her annoyance, they still seemed professionally skeptical.

"There's something else I'd like to discuss, Lisbeth," said the third doctor. "On top of everything else, I have to remind you about the megalomania that seems to have had a great impact on your thoughts about the future. You've often expressed that you have ambitions to climb to the top. That you intend to be a mover and shaker and accumulate great wealth. I'm of the opinion that everyone is allowed to dream big and have great ambitions for their future, but I do think that you went a bit off track here. Do you think your dreams have become more realistic now, Lisbeth? Because if they haven't, life on the other side of these walls will become disappointing and toxic for you to an unimaginable extent."

She forced another smile. These no more than moderately intelligent people were judging her from their own little, mediocre so-called normality. *They* would never make it farther than where they currently were. And they even seemed to be pleased and proud of the fact. Specialist doctors, family men, nine-to-four, day in and day out. They were not on the threshold of any revolutionary thoughts. No groundbreaking ideas. And once they had retired, they would settle down in their tedious lives and wonder why they had never achieved more.

"No, I don't have those ambitions anymore," she lied. "I'll go back to my chemistry degree. You're familiar with my grades, and you've spoken with my lecturers, so you know it's my calling and that I'll be good at it."

Now it was the ward nurse's turn to speak. "I'm only here to give an impression of how I perceive you on a day-to-day basis, Lisbeth. You've done well here, I think. And some of your fellow patients will be very sad when you're discharged. But the reality is that it's far from everyone who has experienced your better side, and you know that full well. I actually think that you've been extremely harsh with some people. If we go all the way back to the time when you were first admitted, we had some very chaotic situations because of you. I'm sure you know that I'm thinking about one incident in particular."

She nodded. Of course they had to bring that up now.

"Well, that was a long time ago. More than a year, right? I'm still sorry about it. It was never my intention to take it so far with that woman."

"She took her own life, Lisbeth. A suicide that affected the whole ward for several months. Some of the other patients grew scared of you, which is why we had to move you around."

"I know it was bad, Karen. But it took me more than a few months in here to understand how much words could impact others who are mentally ill. I've learned my lesson, and I genuinely regret the way things turned out."

She nodded with her eyes fixed on the floor while recalling the triumph it had been to pressure the disturbed woman into stabbing herself in the heart several times with a knitting needle. One less repulsive person in the world who had done nothing useful and never would have. Impure of heart, impure of speech, impure of thought. No reason to shed any tears over her.

"I'm glad to hear that, Lisbeth. I believe you," said the nurse, exchanging looks with the doctors.

Then the first doctor, who was still scratching his eyebrow, spoke again.

"Yes, as you know, we cannot keep you here against your will. But, in my opinion, you're not ready to leave and confront reality." He pushed a piece of paper over toward her. "Having said that, you are free to sign here and discharge yourself. We'll supply you with medicine for the next four weeks and subsequently with a prescription."

She nodded. "Two tablets in the morning and two in the evening. Thanks. I know the routine."

The click from the door to the ward closing behind her sounded entirely different from when she had been given permission to leave temporarily or been on a scheduled visit with her mother. It almost felt like a vacuum behind her sucked all the preceding months in the ward out of her life. It was as if the click itself was life-giving.

Her suitcase was light and she rolled it behind her with ease. She had left most of her clothes in the wardrobe in her room. Nothing she had worn in that institution would be allowed to evoke memories about her time there. She had already put it behind her.

She was strong now, prepared for the next and most important part of her life.

When she reached the avenue with rustling trees, she stuck her hand inside her bag, produced a small plastic sachet, and held it up in front of her eyes. Four times seven blue and white tablets intended to calm her down, dampen her initiative, erase inappropriate mood swings, and dull confusing, destructive thoughts and memories.

She laughed when she opened the bag and threw them down on the ground one by one, leaving a trail like Hansel and Gretel to mark the path she came from and to which she would never risk returning.

"No!" she shouted loudly, causing a couple of stooping patients who were pointlessly getting some fresh air to turn around toward her.

Never, ever, ever would another person be able to manipulate who and what she was or what she stood for.

She would make sure of that if it was the last thing she did.

34

CARL

Wednesday, December 16, 2020

Carl was actually fairly pleased with the situation. The latest lockdown would ensure that they had peace to get on with work. The different teams in homicide would have to isolate themselves from one another. Mona was at home with the little one, all the Christmas shenanigans had stopped, and, best of all, as long as things remained like this, PET would postpone their planned visit to Assad's home indefinitely. In the current climate, no one had any interest in sticking their noses into other people's private affairs unless there was a very urgent reason.

Carl opened the window and had a cigarette. If there was anything he really believed in, it was that nicotine would give all those bloody strains of corona a run for their money.

Rose and Gordon were currently going over the cases on the whiteboard where they had a date for the murder, and Assad was going through Tytte Laugesen's scrapbooks. All in all, he was feeling optimistic.

Carl, for his part, was focusing on the case of the two embalmed bodies. There were more than enough questions to answer on that score. For example, who uses disposable two-hundred-milliliter syringes with long needles? According to his internet search, it could be people who work in agriculture, research labs, or health care. So it was an insurmountable task to find the supplier when there were so many options. The manufacturer could not help them either because there were no distinctive characteristics about the syringes such as production numbers or barcodes.

Carl had no doubt that the latest victims belonged with the others on the whiteboard, because the common denominator was salt. But these cases still stood out from the others because they did not know the exact dates the men were killed, given that they had most likely been kidnapped and might have been killed and buried much later.

There was a video surveillance recording showing that Birger von Brandstrup had been picked up by a white Škoda Superb and not been seen since. It could be forgiven if some people at the time had written off his disappearance as staged. That kind of thing was not unheard-of. He could have hidden away a small fortune and lived like a king in Thailand or some other faraway country.

But they knew better now.

In Franco Svendsen's case, the theory had been that he had died by suicide. On November 4, 2016, after an ordinary busy workday, he had walked down to the beach as he often did to take a refreshing swim in the ice-cold water. But when he did not return at dinnertime, his family grew worried and discovered all his clothes neatly folded down on the beach. Contrary to his usual habits, he had gone in the water naked, which baffled his family, because he was rather modest. All these circumstances gave rise to a genuine concern that he had drowned. His last medical checkup testified to a man in excellent health who had been declared fit and as strong as an ox. Due to the lack of any further evidence, the police went with the theory that he had either died by suicide or suffered an attack of a cramp in the cold water. And that concluded the investigation. But the family believed that it must have been an accident, as they never found a motive for suicide. He had simply been engulfed by the waves in the strong offshore wind. And that was what everyone believed right up until the day when he was dug out of the ground in Skævinge.

Two bodies, each in their grave. But what had they done to deserve their fate, and why were the murders so anonymous in comparison with the others on the whiteboard?

Was it a new strategy? Was the murderer trying to play it safe now? He had still left salt in connection with the victims as a sort of calling card, which pointed to the perpetrator's pride. Symbolic actions like this were often the only leads in cases involving serial killers. He knew that from abroad and recognized the pattern from their own cases. The murders had been committed every two years, each on a slightly later date. And on top of that came the salt. They had lots of leads that could trip up the murderer, and yet they were still completely in the dark.

There were sweat stains under Gordon's arms when he burst into Carl's office. His white skin was flushed with excitement. Rose and Assad followed right behind him, looking just as elated.

Gordon did not even sit down before he began rambling.

"The repair shop owner, Wilder, was killed on Nicolae Ceauşescu's birthday. Oleg Dudek, as Marwa has already pointed out, died on Saddam Hussein's birthday. Pia Laugesen died on Slobodan Milošević's, and Palle Rasmussen on Pol Pot's. And now we can add that the arms dealer, Carl-Henrik Skov Jespersen, was killed on Idi Amin's birthday."

Carl was blown away for once. "Well, that can't be coincidental," he said.

"Ha! Five of the worst dictators in world history on the same white-board. That's definitely no coincidence, Carl. We're way past that discussion."

Assad grinned. "Now we're not only looking for cases in even years such as 1990, 1992, 1994, and 1996, which are the years between the cases we already know. Now we also need to research when the worst vermin in human history were born."

"And if it doesn't lead anywhere, which you might still think, Carl, at least we'll have had fun with a little world history," said Rose. If there was a school dedicated solely to refining sarcasm and barefaced cheek, Rose must have graduated top of her class.

35

PAULINE

Wednesday, December 16, 2020

She could sense movement all around her. Footsteps from several people and the door being opened and closed. Insisting voices and hands being placed on her shoulders, shaking her gently. After a couple of deep breaths, she slowly opened her eyes and saw the outline of two women and Sisle Park behind them looking at her with an impenetrable expression.

"I'm not feeling at all good," she said. "I think that . . ." A wave of nausea rose from her stomach and she suddenly threw up.

The people nearer to her pulled back, looking down at their expensive clothes.

"I'm sorry," said Pauline and threw up again.

"Here, have some water." It was Sisle Park, who had maneuvered herself in front of the others. Had she had the water in her hands all along?

Pauline drank thirstily and it helped. Her eyelids felt less heavy, her stomach calmed down, and she slowly started to take in the scene in which she was the main character.

"Why did you keep me here?" she asked.

Sisle Park tilted her head to one side. Was she puzzled or was she about to strike?

"You poisoned me with that coffee, Sisle. Why?" she asked, looking imploringly at the other women. Did they show any sign of surprise? Would they come to her rescue?

But they all just stood there smiling. Not exactly what she had expected.

Sisle Park's expression was now as gentle as that of the others.

"Pauline, I'm sorry you see it that way. The door over there has a spring lock. And it's very regrettable that no one thought of that. As for the coffee, it's supposed to be the finest Ethiopian arabica you can buy." She walked over to the sideboard and poured herself a cup. "Still warm and smooth as expected. Maybe you're suffering from a stomach bug. There's a lot going around these days."

She took a couple of sips and then turned to the others in the room, thanked them for their help, and told them she would take things from there.

Pauline felt sweat break out on her forehead as the others left. She tried to stand up, but Sisle placed a hand on her shoulder and insisted that she should not exert herself.

Pauline pulled away. "Don't you think I know you replaced the coffee while I was out cold? I'm no fool."

Sisle Park showed no visible reaction, but her voice grew colder. "Let me tell you one thing, Pauline. And I'll only tell you once. I'm tired of your accusations and insinuations." She pulled a chair over in front of Pauline and sat down. "And now I'm going to need you to show me what you've got in that nice handbag of yours that you'd hoped to threaten me with."

Pauline had often experienced how a mood could change with a glance, a gentle touch, a single word. How love could suddenly turn to hate. How interest could turn to apathy. How joy could turn to sorrow.

This time it was aggression turning to anxiety. Sisle had the upper hand. She was much bigger than Pauline, and they were in a room that was remote and soundproof, so she knew it would be best to back down and admit that she had just been playing to the gallery. If she didn't, she sensed that things would end badly.

"Sorry, Sisle. You're right that I came to extort you, but I've got nothing on you. I'm just in a really tight spot at the moment. I'm totally desperate."

"I see. It was certainly a very serious accusation you made. You accused me of murder."

"I'm really sorry. I was just grasping at straws."

"What do you have in your handbag that you thought you could threaten me with?"

"Nothing. Just this." She took out the print and handed it to Sisle.

Sisle read the email slowly and carefully. "But this has got nothing to do with me," she said. "This email was sent to you, wasn't it?"

Pauline shrugged. "I don't remember, but I guess so."

"Don't you think it's best if I keep hold of it so you don't feel tempted to try this trick again?"

Pauline watched as she folded the paper and put it in her pocket. It felt strange and uncomfortable, but what could she do?

"Yes, the entire situation is really terrible just now, and we're all feeling the pressure," said Sisle Park. "This is the third time I'm going to have to send my employees home. But we'll still manage because we're lucky enough not to work in production. We're a sort of knowledge wholesaler, and our customers can't do without us. I recognize that your situation is very different from mine, so, even though you've overstepped the mark, I still understand you in some way."

And what are you going to do about it? thought Pauline.

"You won't be able to get yourself home in the state you're in, will you?"

Pauline stood up and put her handbag over her shoulder. "Yeah, yeah. I'll be fine."

Two wrinkles appeared on Sisle's otherwise smooth face. "Well, I won't hear of it. I'll drive you!"

I'm not getting in a car with her, thought Pauline, and she politely declined. But Sisle was insistent and grabbed her arm firmly.

They walked along extensive, gray basement corridors and up a flight of stairs before reaching the dimly lit, rain-soaked parking lot.

She's not getting me in that car, thought Pauline, scanning the area.

The office building was flanked by a park on one side and a residential area on the other, where light shone from the windows of the big houses.

"Just get in, Pauline," she heard Sisle say from the other side of the gleaming Mercedes.

Pauline grabbed the handle and slowly opened the door. But as soon as she heard the slam of the door from the driver's side, she threw her handbag and made a run for it.

Sisle shouted to her from inside the car to stop, but Pauline did not stop. Once she was in that car, she would be defenseless.

She heard the engine start up behind her. And with the acceleration capacity of a hybrid, it raced across the parking lot, rain spraying from the wheels.

Pauline ran toward the nearest residential street, which featured an almost unbroken line of wrought-iron fences with automatic gates. No one would risk inviting in a stranger in this landscape of self-interest and wealth.

A path opened up between two white mansions about fifty meters down the road, and Pauline saw it as her only escape. The Mercedes braked with screeching tires behind her, the door was flung open, and she heard the unmistakable sound of high-heeled shoes running across gravel. Sisle shouted from behind her that this was insane and that she had nothing to fear. Sisle just wanted to help her get home. But Pauline still did not stop. The sound of the high heels behind her suddenly stopped and Pauline turned around to look. Despite the rain, Sisle was now running in her stockings with her heels in her hands.

What can she do to me with all the streetlights around? thought Pauline as her pursuer gained ground. *Why don't I just stop when I reach the next street and scream at the top of my lungs?*

But the next street proved to be just as inaccessible with its wrought-iron gates. Who would hear her? Who would get up from their cozy, comfortable couch? Who would risk their safety in this affluent area to help a random stranger screaming for help? Who would even be able to hear her from behind their well-insulated windows?

Now her pursuer was so close that Pauline could hear the rain splashing around her feet. She looked behind her for a second as Sisle ran toward the left sidewalk. There was only fifty meters between them, so if she did not cross the street and make her way onto the path opening up on the other side, Sisle would catch up with her before the next side street.

It was a narrow and badly lit paved path between tall hedges, and she could hear Sisle's breathing growing louder behind her. A small square appeared at the far end, again surrounded by houses with closed wrought-iron gates. Which way should she go? Should she continue down the dark path to the right or turn down the street?

"I won't hurt you, Pauline. Just stop!" shouted Sisle, slightly out of breath. The sound of her feet against the wet paving ceased.

Pauline looked back over her shoulder at the woman who was standing only twenty or thirty meters from her with her hands on her hips, drenched from top to toe and gasping for breath. But Pauline did not fall for the charade. Sisle looked very athletic and in shape. In a second, she would rush forward and grab her.

"Let's go back to the car and I'll drive you home. It's only two streets away. Be sensible, Pauline."

Sensible? Pauline nodded. There was no way they were that close to the car, so what was she playing at? Was she trying to lure her into the darkness where anything could happen? Had Sisle purposely chased her in this direction? Pauline was not sure. She had just kept running as fast as she could, and she had no intention of stopping.

When she bolted for the opposite side of the square, she sensed the resources that the woman behind her had spared: Sisle caught up with her in no time and would be able to grab her in a matter of seconds.

Pauline desperately scanned the street in front of her to see if there might be just one house she could head for.

"What are you doing, Pauline?" shouted Sisle right behind her. "What's wrong with you? The car is parked in the opposite direction."

She suddenly caught sight of a house at the bottom of the street that did not have the damned wrought-iron fencing protecting it. It was in a slightly elevated position compared to the other houses, a sanctuary with its glowing windows and beautiful marble steps.

Pauline ran determinedly up the steps to the front door, hammered on it, and shouted as if she could make it come tumbling down like the walls of Jericho at the sound of the trumpets.

It worked, because at the very moment Sisle reached her, the door opened and a large, friendly looking man with a strangely contorted face brought the scene to a standstill.

He looked at them with mild surprise and then turned to Sisle, who now had a firm grip on Pauline's jacket.

"Sisle!" he exclaimed. "Why are you out of breath? Are you racing each other?"

Pauline's skin turned ice-cold. Did they know each other?

"Can I please come in?" Pauline said to a woman walking down the staircase from the first floor.

The man took a step back and motioned that they were both welcome.

"Adam, I'm sorry that we're intruding like this," said Sisle behind her. "Pauline here had a panic attack. She thinks I'm trying to harm her."

The man looked perplexed for a moment and then smiled.

"How strange." He turned to the woman who had just come down the stairs. "Sisle is the sweetest person we know. Isn't that so, Debora?"

Pauline was relieved when the man called Adam offered to drive her home after having consulted with his wife. "You can come if you want, Sisle, and I'll drive you back to your car afterward."

"Good idea," she said. "I just want to make sure that Pauline gets home safe. You've had a rough day, dear," she said, patting Pauline on the shoulder.

When they were all in the car, Pauline thought to herself that perhaps she had wriggled her way out of the situation. She caught a glimpse in the rearview mirror of Sisle, who was sitting in the back. *She must be all right. Otherwise, Palle wouldn't have* . . . Then, after a while, she saw her modest house appear through the windshield.

"I know you probably don't want to help me after what happened today, Sisle," she said. "But I still need to ask you if you could give me a loan. Just to tide me over."

She could see Sisle through the rearview mirror, mulling it over. But minutes later, when they were standing in Pauline's living room, she said yes.

"We'll have to draw up an informal contract, Pauline. I'm sure you understand? A hundred thousand kroner?"

Pauline gasped. Her pulse raced and she felt faint. It was as if the oxygen supply had been cut off from her brain.

"It looks like you're feeling faint again, Pauline. You should take it easy. I'll draw up the contract immediately, if it'll help you relax. But then we'll need to get you to bed."

"Don't you have something to help you relax?" asked the man in a friendly tone.

Pauline looked at Sisle, who had sat down behind the desk and was scribbling something on a piece of paper.

"Thank you. Yes, I've got some sleeping pills in the bathroom cabinet. But I think I just need a diazepam because I'm not quite myself just now. There are two- and five-milligram tablets. I just need two milligrams."

He smiled and returned with a glass of water and two tablets. "These are two milligrams. But I don't think one will be enough. Here you go."

Pauline tilted back her head and swallowed both the tablets in one gulp. Her desperation from the morning suddenly seemed insignificant. There was still some goodness in the world.

"Have another glass, Pauline," he said a moment later as Sisle turned to them with the contract in her hand.

She gulped it down in one go and only then noticed how bitter it tasted.

36

CARL

Thursday, December 17, 2020

It turned out to be a hectic day at work.

The Ragnhild case was partly handed back to Manfred, Bente Hansen's assistant, who had now returned from quarantine, allowing the team to concentrate on the cases on the whiteboard. Assad checked Tytte Laugesen's scrapbooks, and while Gordon and Rose were busy with the dates on the whiteboard, Carl gave his full attention to the two bodies that had been found in Skævinge. At a time when the rest of the country were accustoming themselves to the run-up to Christmas being restricted like never before, the small team from Department Q had more than enough to keep them busy.

Mona stayed at home to look after Lucia while also struggling to convince her older daughter, Mathilde, to spend Christmas with them. Not that she seemed to be getting anywhere with that. But it was worse for Hardy, Morten, and Mika, who were stuck at the clinic in Switzerland with funds that were fast running out. Hardy had made significant progress, but what good would that do him if there was no money left to complete his treatment? All in all, it was not a good time for anyone.

So despite struggling to find the energy to keep going, Carl fought on with the autopsy reports of the last two bodies found in Skævinge and compared them with the photographs and reports from when the men originally disappeared.

One of the men, Frank "Franco" Svendsen, had never exactly been an angel. And he did not look like one either. He was built like an ox with a muscular neck and seemed to have a permanently smug smile on his face that did not show any sign of remorse for the misfortunes he had inflicted on the world. At the time of his death, his company had a dozen ships of dubious origin for scrapping in Bangladesh, in spite of excess mortality among the workforce. The dangerous work of removing asbestos and the many chemical residues in the cargo holds was in large part to blame, but Franco Svendsen brushed off all the complaints and accusations and earned huge sums. If there was a waste product that it was not possible to offload in the former Eastern bloc or in the EU, then he was the man to find a solution somewhere else in the world. There was very seldom documentation for where all this junk ended up, but abandoned mines in central African countries had probably taken their fair share. Right up until Franco Svendsen's disappearance, the company had been doing fantastically well, which was not a given, considering all the rulings against him handed down for environmental crimes back in the eighties.

Franco Svendsen was also a man who quite shamelessly liked to present himself in the media posing in front of his French and Argentinian châteaus. Wealth earned on the back of the desperation and misfortune of others.

The world won't miss that bastard, thought Carl. But then again, in a democracy, even bastards had to be given a fair chance of survival. If not for their own sake, then at least to preserve the humanity they did not give a shit about.

He studied the photo of the remains of the body on the autopsy table. The missing person's report stated that he was a well-built man, which the old photos of him also confirmed, but the photo of the body told a different story. Yes, the man had been lying in the ground for several years, but because the body was preserved by the salt, it was possible to discern how much weight he had lost. Or was he imagining it?

Carl took out his phone and called the coroner's office.

"You don't mention how much you believe the body weighed when it was buried. Is there a reason for that?"

The coroner laughed—something you did not hear often. "How the hell are we supposed to know, Carl? It would be pure guesswork."

"Okay. But if you had to venture a guess? All I see on your table is skin and bone. Is it possible that he was emaciated when he was killed?"

"Yes, it's very likely. We don't know exactly when he was killed, so he might have lost a good deal of weight in the time between being kidnapped and killed."

"Thanks, that's exactly what I was thinking," said Carl, and he remembered to compliment the coroner on the report. That was the best way to maintain good working relationships.

Carl placed the two photos next to each other. The one of the plump man while still alive and the one of his emaciated corpse. The contrast was glaring.

Bloody hell, he thought. *He was almost starved to death before being given the lethal injection.*

Carl took a cigarette and leaned out of the window to allow the smoke to rise up into the air outside. The world seemed dead, gray, and stagnant out there in corona hell. All the newly renovated factory buildings around them stood desolate, like in a war zone. The predominance of parking lots in the vicinity became grotesquely obvious now that they were devoid of cars. There was only a single driver who had strayed into Sydhavnen.

Carl walked over to the desk and picked up the other report. Judging from the many photos, the deceased Birger von Brandstrup was a very different sort of man than Franco Svendsen. Some people might even describe him as a hunk. And even though the man had been married to the same woman for years, he did not shy away from exploiting his good looks by allegedly having many brief affairs, although he had done his best to conceal them. He had been the favorite victim of the tabloids week after week for years, but then he never missed a chance to attend an opening. He was known for flashy cars, and everything about him in general signaled life in the fast lane.

Birger von Brandstrup's body was much easier to recognize when compared to the photos of when he was alive. But still, his body appeared emaciated to a degree that no dietitian would recommend.

Carl knew that Birger von Brandstrup had made a fortune from online betting. Carl had never been one for gambling online—and had never even placed a bet in a betting shop. He would laugh to himself when he walked past one that promised an 85 percent return, because only very gullible people would fall for that. How could they not realize that what it actually meant was a guaranteed 15 percent loss? But then again, that did not sound quite as enticing.

Birger von Brandstrup had been the country's foremost expert at attracting compulsive gamblers and lightening their wallets.

Carl knew, of course, that there were political forces trying to put a stop to the madness, making sure that all the ridiculous advertisements for betting of all types would at some point disappear for good. It was no secret that the time wasted on gambling addiction and associated insomnia was becoming a societal problem that benefited no one except men like Birger von Brandstrup and their personal finances.

Carl shook his head. Here was another man that the world was better off without.

There was a gentle knock on the doorframe into Carl's office, and Rose entered with a complacent smile.

"Why are you looking so smug?" he asked. "Have they reopened the canteen?"

"Funny! No, Carl, but Gordon and I have been researching who committed terrible crimes against humanity and was born in August and December."

"And . . ."

"We began with August twentieth, when Pia Laugesen was found drowned and Slobodan Milošević was born."

Carl put down the von Brandstrup file. "But we already knew that."

She nodded. "Yeah, but then we discovered that the Spanish dictator Franco was born on December fourth, and it's hard not to think that Frank Svendsen—with the nickname "Franco"—might have been killed on December fourth, 2016. That would be just about a month after he was kidnapped. What do you think?"

Carl reached for his cigarettes, but Rose's reproachful gaze made him think better of it.

"I'm not finished, Carl. We also discovered that the biggest bastard of them all, the ruthless Soviet dictator and executioner Joseph Stalin, was born on December eighteenth. So don't you think we can ascertain that Birger von Brandstrup was killed on that date in 2018? And that would be just about three weeks after he disappeared."

Carl picked up the von Brandstrup file again. If the hypothesis was correct, von Brandstrup had been held for a shorter time than Frank Svendsen was before he was killed. And maybe that explained why Svendsen's body looked more emaciated.

"Call Gordon and Assad in here, will you?" he said.

Carl pondered for a moment. It was a huge breakthrough if they had managed to establish a pattern. But where would it all lead?

His colleagues entered the room beaming.

"First, I want to tell you that this is first-rate work, guys. Great effort. Now I think that we're definitely on the right track for establishing a pattern—and maybe even a profile of the killer. Don't you agree?"

Gordon was the first to respond. "Yes. At this point it should certainly be possible to fill in the empty gaps on the whiteboard. If we discover the date of death of some real tyrants, I think we'll be able to link them to a number of suspicious deaths over the years. Of course, that still leaves us with having to find the victims. It's a bit topsy-turvy," he finished, laughing.

Carl smiled at him. "Yeah, what a fate for Franco Svendsen with his life ending on the birthday of his namesake. It just can't be a coincidence, can it?"

"It could still be," said Assad. "But I think that he was selected among a number of possible victims due to his pen name."

Gordon laughed and patted him on the back. "That's something else, Assad. It's called a pet name."

Assad looked at him with a disappointed expression. Was Gordon also going to start correcting him just like the others?

"Pet name? I don't understand. I thought it was a name someone invented for themselves."

"But why did the perpetrator choose these dates?" interrupted Carl. "What is the overall symbolism?"

"It's his way of reminding us about the evils of the world," suggested Gordon.

"Yeah, the victims weren't exactly angels, if you ask me," said Rose. "I certainly wouldn't invite them into my circle of friends."

I wonder if Rose even has a circle of friends, thought Carl. But of course she was right. "If you continue researching the birthdays of infamous people, it isn't inconceivable that we'll be able to find victims to fill in the remaining nine gaps for the entire period of 1988 to 2018. But don't forget that, in the unlikely event that there are several suspicious deaths on the bastards' birthdays, we have to focus on cases where there is evidence of salt."

"I think I'll start with Adolf Hitler's birthday. Isn't that a good idea?" asked Rose.

Assad and Gordon agreed.

Carl was feeling a bit funny. Was he sweating more than usual? It must be because he suddenly felt a twinge of apprehension.

"Something is bothering me now," said Carl. "What if this nightmare isn't over? Our last victim was killed on December eighteenth, 2018, but what about 2020? If someone is due to be killed in 2020, it would have to be after December eighteenth, which means very soon. What evil tyrant has their birthday in the last thirteen days of December? Does anyone know?"

They stared at him in alarm, took out their phones simultaneously, and started searching. There was no time to waste.

After about a minute, they all stopped at once.

Rose was the first to speak. "China's so-called chairman, Mao Ze-dong, guilty of all manner of crimes against his own people and with millions of lives on his conscience," she said dryly. "His birthday was December twenty-sixth."

Carl checked the date on his watch. If their theory was correct, some-one was being targeted at this very moment.

Someone who would be killed in exactly nine days.

37

CARL

Thursday, December 17, 2020

So who would die on Boxing Day?

Was someone being held somewhere just now, starving, oblivious to the fate awaiting them, and without any possibility of raising the alarm? Or was it a case of someone walking around carefree among their loved ones without realizing that this would be their last Christmas together? The intended victim could also be a loner, living in their own little world, just as oblivious to the imminent danger. Carl was convinced that one of these theories was correct. But which one was it? How would they find out in time? They could not just announce that they were looking for a ruthless bastard.

Carl had no doubt that the perpetrator had already singled out their victim, and might even have done so a long time ago. But he also knew that the only chance of preventing the murder depended on him and his team, and that objectively they might as well throw in the towel.

"But can you just give up on another person's right to live if there is any chance of saving them?" Mona had asked him in connection with something unrelated not long ago. And she said that despite the fact that she knew just as well as he did that, in cases like those, they would have to work day and night over the holidays, leaving her alone with Lucia.

Rose did not hesitate to offer the full support of the entire team in spite of the prospect of too much work and no Christmas celebration.

"Of course we're behind you," she had said, and they had all put their noses to the ground over the last few hours to prove the point.

Gordon dealt with background research to uncover new information about the cases they already knew about.

Rose's method had always been to find new ways to approach a case. So if she wanted to fill in more of the gaps on the whiteboard, she needed to uncover new perspectives. She would have to begin with finding new birthdays for dictators that fit the bill. Then she would have to search for cases in which someone had died in suspicious circumstances on those dates. If she then further analyzed these cases and victims, new leads might come up. Who knew the victims, what did they do for work, and what could they be guilty of? And if she had any luck, she might start to build a picture of a potential killer.

While she was slogging away with that, Assad was tasked with following up on lots of loose ends, such as Tytte Laugesen's scrapbooks and Palle Rasmussen's computer. He had to finish that before he could assist Carl.

According to their theory, there were only nine days until someone would be executed, and it was their responsibility to try to prevent it. The four of them agreed that if the murder was carried out resolutely, as in the previous cases, they were facing an impossible task unless they managed to home in on a potential killer. They also agreed that something had caused the killer to change their MO over the years. They seemed to be more cautious now, as if more concerned with making sure that nothing went wrong. Apparently, the killer was unwilling to expose themself to the same degree as earlier. So there was a good chance that the salt would not necessarily prove as obvious as in previous cases. After all, in the two most recent cases, the salt had been hidden inside the bodies, and the murders had not been staged as accidents. The execution of Franco Svendsen and Birger von Brandstrup, and possibly others, had taken place after the victims were kidnapped. And if they went with the assumption that kidnapping the victims had become the killer's favored method, they might still have a chance of finding the next potential victim before they were executed.

And that was Carl's objective.

As he was walking over to Marcus's office, he was stopped by the secretary, Lis, who looked concerned.

"Between you and me, I've been ordered to copy everything we have on the nail gun case, Carl." She pointed at a large stack of papers on her desk. "I don't know what you think about it, but it must be strange for you." She stroked his cheek and smiled warmly. "Well, what I'm really trying to say is that you should look after yourself."

Carl nodded. It was sweet of her, but that was Lis to the core.

And besides, he had read all those files several times before. So what was there to be afraid of?

Marcus Jacobsen naturally understood the urgency of the matter. He had been tormented for years about the case of Maja's little boy, who had been the unintended victim when Ove Wilder's repair shop was blown up. He had thought for a long time that this was a stand-alone incident. But now he had to face the fact that the explosion in the shop was merely a single piece in a larger puzzle of multiple murders. Marcus Jacobsen more than sensed that Department Q could not be mistaken and that Carl and his team were trying to prevent another murder at this very moment.

"Carl, I understand you've been going through cases involving someone disappearing without a trace over the last month and a half and that none of these cases fit your victim profile."

"That's right," answered Carl.

"Is it possible that the person was never reported missing?"

Carl placed his elbows on the arms of the office chair and rested his chin on his folded hands. If Marcus was right, the present case would diverge from the previous cases.

"You're suggesting that it might be someone nobody would miss, but I don't think so."

"No, maybe not. But could it be possible that the family already thinks that the person has died, like in Franco Svendsen's case? Or maybe rather that they suspect that the person has disappeared voluntarily for a time—like Birger von Brandstrup's wife thought he had?"

Carl closed his eyes. "I think the latter is more plausible. But it's also possible that the next of kin have received false information about the missing person. That they're under the impression that they're in contact with that person even though they aren't."

"They might've received fake text messages or emails—is that what you're getting at?"

Carl nodded slowly. "Yes, if the intended victim had left on legitimate business, and if their significant other thinks they have been communicating with them via email, unaware that the replies are really from the captors." Carl waved his hand at Rose, who was standing in the doorway, signaling that she would have to wait a moment. "That's definitely a possibility, Marcus. But then, so are all our suggestions. However, let's assume for the moment that we're correct. How will we get the next of kin to report the person missing? And within the next nine days?"

Marcus gave him a resigned look. "I'm afraid I can't assign any more people to help you," he said. "Everyone has enough with their own cases, and especially now that we have people out sick, in quarantine, or working from home."

"What about using the newspapers or TV? Can't we issue some sort of statement that'll grab the attention of the next of kin?" Carl already knew the answer. That was not something the police did. It would generate endless tips and calls that would be misleading or useless and cost them precious hours.

"Some people just live alone, in case you've forgotten," said Rose. "I live alone, Gordon lives alone, and so do you, Marcus. If the intended victim has no next of kin or friends nearby, it could take a long time before someone reacts."

Marcus sighed and stood up. "If you stumble on a concrete lead, I'll see what I can do. Until then, let's pray for the poor soul. I'm afraid someone is going to be very sad this Christmas."

"I'm most convinced about the last hypothesis, and I have an idea," said Rose when Marcus was out of earshot. "Why don't we invite *TV Avisen* news to the office so they can get an insight into the conditions under which an investigation unit works during corona?"

Carl considered her suggestion. He actually did not give a damn about who they would piss off by bending the rules. If some superintendent or other high-ranking person made a fuss that they were crossing the line, they could just fire the entire team in Department Q or at least fire him. He was not put off by the thought of becoming a professional dog walker or working as a security consultant during the remaining years before his retirement.

"Okay, Rose. You get on that. Don't tell the reporters anything concrete about the cases we're working on. We'll have to improvise when we get to that point. What else have you got? Anything useful?"

She smiled. "Yes, even if I say so myself. Adolf Hitler's birthday was on April twentieth, and Andrea Thorsen was found on the same date in 1994 hanging in her lover's apartment under suspicious circumstances. They pinned the murder on her lover, and he was sentenced to fifteen years but died after having only served five."

"All right. That's a sad story. But I'm expecting a bit more than that before it can make it up on the whiteboard, Rose."

She smiled. "Thank you, Mr. Demanding. I thought as much. So let me tell you that Andrea Thorsen was president of a family company that sold agricultural machinery. Her business slowly went downhill and collapsed due to a long series of unfortunate events. The first was that all these expensive machines—combine harvesters, huge John Deere tractors, seeders, spraying machines, forage harvesters, and others— were vandalized. Someone subsequently broke into her home and stole some very expensive furniture and other unique items. After that, one of the storehouses burned down, one of their diesel tanks was emptied, and then burst pipes caused severe water damage to the buildings. It was a long series of cases that resulted in significant insurance payouts. Of course, all the different assets were covered by different insurance companies, so the payouts did not raise alarms with any one insurance company. But a TV documentary in 1994 brought to light that the insurance payouts totaled more than fifty million kroner, which was an immense sum of money at the time."

"An insurance scam?"

"It was never proven, and the woman appeared to be inconsolable. Or at least when she was in the media. Out of the spotlight, she lived in the lap of luxury with her lover, who I'm sure must have had more than a hand in it. He was no less than an insurance underwriter."

Carl nodded. "And the suicide? You said she hanged herself? But why was her lover put under suspicion?"

"He was in the apartment when she died, out of his head on cocaine. Witnesses testified that he became very aggressive when he used. And the police and judge considered it highly unlikely that she could have done it to herself because she suffered from a severe fear of death and had no reason to challenge that particular phobia, given that she was living the dolce vita. And then there was the safe with seven million kroner in cash, and the idiot had the combination in his wallet."

"And he was sent to prison?"

"Yes, and died five years later. In 1999, as far as I recall."

"Did he die from natural causes?"

"Yes, if a ruptured appendix is natural."

"And now comes the question we all want answered: Why are you linking this case to ours?"

"I was just getting to that, Carl. And it took a very close reading of the file for me to get there myself," she said with an ill-concealed smug smile.

"It was obvious that the lover had been sniffing cocaine because there were at least eight lines ready for his next binge. But when he was arrested, the lover denied that he had cut the lines, and he also refused to tell the police who his dealer was. That was before the trial, when he *was* willing to blabber about all sorts of other stuff, as if that would help him. But before that, the police had analyzed the cocaine in an attempt to locate the dealer. They didn't succeed, but what they did discover was that it was the poorest quality cocaine they had ever come across because it was cut with fifty percent table salt."

Carl whistled quietly to himself.

Now they had case number eight out of the seventeen on their whiteboard.

38

MAURITS

Friday, December 18, 2020

He was woken by his swallowing reflex. A faint, cool stream that caused his tongue to pulsate and the muscles in his throat to contract.

He opened his eyes with great difficulty. His corneas were so dry that it felt as if his eyelids were glued shut.

A blurry figure was towering in front of him. Strong hands pushed his cheeks together and something resembling a baby bottle was pressed against his lower teeth as water dripped from the corners of his mouth and continued to activate his swallowing reflex.

Maurits gagged and sensed that he was about to cough. His head was pounding, and he remembered how he had felt like his head was exploding before he dozed off. It was this throbbing pain that brought him back to the harsh reality of his situation.

Now the figure pulled the baby bottle out of his mouth, turned their back to him, and walked down to face the far wall.

Maurits tried to call, but his vocal cords felt stuck together and he could not manage anything more than guttural sounds.

He had been imprisoned for days without food and with hardly anything to drink. And he had no recollection of having peed over the last twenty-four hours, even though he could not be sure. He looked down at himself and saw a dried-up stain on his underpants. It must have happened while he was sleeping.

Maurits tried to focus on the room but could not collect his thoughts. Did he even know where he was? The only thing he knew for sure was that he had thought days ago that he was destined to die of thirst and hunger. That he was meant to die slowly without any witnesses.

My name is Maurits van Bierbek, he thought, *and no matter what you are concocting down there by the wall, I'm still alive, you son of a bitch.*

The figure turned around and Maurits squinted to moisten his eyes. But it was not until the man stood right in front of him that he could make him out clearly.

He was middle-aged, tall, impressive, and wearing a smile that made his face look twisted, like he had been deformed at birth.

"Let's get some food into you," he said in a deep voice.

He pulled Maurits's left arm toward him and slapped the back of his hand a couple of times before sticking in the needle.

"There you go," he said. "Now you can live a little longer."

Maurits turned his head with difficulty and stared directly up at the drip hanging from the stand next to him.

"In half an hour, we'll try to get some soup in you. I think it'll do you good."

His headache lifted in no time. Maurits closed his eyes in relief and thought that the drip must contain some mild pain reliever. And while his brain was supplied with sugar and salt, Maurits slowly regained his grasp on reality.

But it was a reality he did not want to acknowledge.

He coughed a couple of times and cleared his throat until he sensed that his voice had returned a little.

"Who are you?" he rasped.

But the man did not answer. He had returned to the far wall and stood for a moment moving his arms, as if mixing something at the steel table. Then he took a step to the side toward a long steel ladder that Maurits did not recall seeing before.

There was a metallic scraping sound across the concrete floor as the man pulled the ladder away from the wall. He only stopped a couple of meters in front of Maurits and then extended it to its full height so it could reach one of the runners on the ceiling.

Now Maurits noticed that the trousers the man was wearing looked like the ones carpenters wear, with tools sticking out of large pockets. What did he need them for?

Maurits wanted to get up so that he could kick the ladder over when the man had reached the top. But he could not move. Was there something in the drip that deprived him of the power to move, or had he already grown so weak?

"What day is it?" he asked the man, who was tinkering with one of the runners.

"It's Friday, December eighteenth," answered the man.

Maurits took a deep breath to pump more oxygen into his brain. December 18? How long had he been here, then? He slowly remembered how he had been tricked and the moment when he had woken up in this chair. And he knew that he had been held captive since Saturday, six days ago, which must also be the last time he had anything to eat or drink.

"Are you going to let me loose now?" he asked, because the man was tinkering with the runners and the sliders up there. Could he really be letting him go? Had he been punished enough for whatever crime he had committed?

But the laughter from the top of the ladder made him gasp. It sounded so mocking, so diabolical that Maurits knew for the first time since he had been kidnapped that no matter what lay in store for him in the days ahead, these cold walls would be the last thing he would ever see. What had been hope now became a painful recognition that the rest of his life could be counted in hours. But then why had they not just left him alone so he could die in his sleep when his body gave up?

"Get it over with," he said as loudly as he could. "Kill me and get it over with."

The man laughed again from up on the ladder. He had been twisting and pushing with various tools, but Maurits could not see what he was up to. However, he was sure that it could not be anything good.

A minute later, the man was standing in front of him again. He had an adjustable wrench in one hand and a screw bolt in the other.

"All it takes is using one of these little things in the right place and you won't be able to get any closer than three meters to the table down there. Diabolical, isn't it?"

He pulled the ladder away from the runner and pointed upward. "You can see the screw bolt that I put in there. The slider will hit it and stop, and you won't be able to remove it without this." He dangled the wrench back and forth in front of Maurits's eyes and then pulled the ladder back to the far wall.

"I'll leave the wrench here on the table, Maurits van Bierbek, and the ladder next to it. That'll give you something to think about over the next couple of days."

Mean son of a bitch, thought Maurits.

"Yes, I know what you're thinking. You're thinking that this is torture, and you're right. But we don't torture you because we're torturers—we're angels helping you get to a better place than this world, which you've contributed to poisoning. The ladder and the wrench are merely reminders that if you'd considered your future and what you were doing years ago, you wouldn't be sitting here wondering what's going to happen to you next."

Maurits looked at his twisted face with a look of contempt. "No, I won't have to because I know what'll happen. I'm going to starve to death."

The man smiled. "No, I don't think that'd be very nice of us. We'll look after you for a while yet. And now your soup should be ready."

Maurits closed his eyes. *We'll look after you for a while yet*, he had said.

Yet. Whatever that meant.

39

CARL

Friday, December 18, 2020

"**I'm sorry, Carl**, but I haven't had any luck finding reporters who want or need a police piece at the moment," said Rose. "There's more than enough about the police on TV right now, they said, and I have to say I agree. Apart from the corona-related programs, there are all the old cases that former investigators analyze, shows about traffic police chasing down speed demons, technical reviews of old murder cases, and so on and so forth, from Denmark and abroad. So if we can't offer them anything new or specific, they aren't interested."

"Then damn well give them something specific, Rose. Something to get their blood pumping. And don't hold back."

"Yes, but what? We can't just blurt out that we think someone is going to be murdered on December twenty-sixth, can we? And it wouldn't be fair to worry a lot of different families that the potential victim might be their missing relative."

Carl knew she was right. They could not put the cart before the horse.

He glanced over at the gap on the bottom of the whiteboard. Were they really going to allow management, who had never spent a single minute on a real investigation, to obstruct the best department in the force from preventing a murder? Hell no!

"I'll tell you what, Rose, tell the program planners at *TV Avisen* or any of the news channels, or whoever it is you need to contact, that Department Q is currently working on something big and that the media have to be quick if they want to get in on it. Tell them that this is a rare opportunity to see behind the scenes of our investigation. That ought to make them sit up and take notice. And I don't care who takes the bait. As long as someone does, I'm happy."

After their talk, Carl swung his feet onto the desk and tried to sum up the facts. Everything pointed to the perpetrator being active for almost thirty-five years and having worked systematically to a specific pattern. First and foremost, he only chose to kill every second year, which made good sense, because the more infrequently a killer struck, the greater the chance that each crime would not be connected with the others. Until now, each murder had been committed at a slightly later date in the relevant year, and they were up to sixteen murders over the entire period. And that number might soon be seventeen. At the moment, their investigation suggested that all the murders were linked to the birthdays of infamous dictators and other cynical bastards who had committed crimes against humanity. Carl had no doubt that his talented team would soon identify more of these dates and, hopefully, also the murders linked to them.

But a few questions remained unanswered: What was the overall common denominator between these tyrants and the murder victims? And what was the relevance of salt? Was it merely a signature linking the murders? Was the perpetrator so convinced of his ability to stay one step ahead of the police that he did not shy away from leaving a signature that would link the crimes? Carl had met many conceited idiots in his time, but this one really took the prize for foolhardiness, aggressiveness, and, not least, audacity. And what kind of person would brag about being a killer? Someone who is mentally ill? A callous psychopath? Someone seeking revenge?

Carl took a cigarette and tapped it on his desk. Maybe a few puffs would help him understand how these murders on the whiteboard were connected to the deaths of Tabitha and Ragnhild. They must be connected, given that Ragnhild Bengtsen's body was found next to the two latest victims in the series of ritual murders. But then why hadn't there been any salt in Ragnhild's grave? And why did she kill Tabitha? Could it be that the two women were not part of the grand plan but just collateral damage dealt with resolutely and without hesitation?

Carl sighed and let the cigarette dangle unlit from the corner of his mouth while he racked his brain.

Maybe he should only concentrate on the two latest victims. What kind of people were they? Birger von Brandstrup facilitated gambling and caused people to become addicts. Frank Svendsen polluted the soil, air, and seas, and he sent ships off for scrapping in Bangladesh. Definitely two men who had not contributed anything positive to the world.

"Do you have a minute, Carl?"

It was Assad who pulled him from his thoughts.

"I'll just turn on your TV and go on to TV2 Play. You need to see the latest update on TV2 News!"

He fumbled around with the remote for a second and then a photo of Pauline Rasmussen appeared on the screen, while the breaking news banner text rolled across the bottom: "Actress Pauline Rasmussen, 52, one of the country's most popular cabaret stars, was found dead in her home yesterday. Several sources believe the death to be a suicide."

"They're interviewing the friend who found her," said Assad.

The friend sat stony faced in the studio.

"Yes! Pauline had been feeling terrible for some time," she said. "The recent lockdown was especially hard for her because she had only just rebuilt her faith that she'd soon be back onstage—and then the government pulled the rug from under her again."

"So she was worried about a future with no work?" asked the interviewer.

"Yes, and no money. She had nothing left to live for, and she'd used her savings up over the last year."

"And you found her in bed in her home?"

"Yes, but the first thing I noticed was the pile of pills on her night-stand."

The screen showed a photo of the nightstand with the empty pill bottle, a pile of pills, and an empty water glass. The forensic technicians certainly would not have provided that sort of photo, so it must have been taken by the friend.

"I knew instinctively that something was wrong because the first thing I saw when I walked into the bedroom was all the pills lying there. And she hadn't answered the phone when I called that morning. I thought she must've drowned her sorrows and been sleeping it off. But I was sorely mistaken."

"We invited you here today because we know you have a message in connection with Pauline's death. Care to share?"

Carl wondered why TV journalists always fell in love with stupid phrases like that. Who ever actually said "care to share"?

The woman leaned in toward the interviewer as if she wanted to tell her something in confidence.

"It's the situation in the arts," she said. "Actors and artists have way too many sleeping pills lying around at a time when their lives have been ruined. I think the minister for culture and everyone else who chose to disregard the arts when distributing financial help should seriously think about what they've done. They have a lot to answer for."

Carl looked at Assad with a frown.

"Well," he said. "She was quite a character. First of all, I must admit that I'm very surprised by Pauline Rasmussen's death. She didn't strike me as the type to do this."

"'First of all,' you said?" Assad grinned. Did he already know what Carl was going to say next?

"You're also thinking about the pills, aren't you, Assad? It must've been a very full pill bottle to have so many left on the nightstand and still have been enough to kill her."

"Yes, Carl. Very suspicious! And it also raised suspicions with Sigurd Harms's team, so they looked for something that might indicate a crime.

But all they found were Pauline's own fingerprints. They searched the pill bottle, the bedroom, and the corridor meticulously. She was found with all her clothes on, and her bag had been thrown on the footstool at the end of the bed. Harms went through the contents and there was nothing suspicious in it."

"I bet Harms wasn't pleased with that," said Carl. "Thanks for filling me in, Assad. I agree that this doesn't look like a regular case of suicide. I think it's even more urgent now to get Palle Rasmussen's bloody computer back from NC3. Can't you get Marcus to pull some strings? We need NC3 to restore as many of the deleted files as they possibly can."

Assad gave him a thumbs-up. He was already on his way.

High time to light this cigarette, thought Carl while looking out over the parking lot. He had just caught sight of two young guys with a camera and a microphone rushing in the cold toward the main entrance, when Rose appeared in his doorway.

"They're here now," she said with a reproachful look at the flame from Carl's match.

"They? You mean the TV crew?"

He had only just managed to sort the papers on the desk when the two guys appeared.

"Hi! Erik!" said the guy with the microphone. Carl gave him an elbow bump while the cameraman took up position.

"We're in a bit of a rush," said the reporter, shoving the microphone in Carl's face.

Carl focused on the red recording signal and saw the logo above it: LORRY.

"Rose, come in here for a minute," he shouted, turning his back to the camera.

"Am I imagining things, Rose, or have you invited Lorry to come? A local Copenhagen-based TV station?"

She looked in confusion at the two guys.

"Not as far as I'm aware."

Carl turned toward them and tried to look apologetic, even though he knew it did not work.

"Thank you for coming, and thank you for leaving again so promptly. What we have to say is of national interest."

"But our reports are sometimes shown on other regional . . . ," the reporter attempted, but the cameraman had already gotten the message.

Five minutes later they were rushing back across the parking lot in the opposite direction with the tip that Department Q would make an official statement two hours later on the square in front of the old police headquarters.

"Are you sure that's the right decision, Carl?" asked Rose.

"As sure as night follows day, yes."

"What are you planning to say?"

"Well, our dilemma is that we can't say we're looking for a person who answers to the description of 'bastard.' But apart from that, I'll say it like it is. That we have a suspicion that a very industrious and probably successful person who hasn't been in contact with their family for some time is in imminent danger. So if anyone thinks this might apply to their family, they should contact you directly, Rose."

She did not look pleased.

40

SISLE

Friday, December 18, 2020, late afternoon

She received the call as she was heading home in the dark. The last few days had been hectic, but the years had toughened Sisle up. And no matter what she faced, she had both feet firmly on the ground. Debora had sounded distressed when she called, but then, she was not Sisle. For many years, Debora had been a devoted and loyal servant. But she was in the habit of becoming unhinged. Without Sisle's firm grip on her and her husband's life, they would surely have perished years ago. Most people who had suffered such misfortune would.

Sisle was a hundred times stronger and never doubted herself or her mission. Fate had guided her path. And as long as her instincts and resolve helped her on that path, why would she ever waver?

Now she was again standing in front of the door to Debora's house, where she had put out so many fires over the years.

Debora opened the door, looking pale. "You need to see what we've just seen," she said. "It's not good, Sisle. Not good at all."

Adam was standing in the living room with the remote control at the ready. He appeared to be in shock, and Sisle could already sense that he was nervous about what he had to tell her—and so he struggled to get to the point.

"You have to see the press conference we've just watched. It's almost the only thing on TV2 News just now. We need to discuss what we're going to do."

He pressed the remote. For a full five minutes, they watched the news on the screen, and Sisle could sense that Debora and Adam were constantly gauging her reaction. But Sisle retained her composure.

Carl Mørck, the head of Department Q, was standing in front of the old police headquarters, surrounded by a sea of microphones and cameras. It was so cold that his breath was visible and his shoulders were dusted with snow. His expression was darker than the day when he had come to speak to her at work. And every time one of the reporters tried to interrupt him, he turned his face away. It was obvious from the look on the reporters' faces that his methods were unmistakably crossing a professional line. If this was an attempt to involve the entire country in his investigation, it was certainly doing the job.

Following the statement from the police, the anchor on TV2 News appeared with a serious expression that undoubtedly signaled that this story was not going away anytime soon. It would not be long before a host of experts would be called in to give their opinion on the enhanced resources that would surely be deployed for the investigation.

Sisle and the others did not need this kind of exposure.

"Maybe we should kill van Bierbek immediately. What difference would a few days make?" asked Adam.

Finally, he was speaking his mind.

Sisle looked at him discreetly. *You weakling. Watch what you say*, she thought.

"Maybe Adam is right, Sisle," said Debora, moving closer to her on the sofa. "It's not like we haven't talked about it before. If they get too close, we'll pull the plug and . . ."

Sisle stopped listening. Everything had been happening too quickly over the last few days, but it was pure coincidence. Tabitha and Ragnhild had gone berserk independently of each other. There was no way they could have predicted it. Now Tabitha was dead, which solved the problem of what to do with her. But it had also made their need to stop Ragnhild even more urgent. They had done the right thing by killing her. But who could have known that her body would be discovered so quickly? Adam had sworn that he had covered the grave sufficiently, but he obviously had not. And then there was that idiot Pauline, who had threatened her immediately after. She should not have done that. No one threatened her. And even though the woman had never had anything concrete to link her to Palle Rasmussen's death, her insinuations might still have caused the bulldog from Department Q to return with more questions.

Sisle took a deep breath. "Are you completely sure that you managed to remove everything from Pauline Rasmussen's apartment that might come back to haunt us, Adam?"

"You saw yourself how thorough I was. The paper in her handbag and the shoebox with emails from her bedroom are right here." He pointed to where they were on the table. "That was all I could find. Plus, we were wearing gloves and nobody saw us, Sisle."

"You won't start making mistakes now, I hope." Sisle stared at them until they looked down. "Listen. This Carl Mørck has nothing on us. You heard his statement just now. His department apparently knows that someone is going to die on Boxing Day, but that's all. They don't know who it is, and they have no idea where he's being held. I have no intention of changing my plans or principles because of this. We'll execute Maurits van Bierbek exactly as planned."

"And what if van Bierbek's wife suspects something and reacts to the statement from the police?" asked Debora.

"Why would she? We've made sure there's a good reason why there's no telephone contact between them while he's landing this huge contract in Florida, and she seems content with their alleged email correspondence. Right, Debora?"

"She probably thinks it's romantic that he's expressed his true feelings for her. The last email she sent him seemed almost euphoric. But what do we do if she suddenly changes her mind, starts asking questions, or demands that he calls her on the phone?"

"We'll deal with that if and when the time comes."

"But the police encouraged the families to ask questions that only the

missing person could answer. Adam said that Maurits van Bierbek seemed very weak when he went to see him today. So maybe he can't
or won't cooperate with us if we need him to give us information."

"You're right, Maurits is probably too far gone now. So I don't think
we can force him to give us information we need. He seems to be totally
resigned," said Adam.

"Breathe, Adam. You sound like you're losing it. It doesn't make any
difference if they figure out that he's the intended victim. There's nothing to link anything back to me. And definitely not to you two."

"Are you sure, Sisle? Couldn't they trace your call to van Bierbek or
find something in relation to his kidnapping?"

Sisle could see how shaken Debora was even though she was trying
to appear calm. But that was her problem.

"But Debora *is* right, isn't she, Sisle?" said Adam in support. "And if
the family reacts and doesn't get satisfactory answers, the police will
return to the day we kidnapped him and the exact time when you picked
him up."

Sisle raised her voice now. "Listen up, you two!" They both gave a
start, which Sisle ignored. They would just have to get hold of themselves. "Even if the police have surveillance of the car and manage to
make me out behind the wheel wearing my mask, or if the car rental
company has tracking devices and keeps records for weeks, it won't be
of any help. I used an old Nokia when I called Maurits van Bierbek to
arrange a meeting with the representative of Global Rea Inc., Victor
Page. And both the phone and the prepaid card are now lying at the
bottom of the harbor in Nordhavnen. We only used the rental car for
the first twenty minutes and then moved Maurits into the van. And you
returned the Lexus in perfect condition and on time, Debora, and we
also rented it with false ID and paid with a credit card from CaixaBank
in the same false name. You both know all this, so why do you think
I've started to make mistakes?"

"Are you really saying you've never made a mistake before?" asked
Adam, but he regretted it the moment their eyes locked.

———

Back in late 1987, Sisle had already been keeping an eye on Ove Wilder's Auto for some time. Since she had resumed her university studies, Bjarne's Coffee Shop, just over from Wilder's repair shop, had been Sisle's preferred spot to prepare for the following day's lectures. Like the prices, the usual clientele was not exactly exclusive. But despite the patronage of Sydhavnen's lower classes, the place was characterized by a form of mutual respect that she was not used to from university. These were the people who worked for the lowest wages in the worst jobs, getting up at five in the morning to work their fingers to the bone. Even the country's bad standing with the weather gods did not hold them back. She had seen a lot of purple noses and frostbitten skin in her years there, but she had never heard anyone complain.

Things had carried on this way right up until Ove Wilder's Auto opened and he and his mechanics invaded the coffee shop. Sisle could no longer sit comfortably in her corner concentrating on her studies because of all the filth they came out with. For more than six months, she was forced to listen to them bragging about the insane amount of cheating and fraud they got up to, and all the mechanics' anecdotes about how stupid their customers were and how easy it was to lighten their wallets.

Apart from the extensive fraud, it was first and foremost their disdain and mockery that made her blood boil. When she finally spoke up about her shock and dismay over their criminal activities, the atmosphere at the mechanics' table changed in a split second.

"Listen, lady, you just keep your trap shut and your eyes and ears out of our business, got it?" said Ove Wilder himself, setting the tone for the others. Then he slammed his dirty hand over her folder and pulled it toward him. "This means a lot to you, doesn't it?"

Sisle nodded. The notes in the folder were the result of half a year's work, but she refused to look apologetic. And that was a mistake.

"Don't you live in number seventeen on the next street down? It won't

take us more than three minutes to walk down there and destroy everything you own. We could start with this, for example." He tore the first
piece of paper out of the folder and lit it with his lighter.

She gave a start when the flame consumed it in a matter of seconds,
and they noticed. Their raucous laughter made Sisle see red for a second.
"I might not live very far away," she hissed. "But the telephone box
out there is even closer, and it would be very easy for me to call the
police."

She did not catch who punched her, but she did notice that no one
in the coffee shop came to her aid. The regulars barely looked in her
direction, and Sisle felt completely betrayed for the second time in her
life. So it was the last time she set foot in Bjarne's Coffee Shop.

It took her a good month to acquire knowledge about the layout of
the repair shop and mix the explosives that she intended to use as detonators. Then she had to get hold of the chloroform that she might need
to sedate the victims. She also had to find a way to gain access to the
shop after hours so she could hide the baseball bat and the other items.
Then she needed to connect the detonators to the timer close to the toluene tanks and, finally, position metal fragments in strategic places.

She selected dark corners in the two repair shop rooms where she
could hide, and she practiced tiptoeing across the concrete floor. She
spent a couple of days focused on her aim and the power with which
she could slam the baseball bat very precisely into the backs of the pig
heads she had procured from the meatpacking district.

She finally managed to put together a foolproof plan that seemed to
work on all levels, so she dropped the chloroform. It was merely a matter of acting quickly and not hesitating at all when each of them went
to the changing area after closing time. So unless something completely
unexpected happened, none of the mechanics would have a chance to
react before she knocked them out cold from behind. The detonations
would follow almost immediately, so if she managed to neutralize them
all before the repair shop closed, nothing could go wrong.

However, she had inexplicably failed to notice that one of the mechanics had walked out to the main gate to smoke a cigarette, and it was

pure coincidence that she went to leave through the gate. He looked at her suspiciously and only just managed to react as the hit with the bat across the bridge of his nose caused him to spin halfway around and tumble to the ground unconscious between the wooden fence bordering the neighboring lot and the car parked in front.

In that moment, she realized that time was running out. So Sisle ran as fast as she could out through the main gate and past the salt she had left there, stopping a hundred meters up the road so she could relish her revenge from a safe distance.

And then it happened.

The woman who came running unexpectedly around the corner, wheeling the stroller in front of her, did not hear Sisle's panicked warning shouts to stop. Sisle leaped forward and shouted again, but the woman still did not hear her. And the third attempt to warn the woman was drowned out by the explosion.

The wave from the blast knocked Sisle down, and she passed out momentarily. When she came to, she was completely deaf for half a minute. And when her hearing returned, all she could hear was the woman screaming.

She watched from a distance as flashing blue lights from police cars and ambulances arrived at the scene.

The young woman's screams did not abate for a moment even as the stretcher with the child was carried out to the ambulance. Sisle was devastated.

Had she not had a pact with God? Or was it her destiny to be yet again sorely tested?

When no answer came to her, she promised herself a few essential things in life. She needed to atone for her sin and compensate the young mother. And then she would have to become stronger and richer so she had the means to stop people like Ove Wilder.

She noted the date of the explosion in her diary and subsequently found out that it was the birthday of the Romanian despot Nicolae Ceaușescu.

A devilish thought took hold of her. From now on, she would put all

her effort into selecting her victims and planning their deaths meticulously to ensure that she never again risked the lives of innocent people.
And when she did kill, which for safety reasons she should probably
only do every second year, it was important that no one suspected that
the death was a crime. In that way, she could work undisturbed for the
rest of her life.

Her second killing could very fittingly be carried out in 1990 on Feb-
ruary 16, which was the birthday of Kim Jong-il—the dictator and biggest curse of North Korea. And so Sisle had set in motion her crusade
to make the world a better place.

Are you really saying you've never made a mistake before? Adam had
asked her. If only he knew how deep he had twisted the knife.

What *was* happening right now? Were the two people she had built
her project with over so many years starting to get cold feet? She simply
could not allow that.

"I thought we'd agreed never to doubt one another's efforts, Adam."

Her tone made him squirm.

"Tell me what it is you think I've done wrong. Let's hear it!"

"I'm sorry" was all he could say.

Sisle looked from one to the other. Perhaps she had to consider whether
it was time for them to part ways.

"You mentioned that Maurits is very weak. But how weak is he? Are
you implying that he'll die before his execution?"

"I don't know. It's possible. And that's why I think we might as well
kill him now."

"Stop, Adam. That's the last time you say that. Understood? He will
die on the day he was destined to die—no sooner, no later. You'll have
to feed him better, got it? There's still eight days before we put him
down."

She sat for a moment looking at the shoebox on the table in front
of her.

"Have you read Pauline Rasmussen's emails?" she asked.

"Yes, some of them. She was totally obsessed with Palle Rasmussen."

"And did you wear gloves?"

"What do you take us for?" Adam looked offended.

"Good." She looked at her watch. "I just need to put something extra in the shoebox and then you'll be going for a drive, Adam."

41

CARL

Saturday, December 19, 2020

Carl had barely taken a step back from the podium the previous evening before a torrent of questions had pierced the ice-cold air and twenty microphones held by hands in thick gloves were thrust toward him.

How on earth do you know that someone's life will be in danger on Boxing Day? Why on that particular day? What is the motive? they had shouted from all directions. And regardless of how the questions had been framed, Carl only had one comment—he had already told them what he intended to and was hoping that they would soon be contacted by the family so that the department could intensify their investigation.

Then he had turned toward the grandiose colonnade of police HQ and caught the disapproving gazes of the chief constable and chief superintendent above their face masks.

They had approached him and asked in hushed voices if he had completely lost his mind and whether his boss, Marcus Jacobsen, had been informed about this entirely rash breach of protocol on police media communication.

"Hold back on firing me at least until we've saved this person," he said.

When they had made it absolutely clear that his actions would have consequences, they disappeared into the building, leaving Carl and the persistent reporters behind.

Carl nodded to the crowd and called Assad and Gordon over to him as he made his way to the parking lot.

"There's a good chance they'll crucify you for this, Carl," said Assad.

Carl patted his faithful companion's shoulder. "Then it's a good thing that you'll all still be in the department," he said.

The press conference made the front pages of all the papers, and they could tell the following day that the impact had been significant. Not just because of the many calls from people with a family member who might be missing, but also and especially because of their colleagues, who were disgruntled that everything was now focused on this one investigation that in their opinion was both undeserving and highly unusual. Even though Carl had given Rose's contact number, there was not a single department on Teglholmen or at police HQ that hadn't had its hands full with answering all manner of calls from concerned families as well as lunatics who just wanted to get all sorts of irrelevant nonsense off their chests.

Even though Carl assumed that the missing person must be someone industrious and successful, the majority of calls came from concerned parents of ordinary teenagers who had been missing for only a few hours. The office opposite Carl's had already received several calls an hour from tipsy people on benefits who could not understand why their kid had not returned home after a row the previous evening. And the cursing and swearing of colleagues who had been forced to come to work despite the corona restrictions became inescapable background music in the department.

There was no avoiding that an almighty storm was awaiting Carl, so he ensconced himself behind the closed door of his office and intended to stay there until the end of the day when everyone else had gone home.

Rose's phone in the other office, on the other hand, was oddly silent. After a few hours, she set it directly to voicemail and brought Carl up to speed on what they were doing.

"I've been working with the others for the afternoon," said Rose, nodding to Assad, who was holding the two scrapbooks under his arm.

"Yes, we've been focusing on the Pia Laugesen case. I've been looking at the daughter's scrapbooks, and Rose has been watching some old TV recordings of her."

"Scrapbooks, Assad, not scrapebooks!" said Carl. Assad did not pay any attention.

"I've been looking at interviews with Pia Laugesen from the years immediately before her death," said Rose. "Take a look at this one, for example, from *TV Avisen* news in 2009, the year before she died." She placed her laptop in front of Carl and pressed play.

The well-known interviewer who specialized in financial news was wearing his necktie American style. "Pia Laugesen. You're known for advising the rich to move their wealth to countries with lax banking regulations, helping companies hide their assets to avoid paying taxes, and for your extremely liberal interpretation of tax law. Doesn't that make you partly responsible for undermining the foundation of our society? And aren't you to blame for the average person having to step in and make up for the shortfall when your clients should have shouldered the burden?"

And all the while, Pia Laugesen just sat there smiling with her bright red lips, twiddling her rings and straightening her Hermès silk scarf. She seemed completely unfazed by the interview and kept nodding as if nothing in the world could challenge her integrity.

When the journalist had finished, she flashed her newly bleached teeth.

"Dear me," she said with a condescending smile. "If only we could rid the world of questions like that, you'd soon be out of a job. You have to understand that I need to be completely indifferent to what ordinary salaried workers have to pay. My job is to move wealth around and nothing else. As far as tax law is concerned, it should try to keep up with the loopholes and ambiguous regulations uncovered by my work. I don't understand what the problem is. Envy?"

They saw another couple of minutes of the interview in which the woman did not budge whatsoever.

"I've also found something," said Assad, opening one of the scrapbooks to the middle. "This is from July first, 2010, about a month and a half before she drowned." He pointed at a photo of Pia Laugesen dressed to the nines: open mink coat, another scarf from Hermès, trouser suit, and bangles adorning her arms as if she were a Christmas tree.

Assad pointed at a sentence in the two-page interview that bore the headline "TaxIcon Annual Accounts Top Local Businesses. Pia Laugesen's Empire Soars to New Heights."

Carl read the quote. It would have been enough to get any spin doctor fired in a split second.

The quote read, "I don't give a damn about clients and regular people who don't take precautions with their money. If they can't manage to keep their heads above water, I can't come to the rescue. I certainly can't take responsibility."

"Unbelievably cold," said Carl.

Assad and Rose nodded.

"Doesn't that statement make it quite ironic that she ended up drowning in her own pool?" said Rose.

The irony had not escaped Carl.

"Gordon, get in here!" shouted Rose at the top of her lungs. Was she trying to attract all their angry colleagues?

"Please shut the door, Gordon," said Carl when he came in. "What do you have for us?"

"Just this," he said, throwing a photocopy in front of Carl. It was a full-page ad for Ove Wilder's Auto from an old local newspaper featuring a photo of a wrecked Ford Escort with another photo next to it showing the car looking like new.

"Make your car happier and Wilder," urged the ad, including price examples for regular vehicle checkups, tire changes, and other services.

"What's special about this? It probably isn't even the same car, is it?" he asked.

Gordon smiled and pointed down to the corner at a large black star that read, "Our Prices are Dynamite!" in yellow letters.

"Aha," said Carl.

"Yeah, if you ask me, the killer found out about Wilder's fraud and might even have been a victim themselves. We'll never know because all the paperwork went up in smoke, but the word "dynamite" might hint that Wilder's repair shop was actually blown up. Couldn't that be the connection we're looking for and also tell us about the killer's logic? We certainly have two cases here where the victims have been given a taste of their own medicine as a direct consequence of their own words."

"This case is becoming more and more bloody strange, don't you think?" Carl shook his head in disbelief. "It's enough to drive anyone crazy that we have all these leads from the killer, such as the birthdays of tyrants, hints about the way the victims will be killed, and not least the salt, and still we've got nothing really to go on. The poor person waiting to be killed, and on Boxing Day no less."

"But, Carl," said Rose. "Don't you think we at least have a better understanding of the connection between the cases now?"

"Yes, maybe."

"We definitely have one common denominator for the tyrants and the victims: they were all extremely morally deficient."

"Yes. Now we 'just' need to find a person who has made themselves a guardian of morals and thinks it's acceptable to kill other people." Carl's air quotes hung between them, underlining the hopelessness of their task.

"This is almost religious, isn't it?" asked Assad, but then he was the one most likely to make that sort of observation.

"Yes, but what caused this person to become a holy crusader?" asked Carl. "And where do you look for a person like that?"

"In a psychiatric ward," said Rose. "Or maybe somewhere where it's possible to live in your own little world. I really don't know."

Then the phone rang. It was the receptionist.

"I have a lady here who'd like to speak to Carl Mørck. Can I send her in?"

Carl frowned. "Who is she, and why does she want to speak with me?"

He could hear mumbling in the background.

"Her name is Gertrud Olsen, and she was a friend of Pauline Rasmussen, the woman who took her own life. She has something she wants to show you."

Carl instantly recognized her from the news as she entered dramatically, broad shouldered, heavily made-up, and with her bosom squeezed up into a bodice that would blend in well at Oktoberfest in Munich.

"I found this at my front door last night," she said in a strained voice. "I don't know who left it there, but it certainly gives me the creeps. And I almost didn't dare take it inside because I wasn't expecting any deliveries yesterday, and we have to be careful with all this corona. But I took it inside all the same, and the contents really surprised me. Why was it left there for me? And who left it there? It's a bit of a mystery. And then I thought of you. You're on all the front pages today, and I remembered Pauline telling me that you'd visited her house several times to talk about Palle Rasmussen. So that's why I'm here."

Carl looked at the shoebox. It was small and tattered and had a picture of a pair of brown sandals on one end.

"Please tell me you didn't open it, Gertrud."

She nodded with a look of embarrassment. "Yes, I had to. I didn't know what it was or whether it was for me."

"Have you gone through the contents?"

She shook her head. "No, the whole thing is too creepy. But I could see that there were printouts of some emails from Palle Rasmussen on top."

"Well, I'll be damned," exclaimed Carl.

Rose was already pulling on a pair of latex gloves. She carefully removed the lid.

"Do you recognize the box? Was it Pauline's?" asked Carl.

"Er, yes, maybe. She mentioned ages ago that she was keeping some emails in a cardboard box. This is probably it, right? But I don't understand why she sprinkled all that salt over them."

"What the heck are we supposed to make of this?" Carl asked the others when the woman had left.

"It seems to be pointing in all directions at once," said Rose. "If the police had found it at Pauline's place after her body was discovered, it could have incriminated Pauline in connection with Palle Rasmussen's death. She does vent her anger at his badly concealed interest in other women, and, as we all know, jealousy is statistically one of the top motives for murder."

"So Pauline could have been a suspect for the murder? But they didn't find the shoebox. So where could it have been?" asked Carl.

"That's what I want to know. And as our colleagues didn't find it, it must've been removed from her home before they arrived. Or maybe it was never there. Maybe Gertrud Olsen knows much more about this than she's willing to let on."

"Yes, Gertrud could be lying. She might have sprinkled the salt herself. But, sorry to state the obvious, why would she? She's never even been one of our suspects," said Carl.

Rose looked impatient. "We don't have *any* suspects, Carl. You need to stay open-minded. She could have been in love with Pauline. Maybe she killed Pauline Rasmussen in a fit of jealousy."

"Do we agree that Pauline Rasmussen's killer is the same as in all the other cases up on the whiteboard?"

There was a momentary uncertainty, but they were all in agreement.

"Right, then, listen up, team. There's nothing wrong with being open-minded, but if Gertrud Olsen had anything to do with these cases, why on earth would she voluntarily crawl out of the woodwork at this point specifically? As Rose said, we haven't got anything concrete to go on with the death of either Palle or Pauline, so the perpetrator could be absolutely anyone."

"Hang on a minute, Carl," said Assad. "The way I see it, that woman's arms were pretty damn muscular. I mean, she could easily have bashed Wilder's mechanics over the head or overpowered Oleg Dudek or Palle Rasmussen if she wanted to. Or held Pia Laugesen under the water until she kicked the bouquet. It would've been no trouble for her."

"Kicked the *bucket*, Assad. But, yes, you're right. We can't rule out anything. But I'm more inclined to think that the killer is taking us for a ride."

"But taking us for a ride where?" asked Assad.

"It means teasing us, Assad."

"I think the shoebox is a conscious tip-off from the killer. So I agree, the perpetrator *is* taking us for a ride," said Gordon.

"A tip-off about what?" asked Rose. She was looking tired now.

"Something to link everything that has happened lately," interjected Gordon. "We definitely know that Pauline can't have put the shoebox in front of Gertrud's door because she's dead. And we know that the salt in the box has connected the killings up on the whiteboard. So if we put those two things together, we can safely conclude that it's very unlikely that Pauline ended her own life. The killer forced the pills into her, removed the shoebox, sprinkled salt in it, and then delivered it to someone they knew would bring it in to us."

"Hmm. Have you established a connection between our killer and Pauline Rasmussen's death? Are you all thinking the same?" They all nodded in agreement. "Well, I'm with you all there. But why the hell has the killer chosen to share this with us now?"

Assad scratched his beard. "He's getting to us, and that's what he wants. We need to stay focused before the next person is killed. But it's difficult when we're being pulled in different directions simultaneously. And time is running out."

"I'm leaning more toward the killer being a total nutcase," said Rose. "I think he's getting off on leading us so close to finding out who he is. We're dealing with some crazy lunatic."

There was a knock on the door. Before they could react, Marcus walked in with a delegation behind him of menacing-looking colleagues from other departments. Had the time come for Carl to be pilloried?

"I'm sorry to have to inform you of this, Carl, but this is your formal notification that you're being investigated by a joint narcotics team consisting of colleagues from Rotterdam, Slagelse, and Copenhagen in connection with the nail gun case from 2007, and we have a search warrant for your house in Allerød."

Then a few colleagues stepped forward, headed by Police Superintendent Terje Ploug and, right behind him, the legendary Copenhagen narcotics department's Leif Lassen, alias "Sniffer Dog." This was not a group to be taken lightly.

"Aha," he said when Sniffer Dog handed him the search warrant. "And here I was thinking I was just in line for a bollocking after the stunt I pulled on TV yesterday."

"All in good time, Carl, but this takes precedence at the moment."

He read the warrant. "Has a judge really authorized a search of my house in Allerød? That's crazy. What are you hoping to get out of that? The only people living there are Morten Holland with his boyfriend, and Hardy Henningsen."

Terje Ploug took a step forward, and he did not appear to find the situation comfortable. "We're aware of that, Carl, and we're also aware that they've been in Switzerland for months. We need to ask you to come with us. You may be able to assist us during the search."

Carl looked at his colleagues from Department Q, and they all understood the situation.

This was really happening. And it was serious.

The grapevine never failed in Rønneholtparken. So despite the nationwide ban on gatherings, people flocked to the parking lot between the mass of police cars in front of 73 Magnoliavangen when Carl arrived with Marcus Jacobsen.

"What's happened? Is it true that Morten and Hardy are dead? We haven't seen them in ages," someone shouted.

Carl shook his head and tried to look like there was nothing to worry about—even though he was no longer so sure himself.

An army of men wearing white overalls, latex gloves, and shoe covers were inside ensuring that not even a crumb would escape their attention.

It smelled stuffy, but that was not surprising. It had been months since anyone had been in the house. In fact, Carl was not entirely sure exactly when they had left. He felt a sudden tinge of embarrassment that since he had moved in with Mona almost eighteen months ago, he had only visited Hardy three times. Hardy deserved better than that.

"They're looking for money, drugs, and any digital leads, Carl," said Marcus.

"Are they, now! Well, if they happen to find a fortune, it's mine," replied Carl, laughing. Marcus gave him a look as if to remind him to take the situation more seriously.

They found a lot of interesting things, but none of it happened to belong to Carl. Dental retainers of varying sizes, various sex toys that definitely did not match Carl's sexual preferences, pills that looked like they might be steroids, Hardy's adult diapers, and talc. All things that had nothing to do with anyone else, but that was just the way it was with a house search.

When they were finished with the basement and almost done with the first and second floors, Sniffer Dog pointed to the hatch in the ceiling.

"I've got a hunch about up here," he said, climbing the pull-down ladder in four steps.

"Jesus Christ," he blurted out when he popped his head up through the hatch. "We'll have our hands full with this lot."

Carl looked confused and tried to remember what was up there. He had not been in the attic for years and certainly could not remember when that might have been. But he did remember that it was almost emptied when his stepson, Jesper, had grudgingly come to collect the last of his things.

He climbed the ladder and was greeted by Sniffer Dog's rear in front of a wall of cardboard boxes.

Carl could not believe how many boxes there were. He wondered if they were from one of the many times Mika had moved out and back in with his boyfriend, Morten.

"Well, nothing up here is mine, Lassen," he said. "Do you need to make such a mess? Couldn't you at least shut the boxes again when you're finished with them?"

Total silence is normally the best answer, and Sniffer Dog knew it. He was joined up there ten minutes later by three more detectives. Carl did not recognize them, so perhaps they were from the Dutch police.

An hour and a half later, they called him up.

They had pushed all the cardboard boxes to the sides, revealing a small passage all the way down to the gable.

"It's locked, Carl," said one of them, pointing at a suitcase at the far end. "Can you open it for us, please?"

"No, I can't actually," he said. "I don't know who has the key. It's been up here for years. It's probably something my stepson forgot."

But as soon as Carl had said it, he knew that it was not his stepson's.

They carried the suitcase down to the dining table. It was surprisingly heavy for an unassuming suitcase, so their suspicions were already raised.

Terje Ploug pointed at it and nodded when one of the forensic team asked if he should force it open.

But it was going to take more than a simple effort. Apart from the layers of cobwebs caked around the edges of the lid, it turned out that it was also secured with a yellow substance, which someone identified as some sort of super glue.

"Cut into it from the bottom," said Ploug. But that did not turn out to be so simple either, because the entire suitcase was reinforced with two-millimeter-thick metal plates.

It did not look good, and Carl tried to catch Marcus's eye to reassure him that he was equally surprised. But Marcus just stood there as if paralyzed and watched as his colleagues did their work.

They went to get an angle grinder from one of the vans and started cutting into the bottom. The sparks made the shadows dance on the walls around them.

All other activity in the house had now stopped. Everyone was just standing around waiting, and Carl knew that they would not be waiting in vain. Because the more he racked his brain, the more he remembered how his former partner, Anker Høyer—shortly before he, Hardy, and Carl had been shot down in Amager—had asked Carl if he could help him out and store the suitcase because he was going through a divorce and so had nowhere to keep it himself. And for good reason, Anker had never come to collect it again. How could he have when he was well and truly buried?

"It's Anker Høyer's," he said quietly. "I'd forgotten that he put it up there. It's thirteen years since Anker was killed on Amager. You can see from the cobwebs that it's been up there for years."

Terje Ploug looked at him with an expression of pity. As if Carl was not aware himself that the explanation would never hold up.

"And you have no idea what's inside, I suppose?"

At least ten pairs of eyes looked at him, and more than a few were accompanied by smug smiles.

42

DEBORA

Saturday, December 19, 2020

Adam and Debora had met at a Christian revival meeting in Hurup when they were very young, and the rest was history. Within a couple of years, they had two girls, and then they had a boy, who was everything they could have wished for in a son.

When Isak was fifteen, he had completely outgrown his small provincial school. And it was clear to everyone that if Isak was to be given the chance to live up to his intellectual potential, they would all have to move to a larger town with more opportunities.

Isak had his sights set on the University of Copenhagen, so Adam found a job north of the city where he could develop his talents. At the same time as the girls finished college and Debora had more time to help her husband, Adam started up his own business, which within only a few years proved to be very lucrative. During this period, Isak lived at home and never revealed anything about that part of his mind that would prove to be their greatest sorrow.

Isak was in his midtwenties when he died by suicide and completely crushed his parents.

The first indication that he had been bullied came to light at his funeral. Very few people attended, and only two of Isak's friends from university came. And they were very quiet when Debora tearfully asked them if they could shed any light on why Isak had thrown himself in front of a train.

"He mostly kept to himself," said one of them.

Adam did not understand. "I thought our son was a very sociable guy," he said.

The two friends just shrugged.

Debora was unwilling to leave it at that, and the answers she slowly managed to get were difficult to swallow. Systematic bullying carried out with hateful creativity had been part of Isak's life for years. He had been incessantly mocked for his religious background, his intelligence, his kind nature, and his blind faith in the goodness in others. In the end he could barely open his mouth without there being repercussions. Three of his fellow students had ganged up and instigated the most vicious attacks, and Debora and Adam had a burning desire for revenge.

It was only when they first met Sisle that they understood and learned how anger, vengeance, and punishment could go hand in hand. Adam's business developed chemical products, which Sisle's company turned out to be interested in procuring. And during a couple of fruitful meetings with her, it became clear to the couple that they shared a mutual loathing for people's unfortunate ability to hurt one another.

Isak's three tormenters died together one Sunday afternoon without anyone being able to explain why they had hit a tree by the roadside at full speed. The fact that there were scratches on both doors on the driver's side was never taken as sufficient proof that they had been forced off the road. But they had been. The last of the guys fought for his life for twenty minutes, looking imploringly at Debora and Adam to help him. But it was in vain.

At one point, Sisle told them about her time at university. And because that brought to light some aspects from their own lives, they confided in Sisle what they had done. Maybe they had expected her to be outraged, but she only reacted with sympathy.

In many ways it brought them closer together.

And one November day in 1992, Sisle finally shared her plans with them and her intention to expand her one-woman enterprise by bringing more people on board.

The couple in front of her had sentenced their son's tormentors to death, and it had convinced her that the three of them should work together on similar missions in the future. She told them about her relationship with God and conjured a picture of humanity that God in no way would condone.

Adam and Debora understood. In fact, it was Debora who formulated how their collaboration could become a reality. And Sisle immediately recognized how useful her plan would be.

They moved closer to each other and began recruiting women who understood the psychology of vengeance and justice and would be willing to work for the cause.

Debora took it upon herself to select and teach these women to instinctively come down hard on people who were inconsiderate and uncharitable. And when these women were fully trained and had proven their worth and loyalty, Sisle would employ them in her company and finally release them into society so they could punish the sinners of the world.

Just two years later, their setup had become a full-fledged reality. And the more it developed, the more Adam and Debora felt that Isak's death had not been in vain. Through their son, and with Sisle's help, they had realized that people who did not toe the line deserved to taste their own medicine in the name of God.

It was only later that the couple understood the full extent of what Sisle was capable of and wanted to involve them in.

Debora and Adam were initially not fully sold that Sisle's victims deserved their fate. But as Adam in particular enjoyed being part of Sisle's plans and their execution, Debora slowly came around.

"Sisle is absolutely right," said Adam. "Our work and mission make the world a better place. We have God on our side. And as the Bible tells us, his divine justice can be merciless. And we should follow his example."

————

Over the course of twenty-six years, they had selected fourteen men and women who had ruined the lives of others through their self-serving ways. Sisle had developed and adhered to a series of dogmas that had to be met before a murder could take place. Apart from the more symbolic dogmas, it was an essential requirement that the deaths look like accidents. She had made several mistakes in her first attempt of doling out justice when she attacked Ove Wilder's repair shop, but she had honed her skills since then. Before Debora and Adam joined her, she had killed the kingpin of a gang dealing in stolen goods, a man dealing drugs to kids at the school gates, and a woman who committed insurance fraud. And just as planned, these murders were written off by the police as suicides or fatal accidents.

When Adam and Debora joined Sisle, they immediately accepted Sisle's premise that someone unfit to live would be killed every second year, and that the date should coincide with the birthday of someone who had committed crimes against humanity. She also insisted that no forensic evidence from the crime scene could be traced back to them except their discreet signature: they always left salt close to the victim. Apart from the murder of Oleg Dudek, the factory owner whose hands they cut off, during which the blood suddenly splattered Adam's clothes, they had been extremely careful to avoid even the smallest trace of the victim's DNA on them. They had also made sure that the victims did not suffer unnecessarily.

They changed their method from one murder to the next—bleeding to death, shooting, carbon monoxide poisoning, and drowning—so there would not appear to be a pattern. Sisle only changed one of her dogmas when they singled out Franco Svendsen as their next victim. It seemed that with age, she found more pleasure in dragging out the victims' suffering. The result was that the most recent victims were kidnapped and kept hostage for about a month, during which they were broken down through starvation and psychological torture. Debora found the change more difficult to stomach, but she came around when Adam reminded her how they had stood by and watched a young man die. He also told her that he enjoyed this way of getting to know their victims and admonishing them for their wrongdoings.

Debora took responsibility for recruiting new candidates and always made sure there were four women in training at any one time. They had to go through a long and intense course to show their willingness to pick out and punish sinners in society. And the quicker they proved their worth, the quicker they were hired by Sisle's company. Before they were released into society as angels of vengeance, they worked a regular job at the firm, for which they were well compensated. And if anyone proved unable to keep their mouth shut, they were either paid or threatened to keep quiet, or they were simply silenced.

Debora had always been under the impression that their angels of vengeance would be fully self-reliant by the end of 2020, when they had committed their last murder on Boxing Day.

But she no longer felt sure about any of it.

"What do you think Sisle is planning to do now, Adam?" asked Debora. "What do you think will happen when we've done away with Maurits van Bierbek? I'm actually worried that Sisle is starting to take risks. That policeman on TV certainly seemed to know more than I care for. Then we've got Ruth—or Ragnhild Bengtsen, as the police call her. She went off on her own and risked exposing us. She even came to us for protection. And what about Pauline Rasmussen? She also came to our house, and we had no choice but to kill her. I have a sense that this will end badly, Adam."

"But Sisle said that she'll spend the time after Maurits van Bierbek's death terminating our mission."

Debora nodded. "Yes, Adam, exactly. But won't she have to terminate us too?"

"What do you mean?"

"She's got plenty of employees who can replace us. And how many people has she actually killed? Are you sure she's telling us everything? When it comes to it, do we actually know the real number? And don't you think there's a risk she'll make rash decisions and risk exposing all of us?"

It was as if he were unwilling to make eye contact with her. Was he even paying attention?

"Adam, listen to me! We're suddenly more exposed than we realize, so we have to be very careful. I don't want to end up like Lot's wife."

The comparison grabbed her husband's attention. "Listen to me, Debora. Lot's wife was disobedient. She didn't heed God's commands, so he turned her into a pillar of salt. But you're the opposite of her, named after one of the Bible's strongest women. Don't forget that despite her sex, that glorious woman was also a judge and the wisest of her generation. You've been singled out by God for this mission, and Sisle knows it. Do you really think it was a coincidence that she chose us back then? No, it was because of you and what happened to our poor Isak. We have nothing to fear."

Debora observed her husband for some time. Was that why he had sold his business? When it came down to it, this was what he loved more than anything. Killing, calculating their next move together with Sisle, and being her henchman when the need arose.

"All I'm saying is that we should be careful. You call me wise, but then you should also listen to me. When Sisle has finished with Maurits, we need to be on our guard."

43

ASSAD

Saturday, December 19, 2020

The three consecutive calls had made Assad's head spin. Marwa had told him off for working too much and because everything at home was falling apart. And if he did not live up to his responsibility as the head of the family and make himself more present, she was afraid that Ronia would soon run away and Nella would wither away due to their isolation.

Assad promised that he would step it up, but then the telephone rang for the second time. It was Mona, who could not understand why Carl had not returned any of her calls. Assad had to tell her that the nail gun case had returned to haunt them and that Carl was currently in his house in Allerød because the police were searching it. But he stressed that Carl had appeared calm, so it was probably just a storm in a coffee cup.

Unfortunately, what he said was negated by the third call. It was Carl calling to briefly tell him that a suitcase had been found in his attic containing one and a half kilos of cocaine and more than two hundred thousand euros. He was not being placed under immediate arrest because forensics had to analyze the contents of the suitcase first. And it was that information that made him panic momentarily—because if they did unexpectedly find anything that pointed to him, he would not be able to explain how it had happened.

Assad had no idea how to react.

"And, Assad, you should assume that I'm going to be suspended for the time being and have to hand in my badge and service weapon."

"But then you won't be able to get into the office."

"No, but I've got an idea that you can run by the others, because we can't afford to slow down. My suggestion is that we work with one unit at Teglholmen and one at my house. So if you three agree, I want you to pack the most essential material and meet me at my home as soon as you can, Assad."

Rose took the news hardest. "What the *hell* are they playing at? You don't keep something up in your attic for almost fifteen years if you have even the slightest idea about what shit is inside, do you? You either get rid of it—and there are all sorts of ways to do that, like handing it in to the police—or sell the goods and start channeling the money to secret accounts around the world. So why hasn't Carl done either? Obviously because he has nothing to do with the whole thing. And that's final!"

"But how do you know he wasn't planning to do that when he retires? If you're sitting on dirty money, especially that amount of it, you have to wait for years after the crime before you can enjoy it," said Gordon gingerly.

"What did you say, you idiot? Are you seriously sitting there on your skinny ass, insinuating that Carl is a criminal?"

"No, but I—"

"I don't want to hear another word out of you, Gordon. Don't you know Carl?" She turned to Assad. "And what do *you* have to say, Assad? You look like shit!"

Assad raised his head. "I certainly don't feel very good, if that's what you mean. But I'm pretty sure I know Carl. He told me he would call Hardy and discuss matters with him. Maybe they'll be able to piece together what happened back then."

Assad glanced up at the words Carl had written on the window.

They could so far only tick off the question of the significance of the dates. Which of the other points would enable them to crack the case? Where should they direct their attention? If only he knew.

He took out his folder and put the last of the papers in it. "I'll drive over to Carl now, all right? We'll have to set up a long-term Zoom group. Can you deal with that, Gordon?"

The guy nodded, still red-faced after Rose's outburst.

"Don't look so despondent, Assad. I'm not worried that the police will find anything compromising on me, so why should you be?"

Assad shrugged and looked around Mona and Carl's living room. Were they really going to have to work together covertly in Carl's home with Lucia's toys on the floor and Mona pacing back and forth like a caged animal?

Of course Mona was worried, and so was he. If only Carl knew how worried. Why would he want to continue if Carl was forced out of Department Q? If that happened, it would be easier for him to just find another job. He would get to see much more of his family, and they would not have to deal with the endless questions from PET, which they would expect him to answer at some point.

He tried to push it to the back of his mind because someone was going to be killed imminently—and it was a dead certainty if they did not manage to make some headway. Everything else would just have to wait.

"We've looked at the list you wrote on the office window, Carl. Rose and Gordon are working on several of the points, but I think you and I should focus on the salt. What do you think?"

Carl nodded.

"Your question was why they left it at the crime scene. We need to know why someone would do that," Gordon continued.

"I've actually been thinking about where we got to before Marcus, Terje Ploug, and Sniffer Dog interrupted us. I think it was something or other you said that stuck with me."

"What did I say?" asked Assad.

"Well, Rose had just outlined a motive based on how the killer has seemingly only targeted people with extremely poor morals. People who cheat and commit fraud, people who show no consideration for anything or anyone."

"That's right, and then you mentioned that he acted like some sort of moral guardian. You called him a crusader."

"Exactly. But it was you who put that word in my mind. You said that it all seemed almost religious."

"That's right. Don't you think that an idea based solely on murdering immoral people—and without exception on the birthdays of extreme bastards—seems religious?"

"Sodom and Gomorrah, Assad. That's the story that came to me when I was driving home from Allerød. The world stinks just now, and it can't all be blamed on corona. No, these days people only think about themselves. Just like Anker Høyer when he asked to put his shit in my attic. Selfishness overshadows everything good in the world, don't you see it?"

Assad looked puzzled. "Sodom and Gomorrah? Is that something religious?"

Carl smiled. Obviously not a story an Iraqi Muslim would be too familiar with, but then neither would many Danish Christians.

"It's a sad but engaging story from the Old Testament, Assad. It's about two cities, Sodom and Gomorrah, where the inhabitants acted like pigs and went about whoring and raping at will. I don't know the whole story, but there was a man called Lot who enjoyed God's favor, and God sent down a couple of angels of vengeance to warn him that the towns of Sodom and Gomorrah would be destroyed in a fiery storm and that he should take his wife and two daughters and get out of there before it happened. So Lot asked his wife to give the angels salt, as was the custom with guests, but his wife wouldn't give them her own salt, so she borrowed it from their neighbor instead. When they fled from the town, the angels warned them under no circumstances to look back. But Lot's wife did not obey. She turned around and stared back at the wrath of

God only to be instantly turned into a pillar of salt." Carl nodded to himself. "Yeah, it's a story about how the wrath of God can be connected with salt."

"Now I remember it, Carl. The Koran also mentions Sodom and Gomorrah. I'd just forgotten it. But it's about God's punishment against those who sin and show no regard for common decency. Do you think that's the key to the killer's motive? Because if it is, then he *is* some sort of religious fanatic."

Carl nodded and looked at his friend with affection. It was the first time in ages that Assad had been at Carl's home, and even longer since the two of them had been so close during an investigation.

"I hope it's okay that I was listening in?" Mona had come into the living room without them noticing and was standing with her arms folded. It was obvious that she was dying to say something.

"Assad, I'm sure you know that Carl has kept me updated on the case, so I feel quite confident that I can follow your reasoning. I'm thinking that a truly and genuinely religious person lives with a number of implicit boundaries in relation to what they can and can't do. Fanatics clearly make up their own rules, I get that, but they are still governed by everything their religion is founded on. And that's what makes me doubt whether your killer is sufficiently familiar with what you can and can't do as a servant of God. Contrary to religious fanatics, who almost always refer directly to a specific religion or sect in relation to a violent act, there is no explanation for why this killer views themselves as a servant of God. If you ask me, it isn't a religion but a particular event in the killer's life that set this insane project in motion."

"But what could that be, Mona? That's what we need to know. What sort of person would go down the path of becoming a crazy mass murderer?"

She looked at Carl with a withered smile and tired, heavy eyes. She had not forgotten for a second about the precarious situation she and her family now found themselves in. That much was clear.

She pointed a clenched hand toward them and raised one finger.

"Hypothetically, I think the killer holds a grudge about an old case. And this grudge has only been strengthened by this whole crusade, as you call it, Carl."

Then came another finger.

"And this event that hit the killer so hard dates from so many years ago that you can with some certainty assume that it's from before 1988, which was the year of the first murder you're working on."

And another finger.

"We know that the killer has shown great determination with these murders and so is probably equally as determined in all other aspects of life. I'm thinking that this would require certain significant financial resources, because some of the killings call for an insane amount of preparation and time."

She pointed another finger.

"And we're looking at an extremely patient person who doesn't just go about killing at random. By only killing every second year, they are demonstrating how cautious they are. In my opinion, the killer must be very cunning and extremely well organized."

And now came the last finger.

"When you look at the complexity of the murders, I feel very certain that your killer is also a team player. You're dealing with a leader with disciples around them."

Assad nodded. "An intelligent, patient team player who is probably rich and had once been subjected to something serious that offended their morals. So do you think that he feels a sense of injustice?"

Mona nodded. "Absolutely. And I think that he believes his actions are just. The symbolism certainly points in that direction. The salt is some sort of sign of being God's vengeful angel, and all that strange business with the birthdays of world tyrants is just another way to confirm that these killings are committed in the name of God."

"Do you really think the murderer believes that?" asked Carl. "I mean, chopping the hands off Oleg Dudek, drowning Pia Laugesen in her own pool, injecting potassium chloride into men like Franco Svendsen and Birger von Brandstrup, who were also almost starved to death. It's completely psychopathic, Mona."

"Exactly. But a true psychopath very rarely feels the need to justify their actions."

The phone rang, and Carl's daughter came running in with it in her outstretched hand. Assad almost could not remember the time when Nella or Ronia had been Lucia's age. Had they really once been such innocent little creatures?

Carl frowned when he took the call, and two minutes of almost complete silence in the room felt like an eternity. Then he hung up and looked at Assad.

"I can't remember every detail, Assad. But Gordon and Rose have just about managed to fill all the gaps on the whiteboard. Of the eight cases we hadn't identified yet, there are only two left. The other six all concern people who could be said to have made themselves known in society for all the wrong reasons, and it won't come as any surprise to you that they all met atypical ends on the birthdays of tyrants: Lenin, Gaddafi, Mussolini, Ferdinand Marcos, to name just a few. Maybe you remember the Bobo Madsen case? It wasn't so long ago, 2014 to be exact."

Assad looked at Mona, who seemed to be racking her brain. It was not exactly a name one would forget.

"He died in a horseback riding accident on November 25, 2014, on the birthday of the Chilean dictator and mass murderer Augusto Pinochet."

"Oh," said Mona, suddenly remembering. "Bobo Madsen was the one who supplied payday loans with sky-high interest, right?"

Carl gave her a thumbs-up. "Yes, and it was totally aboveboard. He was a professional loan shark specializing in payday loans. The loans were normally for very small amounts and targeted at regular people with enticing adverts that definitely didn't send any warning signals, but that's the way it is with payday loans. A loan of ten thousand kroner could easily increase to two hundred thousand kroner if the person didn't keep up their repayments, which could be hard due to the exorbitant interest rates that Bobo Madsen charged."

"Okay, yeah, I also remember the debate about payday loans when his body was found," said Assad. "But it didn't change anything, did it?"

Carl snorted. "As long as there are people willing to offer loans, there'll be people who are too shortsighted to consider the consequences. And no, the law wasn't changed."

Mona looked confused.

"But he died in a horseback riding accident, didn't he?"

"Yes, you're not wrong there. He quite literally lost his head when he galloped into an overhead electrical cable that had fallen down into the trees."

"Oh yeah, now I remember," she said. "People made macabre jokes about the accident, didn't they? I think it was to do with his adverts saying that people shouldn't lose their head if they needed money because they could just borrow it from Bobo Finance."

Carl and Assad looked at each other.

So an advert could also turn out to be fatal in a very literal way.

44

MAURITS

Sunday, December 20, 2020

The room was heated, but still Maurits felt like it was freezing cold. His entire body was shaking and his jaw was clenched. However, despite his suffering and misery, he felt an odd sense of calm. *Starvation is a merciful way to die*, he thought. Just like freezing to death, the body adapts to the inevitable. You go into hibernation and your heartbeat slowly stops.

Maurits had always been the first to put on his running shoes in the morning, and he had gone to the gym four times a week—at least before the lockdown. So for many years he had had a stable resting pulse rate between fifty and sixty. But not anymore.

His pulse had increased steadily in the first few days without food or water. It was as if his heart wanted to push every blood cell to the extreme to provide his body with nutrition. But because there was no nutrition to send, his pulse quickly dropped again. Over the last twenty-four hours, Maurits had sensed all too urgently that his bodily functions were shutting down and that his pulse was growing weaker by the hour.

I'll probably die if it drops below twenty-five, he thought. Maurits searched for his pulse on his wrist, and, when he finally found it, he counted again. Twenty-eight beats per minute. It was nothing.

For the tenth time since the man had bolted the slider above him, he stood up with his legs feeling like jelly, gathered all the strength he could muster, and ran toward the far wall to see if the bolt might budge.

The jolt to his torso almost made him lose consciousness, so Maurits huddled on the floor, holding his stomach, and he knew that this would be his last attempt. The ladder and the wrench were still over there on the table in the promised land that he would never be able to reach.

"Dear God, just let me die," he whispered. "Just let me lie here and die on the floor. I'm ready."

Lying sprawled on the concrete floor attached to his chains, he heard a kind of jangling sound down by the elevator door. But he had hallucinated before, so it could be anything: recurring thoughts of moisture on his lips, imagined embraces, memories of past embraces that perhaps he had not appreciated enough. A faint hope of being rescued from above, below, anywhere.

Maurits closed his eyes and just let the sounds be.

"Try to cooperate, Maurits. Stand up. We'll support you," someone said as he felt his arms being pulled.

"He's become extremely weak," said a higher-pitched voice. "What's his pulse?"

"Twenty-seven."

"I'll hold him up on the chair while you fix the drip, Adam."

Maurits tried to open his eyes but did not succeed. If it was not for the flowery scent emanating from the person holding his shoulders, he would have thought it was death itself coming to claim him.

He felt something happening on the back of his hand and then the sudden stream of life flowing through him. It was so powerful that he became nauseated.

"Stop," he whispered. "Go away and leave me alone." But someone held him in a tight grip.

Then he opened his eyes and saw the two hands with bloodred nails that were holding him.

"There you go, Maurits. That's it," said the man in front of him. "Good thing we came by today, don't you think?"

It was the man with the twisted face, and the bastard was smiling.

Now the hands let go of his arms, and he sensed the person behind him straightening up. She walked around and stood next to the big man.

Although her hair, clothes, and makeup were different, Maurits immediately recognized the woman who had kidnapped him. It was the eyes that gave her away. They always did. He had told the camera crew on his various reality series time and again to zoom in on the participants' eyes. The eyes bore witness to people's innermost feelings: passion, disappointment, and fear. But her eyes revealed no such emotion, just cold, empty, and merciless.

"What do you want from me? You'd better keep me alive if you're after money," he attempted. "I have plenty. Give me a number and it's yours. Just give me something to eat and a computer and I'll wire the money to you. And then you can release me somewhere—wherever you want."

The woman scowled. "Do you think I'd have shown you my face if I was going to let you go?"

Maurits did not answer.

"You have to understand that there are very few people I hate as much as you, Maurits."

"Well, thanks, the feeling is mutual," he whispered.

"And my hatred toward you is certainly well deserved. You've been selected from among many candidates who've been in the running over the last two years. No one turned out to be quite as cynical as you."

She bent down, picked up a scrapbook from the floor, and opened it. "Just look at yourself," she said, pointing at the two-page newspaper article. "Look at your smile as you're talking about what you can convince people to do to each other or themselves in your reality shows." She leafed through the next pages and pointed at each of them. Articles illustrated with brilliant photos that showed the successful businessman in a flattering light. At least that was what he had thought until now.

"Do you recognize yourself, sitting there with a flirtatious look as you try to convince the journalist that the participants in your reality shows are free to leave whenever they want?"

"Yes, and they did always have the choice. That's the way it's always been with my shows," he answered in a strained voice.

He was taken by surprise as the large man hit him across the ear. He did not hit very hard, but it still made Maurits jolt.

Be careful what you say, Maurits, you might still be able to get through to her, he thought.

She closed the scrapbook and put it under her arm. "You've polluted the lives of Danes and many others with your twisted morals, and you've tried to convince us that humiliation, adultery, disloyalty, and brutality are character traits worth striving for. You've turned ordinary, insignificant individuals into monsters and made them role models for other weak souls. No one in the media has been able to ignore your perverted ideas. And that's why we have to stop you. I'm sure you realize that now."

"Yes, but why me? I'm not the only one producing TV shows like that."

The man instinctively hit him again, but harder this time. A monotonous ringing in his ear drowned out the sound of his own moaning.

Maurits was about to respond in spite of his pain, but they had already turned around and were walking toward the table at the far wall.

They were talking quietly between themselves, rummaging in a bag and producing things from it that looked like hospital equipment from where he was sitting.

Now the man walked over to him again. Maurits saw his giant hand raised in the air and pulled back in his seat, trying to shield his face with one arm.

"Don't worry," said the man. "We won't touch you again today. I just need this."

He pulled the drip out of the back of Maurits's hand and wheeled the stand with the almost full drip bag down to the table.

"Please give me something to drink," he said quietly. "Even just tap water, please."

The big man nodded and returned with a glass filled with water.

When he pressed it against Maurits's numb lips, he could barely feel the glass. But what he could feel was the water not only streaming from the corners of his mouth down onto his chest but also the refreshing liquid trickling over his tongue and moistening his throat. He craned his neck toward the glass as the man took it away and followed it with his eyes until it was placed back on the table.

Now the woman came over to him. "We've decided to come back at least one more time to feed you, Maurits. But you'll have to do something for us in return."

She spread out her arms, but he did not accommodate her appeal. "I won't do anything if you don't let me go," he said in a clearer voice than before.

She tilted back her head and looked at him down her nose.

"Don't think that anyone is coming to your rescue, Maurits. Don't get your hopes up. So you can either obey and spend your last days without suffering or you can take the consequences."

"My wife will find me. The police will identify the car you picked me up in, and you lot will end your days in prison."

"Firstly, your wife hasn't reported you missing, so no one even knows that you are. Secondly, we've hacked your password and have been emailing your wife on your behalf over the last week. But of course you couldn't have known that. Your wife is still under the impression that you're currently in the U.S. to complete one of the biggest ever takeovers in Danish history. She won't disturb you unnecessarily—in fact, you've asked her not to yourself—so you just write to each other. And she always waits for you to write first. We've kept a very intimate tone on your behalf when replying to her hopeful emails. But you have told her you won't make it home for Christmas."

The woman's eyes seemed to light up when she told him.

"You people are sick," he said bravely as the beacon of hope inside him grew fainter.

"We've come to the point where your wife will probably be asked to pose a new type of question, and you'll have to answer them if you want to avoid us torturing you."

"You can answer however you want. Isn't that what you're doing anyway?"

"Maybe she'll ask questions only you could know the answer to."

Maurits zoned out momentarily. What was the woman saying?

"You're so full of shit! My wife is starting to suspect that there's something up with those emails. I just know it."

"I'll make it easy for you. Will you give us the answers or not?"

The woman in front of him was as cold as ice. Considering how far they had already taken this, his answers would not save him anyway.

"You can do whatever you want with me. You're going to kill me anyway."

But Maurits did not mean it. He did not want to be tortured. He did not want to suffer. All he wanted was for them to leave him alone.

"Tell me when and how you're going to do it and I might cooperate," he said.

"Okay, Maurits. Now you know that you won't be going home for Christmas, but I can promise you that we won't take away your Christmas spirit."

"When and how? Tell me! If you won't, you might as well just kill me right now!" he shouted.

She nodded to the man next to the table.

"Adam is going to hold up a syringe in front of him. This is the one we're going to use. It will hurt, but only for a moment, and then you'll be at peace."

Maurits looked in horror at the enormous syringe in the giant's hand and expected to break out in a sweat. But he knew that it was an illusion, because he was too dehydrated to sweat anymore.

The woman leaned in toward him as if she had something to tell him in absolute confidence. "You're asking when, Maurits, and to that I can only reply that you'll have to wait for Mao."

Maurits breathed in as deeply as he could. "What do you mean? Tell me when," he said again.

"You'll know when the time comes. I never reveal the date to my victims."

My victims, she said. So this was not the first time.

He stared for a moment at the syringe, which the monster down there was holding up proudly in front of him. Then he caught her unwavering eye.

"So be it. You can kill me, but I won't cooperate with scum like you."

"Well, then I suggest you beg God to forgive your sins while you're waiting," she said.

"*My* sins! What about your sins?"

"Maurits, Maurits. God is connected to all souls. But only souls who pray are connected to God. Only they can receive forgiveness. And that is precisely the difference between you and me."

45

CARL

Monday, December 21, 2020

A poke to the stomach, a poke to the chest, and then a warm waft of vanilla across his face. A gentle tug on his cheek, a quiet chuckle, and finally he was torn from the whirling thoughts in which his dream had kept him.

Carl slowly opened his eyes and looked directly into a pair of mischievous blue eyes that emanated endless devotion.

"Time to get down from Daddy's tummy, Lucia. He's not really awake yet," he heard Mona say as she grabbed their daughter and lifted her up.

"It's seven thirty, and I'm heading down to the nursery now with Lucia. Gordon called half an hour ago and asked if you could pop down to the office even though you're suspended. I don't think it sounds like the best idea, but it's your call. He said for you to wait outside and one of them would come to pick you up by the main door as soon as the receptionist leaves her desk. Apparently there's something they're dying to show you."

Carl tried to stay awake. It was that bloody case. He just could not get it off his mind.

"You were really tossing and turning last night, Carl. I had to take an extra melatonin to get a bit of sleep myself."

"It's just that case," he heard himself say sleepily as his eyelids shut again.

"Yes, that really is some case. It's all over the tabloids on the internet. One of them wrote, 'Is Your Neighbor a Murderer?' and another wrote, 'Police Investigator Sends Shock Waves.' They're talking about you as some sort of icon in the force, so you should prepare yourself for being in the spotlight. Get yourself up and have a think about your game plan so you don't get caught out."

She just managed to say goodbye and "wave goodbye to Daddy, Lucia" before he could muster the energy to check his watch.

Carl was not really sure what to make of these latest developments. He had managed to kick-start something he no longer had control over.

But had that not been his intention?

Carl was leaning up against the wall next to the glass façade of the police station on Teglholmen. It was a dark and cold morning, so he straightened his face mask and turned up his collar, which also helped him to remain unnoticed by his colleagues walking past.

Assad appeared at the front door with an expression of defiance and determination. Was it because he resented his boss being painted as a pariah or was it because the case had taken an unexpected turn? Carl was hoping it was the latter.

"Hit me," said Carl when they were inside.

"Hit you? Why would I hit you?" asked Assad with a cheeky smile, elbowing Carl in the side. "We can always have a few rounds later if you insist."

Rose and Gordon were waiting in the office. They had not looked so alert in a long time.

"Look at that," said Assad, pointing at the whiteboard.

Carl sat down and scanned their work.

Apart from a few gaps, the whiteboard was now almost full. They had added dictators including Kim Jong-il, Jean-Bédel Bokassa, Vladimir

Ilyich Lenin, Muammar Gaddafi, Jean-Claude "Baby Doc" Duvalier, and Benito Mussolini to the list of dictators' birthdays.

Rose, Gordon, and Assad stood shoulder to shoulder opposite him like old scientists who had just solved a mysterious and impossible equation and clearly demanded their project leader's unreserved praise and recognition.

"So this is where we've got to now," said Gordon when Carl did not say anything. "What do you think?"

Carl took his time. When the media got news of this case, the prime minister's press conferences would be no match. This would make all the headlines again.

What he saw on the whiteboard was nothing short of madness. In the records going back over two hundred years, there had only been three cases of serial murder in the country. And they certainly had not been as systematic or unusual. This was not a case of defenseless infants or some random junkie prostitutes who had been singled out as easy victims by a sadistic woman hater. The victims here had been carefully selected, and most of them were active and successful members of society. Unlike more conventional murders where it could be established with great certainty that they had been committed with full intent, these cases had all been written off as accidents or suicides. It was sheer luck that they had even been able to ascertain that some of these deaths were murders because they had been committed with such a degree of cunning. So unless the murderer was caught, he would be free to continue unchallenged. And the tragic fact remained that after sixteen verified murders, they had still not succeeded. And it was all the more tragic because a seventeenth victim would in all likelihood be added to the count in only five days. How were they supposed to prevent it?

Carl looked down the list of birthdays and shuddered.

"Those names are enough to make your blood run cold," he whispered as his eyes scanned over names like Ceaușescu, Hitler, and Mao.

He read the years on the whiteboard. There was no doubt now that their theory of a murder every two years held.

Rose looked flushed with excitement, but her skin looked unhealthy, which was no wonder, considering her lack of sleep lately. "We're aware that some of the crimes committed by the victims might come across as insignificant," she said. "But Gordon and I have looked a bit more into their backgrounds, organizations, and networks. And, as we suspected, they've all grossly overstepped the boundaries of decent human behavior."

She pointed at the item "Murder Method" on the whiteboard and chose a couple of the entries.

"The victim in 1990 dealt in stolen goods, but they were always extremely valuable. We're talking about hundreds of millions of kroner a year, which easily exceeds the profit of many listed companies. It was just never proven beyond doubt who stood behind it, so no one was ever punished. Not until our killer struck anyway."

Carl was not sure he liked the term "our."

"Another example," she continued, "was the couple Helene and Georg Bernados, who, for over a decade, starting from the mideighties, ran a ruthless gang that tricked the elderly and disabled out of large sums of money. They paid for it with their lives in 1996 on Lenin's birthday, April twenty-second. And then there was the guy who was killed in 2008 on Mussolini's birthday, July twenty-ninth. He was the owner of a haulage company that drove pigs and cattle to slaughter in southern Europe under horrendous conditions."

It was obvious that Gordon wanted to add something, but Rose continued.

"All these victims were extremely callous. And the more you read about them, the more disgusted you feel," she said.

Strangely, Assad shrugged. "The killer puts me in mind of the camel who farted so much that the air was thick and moist under the rider, but he still managed to get through the desert."

Carl shook his head. Where the hell was the man going with this bizarre comparison at a serious time like this?

"All I'm saying is that just like with the camel, you almost end up liking the killer," mumbled Assad.

"What do you mean?"

"Just think how many mean bastards he has rid the world of. Doesn't that count for something?"

Carl and his two colleagues looked at Assad. They couldn't totally deny that the thought had also struck them.

"But who the hell does things like this? It's complete madness," said Carl. "And how do we move on from here? What about the missing pages in Palle Rasmussen's file, Gordon? And what about the deleted computer files? When can we expect to hear back from NC3?"

Gordon smiled impatiently.

"Well, that's what I've been wanting to say. Even though it didn't amount to much, NC3 managed to restore most of the deleted files. They sent them to me late yesterday, so I've been up all night reading and reading."

At least that explained the bags under his eyes.

"Unfortunately, there are only a few scattered fragments left of Palle Rasmussen's email correspondence, but we already have printed versions of most of it. Even though there wasn't much to go on, it's still surprising how open he is about his sadomasochism in these emails. I found at least four or five where he describes in detail what turns him on. And also one in which someone writes to him that they find him disgusting. If it had been today, the MeToo movement would have strung him up by his balls. He really managed to turn sexually offensive behavior and harassment into an art form. I won't go into detail about what he suggests that people could do with each other's genitals, but I've chosen one example from the day before he died that I think might be a useful lead for us."

He leaned in over the desk and read aloud.

You can forget all about intimate encounters in public places, and stop fucking sticking your nose up places where the sun never shines. What do you take me for, you little tease, are you an idiot? And stop stalking me, you scarred bitch. If you want anything to do with me, you'll have to go all the fucking way and . . .

Gordon looked at them apologetically. "Yeah, that's all I've got of that email."

"*Haqana*," exclaimed Assad. "Well, knock me up with a feather."

Carl wanted to tell him that the correct idiom was "knock me down with a feather" but thought better of it. He suspected that Assad sometimes did know the real idiom and was just pulling their legs. But flippant or not, he was right. This was really interesting.

"Haven't we been thinking all along that this might be a possibility?" asked Rose.

"Yes, I think I considered it the very first time I spoke with Sisle Park. You'd be hard-pressed to find a more slippery sort." Carl nodded to himself. "This appears to explain the connection between the two emails from May sixteenth and seventeenth, 2002. Can you find them, Gordon?"

They sat in silence while he leafed through the file. He stopped and looked at them for a moment before he started reading. "This is the one from May sixteenth," he said.

Dear Palle. I hope you don't feel this is an imposition, but I don't feel like we finished our chat last time. We can meet at Café Sommersko the day after tomorrow, on Saturday, around four, when I'll be in Copenhagen. What do you say? Do you have time? Sisle.

"And this is the one from May seventeenth."

Palle. Your political meeting in Nørrebro Sports Hall the other day made an impression on me. I don't know how to express it, but I would, as you know, love to meet you again. You probably noticed that I sat down in the third row just in front of you and asked someone to move so that I could make eye contact with you. I will contact you ASAP.

"Very interesting," said Carl. "Palle Rasmussen point-blank refuses to meet the sender of the email face-to-face in a public place, which was no doubt symptomatic of his affairs. And he simultaneously mocks the sender and, in my opinion, very consciously tries to provoke her. And the next day in her email from May seventeenth, when she very directly asks to meet him, he doesn't mince his words when he replies that if she wants something from him, then she'll have to go all the way, as we can see in this last note Gordon just dug up. He is no longer just titillated but totally turned on."

"Can we be sure that Sisle Park wrote both the emails?" asked Rose, even though she did not seem to harbor any doubts.

"I think so, yes. And she knew how to get Palle Rasmussen exactly where she wanted him. He's burning with desire for her and can't stop thinking about what he's going to do with her. And so he inadvertently made himself a willing victim. Tying his hands probably just turned him on even more."

"I don't understand any of it," mumbled Assad. "Why would such an intelligent woman sign off with her real name? Don't you think Sisle Park is just being made an escape goat here?"

Carl smiled at Assad's choice of words, but he was right. Why did she do that?

"He calls her 'you scarred bitch.' Is that just an insult, or was she scarred in some way? It should be possible for us to find out," said Rose.

"Are you suggesting that we just strip her down and perform a thorough body search?" asked Carl.

"I'm just saying that if she has had treatment for her scars, we should be able to check up on it."

Gordon shook his head. "You won't get anywhere with that, not with the data protection regulations we have in this country. Any sort of health records would be especially hard to get our hands on these days."

"Sisle Park has a sizable business. She's one of the few women who have managed to break the glass ceiling. Try MediaINFO—there's bound to be loads of articles about her in women's magazines," said Carl.

"I've checked. There's nothing," said Gordon.

"That's odd. Do we have any other details about her life?"

"Born May thirtieth, 1964, as Lisbeth Park in Nørresundby to a

single mother, Dagny Park Iversen. She has written on Facebook that
Sisle was a nickname her mother gave her. She graduated from high
school in Aalborg when she was eighteen. She enrolled in a degree in
chemistry at the University of Copenhagen in 1982 and graduated summa
cum laude in 1989."

"In chemistry?"

"Yeah, followed by an MBA from the University of Cape Town, where
she also lived and worked on and off for almost three years."

"Well, I'll be damned. But if she is so intelligent, why did it take her
seven years to complete her chemistry degree?"

"No idea," answered Gordon.

"What about partners, Gordon?" asked Rose.

"She didn't have any as far as I know."

Rose brought up a photo of her on Google from a conference. "It's
weird. If I were as rich, slim, and beautiful as she is, I wouldn't be struggling so much to find a man."

Carl saw the hurt expression on Gordon's face. When would the boy
get over the crush he had on Rose?

"I'm still thinking about the fact that she studied chemistry," said
Assad quietly. "If anything can cause scars, it's chemicals splashing on
you or exploding near you."

Carl smiled. "I don't think someone like her, someone who managed
to get an MBA, would randomly throw around acid, Assad."

There was a knock on the office door. It was Marcus, standing with
what was now a permanent cloud hanging over him. And Carl knew
what was coming.

"Why are you here, Carl? You're not supposed to be here." He looked
very unhappy. "But we were just about to call you, so seeing as you've
sneaked in anyway, we need to have a little word with you."

"Little word" was not a promising expression. It was as good as guaranteed to include the narcotics team, Terje Ploug, and a couple of people
from human resources.

Marcus led the way past his own office to a small side room that was normally used for questioning people being held in custody. That did not bode well.

The five people present did not exactly look friendly. They looked like the idiot across from them had already been sentenced—and that was not a good feeling when the idiot in this case was him.

It turned out to be a very formal and short meeting. The outcome was not unexpected—he was being charged in what they referred to as the Høyer case.

"As long as the investigation is ongoing, you are not free to leave the country. Oh, and Merry Christmas," said the man from internal affairs who had led the questioning. Sniffer Dog should not have smiled so gleefully at the last remark. Carl did not forget that sort of thing.

"Stay away from this investigation and Department Q, Carl. If I find you here again, I'll have no choice but to let you be arrested."

"You can't be serious, Marcus! Think about what you're saying, damn it. We're so close to a breakthrough in the case. You can't just put a stop to it."

"What you've managed to achieve so far is great work, but you'll have to leave it to your colleagues from this point on."

Carl was speechless. "Last question, Marcus: Do I have your support if I need it?"

"It depends what for."

"Someone is going to be killed in five days. We have a suspect. We need free rein on this."

"Carl." He placed a hand on his shoulder. "You need to use all your energy to prove your innocence. All the cash from the suitcase is currently being checked for fingerprints. If we find just one that's been through your fingers, you risk going down for a very long time. I suggest you go home to Mona and prepare her for what might well be a difficult time ahead for both you and her."

46

SISLE

Tuesday morning, December 22, 2020

She had stood quietly and reflected at this exact spot every year since 1988 in the run-up to Christmas, staring at the little headstone, and now there was one more. Two headstones that rested gently against each other and finally united two tragic fates, which Sisle, and Sisle alone, had to bear the responsibility for.

"I'm so terribly sorry, Maja," she whispered, bending down.

With a gentle touch, she let her fingers glide over the raw sandstone. Not since her student days had she been able to cry over anyone other than little Max, who had been laid to rest here. But now that Maja's name had joined him on the headstone next to his, she felt an enormous tug on her heartstrings.

She had asked herself the same question at least a thousand times. Would she have changed everything, even if it meant that those monsters would still be alive today, if only she with God's help could have spared the little boy? She just did not know. But since that innocent little boy had paid with his life, she had promised herself that methods like setting off explosives, which could risk the lives of innocent victims, could never be used again.

No, after that fateful January day in 1988, her victims had to die alone and in the full knowledge of why.

She turned her head to the empty burial plot next to Maja and the little boy. She had paid for the plot for over thirty years so that one day, when the time came, she could be laid to rest side by side with the boy whom her carelessness had deprived of life. Max would have been a grown man in his midthirties today. She had so far stolen almost twelve thousand days from that little life. Twelve thousand days in which his mother had to live with her unbearable grief and crushed dreams.

Her torment was indescribable.

When Maja killed herself, Debora had asked Sisle if the pain of those left behind due to her other victims did not also trouble her.

That question was the first sign that Sisle was possibly losing her grip on Debora and perhaps also Adam. It was exactly questions like that which could never be asked. Debora knew full well that their victims had been on borrowed time because they had—of their own free will and with their eyes fully open—chosen to go down the path of immorality and carry out their misdeeds. And so neither could Debora allow herself to doubt that the relatives of the victims also carried the responsibility for not having tried to stop their partners' evil and cynical business dealings. *Those who voluntarily live with someone who makes their living from dishonesty, hurting animals, or who lures the poor into financial ruin does not deserve the least compassion*, she had preached time and time again. Was it not true that the victims and their relatives had benefited from a comfortable life facilitated by their despicable and brutal actions? So why should they feel sorry for them when it all came crashing down? All she did was save the children from growing up in a sick environment. She simply could not understand the reason for Debora's question.

Lately, those two had even tried to encourage her to deviate from her principles and kill their victim before his time had come. It was totally against everything their work stood for. And what might the next thing be?

She could easily lose her grip on Adam and Debora, especially now that a busybody policeman was trying to put a wrench in the plan and stop them.

Sisle knelt down and gently placed an inconspicuous bunch of flowers up against the boy's headstone. She wished that she had been able to do this many times before now, but Maja had been alive and could have reacted to the gesture. It had been too risky.

She slowly stood up and zigzagged along the paths between the other graves until she found what she was looking for.

LARS K. PEDERSEN was written on the headstone. The ravages of time had already made it impossible to read the date of death, but Sisle knew it better than anyone. It was the day when God had chosen and spared her. She, the only righteous one of the seven struck by the lightning. She, the only one in the group who could distinguish between right and wrong.

In the first few years, she had spat on the graves of Lars K. Pedersen and the other five, but then one day Debora had introduced her to what she called the just and better path.

Without precisely these people, you would never have discovered God, Sisle. You should be grateful to them that you received your God-given task, for which they had to sacrifice their lives.

"Thank you, Lars," she said, nodding toward the neglected grave.

Now Maja was gone and the police were involved. It was time to let her disciples take over here and start her mission anew somewhere else.

Echoes bounced off the ceiling of the large reception area as she walked toward the elevator in her leather heels. Most of her employees had now been sent home for a few days and only the most senior and trusted were awaiting her up on the third floor, where the meeting room was located.

This meeting was one she had been looking forward to for a long time.

She nodded to the three women from the welfare department who sat looking expectant. Everything was as it should be.

"Welcome, and thank you for making yourselves available on this strangest of days. Do feel free to take your face masks off, and you can keep them off as long as we all remain seated."

She nodded at each of them. What an elite group, what a sight for heaven!

"When my mission is completed on Boxing Day, I will disappear. In other words, I will no longer be among you. But your individual tasks are laid down, as are the plans for the future of the company. As you are all already aware, each of you will be entrusted with disposing of a particular individual, according to carefully planned timetables. I know each of you is already planning how such a murder should be carried out without running the risk of being caught. And you should know that I have complete faith that you will all succeed. From now on, I will act as your coordinator, and, as such, I will need to accept the plans of each person present. The person with the scheme most likely to be completed will carry out the first killing, so naturally you cannot know the exact time for when you will be called upon to act."

She pointed at the person who had raised her hand. Nora. One hundred percent dedicated and at least two hundred percent qualified. The best in the group so far.

"Do you have a question, Nora?"

"Yes, thank you. When will we be informed about the target group?"

Sisle smiled. Who other than Nora could ask the question right in the second before the answer was about to be given? In every way a woman with true leadership potential.

"That is precisely why we're gathered here today. This is the moment I have decided to share that with you."

Three pairs of shoulders fell back into place. The tension was finally released.

"Our goal, every four months beginning in 2021, is to identify a municipal or national politician who has committed an offense against the moral guidelines that must be heeded by every person who takes on the great responsibility that democracy demands of them. Abuse of power, greed, cheating, corruption, disloyalty, violations, lies . . . yes, that's enough to start with. I see you're already nodding."

Nora had her hand up again. Like the two others, she was smiling— presumably in anticipation of release after their long period of training, beginning as aspirants with Debora and subsequently becoming high-level trainees in Sisle's organization.

"What about when we have completed our assignment?"

Once again she had beaten Sisle to the mark.

"I'll tell you. Each of you will be assigned your own personal trainee, whom you will train to replace you and carry out the next killing. Then you'll disappear. You will be well compensated, so you can relocate to another country and finally start a family, if that's what you want. As you have no doubt understood, it's unavoidable that Denmark will go into a state of alert after a certain number of killings of this sort. Regardless of how well you manage to cover up the killings, it isn't possible to kill elected people to this extent without there being a risk of significantly increased investigation and security."

"Like Carl Mørck from Department Q has started just now?"

"Carl Mørck!" Sisle smiled. "Don't you worry about him. Like so many others, his days are numbered. And there are not many left."

47

LAURA VAN BIERBEK

Monday, December 21, and Tuesday, December 22, 2020

There was no sign of Christmas cheer in the van Bierbek family home. The oldest daughter in the family, who was fifteen years old, had been shouting and complaining all day, getting herself into a state that revealed the worst in her, and all because the best shops in the capital were now closed, so she would not be able to get what she wanted.

That was just how Laura van Bierbek was when she wanted something. She had always been a spoiled brat without any boundaries who only needed to look imploringly with her blue eyes at her father to twist him around her little finger into getting his wallet out. And now that he was not here, now that she was forced to be in the house all day, now that she could not go to school and flirt with the boys in the year above, and now that she could not even count on Christmas presents and the New Year's Eve party she and Søsser had been talking about for months, she could no longer control her temper and gave her tantrum full rein.

"Give it a rest, Laura," said her mother in an effort to get her to stop her antics.

Who wanted to listen to that woman? thought Laura. She only bothered to get dressed properly if they had guests; otherwise she just sat there all day long in her slightly too flimsy nightgown with a cigarette in her mouth and a glass in one hand. It was disgusting!

"We'll get Roxan to fix us something delicious. What would you like, darling?" her mother said in an attempt to appease her, but Laura slammed her bedroom door and sat down in front of her laptop. If it had not been for Zoom, she would have gone completely crazy.

Her friend Søsser was especially good company. She knew risqué stories and told her all about what you should do with boys in your bedroom when nobody was looking.

"Hi, Søs. What's up? Are you also dying of boredom?"

Her friend looked at the screen with tired eyes that said it all. "I take it you've heard everything is closed right up until the middle of January?" she said.

Laura nodded.

"What's your dad got to say about all this shit?" asked Søsser.

"No idea, he isn't back yet."

"Where is he? He's been gone for ages now. Is he not even coming home for Christmas?"

"No, it's so fucking annoying. Mom says he won't be home until Boxing Day or the day after. It's all these COVID tests and quarantine that are holding him up."

"Well, at least he'll have presents with him."

"He'd better have!"

"Where is he exactly? Do you still not know?"

"We think he's in California, but Mom's not sure."

Søsser tilted her head a little. She normally had no idea how to look serious, but now it seemed like she had discovered how to do it.

"What's up, Søs? You look weird."

"I'm not sure, but I said to my dad yesterday that he shouldn't expect to play golf with your dad anytime soon because he still hadn't come home. And guess what he said to my mom later that night when they thought I wasn't listening?"

Laura doubted whether she wanted to hear it. She had eavesdropped on their dads when they talked out on the terrace. And she did not like what she had heard.

"He said that he was sure that your dad was messing around with another lady again, and that it was wrong that he didn't just come clean."

"I don't believe a word of it. My mom says he's closing a deal that will make us unbelievably rich."

"Well, then my mom replied that it was all a bit weird because she had seen a policeman on the TV saying they were looking for someone whose name they did not know but who had disappeared. And something about how the family probably didn't know they were missing either. She came and told me afterward that I should probably mention it to you."

"I don't get it. Why?"

"Don't you lot ever read the papers?"

Laura laughed. What a stupid question. Søsser knew full well that they did not.

"What, and you don't watch the TV either?"

"Of course, all the time. Netflix, HBO, Amazon, you know all this."

"No, I mean regular TV. The news and that sort of thing."

"Are you crazy? My mom doesn't watch stuff like that. She just chain-smokes and watches TV series."

"Try and tell her, okay?"

The living room was in its usual state of chaos, which the au pair could not manage to bring to any semblance of order. That was why Laura and her little sister had no desire to be in there. It reeked of smoke, and if Roxan was not quick enough, the room was also littered with half-empty glasses and dirty dishes.

Laura could not figure out her mom, but she also had no desire to know too much about her. Some of the boys in her class had seen a few of the old reality TV programs her mom had been in without much in the way of clothes, and it had embarrassed Laura. Episodes from exotic places where she had been with several guys, and when she talked about them, it almost sounded as if she was proud to have participated, which did not exactly endear her to Laura. Quite the opposite.

But she decided that she would confront her mom with what Søsser had said about her dad, even if just to shake her from her stupor—which it did to some degree. She certainly woke up a little and fastened her kimono.

"Where did Søsser say she'd seen the report, Laura?" She sniffled and wrinkled her brow, causing the thick layer of yesterday's makeup to crack.

Laura opened the terrace door, letting in the freezing-cold air that had spread across the country over the last day, as it tended to help her mom get going.

"Ask Søsser's mom, 'cuz I don't know," she said and disappeared without shutting the terrace door behind her.

A new atmosphere descended on the house a little later, bringing winter closer with it. Her mom whispered into her phone, and over the course of the evening she wrote texts—and the tapping of her long nails could be heard all the way up on the second floor.

"What's she doing?" asked her little sister.

"I think she's trying to get Dad home."

The next morning, their mom looked haggard, with black circles around her eyes and puffy cheeks, just like the time she took hydrocortisone after a breast enlargement that had not quite gone as planned.

But she was at least sober and seemed to be levelheaded.

She had already installed a couple of apps for streaming news and TV reports and was sitting glued to the screen.

"Be quiet for a second, Laura," she said when Laura came into the living room to watch along with her.

The policeman on the screen was a mess, looking almost as disheveled as the wino who sat on the bench in front of the supermarket in the city center, swinging his arms about. A little shabby and unshaven. It was not a good look.

Laura watched her mom fumbling in vain for her cigarettes because she was unable to look away from the man with the stubble.

Then she wrote down a telephone number on the edge of the cigarette packet and called as soon as the press conference was finished.

Only a few minutes later she was saying "yes" and "no," sounding distant, as her eyes began to well up and black mascara slowly started to run down her cheeks.

48

CARL

Tuesday, December 22, 2020

"**Sorry, Carl, but** I have to ask you one more time. Did you have anything to do with that suitcase that you need to tell me about?"

This sort of insistent questioning normally had no effect on Carl. It was like water off a duck's back. But with Mona it was different, and it hurt. He had actually been racking his own brain all night with similar questions, but his hazy memory didn't exactly offer new insight to events lost in the mists of time.

"Seriously, Mona? It was so many years ago, and you know full well how it's been for me since Hardy, Anker, and I were shot. There are gaps in my memory, and, no matter how hard I try, I just have no idea how that suitcase ended up with all that shit in it. Hardy and I did have our suspicions that Anker had his own moral compass, and it wasn't uncommon for us to have to stop him doing something or other: when the blows to someone we had detained for questioning were getting too rough, or when he lied to the chief of homicide, like when his reports were rose-tinted fairy tales. But that he was the sort of hardened criminal the suitcase implies—I could never have imagined that."

Her expression did not convey the relief he had hoped for.

When Mona had left to bicycle with Lucia to nursery, Rose called. She sounded elated.

"The victim we've been looking for is a man by the name of Maurits van Bierbek. No doubt about it. Everything adds up, even the day he went 'missing.'"

Carl knew from the way Rose said 'missing' that she was undoubtedly making air quotes with her fingers when she spoke.

"And also the *way* he went 'missing.' Yeah, everything actually. We've struck gold. So here's the plan: Assad and I are driving to pick you up and then we'll head off. We have an appointment with van Bierbek's wife in twenty-five minutes."

Rose hung up before he had the chance to come up with any objections.

As the three of them drove to the van Bierbek family house, Rose jabbered away nonstop. It was as if it was already Christmas and the call from van Bierbek's wife had been the best present she could have received in this otherwise unforgiving year.

"They hadn't seen any regular TV in ages, Carl," explained Assad. "It was the daughter and her friend's mother who put two and two together; van Bierbek's wife seems pretty shaken by it all."

And that was exactly what she was.

The sense of shock was discernible from a distance, almost as if a fog of desperation hung over the grandiose, Greek-inspired architectural mishmash of a mansion in the most exclusive area of the suburbs.

The woman recognized Carl immediately and almost ran up to him with outstretched arms, as if wanting to cling tightly to someone who might take away her pain. Carl quickly maneuvered to the side to remind her that the corona restrictions were not something that only applied on TV.

"Start from the beginning again," said Carl when she had sat them in front of a window with a vista out toward a parklike garden that would impress anyone from the city center.

It was difficult to obtain a completely intelligible account from the confused woman, so it was fortunate that she was backed up by a teenage girl who did not have the same need to twist every question beyond recognition before she could offer a straight answer.

"A limousine arrived to pick him up on December twelfth. I remember the date so well because it was exactly halfway to this shitty Christmas." The girl looked at them with a seriousness that her mother was in no state to match. "The car was black, and you can see it on the video surveillance. In fact, you can see it driving down the hill. I've saved the file on this memory stick."

She handed it to Rose, and Carl considered adopting the girl on the spot.

"I've also saved all the emails that Mom and Dad have written to each other."

"Have you copied them too, Laura?" said the mother, looking very vexed.

The girl shrugged. That was all she thought about that question.

"You shouldn't just leave your passwords lying around everywhere."

"Why did your dad leave?" asked Rose.

"He'd been talking with someone from an organization in the U.S. that wanted to take over his company. We thought he'd flown to the U.S. to negotiate with them."

"I understand. But the thing is, Laura, your dad never left the country. We've checked. Do you know who he was going to meet that day?"

"Are you saying he's been in Denmark all this time?" She looked down at the floor as she took in this latest information. "But, no, I don't know. I think it was someone from this company." She handed Rose a note.

"Global Rea Inc., Wisconsin, U.S.A.," Rose read aloud. "Isn't that the huge company that produces reality shows for the global market?"

"Yes. But my dad's company is pretty big too. He's developed reality

TV for almost every country in Europe, as well as Asia, Australia, South America, and . . ." She hesitated for a moment when she saw Carl, Assad, and Rose exchanging glances.

This must be our guy, thought Carl. The man produced trash TV and fit the description of someone whom the killer would like to wipe from the face of the earth.

"What's your husband's company called?" Carl asked the wife, who was staring blankly into thin air.

"Unbelievable Corporation. They've developed *Paradise or Hell*, *Reality Prison*, and lots of other shows," she said with something resembling pride. However, Carl presumed it was rather a sign of her elementary awareness of the massive profit that she treasured more than anything else.

"Yes, and *Cougars and Youngsters*, which my mom was in if you'd like to see her without her clothes on," interrupted Laura. She looked at her mom reproachfully.

"Your attorney, Claes Erfurt, is here," interrupted a tiny Filipino woman. "Can I show him in?"

But the man was already rushing over to greet the lady of the house.

"Victoria, what is all this? It's terrible."

Their embrace lasted a few suspicious seconds too long, and Laura rolled her eyes.

"Yes, I'm sorry, but I need to have Claes with me. I need to know what my legal position is just now," said the wife, as if her husband were already dead and buried and that it was far from the worst thing that could have happened.

If this woman doesn't stop, I'm going to have to call Mona and say I'm bringing her daughter home with me, thought Carl.

They did not get much more from the meeting. The attorney was holding the wife's hand, patting it every ten seconds. Maybe his instinctive calculator was already settling the estate. There was no way they would be able to elicit from Victoria's muddled brain who had picked up Maurits van Bierbek and whom he was going to meet.

"Do you have somewhere we could sit and deliberate?" asked Assad.

"We'd like to set up base here, if you don't mind. The atmosphere at police headquarters is a bit strained at the moment, if you know what I mean. And it's very important that we're close by if you manage to get in contact with the kidnappers, Victoria. Unfortunately, we don't have much time."

Laura was the only one who looked happy at the suggestion.

"My dad's office is huge, and no one else goes in there when he's not at home. I can show you where it is. They can stay there as long as they want, can't they, Mom?" She turned on her heel without waiting for a reply.

"Brilliant thinking, Assad," said Carl as he sat down amid an array of photocopying machines, computers, and flashing lights from routers that could undoubtedly carry loads of terabytes in and out of the room.

"Now Marcus can't monitor where you are or what you're up to. And we can just leave Gordon at the office in case something comes up. We can get him to send images of our whiteboard and whatever else we need, and we can print them out on that." Assad pointed at a wondrous machine that probably printed formats as large as A2. If the investigation unit wanted equipment like that, the minister of justice would have to relinquish at least two annual salaries.

Rose looked away from the TV playing in the background. "It's unbelievable! Maurits van Bierbek's company only produced shit TV with the sole purpose of challenging the boundaries of the contestants and the audience. A lot of what he produced bordered on pornographic. And strangely enough, he managed to get TV channels and streaming services across the world to throw their usual morals to the wind and purchase his concepts. I can see on Google that one of them, *Did She Really Say That?*, has been sold to more than fifty countries. And many of them have adapted the concept to local culture and language." Rose shook her head.

Carl was pleased that he had never jumped on that bandwagon, even though it would have proved beneficial in their current situation.

"Have *you* seen any of his shows, Assad?" asked Carl, pushing the list over to him.

Assad scrutinized the titles so thoroughly that it would be easy to think he was picturing the shows in his mind.

"No, my satellite dish doesn't pick up any of these," he said dryly.

"What about you, Rose?"

"I've checked out a couple of them. But there's nothing there really for anyone with even the most basic education. It's nothing but trash. But I do know that several of them are so immensely popular that the more traditional reality programs on the satellite channels have been left in the dust."

"Which means?" asked Assad.

"That they can run for ages as long as there are still enough people who are a few beers short of a six-pack."

Assad looked no less confused.

"I have van Bierbek's company accounts here," said Carl. "His net worth has more zeros in it than I can count. If he really had found a buyer for his company, he would've become one of the richest people in Scandinavia. Which one of you is going to call the company in the U.S. that allegedly wanted to negotiate a takeover?"

"I'll ask Gordon to do it while Assad and I read through the email correspondence between Maurits and his wife. Sound good? And you can look at the surveillance video while we get on with that, Carl."

There was a discreet knock on the door, and Claes Erfurt edged into the room. He was a heavyset man in a far-too-tight marine-blue suit. He finally offered his hand to introduce himself properly and flashed a row of shockingly bleached teeth that could put some of the contestants on van Bierbek's reality shows to shame.

"Sorry for the intrusion," said the attorney insincerely. "Just a small point about you setting up shop here in Victoria's home. Shouldn't you have brought a warrant if you're going to be rummaging through Maurits van Bierbek's private affairs?" He did not wait for a reply. "I think you should have, so it would be best if you pack up your stuff and leave. Can we agree on that?"

Assad stood up and stared at him. "Listen up, stud. Can't you wait for a roll in the hay with the wife until the man *has* been killed? We're actually trying to save him here so you won't have to stretch your trouser pockets to make room for all the millions you're counting on stuffing them with. But maybe you don't want to keep your trousers on? So if you'd be so kind as to tell us what you hope to get out of all this, and if you don't you can—"

Assad stopped when he saw Carl's contorted face.

"What my colleague is trying to say is that you have the chance to give your career a hell of a boost by pretending to fight for your client's life," said Carl. "So I have a suggestion you can't possibly turn down, and then you can leave us alone. As my colleague pointed out to Victoria earlier, we don't have much time."

"Are you sure that was wise, Carl?" asked Rose when the attorney had plodded out the door. "You're going to let him announce to the public that Maurits van Bierbek is the person you said you were looking for on national TV and that we have a strong suspicion that the poor guy will be killed on Boxing Day?"

"Wait and see. As long as there's no mention of Department Q, Marcus can allow himself to believe that the information comes from somewhere else and cover his back. The benefit is that the entire country will be mobilized as soon as the attorney mentions that the family is offering a ten million kroner reward for information leading to the whereabouts of Maurits van Bierbek. And his safe return, that is. Don't you think every Dane will go out of their way to land the reward, especially now during corona, when Christmas is also canceled and they have nothing else to do?"

"Ten million! Marcus is going to have puppies," Assad said hesitantly.

"Have kittens, Assad. But close enough." Carl smiled. Was Assad pulling their leg again? "I agree that it's not normal procedure and that it's an insane amount of money, but Marcus is clever enough to keep quiet as long as our names are not mentioned. We'll be able to get on in peace while the rest of the country plays detective."

"What if the killer throws their principles out of the window and kills Maurits earlier?" asked Rose.

"Are we still talking about Sisle Park as the potential perpetrator?" The others nodded.

"That woman won't compromise on anything regarding her mission. I'm damn sure of it. But obviously she'll realize that we're starting to breathe down her neck. So from the moment the attorney makes his announcement, we'll have to put Sisle Park under surveillance. From now until Boxing Day, we need to stick to her like glue, okay? You'll have to divide the shifts among you as best you can. You have a family, Assad, so you take the day shifts between eight a.m. and four p.m. Rose, you take the evening shift between four p.m. and midnight, and Gordon can take the night shift between midnight and eight a.m."

"I think it's better if I swap with Gordon," said Rose. "If he takes the first shift this evening instead, Assad and I can get on with reading the emails between Victoria and Maurits. I've already arranged with Gordon for him to leave his car parked by Sisle's with the key on the front tire, which means we'll be able to follow her if she leaves the house in her car. He'll just have to go back and forth to Sisle's house in a taxi like the rest of us. He doesn't mind as long as he doesn't have to pay the fare himself."

This was their good old Rose. Not only had she arranged the transport, but she even volunteered to take the night shift. Nothing fazed that woman.

Carl had hoped that Laura van Bierbek had only copied the clip in which her father was picked up, but he had now been staring for half an hour at a grainy recording of a street where nothing had happened except a dog walker passing by who had forgotten the poop bags at home.

"Come on, little car," he said over and over. Maybe they should have asked for a print of van Bierbek's phone calls first. At least then they would have known the approximate time he had been picked up by the fake consultant from Global Rea Inc. But how were they supposed to get hold of a phone record quickly? His experience told him that it could be a very long time before they received it. So his main concern right now was to stay focused and not close his eyes from sheer boredom.

He glanced for a moment at the imposing windows facing a different part of the parklike garden. It would get dark soon, and the workday would have been over under normal circumstances.

Normal circumstances! Carl mulled over the words. Would anything ever be normal again?

Carl pricked his ears. He could hear from the floor below that the seriousness of the situation was finally sinking in for Maurits van Bierbek's wife, who alternated between wailing and ranting about how terrible the whole thing was.

Maybe it was the monotony of the woman's drawling voice that had made him nod off, but he gave a start when his phone rang and brought him back to reality.

"Listen to me, Carl," said Mona in a hushed voice. "The police have just been here with a warrant for your arrest. They asked if I knew where you and your colleagues are. They gave me strict instructions to let them know if I hear from you. I'm sure they're tapping both our phones, so turn yours off and get rid of it so they can't trace your whereabouts. I also want to let you know that I don't doubt your innocence for one second."

He was just about to say something, but she interjected before he could speak. "I know *exactly* what this case means to you, Carl. I know you. You're innocent, so just stay out of sight until you've found the poor man waiting to die. And tell Assad, Gordon, and Rose to look after you and also turn off their phones. Goodbye, darling. See you on the other side of this hell. Kisses from me and Lucia."

There was a beeping sound and she was gone.

Carl breathed deeply. Yes, he had expected his busybody colleagues to come for him at some point, but not this quickly. Carl nodded to himself. The reality he found himself in would get anyone down, but at least he had Mona's unwavering support. That and her heads-up was exactly what he needed.

He focused on the other end of the large room, where Rose and Assad were working their way through the many emails to find even the smallest lead. But no matter how tirelessly they worked, they knew just as well as he did that they would not succeed. Why would the people behind the kidnapping have dropped their guard when writing?

"Hey, you two. I've got to tell you what Mona just said to me." And within seconds they had turned off their phones.

"I'm sorry I've landed you in the soup. But the situation is such that unless you decide to stand down here and now and cease any further contact with me, you won't be able to go home until this is over. It'll probably be worse for you, Assad, with Marwa and the kids at home. So what do you think?"

The dilemma left Assad momentarily dumbfounded. He did not look happy. Then he turned to Carl.

"Well, the thing is, I'm just a bit embarrassed, Carl. I really don't know why you're suddenly talking about soup."

There was a brief silence, and then he stood up and cracked a smile. Then he gave Carl a big squeeze and whispered into his ear that of course he would not let him or the investigation down. Carl had to use all his effort not to break down in tears.

"I'm staying too, Carl," said Rose. "We're with you all the way. But we'll have to pressure the van Bierbek family into letting us stay here."

Carl tried to muster a thank-you, but the lump in his throat stopped the words from coming out.

"By the way, Rose spoke to Gordon while you were taking a kitten nap," said Assad.

"Yes, and he said that no one in Global Rea Inc. management recalls having been in contact with Maurits van Bierbek about buying Unbelievable Corporation. On the contrary, they said that after van Bierbek promoted his latest idea—something along the lines of *Who Dies First?*—it was probably the last merger in the world they would embark on."

"Okay. That does sound like a bad title. Never mind, at least we can rule that out," said Carl. "Just like we expected, the whole merger story was a setup from the beginning. Oh, and did anyone remember to tell Gordon to turn his phone off?"

"Yes. He's using another one with a prepaid card. I've got the number here," answered Rose.

Carl breathed a sigh of relief. "Has he left yet to shadow Sisle Park?"

"Yeah, he left the office twenty minutes ago, and he knows that he might be tailed by the police. He said he'd do everything he could to shake them."

Carl realized that he must have been napping for at least half an hour. He sighed and turned to the screen where the video surveillance recording still only showed the street in front of the van Bierbeks' house in gray and white.

He looked at his watch and considered watching the file from the beginning—and then it happened. A black, gleaming Lexus slowly glided up in front of the entrance to van Bierbek's house. Unfortunately, due to the position of the surveillance camera, it was not possible to see the driver's seat or who was behind the wheel—and there did not appear to be anyone else in the car. Carl noted the time in the corner of the screen. It was exactly ten. Then the recording showed Maurits van Bierbek from behind walking down the steps from the main door with a folder under his arm and getting in the car.

Carl now paused the recording second by second.

"Please give me a clear shot of the license plate," he whispered as the limousine moved forward in small jumps.

Now it turned out toward the middle of the road so that the rear lights came into sight. Carl paused the recording and stared at the license plate: FB 5 followed by four indecipherable numbers.

"Come over here for a minute, you two!" he shouted. "We have the license plate."

Rose nodded when she saw the black Lexus and license plate. She would be able to trace the owner in no time.

Carl leaned back and stretched his arms above his head with the word "success" in his mind. He sat there relishing the only real progress they had made that day. Until Rose returned.

"I'm sorry, Carl. The car was only rented out for a few hours and paid for with a fake credit card under a false name from a Spanish bank. The rental company didn't suspect the woman because the passport she used as ID seemed legit. It was only the following day that they realized they'd been conned. But they were happy that at least the car hadn't ended up in Poland or some other faraway place. The only thing they could remember about the woman who rented the car was that she was in her midforties, but otherwise quite plain."

Carl lowered his arms. "Not exactly a description of our Sisle Park, is it?"

They shook their heads simultaneously.

"Okay, there's not much else we can do other than wait for the attorney's statement on the news, unless Gordon has something for us. I'll call him in an hour. But in the meantime, let me know if you come across anything interesting in the emails Maurits and his wife sent to each other."

"Nothing whatsoever so far," said Assad. "But it seems like the wife is extremely gullible. She buys every silly excuse for why they can't call each other."

"She didn't give a shit," added Rose. "Actually, she asks her husband at least ten times how much he reckons the takeover will bring in. And when he finally replies that it'll probably be around three hundred million dollars, she stops asking about it. She probably ran around the dining table screaming for joy with her arms in the air."

Carl grunted. "Okay, but what next? Can you convince Victoria to put us up for a couple of days? Try to win her over by telling her that we'll get her on prime time TV when things have calmed down a bit. And tell her while her kids are listening that we'll do everything we can to get her husband back."

Rose looked skeptical. "I wouldn't make too much of the latter, Carl. Anyway, don't you think you should focus on your own situation? Have you spoken to Hardy yet? You could use van Bierbek's landline." She pointed at a monstrosity that not only looked like it was gilded—it actually *was*.

Carl nodded. Calling Hardy was the next logical step in that toxic case.

49

SISLE

Tuesday, December 22, 2020

She had been quietly sitting at home in communion with God, just as she usually did when the time had come for someone else to pay for their immoral deeds with their life. In this state of intimacy, the most important element of her ritual was that God was made aware of the nature of the victim's sins and which of Satan's minion's birthdays the victim was destined to die on.

"Dear God, I believe Mao was the most despicable of your creations on earth. He turned himself into a blasphemous demigod who only spared those who posed no threat to his power, just like he mocked you with messages glorifying evil. He allowed his people to die in famines. He executed anyone who challenged his dogma and so-called divine status. And worst of all, he not only seduced his weak people into following him unconditionally, he also seduced the youth of the West. On the birthday of this devil incarnate, another wretched soul will come to meet you, his divine creator, and receive his final judgment. Lord, hear my prayer."

She sat for a moment thinking about what was going to happen in a few days before finally concluding her devotions with her usual thanksgiving.

"I offer you thanks, dear God, for sparing my life when you unleashed your righteous wrath. I offer you thanks for letting me be your
disciple and your sword. I offer you thanks for the task you have entrusted me with and the freedom of choice you have always bestowed
upon me."

She bowed her head and said amen.

Now she was ready.

Maurits van Bierbek had three and a half days left to live. Just over
eighty hours left of a life that had been too long already. In these final
hours, the condemned could realize his situation and either repent so
he could meet God with an open heart or he could deny his guilt and
suffer the consequences of an eternity in hell.

Sisle did not care which path he chose. Her only mission was to remind him that all actions in life have consequences. An eye for an eye,
a tooth for a tooth, as the Bible says.

She crossed herself and stood up from her kneeling position. The
meeting with the three avenging angels she had recruited from the
welfare department had been very successful. And so she was sure that
the purification process in the years to come would be a glory to behold
from a distance. Sisle allowed herself to be enraptured in equal measure
by gratitude and pride.

She went into her living room, turned on the TV, and only just caught
a glimpse of a corpulent man in a marine-blue suit behind the end cred-
its on the news.

That very second her phone rang. It was Debora on the verge of hys-
teria.

"The van Bierbeks' attorney has just been on the news. Did you see
it?" She moaned and continued. "The family has offered a reward of ten
million kroner for any information that can lead to the whereabouts of
Maurits and his safe return. Do you know how many people are already
looking for him? The reporter on the news estimated it to be in the thousands. And they all know time is of the essence."

Sisle pursed her lips. How on earth did any of this change anything?

"Sisle! Are you sure that none of your followers or disciples have caught a whiff of what we're up to? Because if they have, you need to be careful. It's such a big reward, Sisle," continued Debora. "Almost six million Danes now know that they can win the grand prize if they manage to sniff us out. I can just imagine the frenzy this is causing, and it makes me very uncomfortable. Little boys in scout uniforms playing detective, nosy neighbors, old and young people with financial problems, and all the people bored to death with nothing better to do in the suburbs."

"You need to stop now, Debora!"

"But it's just too tempting, Sisle. People are bound to react. Ten million kroner is a lot of money."

"Only you, me, and Adam have any actual knowledge about this. But maybe you two are ten million short, Debora?"

The line went silent at the other end. A little too silent for Sisle.

"I really need you to calm down, Debora, and I need Adam to be with me all the way. Are you listening? I *can't* have you wavering at this point. Are you?"

Despite the poor connection, Debora's breathing was audible and heavy.

"Can I talk to Adam, Debora?"

There was a short silence and then the sound of crackling at the other end.

"Debora seems to be losing her nerve. Can I trust you, Adam?"

"Yes," he answered in a straightforward manner.

"And what if I tell you that you will have to give Maurits van Bierbek the injection?"

"Will I?"

"I want you to keep an eye on Debora over the next few days. Stay at home and make sure that you celebrate Christmas completely normally—to the extent possible this year."

"Okay. But who'll look after Maurits in the meantime? Are you going to—"

"Stop worrying about him. Keep a low profile until Boxing Day. I'll contact you when it's time."

Sisle hung up and pondered the latest developments.

Ten million had been promised. Could they have wished for better exposure? She laughed at the thought of all the people who were now running around like chickens with their heads cut off searching for anything suspicious. The police would be inundated with people reporting anything and everything: drug dens, barns full of stolen goods, moonshine operations, derelict houses, families with questionable relationships. The police would be busy when suspicions turned into reports flooding their helplines. Unbelievably busy! Those poor, poor investigators who had been hoping for a few peaceful days over Christmas.

Ten million! She wondered if this Chief Inspector Carl Mørck would not have preferred a more manageable and conservative development.

What on earth is the man going to do now? she thought as she went down the stairs to her basement. It was light and airy and had been renovated with functional rooms for her maid to easily do the laundry and the ironing. There was also a room for tending to the many flowering bulbs that were stored down here over the winter to be planted out the following spring. In this room, the humidity was constant and it was almost completely dark, which made the door behind one of the shelves almost impossible to spot. She unlocked it and turned on the light to reveal an almost fully equipped chemical lab. In here, Sisle could use synthesis to treat potassium hydroxide with hydrochloric acid or burn potassium with chlorine. Both processes resulted in potassium chloride, which she had used to kill two of her victims—and which she was now preparing for a third time.

She held the beaker up in front of her and looked at the lethal fluid. Injected directly into the heart in sufficient amounts, it would cause immediate death. So-called humane executions were carried out across the world with a cocktail of drugs, causing the condemned to first be sedated and subsequently put in a coma before administration of the final dose of sodium chloride finished the process. But that was not Sisle's method. She wanted her victims to die in full awareness of what was happening, and she did not want to drag the final process out.

Her victims often writhed when the many milliliters were injected directly into their heart. They gasped for air, convulsed violently, and jerked uncontrollably. And when they could no longer breathe—just before they died—she looked at her reflection in their lackluster eyes and condemned them for eternity.

50

CARL

Tuesday, December 22, 2020

"**What's Gordon saying?** Is he in position, Rose?"

"Yes, he's under cover just a bit down from Sisle Park's house, and he says it's bloody freezing."

"He should be grateful it isn't raining. Is she home?"

"There are lights in the windows, so he thinks so, yes."

Carl turned to Assad. "Did you get hold of the floor plan of her house?"

Assad shook his head. "But I know it's over five hundred fifty square meters with a finished basement. So it's a huge place where you could do whatever you want without anyone else knowing. But I doubt she'd be stupid enough to kill her victims in her own home. Plus, she owns several other properties in the area."

"In the area?"

"Yes. Warehouses, rental properties, private houses and apartments, and holiday homes. So if she doesn't leave and drive directly to the property where Maurits van Bierbek is being held, it'll be difficult. There are simply too many options."

Carl had suspected as much. There was not much positive to be said about the last two hours. Worst of all was that there were only two spots suitable for sleeping in Maurits van Bierbek's office, so they had to take turns using the sofa beds. What this meant in practice was that Rose had one of them all to herself, while Carl and Assad had to make do with alternating on the other and putting up with each other's sweat and drool.

On top of that, his call to Hardy in Switzerland had been anything but encouraging because Hardy was, to put it mildly, not doing well. All the experimental procedures his body had been put through, all the pain medication, all the torment his body had been subjected to in the exoskeleton, which he was now trying for the first time, made him unfocused, irritable, and distant. So it was only halfway through the conversation that he grasped the seriousness of the situation that Carl found himself in.

"Really! You're telling me that the suitcase has been in your attic since 2007. That's thirteen years, Carl! Why haven't we discussed this in all the years that your faithful, paralyzed partner has been staring up at the ceiling in your living room? I would think there's been plenty of opportunity, but maybe you didn't think it was important?"

"But I didn't know what was in it, Hardy. You have to believe me."

"Why would Anker ask you to keep his suitcase for him? I don't get it."

"Because his wife kicked him out. And that's why I didn't ask myself what was in it. Why would I? I mean, what do you pack when you're kicked out of the house?"

"Surely the question is more what do you store in an attic. Probably not underwear and socks, right?"

He sounded belligerent, which was out of character.

"How much pain are you in, Hardy?"

"Don't you worry about that, Carl. But you might want to tell me why it never crossed the mind of a brilliant detective like you to wonder what might be hidden in that suitcase. And why you never opened it or gave it back to Anker's wife when he died."

"Maybe I didn't give it back to the wife because she'd kicked Anker out. Or maybe I'd just forgotten about it. I can't remember why, Hardy."

Hardy let out an incredulous sigh.

"Hardy, please do me a favor. Cast your mind back and see if you can think of why Anker would have had all those drugs and money. I'll be arrested soon, and I'd like to be able to give them something that could divert the spotlight from me."

There was a deafening silence. Only Hardy's labored breathing told him that he was still on the other end.

"Will you please try, Hardy?"

He cleared his throat. "I guess I have to, Carl. So I'll try." Then he hung up. It was becoming his habit to end their calls abruptly, and it did not feel good. In fact, Carl had not felt so alone as he did in this moment since he was ten and found his dog at the side of the highway, run over by a car.

His logic told him that there was bound to be a couple of people left in the force who still held him in some esteem, but a little old-fashioned comforting would not have gone unappreciated at this moment. A squeeze on his shoulder, someone pressing their forehead against his, a friendly word, the kind of closeness that does not question certain things. So what was wrong with Hardy? Why was he so cold?

Assad came in, sat down in front of him, and looked him straight in the eye.

"I want you to know that Marwa and I are writing to each other even though we're both staying low at the moment. We have a couple of Arabic email addresses we rarely use and that only we know about. Turns out they're very handy in our current situation. She'd just written something about you."

"What did she have to say?"

"That the police came by our place asking for me. They've given her strict instructions to contact them if I get in touch. And they told her that it could became very problematic for me and my family if I don't turn myself in and tell them where you are."

Carl scoffed. "Problematic for you and your family, my ass. Don't you know what this is, Assad? It's police-state methods that have no place in Denmark. They can't charge you with anything in this case, and they can't blame it on your family that you work for me or Department Q for that matter."

"But that's exactly what they can do, Carl. They'll come back, and if Marwa can't give them any news about you, they'll do another check on their residency permits. That's exactly what they said."

"Those bastards! Well, you can write back and tell her that I've driven up to my parents in Vendsyssel and am hiding out there. It'll be fun when my old mother insists that they come in for coffee before she can be bothered to hear what they want. And taste her cookies and hear the story about the time she drove all the way to Løkken alone on a tandem bike. She'll wear them down before they even get to the point."

"Hmm. I'll tell her that."

"I can sense that you've got something else on your mind. Spit it out, Assad."

"Are we still agreed that we believe there is a connection between Sisle Park and Pauline Rasmussen?" asked Assad.

"Yes. Because of the salt in the shoebox."

"And because there was also salt in the graves next to Ragnhild Bengtsen's grave. That gives us a connection between her and Sisle Park."

"Yes. Especially because it makes it more than probable that the two bodies next to Ragnhild's grave are directly linked to the other murders."

Assad thought for a moment and scratched the stubble that had grown significantly since they went undercover.

"And we also agree that there's a connection between Ragnhild Bengtsen and her victim, Tabitha Engstrøm, right?"

Carl smiled. "Yes, definitely. No one would kill a totally random stranger in that way, would they? But where are you going with all this?"

"Well, do we also agree that Tabitha Engstrøm's notebook clearly states that she's part of some form of brotherhood or sisterhood, or whatever we should call it, and that she mentions several of the people in the group by name?"

"Yes."

"And do you think Manfred or someone else from Bente Hansen's team has spoken to any of the people Tabitha mentions?"

"I'd assume so."

"Okay, so you're not a hundred percent sure if they have. You're just assuming?"

"Yes." Carl nodded.

"The thing is, we know that some of the names Tabitha mentions are aliases. She says so herself. But do we know if they're *all* aliases?"

"Yeah, don't we?"

"So here's the thing. I've been searching for the woman Tabitha refers to as Debora. It's such an unusual name in Denmark that we should try to contact all women with that name. Maybe we'll find someone who is connected in some way to Sisle—just like we've made connections with all the other women."

"But even if we find her, it's far from certain that she knows where Maurits van Bierbek is. Or that she's even an accomplice to Sisle's crimes."

"I think there are many similarities between the motives for the things Tabitha did and the things Sisle is doing. Don't you?"

"Yes. It makes sense that you're looking for Debora. Have you checked the national register?"

He nodded. "There are even fewer Deboras in the Copenhagen area than I'd expected. Apparently the name really is uncommon."

"Have you contacted them?"

"Yes, all of them. Three of them don't actually use that name, and a couple of them were too young. Maybe it's one of those names that have come back into fashion."

"So it *could* be an alias like all the others in the group."

He nodded. "Or she's just lying low. Maybe she's just registered everywhere with her Christian name and a simple 'D' for her middle name."

"I've called my neighbor from Maurits's landline," interrupted Rose. "So now I know that the police have also paid me a visit at home and contacted both my neighbors to ask if they know where I am. They were given strict instructions to contact the police the second I return home." She laughed. "They'll be a long time waiting for that to happen."

"What are you planning to do after Boxing Day, Carl?" asked Assad.

"If we find Maurits van Bierbek in time, I'll dance the fandango in Marcus Jacobsen's office."

"And if we don't?"

"Then I won't be dancing, but I'll still report to his office."

"I'm heading off now," said Rose, throwing an oversized scarf around her neck and putting on her coat.

She was going to relieve Gordon; Carl had forgotten all about the shifts.

He looked at Assad and knew they were thinking the same thing. One of them could take over her bed while she was watching Sisle Park's house all night. Brilliant!

Rose hesitated for a moment on her way out the door, turned around, and looked at them.

"And by the way, you two, don't even think about using my bed!" She tapped her nose. "This'll give you away, and I'll be pissed off if you do."

Carl could all too clearly picture the scene. Better to just rough it on the floor.

51

MAURITS

Tuesday, December 22, 2020

For a time when he was very young and felt most uncertain and at a loss, Maurits had begun counting. And it did not matter what he counted. If he was sent to the principal's office because he had talked back to the teacher again, he would count the books lining the bookshelf behind the principal as he took his telling off. If he lost himself in the eyes of a pretty girl, he counted how many times she blinked to avoid revealing how shy he felt. And for some years, all situations could be made more bearable in this way—so long as there was something he could count. The habit had worn off over the years as Maurits learned to cope without the counting. And it had stayed that way until now. Isolated from the world and resigned to his powerlessness to avoid the certainty of his physical demise, he suddenly heard a voice counting again.

Maurits shook his head and tried in vain to open his eyes, which seemed glued shut.

Was it him counting? And if it was, what was he counting?

"What are you counting, Maurits?" he heard himself say.

Was it the seconds counting down? Was it his increasingly diminished pulse, or was it an echo of his granny's grandfather clock defiantly keeping time that could never be again?

Over the last few days, he had tried for several hours to keep track of time. For the condemned, it was the black hole of eternity that awaited—the sole goal to which the seconds marched on. Despite the unavoidable shutting down of his brain, there were still fragments of thoughts that he could not shake off. Perhaps that was why he was counting—to drown out the noise in his head.

He did not understand. Why did he have to be killed?

It went without saying that he could have been a kinder person. Of course he could have put the well-being of others before his own just once in a while. Of course he could have been more constrained in his desire to create sensational entertainment.

But had the game not always been voluntary for those who took part? So why was he here?

Maurits writhed to the side. His empty intestines were burning with stomach acid. His throat felt raw.

Why could he not just be left in peace? How long would they prolong his agony?

He gasped suddenly and opened his mouth wide. Everything that evil bitch was trying to convince him of might not actually have anything to do with reality. Everything she was holding him accountable for, everything she was mocking him for and was angry about was maybe not the real reason he was being held here. There was no doubting that the woman hated him, but that was of secondary importance. It was so obvious to him now. The real reason he was being held hostage was a combination of things. But when push came to shove, it was definitely his money she was after. And now she was keeping him here in his torment while she negotiated the ransom. That was obviously what she was doing. And the ransom was guaranteed to be close to the maximum of whatever cash his estate could raise. That was undoubtedly why it was taking so long.

He attempted to smile but held back because his lips were cracking. She had probably demanded one hundred million kroner. That surely would not be a problem. But Victoria had probably resisted the negotiators. She was like that when it came to giving something up.

Maurits breathed more deeply and freely than he had for days. For a moment it felt like he had managed to fight off his pain and convulsions.

He tilted back his head and tried once more to open his eyes but failed again.

He sat like this for a while, his mouth gaping and his head tilted back. Then he heard himself counting again.

He found it odd. What ominous signals was his subconscious so occupied with transmitting that he had to try to block them out?

He held his breath for a moment and then it came to him.

Why did they want him to help answer questions in an email to Victoria? Maybe it was because they were trying to prove that they really did have him.

Bullshit, he thought. If they were, they could just have taken a photo of him with a newspaper to prove the date. Was that not the normal procedure when someone was kidnapped?

Maurits closed his mouth and let his head fall forward and down toward his chest.

Then he started counting again as sounds from the elevator by the far wall slowly became audible in the room.

"One, two, three, four . . ."

52

CARL

Wednesday, December 23, 2020

"**Wake up, Carl**. I'm off to relieve Rose. It's seven o'clock."

Carl raised his head a little from his pillow and felt the cover sticking to the corners of his mouth. He tried twisting his body a little, but his hip was hurting after a night on the concrete floor.

"Bloody hell" were the first words he spoke that day.

"You must've slept well, given the way you were snoring," said a surprisingly light voice.

From a state of feeling free from everything—free from the cold, free from accusations, free from the choking grip of corona—reality hit him like a hammer. He had never felt so tired, battered, and unwell as he did this morning.

"Slept well?" he asked, puzzled, while trying to focus on what it was Laura was waving in front of his nose.

"Assad made it," she said with a smile as the smell of the coffee made Carl's nostrils flare.

"It's not too strong, Carl. It's safe to drink," said Assad from the door as he put on his shoes.

Carl nodded, leaned on his elbows, and took the cup.

"Is there sugar in it?" he asked tentatively.

"Just a little," said Assad convincingly.

Carl took a sip, which in a millisecond of reaching his throat made it constrict, setting off a coughing fit.

"Yes, it's good, isn't it?" asked Assad, while Carl tried to stop spluttering. Never had coffee been so insanely strong and sickly sweet as this brown substance that he had been tricked into drinking.

"It's a great pick-me-up," continued Assad as he put on his coat and left.

"Now it's just the two of us," said Laura, standing right in front of him. "Mom is at the attorney's office and took my sister with her."

She handed him a bowl whose contents Carl could not quite make out.

"Mom's favorite kefir," she said, looking like she was just about to feed him.

Searches for videos of Sisle Park did not generate many hits. She rarely made appearances in public, and they were usually limited to brief statements on topics that were so general that they did not offer any potential leads. She was always well-dressed in black trouser suits and white blouses, with her hair styled short, with no place for any flyaway strands. Her appearance was as controlled and neutral as her conduct and words. An overall picture of a woman whom no one would suspect of committing these heinous crimes.

Where and what were her weaknesses? Where was the crack in her armor that would allow them to discern her true nature?

"I've seen that lady before," said Laura from behind him.

Carl turned around with a jolt. He had not heard Laura van Bierbek come into the room this time.

"Seen her before? What do you mean, Laura?" he asked.

The girl pointed at the screen. "She came here one day when Dad was at work. She said he'd forgotten an important document at home and she was supposed to pick it up and take it back to the office."

Carl frowned. What the heck was the girl talking about?

"When was this, Laura?"

"A long time ago. Just after the summer holidays, I think."

"Did you let her in?"

"A total stranger? Of course I didn't. I told her that I'd call Dad and ask him if it was okay."

"Good move, Laura. What did she do next?"

"She took a step back and looked at the name on the house. Then she apologized and said that she'd got the wrong address. She was apparently supposed to go to the neighbors'."

"And did she?"

"I looked out the window, but she didn't. She just drove off. So I called Dad, and he had no idea what I was talking about. He certainly hadn't asked anyone to pick anything up."

"What do you think she wanted?"

"I think she was a con artist, and so did Dad. She kept staring around her when she was on the front steps, as if she wanted to check if we had surveillance cameras and stuff."

"But there are. That's not exactly a secret with this house."

"No. My dad and I went through the video surveillance that night so he could see what she looked like. But it didn't show her face, and the car was parked in a way so you couldn't really make it out. But I remember her hair being longer and darker than it is just now on your screen."

Carl nodded. There was no doubt Sisle Park had wanted to familiarize herself with the interior and exterior camera angles.

"Did you think she would come back to steal something?"

"Yes, but Dad said that she was welcome to try because she wouldn't get anywhere." She pointed at the frozen image on the screen. "Who is she?"

"We're not quite sure yet, Laura. But we're going to find out. Can you show me the video of when she was here? I assume you've got a digital copy?"

She smiled and said that she did not think they kept the surveillance footage for so long. But she would have a look.

———

"Who is she?" the girl had asked, but the question they were asking themselves was who was she *really*. Who could they ask? Sisle's employees? He shuddered at the thought of trying to get anything out of the types he had seen at her company. They would probably rather chop his head off than allow him to stick his nose in their boss's affairs. In the end, he decided to call the chemistry department where she had been a student. And when no one answered, he called a few people with the same unusual surname. But no one knew anyone by the name of Sisle or Lisbeth with that surname.

Carl realized for the tenth time that day how stuck they were. It felt fatal. December twenty-sixth was now only three days away, and it was looking more and more likely that they would have to neutralize Sisle Park to prevent the murder of Maurits van Bierbek. But how could they do that within the law? They could not just burst into her house and arrest her without compelling evidence. They could not just grab her and let time take its course. And who could even know if she was going to be personally present when the murder was committed? When he thought about Pia Laugesen's death and the way she had been forced under the water in the swimming pool until she drowned, he found it hard to believe that a relatively slightly built person like Sisle would have had the strength to handle such a strong and sturdy woman.

And if there had been a third person present, how were they supposed to establish who that person was and how they had managed to get so close to Sisle Park that they had made themselves an accomplice?

Palle Rasmussen's characterization of Sisle Park as a tease, stalker, idiot, and scarred bitch certainly was not flattering, and he was way off the mark in calling her an idiot. But could the other supposed character traits help them in their search?

It was almost twenty years ago that he had written it, and naturally she would have changed over those years. But maybe the root of her insane quest could be found in those years before she developed her current persona.

Carl was studying her brief résumé. Sisle was baptized Lisbeth Park, and of course they had searched for that name both with and without an "h" at the end of her first name. But they had only hit dead ends. In spite of the unusual surname, no one matched the Sisle they were looking for.

Carl wondered how this young woman had ended up continuing her studies in South Africa and stayed there for years. What was her relationship with the country? Was South Africa a country where she could specialize in her chosen field? Or was she running from something?

Carl could imagine anything when it came to her. But it surprised him all the same that she had walked right into the lion's den to check out the position of the surveillance cameras at the van Bierbek residence. She might have worn a disguise and a wig, but when a fifteen-year-old girl is watching, all disguises fail.

But maybe *he* could pull off wearing a disguise that would allow him to move freely and investigate a few things.

He got up and looked at himself in the corridor mirror outside Maurits van Bierbek's office. He had not expected much but was still disheartened by the sight of a shabby, elderly man with unkempt thinning hair that had turned gray—but not the shade that would put anyone in mind of George Clooney.

"Laura!" he shouted a couple of times before she appeared in front of him with a piece of paper in her outstretched hand.

"What's this?" he asked as if he did not already know.

"August twenty-ninth, 2020, two thirty-two p.m." it read in the corner of the blurry color print of what the surveillance camera had recorded when Sisle Park had turned up unannounced.

"I'm sorry, but it only shows the top of her car and a little bit of her. And this is the clearest image I could find. And look at her hair—I was right. It's long and brown, but I'm sure it's a wig."

The car looked like it was quite a few years old. Apart from its yellow finish, the only distinguishing feature was a roof rack of the type that can be bought for a song from any basic hardware store.

"Thanks, Laura. This is helpful." He gave her a look as if she were suddenly his very best friend. "You wouldn't happen to have a phone I can borrow for a few days?"

"Er, I only have my own."

"Well, that's all right."

She took a step back and looked shocked. "What do you mean? I can't go without my phone, and especially not now."

"Can't you just use the landline if you need to speak with your friends?"

"That's not the problem." She looked at him as if he were a hopeless case. Had he never heard about texts, emails, Twitter, Facebook, Instagram, YouTube, TikTok, and Snapchat?

"Maybe I can rent it? Just until Boxing Day."

She bit her lip. "It'll cost you five hundred kroner a day."

Carl gulped. "I was thinking more along the lines of five hundred in total."

She gave him another incredulous look.

"Do you have anything in the house I could dye my hair with? And would any of your dad's clothes fit me? I need to go for a drive, and I really don't want to be recognized."

An hour later, a tired and weary-eyed Rose came into the office after her night shift. She had only just managed to throw her coat on the floor and collapse on the sofa bed when she caught sight of Carl.

"What the hell!" she blurted out. Carl had expected no less. He had used some of Victoria's old hair dye and when he had rinsed out the remnants, his hair had stuck out like a scarecrow's. So Rose's reaction was no surprise. He had even given himself a shock when he saw the red-haired man looking back at him in the mirror.

"Yeah, it's certainly not the color Mom uses these days," said Laura when it was all too late. Carl could not believe it.

And to finish off his highly unusual appearance, Laura had equipped him with an outdated suit, tie, white shirt, and shoes of the type Carl's father would have sneered at.

"You look good," Laura had tried to convince him. Rose was not one to soften a blow, however.

"Mission accomplished," she mumbled. "You certainly don't look like yourself. Actually, I've never seen anything like it before, thank god. What are you up to?"

"Thanks for the reassurance," he said. "I need to get out and look into some things. How did Gordon get on with his shift? Was he freezing to death?"

"I think so." She yawned. "He'd already left by the time I arrived."

"Okay, poor guy. It sure was cold. Did you ever get around to investigating Sisle Park's time at university?"

"Er, why do you ask? It's not like we got the memo to do it. Aren't you supposed to be the one doing the delegating?"

"So you didn't?"

She shook her head and pulled the blanket over her. Carl could just as well have slept on that sofa bed instead of the hard floor. She did not even care to check.

Laura took Carl to a huge garage and pointed to a conspicuous Alfa Romeo parked to one side.

"No one is going to miss that," she said. "Dad gave it to Mom five years ago, and his mechanic has given it regular checks since then, but she's hardly ever used it in all the time I can remember. She always says there's no point in having a driver's license when you can just call a cab. And it's just as well because she's always a bit drunk."

Carl got in the car, which was quite challenging for his sore hip because it was low-slung. Half an hour later, he parked in front of the chemistry department at University of Copenhagen. It was more than thirty years ago that Sisle Park had studied here, so he could hardly expect anyone to be remaining from those days. But he might get lucky and find someone bright enough to unearth something from the records.

The front door was open, but the empty hallways did not hold much promise. Not only was there a lockdown, but it was also the Christmas holidays, so it was no surprise that the place seemed completely abandoned. *How does a society move forward if everything has been totally shut down?* he thought as he stared into one laboratory after another filled with flasks, bottles, and steel sinks that shone as if they had never been used. An indistinct smell of metal and chemicals hung in the air and reminded him of the time when Hardy had been staying in his living room.

"Is there anyone here?" he shouted a couple of times, only to be greeted with his own echo. He tried a few locked office doors. It was not surprising that no one had answered his calls.

"Shit," he said out loud. Then Laura's phone rang.

"Hi, Assad. What's up?"

"Sisle Park has just driven off from her house. I'm sorry but I didn't manage to follow her because the key to Gordon's car had fallen down on the ground and I couldn't find it."

"Shit," said Carl again. They really were not having much luck today.

"Do you want me to see if I can get inside the house?"

"Do you mean break in?"

"Er, yes, something like that."

"There must be alarms everywhere, so I wouldn't recommend it, Assad. Before you know it, there'll be a couple of angry-looking security guys. And that's nothing compared to how Marcus would look. You can sneak around the house and see if that pays off, but I doubt it."

"Okay. Then I'll just stay here until she comes back. I'll wait in Gordon's car and hope, Allah willing, that the ice will melt from my beard." He laughed.

Carl was leaning up against the corridor wall when Assad ended the call. Right now he really just wanted to turn himself in to the chief of homicide and get it over with. Then he could relinquish responsibility to Marcus and his colleagues. What could Carl really do in the current situation anyway? He looked at his reflection in the window opposite. The hideous red hair was one thing, his despondent expression another.

If you just give up and turn yourself in, you'll kill Bierbek. Are you ready to do that? he asked himself. Laura would lose her father and a despicable person would succeed in her evil endeavor. If he turned himself in now and abandoned the case, Department Q would suffer a blow from which it would probably never recover. And then there was his own personal issue. What had Sniffer Dog and his colleagues unearthed that had made his situation so bleak?

He smiled at his reflection. The dye would probably wash out. A few hours' good sleep in Rose's bed tonight and the circles under his eyes would disappear. He would just have to man up and show them all that a local boy from Brønderslev could still keep his feet firmly planted on the ground. It would make his father proud.

He decided to try one last time to see if anyone was around.

"ANYONE HERE?" he shouted, and he finished with a piercing whistle, which he had taught himself at police academy.

The metallic sound of a door being opened and slammed shut echoed from one of the side corridors, followed by the hurried footsteps approaching. Seconds later a dark-haired woman appeared, wearing an expression of disdain and anger.

"How on earth did you get in here?" she asked, squeezing her phone as if she was just about to call for assistance.

"I walked in through the unlocked door." He pointed down the side corridor without knowing if that was actually the direction he had come from.

"Then I'll have to ask you to turn around and leave by the same door," she said, critically scanning his disastrous hair and foppish clothes. "You definitely have no business being here."

He felt optimistic. Only an administrative employee would make such a fuss. She was literally exuding ownership of the entire institute, so he just had to play his cards right.

"You're not completely wrong. I'm not a student, not a lecturer, and I'm not here from the ministry of education or some so-called unbiased consultancy service to analyze the running and effectiveness of your department. But I do have this . . ."

He pulled out a worn ID from his pocket and held it up so close to her face that she could see every minute detail.

She turned her head slightly, but she did not take her eyes off the ID. The word "POLICE" had a tendency to have this wonderfully paralyzing effect on people.

"Yes, nothing too serious, but I really need to get hold of some information," he continued. "I'm sorry to disturb your Christmas peace, but, as I'm sure you're aware, police work doesn't stop for the holidays. I'm afraid that's just our fate."

He made sure to try to look forlorn, as if he had a pair of crying children at home missing their dad.

He jutted out his elbow in a corona greeting. "Chief Inspector Carl Mørck. Sorry I didn't have the chance to introduce myself."

She hesitantly bumped his elbow with hers.

"Tatjana Kuzlovski Kristensen," she said, trying to look like she did not wish he would just take a hike. "What's all this about?"

"Well, that's just it. I need some information about a student who graduated from here in 1989. Summa cum laude, mind you."

Her broad smile did not look promising.

"Yeah, I know it's a long time ago. Too long, right?"

She nodded with the same smile still on her face. "You do realize that's thirty-one years ago?"

"Well, it's not the hardest calculation in the world. So what do you suggest?"

"Certainly not to go barging into a department where everyone has been sent home."

"Are there any archives?"

"Probably," she said. "But I've got nothing to do with them. Why don't you talk to someone who worked here back then? An old lecturer should be able to remember a student who graduated summa cum laude."

"And where would I find one?"

The address she gave him was not in a fancy location, but when Carl arrived at the retirement home where the almost ninety-year-old widower, Torben Clausen, had spent the last ten years of his life, he thought it looked cozy enough. The former lecturer had his entire world encapsulated within just twelve square meters: a bed, a bookshelf full of scientific literature, an armchair covered in purple velvet, and quite a lot of other monstrosities from a bygone age. Not too different actually from the sheltered housing where Carl's equally old ex-mother-in-law, Karla Alsing, had lived in all the time that Carl had worked at Department Q.

Torben Clausen looked at him with eyes that were so plagued with cataracts that it must be near impossible for him to discern his surroundings. The wrinkles around his eyes bore testimony to a life that had not always been easy.

"So, you're a chief inspector," he said three or four times to let it sink in. "Not so often I have one of your sort visiting." His false teeth rattled as he laughed quietly. "In fact, never."

Carl got straight to the point. "Can you remember a student called Lisbeth Park? She graduated in 1989 summa cum laude from the department of chemistry. You were a lecturer there at the time, so maybe . . ."

Clausen's straining eyes flicked from side to side as if looking for a spot to rest on.

"I thought that maybe you . . ."

The old man turned to the window, and the gray light hit his face. "Yes, she was a talented one. Talented and a mystery to everyone. I remember her all too well."

"All too well?"

"She was the only one from what I called my 'elite team' to survive a lightning strike in 1982."

"Lightning strike? The only one? What do you mean?"

"Exactly what I said, young man. Seven students were hit by lightning in Fælledparken just next to the department." His lower lip started quivering without any warning. "Ohh," he said, gasping for breath. "I haven't thought about it for a long time. And I didn't think it would have such an effect on me." He wiped his blind eyes.

Carl nodded and tried to jolt his memory. Regardless of how dramatic this event sounded, he could not recall it. But then he had only been seventeen and his mind was on other things entirely.

They sat in silence for a minute or two until the old man had regained his composure.

"You see, it was my fault. I was the one who suggested that we take the lecture outside, God forgive me." He cried a little again.

"Suddenly the sky went dark, but I didn't anticipate any lightning, and the first strike took me by surprise. I didn't pay it much attention because my students were in the middle of a heated fight, and I was more concerned with their screaming and shouting. Well, in fact it was only Lisbeth Park who seemed completely enraged. She was by far the best student on the team, and she accused the others of having stolen her notes. And also something about them bullying her and perhaps even something about one of them having betrayed her. But I'm not so sure about the last part. But she was incensed, and the others laughed at her. I was watching from a distance and about to walk over and intervene but then the entire sky lit up and a horrible boom almost burst my eardrums. The rain started in the same instant, and the next thing I remember is kneeling down with the water rising around me and my students in front of me lying lifeless and charred in a circle around the crater the lightning bolt had created. I was in a state of total shock. The sort that haunts you in the middle of the night no matter how much time has passed."

"And Lisbeth Park?"

"She survived. I've no idea how. I was told that she was thrown by the impact."

"What happened to her?"

"I don't really know, because she disappeared for several years before returning to finish her degree. Summa cum laude, as you already know. I know that she had spent some of the time she was away in South Africa, and she certainly knew a lot when she returned that she hadn't learned at our department."

"You said that she was angry with her fellow students?"

"Yes. Now that we're talking about it, I do recall that she time and time again accused her fellow students of stealing from her analyses and papers. The confrontations resulted in a lot of mockery and denial. She even complained to the head of the department, which is why I know. Maybe she was bullied by the others after her accusations, or maybe they simply froze her out. And then there was that thing with a young man who betrayed her. It's coming back to me now."

"Were you hurt as a result of the lightning strike?"

"No, but as I said, I was in a state of shock. And just after they had rushed her to the ambulance, I suffered a heart attack. I'm sorry I'm telling you all this in the reverse order, but the paramedic who took her to the ambulance, also saved my life. I'm old now and I don't have long left, but I've always been deeply grateful to that paramedic, and every Christmas I've sent a present to him and his family." He pointed at a small tiled table in the corner. "The present is there on the table. But I guess it'll have to wait because everything is closed."

"You don't remember what happened to her immediately after the accident?"

He shook his head.

"About two years ago, Martin reminded me about some details regarding the accident. He'll probably be able to tell you more. He also asked questions that I couldn't answer."

"You mentioned that he saved your life?"

"Yes. He was the first at the scene. And thank god for that. He's retired now, but he thought he'd like to write his memoirs and wanted to include the event. It made quite an impression on him . . . yes, even on him."

"I gather you have his address."

The old man sat quietly for a moment trying to get the images out of his head before answering. "You mean Martin's?" He pointed at a small red notebook that was the only thing on his desk. "His address is on the first page. You'll have to read it yourself because my eyes aren't what they used to be."

Carl nodded. "Maybe I can bring your present to him myself?"

It was the first time he saw the old man smile.

53

SISLE

Tuesday evening, December 22, and Wednesday, December 23, 2020

Who did they take her for? Did they really think they could keep her house under surveillance without her noticing? Were they not able to work out that her property was equipped with motion sensors everywhere and that she had heat sensors on her roof picking up not only on movement in the vicinity of the house but also revealing the outline of anyone who tried to get close?

A fairly new VW Golf had been parked a bit down the road the entire afternoon. Not strange in itself, but considering the police press conference on TV and the huge reward being offered, she could not allow herself to overlook even the slightest unexpected change around her.

Later in the afternoon, she caught sight of a pale man and photographed him a couple of times while he stood hiding behind a tree, staring up at her house. He appeared to have time on his hands, because in spite of the inclement weather he did not move from his position, except for a few minutes when he sat in the car.

"Are you having your lunch?" she asked aloud, checking her watch. Exactly ten minutes later he resumed his position behind the tree, so it seemed she was right.

Who are you? she wondered to herself when he pulled out a camera and pointed it toward the house. Sisle moved back from the window with a start and stood for a moment pondering over this man. Who could know something that might explain this surveillance? Not one of her employees had a man in their inner circle like this—the sort of man who could most aptly be described as death warmed up. And she could be certain because she had a file on each employee at Park Optimizing containing personal data that might prove useful in exactly this sort of situation: medical history and health records, their résumé and other background information prior to employment with her, Debora's progress reports from when they had been under her wing, family relationships, finances, photos of all family and close friends, hobbies, psychological profiles including their strengths and weaknesses, and much more.

But a skinny and especially pale man like this one was not someone she had come across in those materials. So who had stationed him out here?

She called Adam, who answered almost immediately.

"In a moment, I'm going to send you a photo of a man who is watching my property. Let me know if you recognize him."

He called back a minute later.

"No, I don't know him. Do you want me to try a face recognition assessment? I can use a VPN connection so it looks like I'm in the U.S."

"No, don't bother. The bird might have flown by then. Just get over here pronto."

They approached from behind, and the guy let out a shout when Adam secured him in a grip under his arms and up around the back of his neck, forcefully pressing his head forward.

"What are you doing?" he moaned as Sisle stepped in front of him. "Let me go."

"I ask the questions around here," said Sisle. "You have my house under surveillance. Why? Who are you?"

Sisle nodded to Adam, who loosened his grip.

"I'm not watching your house. My girlfriend lives next door and I think she's cheating on me, so let go."

Sisle nodded again and Adam fully released his grip on the man.

"Really! What's her name?"

He hesitated for one second too long. "What's it got to do with you? Who are *you*?"

Sisle stepped closer to him. Where had she seen this man before?

"Do you have any ID on you I can see?" she asked.

He smiled contemptuously. "Over my dead body. You've got no right!"

"Over your dead body? That could be arranged. Would you do the honors, Adam?"

The pale streak of a man should not have been taken by surprise when he took a massive punch to the back of the neck, and his blue eyes turned a shade of gray as they tried in vain to stay focused on Sisle.

"What are you doing?" he stammered when Adam rummaged under his jacket and fumbled in the inner pocket.

"Nothing here," said Adam, as he carried on searching the guy.

"Just tell me who you are here and now and you might just spare yourself any further problems."

He seemed very perplexed and lowered his head. He still refused to answer, but his fear of another blow was something he could not hide.

"Things could get nasty if you don't help us out here. You see, I can't have someone spying on me without knowing why or who they are. Your choice, or do you want another beating?"

He shook his head. "I don't know why you think I'm spying on you. I've just—"

Adam punched him again. Harder this time.

Adam laid the unconscious man on the daybed at the far end of Sisle's bedroom and fixed his wrists to his belt behind his back with a couple of cable ties.

They found his vehicle registration in the glove compartment, and under the seat they also found his wallet containing ID that was more worrying than they could have anticipated.

"Damn it, Sisle! He's a policeman," said Adam when he came in with the ID in his hand. "You can't keep him here. We need to get rid of him somehow or other."

Sisle studied his ID card. "Gordon Taylor, lawyer and police assistant," it read.

She googled his name on her iPhone and found what she had expected. He was standing in several photos next to his boss, Carl Mørck. And then she found a couple more photos showing Department Q grouped together: only four people in total. Quite worrying when she had read about the effectiveness of the department and how many cases they had solved.

She printed a couple of the photos and placed them on the desk.

"I've got a bad feeling about this," said Adam. "Carl Mørck has identified you as the person who has kidnapped Maurits van Bierbek, Sisle. You do realize that, right? I seriously think that the risk of them coming down hard on all three of us is now imminent and greater than ever. So shouldn't we kill Maurits van Bierbek and this guy and then lie low for a long time?"

Sisle's eyes narrowed. "As far as I remember, it wasn't too long ago that I tried to impress on you and Debora that I do *not* change my plans. And as far as Gordon Taylor here, let me see if I can't twist us having him to our advantage. In the long term, we can do what we want with him, but Maurits van Bierbek will have to wait until Mao's birthday on Boxing Day. Understood?"

"But what do you think Carl Mørck will do when he discovers that this one hasn't reported back? If he just simply vanishes from the face of the earth, Mørck will force his way into the house. And I assume you don't want that, right?"

"Let him come. The guy will be gone tomorrow morning."

"Where to?"

"We could put him in with van Bierbek for the next few days, couldn't we?"

Adam looked more than skeptical.

———

Sisle gave the police assistant an injection that would ensure he did not gain consciousness for hours. So things were peaceful, especially now that Adam had gone home—albeit grumbling, contrary, and wholly dissatisfied that his opinion had not been taken into account.

It would not take many of those sorts of murmurs of discontent from Debora and Adam before Sisle could see the advantages of ending their association. The new setup she was kick-starting in the New Year was going to be led by new disciples of a far higher caliber than the recruits Debora had provided in the last few years. In fact, she did not need any more recruits. And when she considered her own organization, there were at least forty suitable candidates who could be sent out to complete their own missions over the next twenty years. And that was as far as her plans went. So as soon as Maurits van Bierbek had been killed, Adam and Debora would have outlived their use.

Sisle sat down at her desk.

All the preparations had been made for executing Maurits van Bierbek. In this last phase, with the instruments for the actual execution ready, the only thing that remained was to formulate the judgment itself and the justification for it. The verbal issuing of the final sentence was something she had started in 2016 when it was Franco Svendsen's turn to be killed. But just before she was about to give him the lethal injection, her words failed her. His terrified eyes had implored her, and his tears resulted in one wretched moment of doubt that was enough to ruin even a well-rehearsed sentence.

As a direct result, she had written down what she wanted to say when it was time for Birger von Brandstrup to die, and everything went smoothly with the declaration of his sentence. And that was exactly how she wanted things to be when they put down Maurits van Bierbek. Controlled and dispassionate.

Sisle smiled. Her disdain for van Bierbek meant the words almost wrote themselves.

———

A ray of light shone over her bookcase close to midnight, so Sisle stood up from the desk and just caught sight of a taxi turning the corner on her street. She looked down the road toward the gray Golf that was still parked there; they would have to get rid of that. She was thinking that they could do it tomorrow, when she spotted another figure down there by the car. And this one also seemed to be looking up toward her house.

The figure moved momentarily out of the shadows, stopped briefly under the light of the streetlamp, and looked around. It was a youngish woman who, judging by her body language, was puzzled about something. Was it perhaps because she had expected to meet Gordon Taylor?

Sisle took her night-vision goggles and caught a glimpse of the woman's face before she returned to the shadows.

It only took a quick glance at one of the printed photos of the Department Q group before Sisle had identified her as one of them.

There was no mistaking that the group was closing in on her.

Sisle got up at six o'clock the following morning and confirmed that the woman was still in position. *What a shame there has been nothing for you to see and report back on*, she thought. She was probably going to be relieved by someone else soon.

It happened at exactly eight o'clock. Just as she had expected, the third person from the group of four turned up. A dark, broad-shouldered man of less than average height whom she immediately identified as Hafez el-Assad was now standing behind the Golf, talking with the woman. They were probably discussing where Gordon Taylor had got to, as he was probably supposed to take the shift after this one.

Sisle smiled. She had checked on the sedated man several times during the night. Lying there like a stranded porpoise, he exhibited absolutely no visible or audible signs of life apart from the odd faint sound of breathing.

The next changeover down at the parked Golf would probably be at four o'clock this afternoon, when Assad would be relieved. And when Gordon Taylor failed to arrive, it would stir things up one way or another.

There was direct access from Sisle's house to the garage. However, the route from her bedroom at the back of the house to the garage door went through four living rooms, a corridor, the kitchen, and the utility room, which was an impossible distance for Sisle to carry an unconscious man—even if he was almost just skin and bone.

So she gave him a big push and he rolled down with a bump onto a heavy blanket she had placed on the floor. He landed on one shoulder and let out a sigh, but he was still unconscious.

Sisle pulled her Persian rugs to the side a little and dragged the man through the various rooms while the sweat started to trickle down from her armpits. When she reached the garage, she was already tired and took the five concrete steps down to the garage floor with one almighty tug at the blanket. She heard the back of the man's head hitting the concrete edges of the steps, but what choice did she have?

At ten o'clock, the man from Department Q had moved sufficiently close to the house for her to make her move. *This is my chance*, she thought, and she rushed out to the garage, opened the garage door, and with her foot on the gas sped past the man, leaving him fumbling with his ass in the air looking for something on the front left tire of the Golf.

She did not have far to drive.

But there was no way they could know that.

54

CARL

Wednesday, December 23, 2020

The retired paramedic, Martin, had no less than three surnames and just as many litters of children all in the one place. Or at least there were six or more functioning children's bikes in front of the open kitchen door of the terraced house in Albertslund. There was a mighty racket coming from inside, so when Carl rang the front doorbell, there was no reaction. The bell was simply drowned out.

Instead, he just went in and stood there like an unexpected and unknown guest in the living room with the present held out toward eight people, large and small, who suddenly stopped in their tracks, holding Christmas decorations in their hands, staring at him in confusion.

"Sorry for intruding," he said. "I'm supposed to deliver this from Torben Clausen for a Martin. Is that one of you?"

The only real possibility, a man in his early sixties, came down from a chair and left the Christmas tree star hanging to one side.

"That's me," he said, then stared at Carl's mouth in apparent shock that he was not wearing a face mask. "You can put it there on the table. I don't think we should get too close to each other."

Carl put a hand up to his mouth. "Sorry, it's so easy to forget," he said, fishing out one of the blue face masks he had been carrying around in his pocket for months. "Do you have five minutes, Martin?" He pulled out his invalid ID badge so everyone could see it, and the effect was brilliant. The older children fought to get closer so they could get a better look, while the adults had their eyes fixed on their host as if he was already under arrest.

"I know it looks like there are too many of us gathered together, but we do actually all live under the same roof. That means it's okay, right?"

Carl smiled underneath his mask and hoped the man could sense it.

"Relax, I'm not here about the restrictions on gatherings. I'm here about Lisbeth Park. Torben Clausen has just been telling me that you were the first person on the scene after the lightning strike. Look, do you have a few minutes? I have some questions in connection with that event."

"I've experienced a lot in my years as an ambulance driver and paramedic, but that day back in 1982 stands out. Try to imagine it. Six bodies still steaming and smelling like roast pork. Six people that just moments before had been as alive as you and I. And just one survivor."

"Lisbeth Park?"

He nodded and gave a detailed account of what had happened.

"So you're saying that she was happy the others were dead?" Not exactly anything that would surprise him in her case, but he was curious.

"Yeah, that's what she said. Her exact words were 'If I can survive this, then with God's help I can survive anything.'"

Carl nodded. She had certainly tested that hypothesis ever since. But Carl would put a stop to that. He hoped.

"Torben Clausen told me that you've started writing your memoirs and that the accident—and the fate of Lisbeth Park in particular—has been on your mind. What have you found out about her? Can you tell me?"

The rugged man gave a cheeky smile. "So long as you don't steal my story and publish it."

"I promise. What happened to the girl after what you've just told me?"

"I drove her straight to Riget Hospital, which was just minutes away. She was admitted to the trauma center and then to the neurological ward. She was there for a few days and then transferred to the county hospital in Glostrup for further treatment. She was finally admitted to their psychiatric center. The psychiatrists wouldn't tell me much, but I did manage to winkle out of them that she allowed herself to be admitted for a period of almost two years after suffering some intense and irrational episodes. Apparently her brain was heavily affected by the lightning strike."

"Almost like electroshock, right?"

"No, far from it. Lightning can produce both gamma rays and X-rays and have a charge of several hundred million volts and a current of approximately ten thousand amperes. Electroshock doesn't come close to that."

"So what do you get with electroshock?"

"Something entirely different. Normally a direct current of four hundred and sixty volts and zero point eight amperes."

"Okay. But then why didn't the lightning kill her?"

Martin shrugged. "She must have been standing exactly at the right distance from the strike. And in contrast to ECT—that's electroconvulsive therapy—which lasts between fifteen seconds and one minute, the discharge of lightning lasts only a quarter of a second as far as I'm aware. If the discharge had lasted as long as ECT, she would probably have been burned to a cinder."

"Have you spoken with Lisbeth Park recently? I suppose you know that she calls herself Sisle Park these days and is a successful businesswoman?"

"Yes, I know quite a lot about her. But I haven't spoken with her. I've tried to get an interview with her a few times, but I've always been given a point-blank refusal by whomever I spoke with at her company. It's a shame because it's a very interesting story. Especially given the path she's taken in life."

If only you knew, Martin, thought Carl.

––––––––

When Carl called the psychiatric center in Glostrup to make an appointment, he was told that the place had changed a lot since 1982. Back then when Lisbeth Park was admitted, it was called Copenhagen County Hospital Nordvang, but since then, not only had the name changed but also the psychiatric principles and management structure.

"If you have questions about patients who have been committed here, there are standard procedures that you'll need to follow before being given access to a patient's records," said the secretary. He realized it would make no difference how much he stressed the importance of his inquiry or said that he was investigating a case that could have dire consequences if he did not receive a little help as quickly as possible.

"It's the Christmas holidays and we're short-staffed because a lot of people have been sent home due to COVID-19, but you might be able to get a reply sometime in January."

Carl wanted to explode but he could not muster the energy. It would make no difference anyway.

"Can you tell me the names of the doctors working there in 1982? Please," he begged.

"You'll have to search the internet," came the reply.

Thanks for nothing, thought Carl.

He stopped at a gas station, bought a pair of reading glasses, strength plus two, a hot dog baguette, and ten nonalcoholic Carlsberg Nordic beers and began surfing on Laura's tiny phone.

I should have bought strength two point five, he thought, squinting. It was not easy to track down retired psychiatrists. He did find references to many doctoral theses written by psychiatrists, and also mention of a few who had worked at Nordvang in the eighties. But the ones who were not already dead had withheld numbers.

He thought better of waking Rose to get her to search. Gordon would be a safer bet, so he called the temporary number.

He waited until the phone went to voicemail. Then he tried again, still with no luck.

It was out of character for Gordon to leave his shift early and then just head home to sleep.

Carl sighed and squinted at the screen again. Not many of the doctors who had been at Nordvang in the relevant period had stayed very long. But that was just the way it was with doctors. They were promoted, switched fields, were offered better incentives, and changed jobs. It definitely did not resemble the police force.

Carl started searching for psychiatric nurses instead, and after half an hour he came across one called Karen Jochumsen who had worked over many years at Nordvang as a charge nurse and, thankfully, also in the period he was interested in. She had retired after a few extra years as an agency nurse, and from the phone it seemed like she did not mind the diversion from her usual humdrum existence.

"Lisbeth Park!" It sounded as if she drew a deep breath.

"If there's one patient I remember clearly, it's her. But you have to understand that just like the doctors, I'm bound by confidentiality and can only talk about her illness and treatment providing she gives her consent."

Carl knew that Sisle's consent to discuss her mental health was the last thing anyone would ever manage to obtain.

"Of course, I understand. But maybe you can refer me to one of her doctors? It is a police matter after all, so don't you think I might be able to get a bit of help?"

"Oh, well, I must admit that you've got my curiosity now. If you do manage to get access to her records, please get back in touch."

"It sounds like you've been wondering what happened to her."

"Of course I know what happened to her. I've seen her on TV a few times over the years, and it's impressive what she's managed to achieve. But then she was *very* special."

Carl thought that her emphasis on the word "very" was an invitation for him to challenge her on her opinion.

"So you had concerns about her, Karen?"

The pause was long enough to get his hopes up that she might fall into his trap.

"I'm not allowed to say anything about her stay at Nordvang. But if I'm honest, no one who worked on the ward really understood her. We knew that she'd been through a lot, but she had actually suffered more damage from the lightning strike than we first thought. But again, you'll have to ask someone else about it."

Carl gave up. She was too professional to be manipulated.

"Could you maybe give me the name of a doctor so I can try to get access to her medical records?"

"I could give you several names, but I'm only in contact with one of them. And he is the one who could help you most, come to think of it. His name is Thorleif Petersen, and he was the consultant psychiatrist on the ward. In the last few years, he's had his own practice and taught forensic psychiatry at university on and off."

The address she gave Carl turned out to be close to Maurits van Bierbek's house in Gammel Holte, so he decided to pay the doctor a visit.

I should've been a doctor, he thought, comparing his own house in Rønneholtparken with the three-wing whitewashed farmhouse leading directly onto paddocks and frozen pastures.

"My husband is out with the Icelandic ponies. Third path to the right in between the paddocks. You'll have to speak up because he's become a bit hard of hearing with age," explained his white-haired wife, who could easily fit a size 2, unlike Carl's own mother, who didn't have the luxury of a healthy diet.

Carl looked down at his shoes as he trudged through the mud. He had to admit that a couple of days' rain was more beneficial to the soil than it was to his shoes, which soon filled with mud, reminding him how bloody cold it could be in Denmark.

"Hello there!" he shouted at a suitable distance when he saw a head appear over the backs of a group of ponies waiting for treats.

A man with eyebrows so bushy that it was impossible to focus on anything else stepped out from behind the ponies. He stood with his legs wide apart in insanely long rubber boots, looking at Carl as if he were one of his patients.

Carl introduced himself a couple of times with increasing volume, showed his badge, and received an accepting smile. This man definitely had plenty of good experience working with the police.

Carl told him who had given him the address, and he received another smile, which bore witness to the high esteem in which he held Karen Jochumsen.

But the smile soon evaporated when Carl mentioned Lisbeth Park.

"What about her?" he asked, sounding suddenly hostile. He knelt down and raised the hind leg of one of the ponies. "I'm afraid it's laminitis, as far as I can see. Do you know what that is?"

Carl nodded. Everyone who had grown up in the countryside knew that. "I'm sorry to hear it. He looks healthy enough otherwise."

The man stood up and stroked the horse's muzzle. "He's been a good boy, but I think the vet will have to put him down tomorrow. It'll be a sad day." He patted the pony on the chest and led him to a paddock on the other side of the path.

"What about the others? Do they also have laminitis?"

"I hope not. But if they do, I'm entirely to blame."

"Feed or grazing?" asked Carl.

The doctor frowned, and a hint of respect showed in his eyes.

"I grew up in the countryside," said Carl, guessing his question.

"Can I offer you a little drop inside? It's a bit cold today." He looked at Carl's muddy shoes and smiled.

"I'm not at liberty to say anything about the patient or her treatment, unless there is a risk to life by my withholding information about her."

Carl sniffed the whisky that Thorleif Petersen had poured. It was proving to be a rewarding talk. He explained in detail what Department Q had pieced together and what the current situation was for the kidnapped Maurits van Bierbek.

Thorleif Petersen's professional mask disintegrated.

"Ohh, that sends a shiver down my spine," he said. "I must admit that she was the most complicated case I've ever come across. It's terrible that we didn't manage to neutralize her before letting her go."

"Neutralize?" Carl was reluctant to ask exactly what he meant by that. "Tell me about her. How did she turn out the way she did, in your opinion? And what are her weaknesses? We've only got three days to prevent another murder."

"What's that?" He held one hand behind his ear.

"We only have three days to prevent another murder."

"Can't we get a judge to issue a warrant for her arrest?"

"Everything we have on her is built on assumption and speculation. I'm convinced that we're right, but it's not enough for us to have her arrested."

"You asked me who she is. I can tell you that she came to us from Glostrup County Hospital, and before that, she had been admitted to the neurological ward at Riget Hospital. The latter tried to ascertain the damage to her nervous system and brain following the lightning strike, but they didn't get very far. The scans showed that certain areas where the tissue is most sensitive were affected, but the neurological and neuropsychological aftereffects of such an impact often don't show for some time. So we don't know if her cognitive and emotional state was a result of the accident, but she was without doubt a very special case. And when she was transferred to the burns unit at Glostrup County Hospital, they discovered a dead fetus inside her."

Carl struggled to fit all the new pieces into their grand puzzle.

"I'm thinking that she may have already been insane," suggested Carl, and the doctor nodded.

"Naturally, she took the removal of the dead fetus hard. She talked about how God's punishment had struck her and the child because she had become involved with the devil who had impregnated her. She said that he had betrayed her with another woman in her class and that she had wanted him and several others in the group to die a violent death. She repeated over and over that the lightning had provided the answer.

And she increasingly blamed the man who had betrayed her for the death of her child."

"Do you think she wanted the baby?"

"She didn't even know she was pregnant. But the damage was much more severe than the loss of the child because her uterus was so inflamed and injured that there was no saving it. She'd never be able to have children, and that was the state she came to us in. Incredibly angry and vengeful. Talking about evil and God and revenge incessantly. I was called in because my colleagues were worried that she might be a danger to her surroundings. She certainly was hard on some of her fellow patients, and one of them allegedly took their own life because of her. So in some way they were right."

"But she hadn't committed anything that might be understood as some form of criminal offense at that point, had she?"

The doctor sighed and poured them another whisky. He downed his own and licked his lips while seemingly searching for an answer.

"Sisle Park was not committed against her will, and no one had requested for her to be. She was there voluntarily. I took her voluntary stay with us of around a year and a half as a sign that she wanted to get better and function normally in private and public."

"But then she discharged herself?"

He nodded. "How many people did you say she's killed?"

"Premeditated?"

He nodded.

"At least twenty-two people and possibly more. And that doesn't include the indirect victims of her actions."

Thorleif Petersen buried his face in his hands. "It's terrible. Just terrible. We should've stopped her. We should have seen it coming. But how could we?"

"Sisle Park is probably a different person from the Lisbeth Park you met. She's clearly developed aspects of herself that only function via specific rituals. Otherwise this Maurits van Bierbek would probably be dead already. There's the fact that the murders can only happen on the birthdays of despots. Then we've got the salt at the scene of every murder, which is an obvious allusion to God's judgment on Sodom and Gomorrah. The entire pseudo-religious element and the methods all indicate something highly ritualized. Is it possible that she also suffers from OCD? I mean, everything she's done points to compulsive ideas and actions."

The doctor straightened up in his seat. He was as pale as a sheet. "We discussed the possibility several times during conferences, and also that she had schizophrenic characteristics, but she managed to convince us otherwise every time. We focused instead on what had happened to her with the accident and the dead fetus. And we became convinced that her main issue was major depression. But now that you mention it, I'm sure that she suffered from OCD—and still does. Based on what you've told me, I would now view her as both a schizophrenic and someone with a serious obsessive-compulsive disorder in addition to lots of other disorders. The woman is deeply troubled. But all this, combined with her compulsive ideas, which she justifies in a quest against bad morals and ethics, makes for a deadly cocktail."

Carl nodded. "With what you know about her now, what would you think her biggest weakness is?"

The doctor stared blankly into the distance for a long time. Then he took another whisky while still looking at a loss.

"Do you think she takes medication for any of this?" asked Carl.

Thorleif Petersen seemed to wake up from his trance. He still looked distressed and melancholy, but at least he was present again. "With everything you've told me, I can say it's almost certain that she doesn't take any medication. There's nothing to indicate that the extent and violent nature of her actions have waned in the least. She may have taken sedatives once in a while—after all, there are two years between each murder—but definitely not in the lead-up to a murder. And that's where we are now if I understand you correctly."

He leaned forward toward Carl. "You mentioned the small child who she inadvertently killed. That, combined with the flowers and the money she sent the mother, and not least that she had lost a child herself and will never be able to have one, that is her Achilles' heel. Believe me, if you really want to get to her, that's your best bet. Use it against her."

Carl nodded. Then his phone rang. He did not recognize the number even though something told him that he should.

"Hello, Carl Mørck speaking," he said.

"Gordon never made it home last night." It was Rose, and she sounded like she was panicking. "He disappeared on his shift, Carl. And Assad told me that Sisle sped away from her home this morning. She's taken him, Carl. I just know it."

55

GORDON

Christmas Eve, Thursday, December 24, 2020

Gordon's body woke bit by bit. First with a thumping pain in the back of his head, followed by the feeling that his ankles and wrists were being squeezed tightly, and that both his hands and feet were numb. Then he felt the nausea and his body almost screaming out for hydration and a less uncomfortable position.

He opened his eyes knowing full well that his situation was hopeless, but Gordon was not fearful. He was angry. Angry at his carelessness and at having been taken by surprise. He should have made a run for it straightaway when he sensed something moving behind him. He was quick on his feet and could run a hundred meters in fourteen seconds. So why had he not done it?

Now he looked up. He took in the bare walls and a table at the far end of the room next to an elevator. It was quite a wide elevator as far as he could make out. Perhaps a freight elevator. He tilted his head back and noticed the ceiling had a couple of runners stretching almost down to the far wall. It looked like a room that had had some sort of industrial function. With such a high ceiling it could well be a sort of warehouse. He could clearly picture a truck driving around among four- and five-meter-high metal shelving units, taking pallets from the shelves, and driving down to the far end to load them on the elevator.

He tried to wrestle himself free of the cable ties securing his feet to the legs of the chair and his arms to the back, but their tightness made moving painful.

Then he heard a sound from behind him like someone sighing or attempting to articulate very weak vowel sounds. He tried to turn around, but his back was as stiff as a board.

"Is there someone there?" he asked, and he heard the same sighing sound.

"Damn it!" he exclaimed when he tried to twist again. For every jolt to the right, it felt as if a knife were jabbed into his back. What had happened to him?

He moved back and forth, each time with a slightly bigger jolt to his right.

"I can hear you behind me. Is it you, Sisle Park?"

But there was no answer. He finally managed to twist himself so far to the right that he could make out a body slumped over in a chair that like his was also fastened to the floor. It looked strange, but the poor person seemed to be secured in place by a couple of chains that appeared to come out of his back and straight up to the ceiling.

"Maurits van Bierbek?" he asked tentatively. He was sure it was a man at any rate—there was no mistaking the beard growth or the urine stains on the front of the loose underwear. Nothing about this man bound in armor radiated any of the sort of prosperity or energy one might have expected from a person like Maurits van Bierbek. He looked like an emaciated prisoner, thin and helpless with pale, dry skin and greasy strands of hair flopping down over his forehead. His lips were chapped, legs and arms discolored, and his chest strangely still. The second hand on his wind-up Rolex had stopped, indicating that he must have been sitting there motionless for a very long time.

But he was alive.

————

Gordon wet himself a couple of hours later. He had managed to hold it for a long time—almost ready to scream in desperation, but what was the point when no one could hear him?

Since high school, he had made a big deal about being able to hold it longer than anyone else. And when he did finally give in, he impressed and entertained his friends by being able to pee for several minutes before his bladder was empty.

I must have been here for a long time, seeing as I couldn't hold it anymore, he thought as he watched the puddle of urine on the floor slowly make its way toward the far wall.

It had been very close to the end of his watch on the night of December twenty-second when he was attacked. Under normal circumstances, he could hold it in for at least a day, so he reasoned that he must have been unconscious for over twenty-four hours and was now sitting here helpless on what was likely Christmas Eve. Unless they had injected him with something that obstructed his autonomous bodily functions. What a dreadful and miserable holiday.

He turned to Maurits van Bierbek, who had not moved in the last few hours. According to Department Q's reckoning, he only had two days left to live. A horrible thought—but where did that leave Gordon? Was he destined to share van Bierbek's fate?

When Gordon realized the likelihood of this, he started crying. It came suddenly and unexpectedly, and it felt embarrassing. He knew why he was crying—of course he was scared of dying, but it did not make it any better that he had experienced nothing but disappointment in love. He had never had the chance to tell a woman that he was completely hers, just as he had never received a declaration of boundless love. Two people choosing each other for life without fear of betrayal.

Gordon had been in love many times. Always from the sidelines and without acting on it. And now that he had turned thirty-two, he had outgrown the phase when it was apparently easy to find a girlfriend. He could understand why when he looked at himself in the mirror. How often had he gone to a tanning salon, only to realize that he could not tan? How often had he stood sweating in front of the same mirror with dumbbells in his hands, only to realize that he would never bulk up? Some people said that Gordon Taylor looked nice, but not nice enough apparently for someone to fall for him head over heels.

And now he might never experience that.

"Maurits?" he shouted as loudly as he could. He did not want to be alone in this forsaken place. If only Maurits would wake up.

But Maurits barely moved.

Then there was a deep humming from the elevator down by the far wall. And when he pricked his ears, he could hear the clicks from above every time a relay on a new floor was activated.

Gordon counted to five before the elevator reached their floor. Could this mean that they were five floors belowground or that someone had taken the elevator from a higher floor? Would he be able to tell when it went up again?

Then the elevator door opened.

He immediately recognized the slender woman, Sisle Park, and saw a giant of a man behind her. He was almost twenty centimeters taller than she was, and she was not exactly short. His face was contorted and his eyes were not aligned. *Clearly a birth defect*, thought Gordon. Was this the man who had knocked him out in the dark? The closer he came, the more convinced Gordon was. It was him.

"I see you're awake, Gordon Taylor. What a pleasant surprise," said Sisle Park, making sure to avoid the puddle of urine.

She walked all the way up to him and smiled gloatingly when she noted the dark stain on his trousers.

"I'm sure you'll get used to that," she mocked. "Have you had a chance to say hello to your friend here? Wasn't he happy to see you? And weren't you happy to finally discover where he was, seeing that you've been so desperately searching for him? We've bolted your chair to the floor, so you'll have to make an effort if you want to look at him."

Gordon scowled, considering whether to spit in her face, but he thought better of it as the giant took a few steps closer.

"Are you going to hit me again?" he asked. "You fucking don't hit someone who is defenseless. Even *you* wouldn't do that, would you, Sisle Park?"

She did not react to his sarcasm. "We've had time to check up on you since we brought you here yesterday morning. So you've been with Department Q for almost ten years, and I imagine you've given Carl Mørck his money's worth, given that you're still there. A law graduate with good grades and yet you chose to become an investigator with the police. Not the path one might have expected if you ask me, but it does tell me that you're very dedicated to your work. I respect that. So I've decided to give you the opportunity to follow Maurits van Bierbek's case to its conclusion."

Maybe she expected a reaction from Gordon, but he was not going to let this bitch know what he thought about her or her sick ideas.

"We'll kill him at noon the day after tomorrow. And when he's dead, we'll remove him from here and leave you with the hope that your colleagues from Department Q will find you. I think it's highly unlikely, but let's see. I'd hate to deprive you of the hope."

She nodded to the large man, who fetched a drip stand from over by the far wall and attached a drip bag to it.

"Just give him as much as he can take, Adam," she said coldly. So, the giant was called Adam. Probably the same man who had helped her drown Pia Laugesen. There was no doubt Assad had come to the right conclusion, because this man would easily have been able to hold the strong woman under the water in the pool for as long as it took.

Adam stuck the needle from the drip into van Bierbek's hand and waited. After some time, he started breathing deeper, and they slapped his cheek and told him to wake up. Adam kept slapping him harder and harder until he finally came to.

56

CARL

Christmas Eve, Thursday, December 24, and Christmas Day, Friday, December 25, 2020

Christmas Eve was not proving to be a joyful day in Department Q's makeshift office at Maurits van Bierbek's house.

They had lost all contact with Gordon and were consumed with worry. Rose was in a state of shock and constantly blamed herself. Why had she not immediately raised the alarm when she realized that Gordon was not there when she came to take over his watch? If she had, they would have probably been able to procure a search warrant for Sisle Park's house, and they might even have found her there and brought the whole sorry saga to an end. With luck they could have also forced out of her where she was keeping Maurits van Bierbek. Someone in the police was bound to have helped them, because one of their own had been kidnapped in the line of duty.

Carl could feel Rose looking at him with a hint of reproach. But if they had raised the alarm, it would inevitably have caused no end of problems for all of them, and it would not have helped Gordon one bit. Quite the contrary. Carl would have been arrested, and the others would have faced serious consequences—possibly even leading to them losing their jobs.

It really was a terrible dilemma.

"I'm breaking into her house," said Assad. "There's no stopping me this time."

"I don't think it'll help Gordon when Sisle Park finds out about it. And if you don't find the exact address where van Bierbek is being held, or what's happened to Gordon, it wouldn't make much sense anyway, would it?"

Assad looked despondent. It was obvious that he was feeling exhausted. They all were.

"Have you contacted your families to wish them merry Christmas?" asked Carl. They both smiled tiredly. He had not been in contact with Mona either since they had gone into hiding. She had been the one to ban him from contacting her. But he was tempted to give in.

"I called Gordon's parents," said Rose. "Gordon usually talks a lot with them in the run-up to Christmas, so they must've thought it odd that he hadn't been in touch. They are the type who might raise the alarm with the police, so I thought we'd better nip it in the bud. I told them that he's in love with a woman at the moment, so they shouldn't worry that he hasn't called them." She let out a deep sigh. "His mother had certainly not expected to hear that news, and she sounded so happy about it that it was almost embarrassing. I feel ashamed, but what else could I do?"

There was shouting coming from the living room below. Maurits van Bierbek's two daughters naturally had their own frustrations to deal with. The younger sister was crying, and Laura was yelling at their mother. What else could one expect? It was Christmas Eve without the trimmings: no presents, no family, no dad. And someone had to take the blame.

"Give me some ideas," said Carl. "We need to think out of the box. You've been looking for someone called Debora, Assad. Did you get anywhere?"

"I don't think there's any hope there, Carl."

"I feel completely numb. Obviously Gordon can't get in touch with us, or he would've done it ages ago. I simply can't shake that thought," said Rose quietly. "Do you think she might have killed him already?"

When had they last seen Rose welling up? Carl could not remember.

"No, I don't think so. That would be out of character for Sisle Park, Rose. She doesn't kill random people. She has a plan. And with everything we've learned about her mental state, we can be sure she won't stray from it. And we didn't find any salt close to Gordon's car, did we?"

Rose tried to look relieved, but she was not convincing. "There was no salt in van Bierbek's driveway when he was kidnapped either. And two of the cases only turned up salt when they were dug up." She put both hands in front of her mouth and breathed deeply into them. Was she starting to panic?

He should not have mentioned the salt. Rose was right—it was irrelevant. "But listen, I'd be surprised if Sisle Park doesn't reveal what's going on with Gordon. She's brazen and arrogant. And if we assume that she's the one who's kidnapped him, she will—"

"She *is* the one," interrupted Rose.

"If that's the case, I'm hoping that she'll give us a heads-up about what she's up to."

"How is she supposed to do that when our phones are turned off? And she doesn't even know where we are, Carl, so you can't exactly expect a courier to turn up with a message, can you?" Assad looked at him with his big eyes. And he was unfortunately right.

Carl fumbled behind him for his coat, which he had thrown over the back of the sofa. "I'll be quick," he said, and he took out his phone from the pocket.

"Are you planning to turn that on? Are you out of your mind?" Rose shook her head. "This area has lots of towers. You've got no more than ninety seconds before they trace you, Carl. You can rest assured that they're ready and waiting. Narcotics have endless resources when it comes to serious cases. If you want to check something, why don't you use one of van Bierbek's computers?"

"I just want to check if there are any messages or emails from her. It'll only take a minute."

He turned on the phone and counted the seconds while Rose and Assad tried to explain that police HQ were no doubt reading his emails anyway and so already knew if she had written.

"And you can be sure that they've also sent you emails bugged with spyware, so please don't," said Rose in vain. Carl just *had* to check.

It took him thirty precious seconds just to get the phone up and running. Despite Rose's ardent protests, he opened his email account and was faced with an almost endless stream of emails. Emails from Marcus Jacobsen, emails from Sniffer Dog and his team, emails from his parents wishing him a merry Christmas, and at least ten other Christmas messages from family members, one email from Hardy and one from Morten, and lots from people who wanted to earn ten million kroner and believed that they had the one tip-off that would reveal the whereabouts of Maurits van Bierbek.

Carl began to sweat.

"You need to stop this, Carl. *Now!*" shouted Rose, but Carl did not stop.

"I just need to check my messages. It'll only take a few seconds."

But that was not the case. Far too many people wanted to get hold of him. Far too many Christmas-related messages. Some from people who sounded very worried about him. It was almost touching.

"*Stop,* Carl!" It was Assad, who stretched out his hand to grab the phone. A push of a button and he had turned it off.

"That was almost three minutes, Carl. Are you out of your mind? Your generation is simply so stupid when it comes to anything to do with the internet. Did you really have to download your emails when you could've just checked them on the computer here?" said Rose. "And where do you suggest we sleep tonight? Because you can rest assured that they've already traced where you are—and us for that matter."

Carl stood up without a word and walked down to the living room, where Victoria was bracing herself to get in the Christmas spirit. Meanwhile, poor Roxan was darting around hanging up Christmas decorations—without making much of an impact in the oversized room. A plastic Christmas tree with electric lights had already been positioned on a huge Persian rug. If the situation had been different, it might have been tempting to dance around the tree.

"Excuse me, Victoria. We have a situation. We think that a lot of police cars will be arriving any minute to look for us. Unfortunately, we've got a terrible suspicion that the police might be mixed up in your husband's kidnapping. What can we do to make sure they don't find us?"

She straightened her blouse several times before being able to speak. "The police?" she exclaimed while looking like she had seen too many crime dramas. Everyone knew that corrupt police were the most dangerous people to mess with. She looked skeptical.

Had he taken it too far?

"There's no need to be scared. They're not after you," he said to appease her.

"But why would the police do that to Maurits? I don't understand."

"Don't worry about that just now. I'll explain later. Do you have somewhere we can hide where they won't find us? They'll probably have a dog unit with them."

She looked terrified. How was she supposed to fool them if they brought dogs?

Once again, it was Laura who came to their rescue. She had clearly been listening and did not find Carl's explanation very believable, but she smiled as if this was the coolest thing that could happen on a totally ruined Christmas Eve.

"There's an ATV Hunter quad bike out back. Dad uses it to race around the grounds. The dogs won't be able to trace you on that. We'll just say that you all popped by to ask a few questions."

Carl took charge of the situation. In just four minutes the team gathered all their things to make their getaway—just as they caught sight of the blue flashing lights dancing in the distance.

"This is not a Christmas I'm going to look back on fondly," said Carl as he started up the quad bike with Rose and Assad hanging on the back as best they could, with all their stuff in tow.

"But you'll never forget it, Carl," said Assad in an attempt to cheer him up.

After a few minutes they had reached a sheltered spot behind a windbreak, and Carl wasted no time in removing his SIM card from his Samsung and scrolling through his texts while the other two looked on.

"I think you should drop the text messages, Carl," said Rose. "It's more likely that she would send an email, because it's the simplest thing in the world to set up an almost untraceable email account."

Carl sighed. The sheer number of unread emails seemed insurmountable. "Will I even be able to read them without the SIM card?"

Rose nodded. She was familiar with his phone settings.

Most of the emails in Carl's inbox had no subject or, even worse, it was the same old subject from an old email thread that had never been updated, so it was impossible to know what the new email was about. Bloody annoying. Some people never bothered with a subject—and especially not those who were only out to get him. Unfortunately, they were in the majority.

"Don't waste time on those emails, Carl. Some people just jump to conclusions," said Assad half an hour later. He pointed at the blue flashing light that rose up into the sky in the distance and then disappeared.

Carl nodded. If this was the depressing Christmas far from home in the back of beyond, he hardly dared to think how the new year would pan out once he had turned himself in.

"Stop!" Rose grabbed Carl's wrist and stopped him from scrolling. "That one. Try to open it, Carl," she said, pointing.

He looked at the subject: "Answer to your inquiry."

Carl opened it and revealed an email with two photos on the page.

It felt as if the dark, cold winter penetrated them to the core in that instant. The white mist from Assad's mouth stopped. Rose tightened her grip around Carl's wrist. And Carl moved the phone right up to his face in an attempt to grasp exactly what he was looking at.

The text was to the point:

Stay away if you want your colleague back alive!

They were all glued to the photos that accompanied the text.

"Oh god, no!" exclaimed Rose.

The first photo was taken from behind the two men, who were each sitting on a metal chair. The quality was good, so there was no mistaking that one of them was Gordon and that his hands were secured to the chair with cable ties. And it was equally obvious that the other person, who was slumped forward in the chair, had a piece of metal armor around his body that was secured with chains to the ceiling.

The second photo showed the two people from the front. Gordon was staring straight at the camera with a strange expression of hatred and defiance. His eyes were tired and bloodshot, but they still exuded a spark of danger that did not bode well for whomever it was unleashed on.

"Thank god! He hasn't given up," said Rose, relieved.

But Carl did not share her relief, because no matter how indomitable Gordon was, he was not the master of his own fate. If Carl and the others heeded Sisle Park's warning to stay away, Maurits van Bierbek was sure to be dead in less than forty-eight hours. And if Gordon witnessed the deed, why would she let him live?

Carl was convinced that Sisle Park had no intention of allowing them to stop her, and he was just as convinced that Maurits van Bierbek would not be the last person she killed.

Carl stared intently at the images. Was there any way these photos could help them? He doubted it, because Sisle Park did not appear in any of them—and so they still did not have irrefutable evidence that she was behind it all. So even though they knew what she was up to, and even if she wiped Gordon from the face of the earth, only one thing would stop her in carrying on with her insane endeavor: her death. Carl was convinced that was how her mind worked.

"We can't see the details on this lousy small screen, Carl. We need to get back to van Bierbek's house and enlarge them as much as we can."

"So you really think there might be something on these photos that can help us identify where they are, Rose? I just don't think Sisle Park is that stupid."

———

They waited until well after dark before they got on the quad bike and slowly made their way back to the house, trying to be as quiet as possible.

They could see through the garden window that the Christmas tree lights were still on, and a small pile of wrapping paper on the floor was the only evidence that at least there had been some sort of Christmas celebration.

"I heard you coming," whispered Laura from one of the second-floor windows. "You can come in. The police are long gone."

She ran out to meet them and immediately started telling them what had happened when the police were there.

"Mom was crying the whole time, saying that you had been here against her will and taken off on Dad's quad bike. She was actually really good—I was so impressed. She lied and cried and if I hadn't known any different, I would have believed her." She laughed. "Now at least I believe her when she says she's an actress."

"What did the police do when she said that?"

"They searched the whole house. They found the hair dye in the bathroom. So they might be looking for you with red hair—but I did tell them that you'd already washed it out."

Carl nodded. If that was possible, he would do it on the spot.

"The dogs were onto your scent the entire time, but they lost it about fifty meters from the house. It all added up with Mom's explanation, so they believed her and made her promise to contact them immediately if you came back."

"Do you think she would?"

"Not after you told her that the police were involved in Dad's kidnapping. Just before she went to bed, she said that if they returned she'd kick their asses." Laura laughed so hard she cried. She obviously really wanted to see that.

"What did they say about me?" asked Carl.

"They said that you were dangerous, that you're a drug smuggler and involved in the deaths of people here and abroad. That you have to be captured before you can do any more harm."

Carl exhaled heavily. What proof did they have for all this shit?

The large screens revealed many details they had not been able to see on Carl's phone.

The room where van Bierbek and Gordon were being held seemed to be newly renovated. The steel runners on the ceiling were shiny, and the walls were painted an even white. There were no scratches or marks on the concrete floor or the far wall. The elevator had shiny, double-steel doors.

"Maybe it's just been built?" suggested Rose.

"Yes, or it's never been used. What do you think those runners on the ceiling are for?"

"It's hard to tell, but I don't think they're part of the original interior." Rose pointed at the chains hanging down from the runners. "This is her satanic invention, I'm sure of it. The victims can move—but not as freely as they want to. Look at the bolt up there on the runner. It prevents her prisoners from moving more than a few steps. It could be a runner controlled remotely to transport goods from the elevator into the room," she suggested.

"No, I don't think so, because there would have needed to be more of them," said Assad.

They spent a long time looking at every small detail on the photos: van Bierbek's drooping jaw, the veins showing under the skin on his hands, his emaciated body, and his shoulders exuding despair and resignation. The chair he was sitting on was the same type as the one Gordon was on. An industrial steel construction that could withstand anything.

"Who uses chairs like that?" asked Carl. "Some kind of machine shop?"

"Look at the legs. There's a small metal plate welded onto them so they can be bolted to the floor. Judging by the rust, the metal plates have always been there."

"Where would someone need solid chairs bolted to the floor?"

"I'm thinking a machine shop like Oleg Dudek's. I'll call his foreman and ask if he recognizes them," said Assad.

While Carl and Rose continued scrutinizing the photo showing the captives from behind, Assad went over to the far end of the office and called from the landline.

"What else can you see, Rose?" asked Carl.

"It's a freight elevator. I'll enlarge that area of the photo." She pointed at the double steel doors and a logo that was barely visible.

Carl squinted. He would give anything just now for a pair of super-strong reading glasses. "Do you agree that it doesn't look totally new?"

Rose nodded and changed to the photo showing Gordon and Maurits van Bierbek from the front. Rose enlarged the photo as much as possible without compromising the detail.

"Focus on the floor and then up the far wall and back along the ceiling, Rose," said Carl.

Rose began by focusing on the floor. Apart from the stains around van Bierbek's chair that showed how often he had wet himself and where the stains closer to him became increasingly darker, there was nothing of note.

"You can tell how his urine has grown more concentrated," said Carl. "He's obviously heavily dehydrated—perhaps to the point that he's dying. But I still think that Sisle will keep him teetering on the edge until the day she plans to kill him."

Rose moved the focus to the end wall, which was completely devoid of any distinguishing marks. No electric sockets, no old nails or screws that could give away the age of the room. No furniture or decoration.

"Now focus on the ceiling," said Carl. "You can see that the runners don't go all the way down to the far wall, so you might be right in saying that they were added later with the sole purpose of keeping the prisoners in position. They're definitely not for moving goods."

"If the two previous murders from 2016 and 2018 of Franco Svendsen and Birger von Brandstrup were committed here—in contrast to all the earlier murders from Bobo Madsen and the riding accident in 2014 and back—this is probably a place that Sisle acquired in 2016 or not long before that," said Rose.

"So you think that Sisle Park acquired this place sometime between Bobo Madsen's and Birger von Brandstrup's deaths?"

"Yes, sometime between 2014 and 2016." She stopped and looked at him for a moment. "This could prove difficult to establish if we don't get help from Marcus Jacobsen and Co. It's Christmas Day, Carl. We might only have twenty-four hours left."

Carl nodded. They *had* to get to the bottom of it. "Try to move back along the runner on the ceiling again, Rose."

They did not dare even blink as they scanned the shiny steel runners. They were bolted to the ceiling with stainless steel brackets that stuck out on both sides and were attached to the ceiling with industrial screws.

"I think there are ball bearings inside the runners," said Carl, "so that the sliders attached to the chains can move easily."

"So you think van Bierbek has been able to move around in the room before he became too weak?"

"I don't know. I guess the bolt in the middle of one of the runners would have made it difficult." Carl shook his head. The woman was not only raving mad, she was also an all-out sadist. That was becoming increasingly evident.

They began to inspect the photo at two centimeters farther along from the bolt. Rose froze. "Wait! Can you see those marks on one of the runners? What do you think they are?"

Carl did not know. "Something appears to have been wrenched into the runner. Maybe to make the slider fall out."

Rose tilted her head to get a better angle and nodded. "Of course. Van Bierbek has attempted to wrench one of the sliders out of the runner."

"But how? Is he a contortionist or something?"

"Carl, look at that!" Rose peered so closely that her nose almost touched the screen. "Here, right behind the marks. The manufacturer's name is embossed in the runner."

"I'm afraid I can't see that, Rose."

"Well, it isn't very clear, but I think the second word is 'Steelware.'"

She zoomed in even more but zoomed out again when it did not help. "The first three letters are 'Mex.' Does it say 'Mexita'? It sounds like a terrible pop song from the eighties."

Carl googled the name, and the result sent a shiver down his spine. He pointed at the website.

"Do you think this might be helpful, Carl?"

"Maybe," he said hesitantly.

"Are you getting anywhere?" asked Assad from behind them. "I certainly am. I woke up Dudek's foreman—who sounded like he had a real hang-up."

"A real hangover, Assad," said Rose.

Assad frowned. "Well, what she said. Anyway, he sounded really out of it. But I sent him a close-up of the chair van Bierbek is sitting on, and he saw straightaway that it is similar to the chairs that were bolted to the floor in front of some of Oleg Dudek's machines. He said that all the inventory and tools from the factory were auctioned off when Dudek died and the factory went under."

Rose and Carl stared at him in disbelief.

Even though Sisle Park did not appear in the two photos, this new information confirmed a link between the scene in the photos and the earlier crimes of the supposed serial killer.

There was no way Marcus Jacobsen could ignore this.

57

GORDON

Christmas Eve, Thursday, December 24, and Christmas Day, Friday, December 25, 2020

Sisle Park and her hard-hitting henchman had stayed the night before until Maurits van Bierbek began breathing more normally again. They had wished both their captives a merry Christmas and promised that one of them would return the following day. They would go back to Adam's house and celebrate Christmas, and Sisle would remain there until it was all over.

"Your colleagues in Department Q are probably going to be bored, but at least they can entertain themselves with the lights going on and off in the different sections of my house. I can control them with this app." She held up her phone and pressed one of the buttons. "There we go," she said. "That's the lights activated on the second floor. They must be wondering who's sneaking around the house. And no doubt they're also wondering what's happened to you. Why don't we give them a clue?"

Gordon did not reply but merely stared at her in hatred as she took a photo of them first from the front and then from the back.

She's playing with fire, he thought. *Perhaps she had no idea how much you could enlarge a photo taken with a good camera phone. She'll give them more of a clue than she bargained for.*

———

He felt less optimistic when Sisle Park and Adam returned the following morning. He had had to empty his bowels during the night, and over the last few hours his skin had begun to sting. Van Bierbek had grunted a few times earlier that morning, but there had been no communication between them.

Gordon's two captors greeted him coldly, walked around him to avoid the smell, and gave the drip to his cellmate again. There was no doubt that there was more than just sugar and salt in the drip because, only a minute later, van Bierbek began coughing and tried to sit up straight.

Gordon turned around and saw that van Bierbek had now regained some of the color in his cheeks. His eyes were moving behind his eyelids and his breathing had become more staccato. He tried to say something a couple of times that sounded like "oh no, oh no."

He slowly opened his eyes and squinted at the light from the ceiling. Now he clearly exclaimed, "Oh no!" as if he was once again aware of his hopeless situation.

Then he saw Gordon sitting in front of him, twisting in the seat to try to catch his eye. Van Bierbek did not react immediately—perhaps he could not fathom what he saw—but then his eyes moved down to Gordon's hands fastened to the chair. His expression turned even darker, a pain seemed to jolt down his neck, his lips quivered, and he started sobbing. There were no tears in his eyes, but that only made the sight even more agonizing. He had just realized that the presence of this person in front of him did not improve anything about his own situation. On the contrary, he seemed overwhelmed by the questions Gordon's presence presented.

He stared fearfully at the drip hanging next to him. Perhaps he was expecting the poison to penetrate his veins in the next moment. That this was his final hour.

Or perhaps he actually knew what Gordon knew—that he was not destined to die until the following day.

He was clearly trying to control his crying and gasping for breath.

Apparently he was not one for displaying his fear and desperation. He switched his focus to the two people walking back and forth at the table down by the far wall. Gordon looked in the same direction and tried to figure out what they were doing. A couple of glass flasks were lined up and arranged as if being displayed. Then they cut open two plastic bags and produced two large syringes from them.

Two syringes!

Gordon was sweating now. Sisle Park's two previous executions had been carried out with an injection of potassium chloride. Was that what they were preparing for just now, injecting the lethal substance directly into their hearts? Yes, Sisle Park had said that she would let him live on after Maurits van Bierbek was killed. But could she be trusted? Was this callous woman so evil and sadistic that she might decide to kill Gordon first so Maurits van Bierbek could see what awaited him?

Now it looked like they were removing full plastic bags from a cardboard box. Adam took a pair of scissors and started cutting them open. He emptied the contents one by one into a large plastic container. When he had finished, he poured a large amount of clear liquid into the container— perhaps water—and started to shake it while Sisle Park placed a large funnel on the tabletop.

Oh god! he thought. *They're preparing a saline solution. Was this the primitive method they used to preserve Franco Svendsen's and Birger von Brandstrup's bodies? A funnel in the mouth and then just pour until the emaciated body could not hold any more?*

Gordon no longer felt the infernal stinging from his anus, but he did notice that he was wetting himself again.

"Whoopsie-daisy," said Adam when he walked past him seconds later to check on van Bierbek's drip.

Gordon writhed in his seat, but the cable ties around his wrists only dug in deeper.

Will I end up with the same indentations on my wrists that Palle Rasmussen got when he was fastened to the wheel of the car as he slowly lost consciousness? he thought, and the idea of having anything in common with that man sent a shiver down his spine.

"I'll just give you another shot, Maurits," said Adam behind him. "We need to get you in good shape so you're ready to receive your sentence while you're still fully conscious."

"It won't happen, Maurits," Gordon heard himself say aloud.

He could hear Sisle Park laughing from down at the far end of the room.

"We'll see, Gordon Taylor! We'll see!" she shouted. "You have to remember that Maurits van Bierbek is too good a catch to let go. This is a man who deserves to be wiped from the face of the earth."

"It would be better if it was you!" he burst out.

She walked up to him. "Really, do you think so? We both know that you're wrong, don't we? The man behind you is an amoral, selfish, greedy bastard who infects other people with his low standards. He brings out the worst in people, robs them of whatever iota of intelligence they might have had. There's nothing good to say about Maurits van Bierbek. We're going to put a stop to his crimes against humanity, so don't feel sorry for him. You probably know when it's going to happen, so why don't you tell this monster once we've gone."

Gordon heaved a sigh of relief. So they were not going to make an example of him and kill him here and now. But his relief was short-lived. He still did not know what was going to happen after midnight.

"Right, then, Maurits," said Adam, still behind him. "You're ready now. You'll feel better in half an hour. I've given you a good pick-me-up cocktail, and it'll soon have your heart pumping stronger and faster. I've also given you liquid and minerals to stimulate your circulation. How does that sound?"

"Can I please speak with my children?" asked Maurits, voice still weak.

Would a monster ask something like that? Gordon was well aware that the person behind him was cynical. But was there more to the man? Or was it just the situation making him emotional?

"What are you talking about, Maurits?" asked Sisle Park. "Do you suggest we bring them here? Or do you want us to set up a Skype call?

Or maybe you'd rather contact them via WhatsApp or Zoom? What do you suggest? That we simply call them?"

"Yes," he moaned. "Please."

She laughed. "That's not going to happen, Maurits. You'll leave this life without any comfort or love. And we'll make sure that not even your new roommate's colleagues will be able to find you when we're done. That's a guarantee."

"I hope you burn in hell!" he said hoarsely.

"Not likely. I have God on my side. God is not without fault, so sometimes he creates freaks like you. But then he makes up for his mistake and gives the sword of revenge to someone who can take care of people like you. No, hell is reserved for you and your sort."

Gordon began laughing. "Don't listen, Maurits! She's insane. Does she look like a messenger of God? Look at her. Look at the madness in her eyes."

She came down on him in seconds, slapped him, and spat in his face. "You know nothing about me, Gordon Taylor!" she shouted. "NOTH-ING! Got it?"

"I know more than you care to think. You're the serial killer striking every second year on the birthdays of the worst tyrants in human history. You think that you're God's avenging angel, a guardian of morals who justifies her deadly actions in reference to Sodom and Gomorrah by using salt as her trademark."

She used her nails when she hit him again. Gordon jerked to the side and felt the warm blood trickling down his cheek.

Then he straightened up and lowered his voice. "You're also the woman who killed a small child when you started your sick crusade. Ove Wilder's repair shop, remember? And you killed the boy's mother with the unbearable grief you left her to cope with for the rest of her wretched life."

"SHUT UP!" she screamed and hit him again. This time with her fist clenched.

Gordon shook his head, and the crazy expression in her eyes told him intuitively that he should obey, but he could not help himself. He just had to twist the knife in her heart one more time.

"Maybe it was God's biggest mistake that you didn't die in the explosion. But I guess that was the same with Satan, the fallen angel. God didn't manage to strike him down either. As you can hear, Sisle, I know everything about you worth knowing. And my advice to you is to take the consequences of your fall and stop this nightmare here and now. Turn yourself in and take your idiot of a sidekick down with you. It's the only way you can make the world a better place, and I'm sure God agrees."

It was not the first time he had experienced a powerful blow to the neck from the man behind him. But this time he did not pass out. He only pretended.

58

CARL

Christmas Day, Friday, December 25, 2020

"**I couldn't care** less that it's Christmas Day. This is the police you're talking to, and I'm telling you to drive down to the factory ASAP. Got it?"

Carl was furious. You'd be hard-pressed to find a more uncooperative and annoying idiot. The sort of man in his midforties who always had to be right. The sort who point-blank refused to deviate from his schedule when circumstance required it.

"I'm at my holiday home," he replied matter-of-factly. "It's fifty kilometers to Åbenrå, where the factory is located. And it's not even certain that we installed those runners. The company is German, you know, and—"

"If you don't get up right now and rush down to Åbenrå to find some answers, I promise you that you'll be charged with obstructing an investigation and also being an accomplice to a death. If you prefer, I can send a couple of police officers to escort you down there. But damn well rest assured that we'll bill you for our time. Understood?"

"Yeah, but . . ." He was just about to start complaining again, but Carl stood his ground.

"If you don't get over yourself right now, I'll call the owners of

Mexita Steelware and suggest that they find a new CEO pronto if they want to avoid being splashed all over the media for the next couple of days."

The man finally gave in and shouted to someone that he had to go to work. There were ardent protests from the background. Apparently his wife was just as lacking in solidarity as her husband.

"Did you convince him to go?" asked Rose from the corner where she and Assad were working.

Carl nodded and walked over to them.

"Unfortunately, he didn't know if they'd be able to find the original order for the metal runners. But it might be helpful that we've been able to narrow it down to within a couple of years. What an idiot."

He tried to shake off his annoyance and turned to Assad.

"How are you getting on? Have you managed to get a better overview of Sisle Park's property portfolio and rentals?"

"The properties, yes. I made that list the other day, so it's here." He handed it to Carl, who skimmed it. It was a very long list.

"The problem is that all the pending property sales didn't always go through. Look at this one, for example."

Assad handed him a piece of paper regarding Park Optimizing's preemptive rights to a plot that was still under development.

"Development? What exactly does that mean?" asked Rose. "Could it mean that there's already a building on the site waiting to be demolished? It doesn't tell us much, does it?"

"Yes, we need more than this, Assad. Look for old surveillance photos that show the sites. Street view, Google Earth, anything. I also don't think we can call this document a conveyance agreement. Isn't it more some sort of preliminary agreement? Are there many of these types of documents?"

"Perhaps twenty-five. We're not quite sure yet. It'll be a huge task, as the male camel said when he came across a herd of wild females."

"Thanks for the parable. I can picture it clearly. What do you think she wants all these plots for?"

Assad shrugged. "Who knows? Maybe they're just investments. The profits from Park Optimizing run into the millions annually, so instead of paying negative interest in Danish banks or taking risks with stocks and shares, she might've seen property as a better investment. Land has always been a good bet."

Carl sighed. "Jesus! And you said that there might be rentals on top of her property portfolio?"

They both nodded.

Carl did not understand. "If all this holds, why the hell did she bury the bodies of her latest victims on public land? She could've just chosen one of her own plots."

"But don't you think it would've drawn unwanted attention to her if they'd been found on one of her sites?" asked Rose.

"But in that case, she might also be holding Maurits van Bierbek and Gordon captive somewhere that's not in her name. So how are we supposed to locate it, and in such a short amount of time?"

"Good question, Carl, but we believe we're looking for a larger building," said Rose. "The large freight elevator indicates that it's a place that's intended to receive a lot of goods and pallets, and also that there must be several floors—maybe even underground."

"Does she have any buildings of a considerable size?"

"Not apart from her headquarters, which doesn't have a goods delivery entrance. There is a basement, but we can't spot any gates or loading bays that would be large enough for pallets or a delivery van. But to complicate matters even further, the Land Registry records show that she also owns another company, Iversen Optimizing, named after her mother's maiden name."

"Does that company also own property?"

"No, it's a holding company with several owners," answered Assad. "So I looked into it the other day. And here comes the interesting bit. This holding company has a subsidiary called ISAK, and the co-owners of that company are named Adam and Kirsten D. Holme. I didn't give it much thought at first, but then Rose took a closer look at the ownership. It turns out that the husband used to own a company that he and his wife are still minority shareholders of. And guess what we discovered when we searched for the wife's business roles online? One of them listed her full middle name: D for Debora."

Carl was speechless.

"Well, we've finally got our link between Sisle Park, Tabitha, Ragnhild, and everything else connected to Debora's secret society," said Assad. "And we also have an address not far from Sisle Park's."

Carl punched the air. They finally had a concrete lead.

"We haven't found any properties listed under the company ISAK," continued Rose. "But it also has a couple of subsidiaries."

Carl took a deep breath. "Why don't we pay this Debora a visit right now."

"Good idea, but there are a few things we need to consider first," said Assad with a serious expression. "What'll happen if we just rush down and turn up at their door? Won't we be putting Gordon's and Maurits's lives at risk?"

Rose nodded enthusiastically. "Maurits will be killed tomorrow if we don't act. That's a given. And it could happen as early as ten seconds after midnight. But would Sisle Park risk us finding the building before then? I don't think so. So if we reveal too much of what we know about her accomplices and make them reveal the place where the two poor guys are waiting on the steel chairs, Sisle Park will definitely make sure that Gordon and Maurits are moved—and not necessarily alive. So no matter what we discover, we need to be very careful. We don't have any other choice."

59

ADAM/SISLE

Christmas Day, Friday, December 25, 2020

The final days before the execution of Maurits should have been a time of expectation and joy, just like the many times before when they had killed someone. Every single time, Sisle had felt happy and exalted at the complexity and her own cleverness, and at how smoothly everything had gone—even though not every murder had been easy to plan and carry out.

But Sisle did not seem at all pleased this time. It was obvious that Gordon Taylor had filled her with an all-consuming rage.

Yesterday, they had celebrated an otherwise normal Christmas Eve. They had eaten a simple meal, honored the couple's dead son, Isak, with a silent prayer, and congratulated one another on having almost completed everything successfully. Finally, they had thanked God sincerely for having stood by them through everything. It had all in all been a good evening.

But Adam had still felt that the encounter with Gordon Taylor and his verbal attacks on Sisle had gotten to her. Sisle's movements were stiff and staccato and she sounded absentminded. She kept repeating that she had not heard words that shameless since before the lightning struck her.

"You heard him yourself, Adam," she said as she paced back and

forth in front of the sofa where Adam and Debora were sitting, their
faces lit by the glow from the fireplace. "All his satanic words and his
scornful face."

"God is testing you," said Adam. "Gordon Taylor is trying to frighten
you into thinking you're under attack. But what did he have on you
apart from his theories? Nothing. Nothing at all! And what could happen, anyway? No one knows where Maurits and Gordon are. He was
just trying to sow doubt in your mind. It's the work of the devil."

"Are you absolutely sure that no one knows, Adam?" interrupted
Debora. "Carl Mørck's team are closing in, and they know that Sisle might
be behind the killings. And Gordon Taylor has seen you, and he knows
your name. Things could take a turn for the worse before we know it."

He nodded.

"And don't forget that it isn't only Sisle who's in the line of fire. We
are too, Adam. How do you think we'd cope if we were sent to prison?
Separated and not allowed to see each other for many years. Tell her,
Adam!"

Adam did not know what to say. He hated being stuck in the middle
of these two.

Debora shook her head at his silence and turned to Sisle. "Can't you
see deep down that things are coming to an end, Sisle? It's only natural
that you're angry at yourself because we didn't put a stop to this in
time. Isn't that what all this is about?"

Adam watched Sisle as she slowly turned toward Debora. The anger
seemed to have been erased from her face, and she shook her head slightly
while smiling gently.

"You're probably right, Debora. You often are. And I do appreciate
that you can be so insistent. Sometimes it's been good for us to clear the
air. And just look at the rewards of your insistence and stubbornness."
She spread out her arms as if embracing the living room and the adja-
cent areas. "The ideal school for my recruits, right here. What would I
have done without them and without you?"

She stepped closer and stroked Debora's cheek. It was obvious that

Debora felt uncomfortable with the caress, but she did not say anything.

Then Sisle turned to the fireplace, stirring the fire with the poker and nodding.

Adam smiled at Debora's way of disarming Sisle and restoring the good mood of the evening. Now the only question remaining was what Sisle would decide to do. Would she admit the seriousness of their situation and bring forward the killings to tonight, just like he and Debora had proposed several times before?

He was stopped in his thoughts as Sisle spun around and swung the poker at full force directly into his temple.

It was strange to see them like this. Silent, and in Debora's case still with a look of shock on her face.

A little blood trickled from her head, while Adam's thick skull had withstood the blows. But there was no mistaking that they were both dead.

Sisle took a closer look at them. Adam's head was twisted down toward his shoulder, and his face no longer looked so contorted. It was almost sad that he was gone, this loyal man. If it had not been for Debora and her incessant demand that they should complete their mission ahead of time, Adam might still be alive.

"That was silly of you," she said aloud, closing Debora's blue, staring eyes. "Silly, silly, silly Debora. We could have sat together tomorrow and toasted our last mission together, but I could sense that you didn't want to."

Sisle wiped the blood off the poker onto her dress. Then she sighed and put it back in the stand in front of the fireplace.

Sisle was free now. These two could no longer harm her, and when it came to it, there was no reason for her to allow them to weigh her down in her new life. Whatever reminders there might be in the house of their shared project would soon be history. The fire would consume everything. People would say that the Christmas tree had been placed too close to the curtains. Some would say that they had been thought-less, while others would think it was strange to light the candles on the Christmas tree after Christmas Eve.

She fetched some methylated spirit and acetone from a cupboard in the kitchen and took some lighter fluid next to the fireplace and gener-ously doused it over the furniture and carpets, making sure to place the bottles back where she had found them. She then took two canisters of gasoline from the shed next to the carport and doused the rest of the house with most of the contents before returning the canisters. Maybe that would confuse the fire brigade a little when they tried to ascertain how the fire started.

She started humming "O Christmas Tree" and pulled the tree closer to the curtains. She had lit half of the almost-burned-down candles when through the window she caught sight of blue flashes lighting up chim-neys and roofs in the distance.

Police, fire brigade, or ambulance? It was impossible to know, so there was no point worrying about it.

She opened a couple of windows to feed the flames and heard a siren in the distance, which made her hesitate for a moment.

Could they be coming for her?

She shook her head at the ridiculousness of the thought. Of course it had nothing to do with her. No one had any idea that she was staying here, and it was impossible to know that Adam and Debora had any connection to her. How would they even have the couple's address? She shook her head and smiled at her momentary alarm.

She was lighting the remaining candles as the flashes and siren drew closer.

It is odd, though, she thought. *It's probably just someone ill who has called for help. Or a small insignificant fire somewhere.*

She laughed for a moment. She would give them a real and anything but insignificant fire. Once it took hold in such a large old house, with all the heavy furniture, carpets, timber framing, and wooden paneling, they would have a literal inferno.

The flashing lights were approaching too quickly now, and Sisle's defense mechanisms took over.

Just to be on the safe side, she thought, pushing the Christmas tree into the long, acetone-soaked brocade curtains, whose fabric was dense enough to fuel the flames.

She glanced one last time at the two bodies, whispered a quiet good-bye, and made her getaway in her car.

60

CARL

Christmas Day, Friday, December 25, 2020

They had been driving for some time in the wake of an ambulance that appeared to be in a hurry to reach the same neighborhood. It stopped in front of a house where the wife was standing outside waving her arms above her head, screaming desperately that her husband had collapsed and was not breathing.

Only then did they notice the ominous pulsating red light in the sky above the roofs a little farther away.

When they turned down the road, they knew immediately that the flames were coming from exactly where they were heading. Carl had witnessed many fires over the years but never in such a large, magnificent house with so many historic details. It was really a sad sight, and it only took a glance to realize that the fire brigade would not make it in time to save anything worth mentioning.

The reflection of the flames on Rose's face accentuated her frustration.

"We're too late," she said, cursing as a couple of windows exploded and sent pieces of glass raining down over the neat front lawn and the spruce-covered flower beds.

"Imagine if Gordon and Maurits van Bierbek are inside," shouted

Assad, darting back and forth with a terrified expression to see if the whole house was engulfed in flames.

Assad ran back to the others. "There's a yellow car in the carport similar to the one Sisle Park was driving when she carried out the reconnaissance at the van Bierbek home," he said.

Now the heat emanating from the house was so intense that those residents from the street who had come to see the spectacle had to gradually fall back.

Carl pulled out his invalid ID and talked to the closest spectators. "Does anyone know if there's a basement under the house?"

Someone answered no, and several others agreed.

"Thank god," sighed Rose.

But then where were Gordon and Maurits van Bierbek?

"Do any of you know the occupants?" Carl asked the crowd.

"Not very well," answered an elderly woman, who explained that she was the one who had called the fire brigade and that she lived across the street. "They mostly kept to themselves."

"Well, I wouldn't quite say that," interjected a graying man next to her. "They had lots of visitors," he added without taking his eyes off the flames.

"Lots of visitors? Can you elaborate?" asked Carl.

"Mostly young women who came once a week—and always at the same time."

"Okay. Did you ever see any of their faces? Would you be able to recognize them if I show you some photos?"

The man nodded and instinctively ducked his head as another window exploded.

Carl snapped his fingers at Rose and asked her to show the man her photos of Ragnhild and Tabitha.

She had to wave the phone right in front of his face to get his attention. He pulled a pair of glasses from his breast pocket and brought his face close to the screen. "Yes," he said simply, removing his glasses again.

"Yes what? You recognize them?"

He nodded and said that he had not seen one of them for some time, still not taking his eyes from the mesmerizing sight.

"Okay, then I think it's safe to assume that the occupants of this house are the same people we're looking for," said Carl to Rose and Assad.

"Are you talking about Debora and Adam?" asked the man. "I'm afraid they might still be in there. That would be awful—I can barely imagine a worse way to die. Why in the world did this have to happen to them?" He paused for a while and looked directly at Carl for the first time. "But the woman who was with them this evening drove off in a rush. I saw her when I was returning home from walking my dog a little while ago. Doesn't that seem strange?" He nodded without waiting for an answer. "I think you should get hold of her and ask what happened," he ended matter-of-factly.

Carl thought he sounded like a retired civil servant.

"Can you bring up a photo of Sisle?" he asked Rose in a hushed voice. And Rose was on it in a second.

Sisle Park looked good in the photo—the epitome of a successful businesswoman, the archetype of a participant on the TV program *Dragons' Den*. The kind of woman who creates a toxic cocktail of envy and admiration that brings out the worst in people.

The man nodded. "She didn't look like that today, but I have noticed how she can dress up."

"So this is the woman who drove off not long ago?"

"I don't want to sound overconfident, but let's just say that I'm ninety-nine point nine percent sure."

"This is when we call Marcus," said Rose. "We *know* that she's the one behind it all, and we have to stop her. Marcus has to put out a call for her arrest, are we agreed?"

Carl nodded. "You take care of that call, Rose. I'm sure our friend here can give you a detailed description of her clothes."

The fire engines arrived, and the firefighters immediately set to work.

"You'd better get out of here, Carl," said Assad when he saw that the police had also arrived.

Carl shook his head. "We need to know if there's anyone in there first." His eyes followed Rose as she walked off to one side and made the call. Meanwhile, a couple of firefighters in asbestos suits came out of the inferno carrying two charred bodies and laid them down on the ground. The crowd looked horrified.

Carl flashed his ID to the firefighters and squatted in front of the bodies. It was a ghastly sight, and they smelled heavily like burned spit-roasted pig.

"What happened?" he asked, staring at the two heads almost touching each other in an awkward position. Only an hour ago it would still have been possible to extract information from these two heads, which would have meant that they could save Maurits van Bierbek and Gordon. Such was the irony of fate. All too often Carl had wished for nothing more than to be able to delve into the minds of those who had lain lifeless in front of him. All the answers extinguished by death, all the explanations that would never see the light of day. Gone forever!

And where was Sisle Park now? The only place they would not have to search was at her own home. Like the cunning fox she was, she would find a new den.

The police had finished cordoning off the area to keep people at a distance. And Rose and Assad nodded imploringly toward Carl. It was high time for them to get going.

They pulled back from the crowd and walked a safe distance away.

"Just an hour before and we'd have been in time," said Rose.

Carl nodded. And now that bloody CEO for Mexita Steelware, who had wasted their time, might be the only person who could help them.

Carl took out his phone and dialed the number.

"Are you at the factory?" he asked.

"No, I asked my manager who lives in Åbenrå to go over there and search the archive," he said without the slightest hint of embarrassment.

"So you're not down there?"

"No, I'm at home. He'll be much better at that sort of thing than I would."

Carl could feel the rage growing inside him. "Are you insane? If you knew that all along, why the fucking hell didn't you mention him earlier? Now two people are dead. And you should know that if anything could've prevented it, it would've been you getting off your ass quicker."

Assad tugged at his sleeve. "We wouldn't have made it anyway, Carl," he whispered. "Stroke his muzzle. It always works." He demonstrated by stretching his hand high in the air and making a petting gesture. That man always had camels on his mind.

"Well, what's done is done," said Carl with strained composure. "Give me the man's name and phone number and I'll take it from here."

"What did Marcus say, Rose? You didn't look happy," asked Carl as they were driving back to their base in the van Bierbek home.

"He said he's putting out a warrant for her arrest straightaway—along with yours, in fact."

Carl frowned. What the hell was that supposed to mean?

"And Marcus also said that we'd be on the news within half an hour."

Carl was shocked, to say the least. "Didn't you tell him that I'd turn myself in when this is over?"

"He didn't care. I think he's under a lot of pressure just now, Carl. He said the Dutch are watching his every move."

"The Dutch?"

"The police from Rotterdam investigating the murders in Schiedam, remember? You know they think that they're directly linked to the murders in Slagelse and what happened out on Amager when you were shot down."

"But I don't have anything to do with that ancient case. Why doesn't Marcus believe me? It's bloody crazy." His disappointment made him feel physically sick. Had Carl not always been there for Marcus every time he needed him? When his wife became ill and died? When Marcus decided to leave the police—and subsequently return? Had all this really just been forgotten?

"He also said that they've found your fingerprints on several of the banknotes in the suitcase from your attic. He's not on your side anymore, Carl."

That was a real blow.

Carl stared at the GPS in the car and let it direct them the rest of the way. Just now he barely knew what to do with himself. Did his colleagues on the other teams seriously suspect him of being an accomplice to murder and selling hard drugs? They must be out of their minds.

"HQ have arranged to bring home Hardy, Mika, and Morten from Switzerland so they can question Hardy."

Carl couldn't believe his ears. "Do they suspect *him* now too?"

"No, but they think that he suspects you, Carl. I'm sorry."

Carl stared at the road and the city that slowly came into view ahead. He felt completely empty inside.

"Did you get any further with that factory manager, Carl?" asked Assad tentatively.

Carl sighed. This was all too much at once.

"Yes," he said, nevertheless. "The manager was an old fella from Southern Jutland whose dialect I could hardly understand. But thankfully, he was much more cooperative than his CEO." Carl composed himself. Either he threw in the towel now or he manned up for the final round.

He wiped the sweat off his forehead and tried to regulate his breathing. Just half a minute later he already felt ready to carry on.

"Yes," he said. "The manager knew a lot, but unfortunately he wasn't able to find information on the runners on the spot. Not only because they were installed several years back but more because we don't have the address. He also said he was convinced the work was carried out externally, because he didn't recall their company being called out to do it. And if it was the company's own workers who carried out the work, then it couldn't have been in Jutland because that's his area. But he's still searching."

"Christ," exclaimed Rose.

It was not looking good; now Gordon's and van Bierbek's lives depended on an old fella finding information from dusty files.

The van Bierbek house was engulfed in darkness inside and out. Why
turn on lights in rooms no one was using? Why play music or stream
TV series when those living in the house were counting down the hours
until the most important member of the family would die?

Rose knocked gently on the doorframe to the living room, where the
girls sat petrified on each side of their mother. The younger girl had evidently been crying, and the older girl, Laura, was sitting with her mouth
clenched, staring blankly ahead.

All three of them looked up at Rose, but any sign of hope was quickly
extinguished from their eyes when she shook her head. Then Laura also
started crying. Carl walked over to the door and was about to explain
the situation and that there was still hope, but he was stopped by Victoria's steely gaze.

"We've just turned off the TV, Carl, so we know all about how the
police are looking for you." She looked away from him and over toward
the door to the kitchen. "You have to understand that we don't want
you here."

"Just a minute, Victoria. I'm not sure what I'm supposed to understand. I haven't seen it."

"You're a bloody murderer yourself!" screamed Laura suddenly. "Get
lost! I hate you!"

"Yes, you need to leave, Carl. The rest of you can stay. But not him,"
added Victoria.

"You're no better than that Sisle Park, who's got our dad!" shouted
Laura.

Assad stepped forward and descended the three steps down into the
living room.

"Let me tell you something, you ungrateful . . . ," and then he said
something in Arabic that was better left untranslated. "Carl is only a
wanted man because instead of turning himself in, he's been working

day and night to find your dad. He's put this investigation above every-thing else—including himself."

"Be that as it may," sounded a voice from the kitchen door. It was Claes Erfurt, Victoria's meddlesome attorney. "But our agreement no longer stands, Carl Mørck. The police are offering a reward for informa-tion about you. Not quite as good as that for Sisle Park, but enough to stress the seriousness of their accusations. We can't justify harboring a wanted killer. I'm sure you understand. We'll give you fifteen minutes to collect your things and then you need to leave."

Had he said "we" can't justify? Had he already taken his seat at the head of the family table?

Carl turned to the girls and their mother. "Your dad isn't dead yet, and the three of us are the only ones who can—"

"Get the hell out of this house." Claes Erfurt was now holding his phone in his hand, ready to make the call.

This was all too much for Assad, who threw himself at the attorney and grabbed his throat, silencing him in one fell swoop.

"Give me that phone," said Assad as the attorney's pudgy face be-came visibly redder. Assad turned to Carl and nodded. "Tell them what's happening just now."

Carl knelt in front of the girls.

"We're convinced that your dad is alive. And one of our best friends is being held with him. We've seen a couple of photos of them. We will do everything we can to find them both in time. But that is going to require help. And whom can we rely on? The man who has put out a warrant for my arrest is my boss. He also wants to solve this case, and he knows what is going to happen to your dad, but he doesn't know that one of his employees, our friend Gordon, is also being held by the same person. We'd like to tell him, and we'd like to get more people on this case, but we can't actually see how that would help. We're wait-ing for a call from Southern Jutland that might give us the break we need. So please give us some time. And no, Laura, I haven't done what they're accusing me of, and I will convince them of that when all this is over."

Rose interjected: "Victoria, the man whom Assad has locked in his grip has no actual intention of getting your husband back. Can't you see that he's obviously obsessed with you and is only waiting to take Maurits's place when it's confirmed that your husband is dead?"

"NO!" screamed Laura. "I hate that idiot, Mom."

"We're going to have to incapacitate him until sometime late tomorrow, Assad," said Rose.

61

GORDON

Christmas Day, Friday, December 25, 2020

"**Are you awake**, Maurits?"

Gordon's throat was parched and his lips stuck to each other. Had he even said it aloud?

"Are you awake, Maurits?" he tried again. The constant light in the room was beginning to feel like torture, and Gordon had not slept since he was brought in here. Behind him, Maurits appeared to be so drained of energy that he was half-unconscious most of the time. Gordon envied him.

"If only I could slip into nothingness like you, Maurits," he whispered. It was so hard to be awake all the time. The thick saliva in his mouth felt like glue. And, once in a while, when he managed to swallow it, it felt like it blocked his throat. He sighed and sensed the unpleasant smell of his own breath. Was that how people smelled just before they died? Was the decay trying to escape from the inside?

"Maurits, can you hear me?" he tried for at least the tenth time that day. Or was it night? How close were they to Boxing Day now? Was it already past midnight? Were there only minutes left?

Gordon was suffering. His entire existence was built on knowing. His parents had chuckled and praised him as a boy when he was able to come out with a piece of information at dinner that he had not learned from school or them. It felt motivating for him, so as a child he had gathered all the knowledge that could generate praise and admiration. He had brought the habit with him to Department Q, where no problem was ever allowed to feel more insurmountable than a small bump on his quest to find the truth.

And now he could not answer even the simplest question. It was of utmost importance for him to know what day and time it was. One glance at his wrist, behind his back and out of sight, would give him the answer instantly. So in his current situation a simple wristwatch with the date and time seemed to be the most important invention of all time because it held the answer to how long it would be before they died. So close and yet so far.

"Maurits, wake up. We have to talk," he said as loudly as he could, hurting his dry throat. But was there a reaction?

He held his breath and listened intently.

"Mmmmm," he heard behind him.

Gordon strained his head around toward Maurits van Bierbek and looked directly into his open, bloodshot eyes.

They nodded to each other. The feeling of not being alone in the universe for a second almost brought tears to Gordon's dry eyes.

"Is it now?" asked Maurits with a voice so feeble that the words came out as a whisper.

"We're alone," answered Gordon. "It's not now."

"They said I'd have to wait for Mao. Do you know what they meant?"

He slumped a little forward while his question echoed in Gordon's head. What should Gordon answer? Was it heartless to avoid answering, or was it heartless to tell him the truth?

"So you don't know, Maurits?"

It took him a long time to respond with an immensely slow shake of his head.

"And you want to know?"

"I do, yes." It was the ensuing "please" that swayed Gordon.

"Mao was born on December twenty-sixth, Maurits. That's the day they're going to do it."

Gordon was ashamed. *The day they're going to do it*, he had said. Did he really think he could get away with saying just that?

"So they are going to kill me?" asked Maurits quietly.

Gordon looked him in the eye and nodded. Then Maurits closed his eyes and nodded along.

"Mao's birthday. When? Is it Boxing Day soon?"

Gordon realized that Maurits was no longer afraid. He was resigned to his fate, had given up on his life, and maybe even wanted to get it over with as quickly as possible.

But Gordon did not feel the same. When he had lashed out at Sisle Park, she had altered her manner toward him. First he had thought it was out of respect, but he soon changed his mind.

I shouldn't have taken it so far with her. I should have kept my mouth shut. Now she won't let me live. I just know it.

"We're going to die together, Maurits," he said, trying to keep his voice steady.

"On Mao's birthday?" Maurits asked with a smile. "Hasn't Boxing Day already been?"

Gordon shook his head. That was not possible—or they would not still be alive.

Gordon closed his eyes and prayed silently. *Dear God, please look after us. Let Carl, Rose, and Assad arrive in time. I'm too young to die, as I've explained to you before. There are so many things I haven't done yet. So please help us, dear God. Amen.*

It felt good for a moment. But only for a moment.

"Mao's birthday," Maurits said quietly again. "I don't understand. Can you explain?"

Gordon nodded.

"Yes, it's tomorrow, Maurits, or maybe even already today. I have no concept of time anymore. Maybe it's night now, maybe it's morning. I have no idea."

A click from the elevator relay made him start. Then another, and then another. And every time he heard it, his entire body shuddered.

Then the elevator door opened.

Gordon half closed his eyes to avoid the full impact of the shock—because the sight of Sisle Park entering the room was truly shocking.

He lowered his head only enough so that he could still just follow her movements through the small gap left under his eyelids.

She did not say anything. She stood there staring at them.

And she should just stay where she was. Not come any closer to them. Not now.

Then she flicked out her arms. Gordon had not seen the blanket in her hands, which she now spread out on the floor.

Moments later, she had taken off her coat, lain down on the floor, pulled the coat over herself, and gone to sleep with a sigh.

62

CARL

Boxing Day, Saturday, December 26, 2020

The minutes felt shorter and shorter as time was running out, and the desperation was growing. If anyone in the house had slept that night, then Carl had certainly not noticed it.

Rose had endlessly paced around her comfortable sofa bed, torturing herself hour after hour by looking at the photo Sisle Park had sent them.

"We've got nothing to go on but the runners and the freight elevator, Carl. There's just nothing else. Where did we go wrong with this investigation? I just don't get it. Would it have been different without corona?"

"It would have been different if it hadn't also been Christmas and then all this business with me."

Carl let his gaze wander out into the gray of the fading night. The sun would soon rise with its faint December light and threaten the arrival of the day on which the unspeakable would happen. Two hostages, one a dear friend, were unlikely to see another nightfall when the sun disappeared again below the horizon.

Carl looked at his watch for the fiftieth time as it greedily ticked toward the end. The time was now eight fifteen a.m., and the man from Åbenrå still had not called back.

Then he called Marcus Jacobsen's private number from his own phone.

The chief of homicide sounded drowsy, but he became fully alert the moment he heard who was calling.

"I wouldn't have expected this of you, Marcus," said Carl.

"Ditto, Carl."

Carl's head fell toward his chest. "Marcus! You know everyone is innocent until proven guilty. Isn't that what we all had hammered into us at police academy and constantly ever since?"

"Yes, but we've found your fingerprints on many of the banknotes from the suitcase, Carl."

"So I heard. But have you—the man who was our best detective back in the day—not even considered that Anker could have planted them there?"

"Why on earth would he have done that?"

"Don't you think you should be able to work that one out yourself? But how many banknotes did you find Anker's fingerprints on?"

"On enough, I imagine."

"On enough? Thanks for the definitive answer. But I'll tell you this much—you've obstructed our investigation in Department Q with this false accusation, and you'll come to regret it if things end badly. In a few hours, Maurits van Bierbek is going to die, and for your information, Sisle Park has also taken Gordon hostage."

"Yes, we know. When we put out a warrant for her arrest, she sent us a photo where we could see them sitting in the room. We're doing everything we can to find them."

"There's also a huge risk that she'll kill Gordon. Have you thought about that?"

"We don't think that's likely. It doesn't fit with her profile. We have a team of psychologists working on it."

"I see. Well, seeing as you know all that, we could give you a helping hand. Don't you think that would be a good idea? Maybe also for Maurits van Bierbek's sake—and his family's."

"You're trying to make a deal. I know you, Carl, and the answer is no. You won't get any immunity. We're going to arrest you the minute we locate you regardless of what you offer."

Carl was suddenly aware that Marcus was talking more slowly than usual. He was attempting to anticipate what Carl would say and already question it before Carl had even had a chance to respond. And he knew that Carl would protest and argue, keeping the clock ticking. He knew it!

"You're not at home at all, are you, Marcus? Are you working? Do you have someone sitting next to you just now trying to trace where I am?"

"Of course I'm at ho——"

Carl terminated the call straightaway and looked at the stopwatch. It had not taken more than two minutes. There was no way they could have completed the trace.

"You need to eat something, Carl. The rest of us can't think with your stomach rumbling so much." Assad already had a plate of food ready. It was leftovers from the Christmas dinner Laura had put out for them the night before. And even though Assad had heated it up, the last thing Carl wanted to eat on an empty stomach was dry duck and roast pork with the corners turned up.

"I can't eat anything just now, Assad. Maybe a bit later."

Then Laura's phone rang in his pocket. It was the manager from the factory in Åbenrå.

"Yes!" shouted Carl by way of answer.

"Sorry to ring so early." The man sounded genuinely guilty. Early? When the hell did people in Åbenrå get up?

"Have you found anything? Tell me you have!"

"Yes. It's still not clear where the runners were installed, but I can see that the job was booked by an Adam Holme and carried out on October fifteenth and sixteenth, 2016, by a fitter from a company we no longer work with. I thought maybe you could call this Adam Holme. I've got his number here."

No, no, no, raced through Carl's head. They were running out of time.

"What was the name of the fitter. Do you have it?"

"No, but I can give you the number of the company where he worked. But why don't you just call Adam Holme?"

"Because the man is currently lying totally burned to a cinder on a slab with forensics next to his wife. That's why. But thanks, we don't have much time."

He took the number of the installation company, slammed the phone on the table, and swore.

"Rose!" he shouted. "Quick! Get me everything you can on an installation company called Lang and Sons. They're based in Vanløse." He turned to Assad. "I will have something to eat now."

He looked at the congealed gravy and was reminded of the psychiatric hospital in Brønderslev just down the road from his parents' house. His mother had worked there at one time as a cook, and there was often leftover gravy.

"Lang and Sons was declared bankrupt in 2019," said Rose. "It was reestablished last year under the name Lang's Sons. I've got the number here for a Sigurd Lang, who is the current CEO."

He dialed the number immediately. "Rose, you call someone else from the company. We simply have to get somewhere with this lead."

The telephone rang at the other end for what seemed like an eternity before going to voicemail.

"Any luck, Rose?" he shouted.

"Voicemail. Closed for the Christmas holidays. Opens again January fourth."

"God damn it!" he exclaimed, deciding against the gravy. "Find me the private address for the CEO and we'll drive there."

"There is no address!"

"Sigurd Lang. How many people have that name? It can't be that hard to find."

"I'll call someone called Gerda Lang, who lives in Hvidovre. Maybe she knows him," she answered.

God, let her know him, thought Carl.

A minute later and Rose was talking to someone. "Yes, yes, yes!" she said excitedly. "Yes, yes, yes!"

When she hung up, she turned to Carl and Assad.

"Gerda is the mother of the three sons who took over the company, and she was able to confirm that they definitely hadn't fitted those runners because the company did a different sort of work altogether. And she knows that because she was the one running the company for the last few years while her husband was ill and until he died. That sort of work was something they outsourced to two Polish guys who traveled around doing whatever available work there was from various companies who needed fitters."

Carl felt his blood pressure increasing. Casual workers from Poland? Were they not all Catholics and so must have long since traveled home for the holidays to celebrate with their families in Wrocław or Katowice or wherever the hell they came from?

He put his hand to his head. "You didn't happen to get any contact details for those two, did you?"

"Yeah. One of them lives here in Denmark. His name is Jurek Jasinski and he lives in—"

There was a crash, and they both turned to face Assad, who was standing with his hands empty, a broken plate in front of him and gravy over both his shoes.

"Say that name again, Rose." His eyes had never bulged so much before. A few millimeters more and they would pop out.

"Jurek Jasinski, he lives in—"

"Come on, you two," he insisted, and he left a trail of gravy leading to the terrace door.

Assad leafed through his notebook while Carl put Victoria's Alfa Romeo through its paces.

"Jurek Jasinski is the same man I called yesterday and asked about the metal chairs. Unbelievable. I originally talked to him on December seventh to get more information about Oleg Dudek. You remember, the one whose hands were chopped off in one of his machines. He did tell me back then that he'd been forced to try his luck in Copenhagen when he was fired, but I never found out what he did."

Carl could hardly think.

"Nobody could have known that a Maurits van Bierbek would be kidnapped five days after your meeting with this guy, Assad. So stop looking so worried," said Rose.

"I could've asked him what he did after his time with Oleg Dudek!"

"What good would that have done? Gerda Lang told us herself that he and the other Polish guy only did work for them for a short time. He's probably worked at numerous places since then."

"Why the hell isn't he answering his phone?" grunted Carl. "If he's gone to Poland for Christmas, I'm going to explode."

"He might well have, Carl. He was very relaxed about corona. None of us wore a face mask when I was there. On the other hand, he was drunk as a punk when I called to ask about the metal chairs."

All three of them sighed when they parked in front of the little yellow light-concrete house. No light behind even a single window. The front mat had been kicked halfway into the plant bed next to the door.

No car in the driveway and the mailbox was overflowing with junk mail, which had probably been sticking out there for days in the icy, windy weather.

They rang the doorbell, banged on the door, peered through the widows. Nothing.

It was only when they were sitting back in the car and Carl had started the engine with a lump in his throat so big that he had to keep trying to swallow it that Rose noticed something.

"Stop!" she shouted, pointing at the front door. A disheveled figure of a man with greasy, bright red hair had emerged, wearing a half-open dressing gown and patterned underpants, and was standing looking at them drowsily.

63

SISLE

Boxing Day, Saturday, December 26, 2020

She woke up after a dreamless sleep and stretched contentedly while remembering where she was and why she was lying on a concrete floor.

The two figures a little distance from her were both slumped forward on the chairs. The first one with half-closed eyes, the second apparently unconscious.

She looked at her watch and was puzzled. Was it really eleven thirty? She had not slept so long for years.

Well, well, she said to herself. But then the previous day had been satisfactory. She had put a permanent end to a chapter in her life that was no longer tenable, and, in a moment, she would look online to see what was written about the fire and, hopefully, also see the names of the victims.

"Sad for them, but I had warned them," she said, standing up with the blanket she had slept on in her hand.

She turned to the table and looked at the various concoctions. The injections were ready, the drip on the drip stand, and the saline solution in the bottle. The rest would just be a formality.

"Dear God," she said. "I thank you for the clarity you have given me. For having been your just vessel in an age where Satan reigns on earth. Thank you for giving me strength and teaching me about the deception of man. Thank you for giving me the ability to see falsehood when I meet it. Some say that egoism should be forgiven because there is no cure. But you and I know better. There is a cure, and that cure is death."

She turned around and stretched her arms above her head. "Here before me sit two wretched souls in whom Satan resides. They are at the mercy of your judgment with me as your vessel. And I will lead them until they have understood their sacrilege so they can face death and hell without any doubt, and with the full remorse you deserve."

She stepped closer and bent down toward Gordon Taylor's exhausted body.

"You're awake, Gordon. That's good. You'll be my witness of truth that everything takes place in a dignified manner."

He raised his face toward her. He was so full of anger that his lips were trembling.

"I will shortly give you both a small drip that will wake you up. Just a quick injection to make the body function as long as I need it to. I'll start with Maurits. It is after all for his sake that we're here today. He looks like he could do with a little pick-me-up."

Then she walked over to the table and grabbed the drip stand. There was no doubting that the solution would wake van Bierbek in seconds. Even Franco Svendsen, when he was extremely close to death, had been quickly but temporarily revitalized. It had been so effective in fact that he had started begging for his life and imploring for mercy. It had been very pleasing, and she wanted it to be just the same with van Bierbek.

She felt Gordon Taylor's eyes killing her with every step she took, and, when she passed him, she heard him mumble but could not make out what he said.

The needle glided into the largest vein on the back of Maurits's hand as if his skin were butter. The skinnier his body had become, the more visible his veins were, and Sisle was particularly happy with this side effect. Everything had to go smoothly, even this preparation stage.

She squatted down in front of his face and waited. The almost imperceptible movement of his eyelids should improve greatly within less than a minute. But when a minute had gone by and there was no visible improvement, she increased the speed of the drip.

She thought she detected a hint of a sigh after a few minutes, but she did not like it. It had never taken this long before.

"Come on, Maurits," she insisted, slapping him across the cheek.

"Bitch," came a whisper behind her.

She spun around on her toes and caught Gordon's eye.

"Are you talking to me?" she asked.

"Yes, you bitch," he said again very weakly.

Sisle stood up.

"Perhaps you're sitting there under the illusion that you're going to get off. But, Gordon Taylor, you've slandered me with your satanic and scornful words, and for that you'll share the same fate as Maurits. Do you understand what I'm saying?"

He nodded, but his expression was unchanging. No visible regret, no fear.

Now Maurits began to hyperventilate with short, ineffective gasps. Perhaps she had already given him more than she should have. She stood up quickly and pressed the clamp on the tube so the drip stopped running.

"Maurits, wake up!" she shouted, and she shook him so his head dangled from his neck. He seemed to be having an allergic reaction, but she did not know what to do about it.

She squatted down next to him again, took his hand in hers, and began to stroke it as if he were a child who would not stop crying.

"There, there, Maurits. I know you can hear me. Don't be scared. There, there!"

She continued this way for a long time while the man behind her ceaselessly whispered, "Bitch." It made her think of Adam and how he used to be the one who could keep order.

"But I don't need him anymore," she said aloud, and she began stroking Maurits's hair.

"You must hear what I have to say, Maurits. It's important. I've prepared it so well, so you simply have to."

Then she took out her piece of paper and began reading aloud while taking van Bierbek's hand and stroking it again.

When it was clear that there was no sign of life coming from him, she stopped with her speech.

"It's Satan poking his horned face between us," she said, looking up at the ceiling.

"Make him stop, O God, and let Maurits come back to this place where we are. Back to the use of his senses. Back to receive his sentence."

After almost half an hour, when the time had passed midnight, Sisle sensed for the first time in all these years that the devil was getting the better of her. She had never felt his toxic breath so close. She turned to Gordon, sitting there with his half-closed eyes, and knew that the devil was residing in him.

She pulled out the needle from Maurits and within half a minute had stuck it in Gordon's hand behind his back. He stretched his fingers in an effort to defend himself, but his efforts were weakening, so it was hopeless.

This time it took less than a minute. Gordon's eyes opened wide, he coughed and cleared his throat. He took deep, jolted breaths, and with each new inhalation his strength and willpower returned.

Despite the cable ties around his ankles, his legs were moving like drumsticks. His knees were jerking up and down, and he was now breathing like someone who had held their breath too long underwater and was finally fighting for air.

"Well done, Gordon Taylor. Now I know it works." She patted him on the cheek, pulled the needle out, and placed it back in Maurits.

"Your turn, Maurits," she said, checking the pulse on his neck while looking at her watch and counting.

The pulse was definitely weak, but his heartbeat was regular, and it looked like a little color was returning to his cheeks. Perhaps it would just take half an hour, in which case they would simply have to wait.

"Leave us alone," said the voice behind her. It sounded clear and determined.

"Shut up! If you carry on, I can just as easily sedate you again, Gordon Taylor."

"Leave us alone and disappear. Make a run for it, hide in the jungle on the other side of the planet, or you'll come to regret it."

She smiled. It was actually very amusing to end people's lives in this atmosphere. It was new for her.

"You're being hunted, Sisle Park. And when you're caught, there will be no mercy for you. You do know that, don't you? There's no going back to your normal life."

She shook her head indulgently. "Maybe you think that Department Q has hurt me, but it's quite the opposite. You've helped me make some important decisions. When you're sitting cold and stiff with your friend here, I have every intention of following your advice. So thank you."

"I hope you rot in the jungle, you monster. But they'll find you if you haven't already decomposed before then."

She laughed. "My dear friend, everything is ready. A private plane to Poland and from there a rented car to Brussels, from where there is a direct flight to Nigeria. A completely immoral and corrupt country more than happy to welcome multimillionaires with the right sort of passport in their pocket. And the country is huge, with endless opportunities. You'll see, there's a very interesting life waiting for me."

She could see it in him. His brain was not yet quite ready to understand the essence of what she told him. Would she continue her crusade on the other side of the world? Was she going to start killing on foreign ground?

"I can see you're thinking so hard it hurts, Gordon. But the answer is simple. Yes, I'll continue."

He sighed deeply. His thin face radiated nothing but powerlessness. He was right where she wanted him.

"Everything you're doing is blasphemy," he said hoarsely. "You're blaspheming against the God you pray to. Don't you know the Ten Commandments, Sisle Park? You obviously don't, because you're breaking them."

"Shhhh. Be quiet. Can't you hear? Maurits is breathing heavier now."

"You shall have no other gods before me. But your god is yourself. You shall not take the name of the Lord your God in vain. But you do it constantly. Keep the Sabbath day holy. Yet you killed both Palle Rasmussen and Franco Svendsen on a Sunday. You shall not kill! Do you need me to say it twice, Sisle? YOU SHALL NOT KILL!"

"Ah, I can hear you've learned your little catechism. But think about all the times God chose His servants to kill. I am one of His angels on earth who—"

Then Maurits van Bierbek coughed faintly.

"Are you with us, Maurits?" she said, slapping him across the cheek.

"Mmmm," he answered.

She resolutely walked down to the table and filled the two syringes with the deadly fluid. It looked so innocent, as clear as water, so refreshing.

She then attached the thick tube to the large container with the saline solution. When they were both dead, she would stick the tube as far down their throats as she could—and there was at least three to four liters of concentrated saline solution for each of them. Not exactly a final embalming, but there was nothing wrong with the symbolism. And finally she would sprinkle a little pile of salt on the floor in front of each chair.

In a moment, Maurits would look at her with more awareness. Then she would give him a little drop more from the drip and read her death sentence to him.

And then she could move on to her next victim.

And in an hour, she would be gone.

64

CARL

Boxing Day, Saturday, December 26, 2020

Jurek Jasinski had been drinking heavily since December twenty-third because "his woman" had been annoying him. One and a half bottles of 88 percent Balkan 176° vodka had a hell of an effect, and Jurek loved it.

After they had been arguing for over a week, Jurek could not take it anymore and went to work on the ten elegant and slender bottles that he had otherwise planned should see him through the next year.

By the following day, she had already had enough and left Jurek to his own fate, taking the train to Horsens, where her sister lived with her husband.

That was the gist of Jurek's explanation of why he had not immediately reacted to the heavy knocking on his door.

He was unsteady on his feet when he led them into a living room that reeked of sweat, cigarettes, and booze.

"Would you like one?" he smiled cheekily, not waiting for a reply before he downed a shot himself. He was clearly a seasoned drinker.

"I suppose you remember me, Jurek?" asked Assad.

Jurek nodded and laughed so hard the spit sprayed from his mouth. "Our little talk about metal chairs and Oleg Dudek. What more do you want to know about that bastard?"

"Have a look at this photo." Assad held Sisle Park's photo of the two hostages up in front of him. "Don't look at them. Look at the runners on the ceiling." Then he gave him a new photo where the runners had been enlarged.

"What the hell is that?" He rubbed his sleepy eyes and fumbled for a pair of glasses lying between cigarette butts and used kitchen towels.

"Don't look at the men. Look at the runners, Jurek. Isn't it true that you fitted them with a colleague a few years ago?"

"A few years ago?" Now he looked like someone who needed something even stronger than Balkan 176° to give him a kick start.

"It was definitely before 2017," said Assad. "Our guess is 2016 or before."

"Those runners?" He pointed with a nicotine-stained finger directly at them. "Let me tell you why I remember them. They were positioned too bloody close together. If you needed them for any sort of hoisting, why the hell would they be so close together?"

Carl held his breath for a moment. "You recognize them?" he asked with his pulse racing.

"Bloody stupid to place them so close together," he slurred. Now they just had to get his memory up to full speed.

"We need to know immediately where you installed them, Jurek. We don't have the address, and if we don't get it, the two men in the photo will very soon be dead." Assad hesitated and sighed. "If it isn't already too late."

"Maybe they deserve it?" Jurek grinned.

"One of them is our man, so no, they don't both deserve it. But come on! Do you know where it is?" asked Carl, very tempted to grab the collar of Jurek's dressing gown and shake the booze out of him. But then Rose tried her hand.

"You're a handsome man, Jurek. And I'm sure your wife is a fool to let you sit here alone over Christmas. But now that she's gone, how would you like to earn a thousand kroner so you can keep drinking until she comes back? What do you say?" She waved the banknote in front of his face.

"What are you asking me to do?" he grumbled.

"Tell us where you installed those runners. Think as hard as you can!"

He leaned forward with his hands folded over his chest, his boozy breath coming out in a thick wave that almost knocked Assad over.

"Where was it, where was it? *Kurwa, kurwa!*" He rubbed his temples and shook his head as if that might help his inner timeline fall into place.

"Was it in Copenhagen?" asked Rose, waving the banknote.

He nodded.

"It took us three days to install them because the bitch who hired us sent us home after a couple of hours every day and because the concrete in the ceiling was pure *gówno*."

"*Gówno?*"

"Shit; don't you speak Polish? It was such hard *gówno* that we——"

"*Where*, Jurek? *Where?* That's all we need to know," insisted Rose. She started to move the banknote back toward her purse.

"Hold on! It was just outside Copenhagen, northbound on the motorway. It was odd because the building wasn't finished. There was an elevator and several floors belowground, but only one floor aboveground. You would've thought it was in Warsaw back when the Russians were there—they also left half-finished buildings."

Rose slammed the banknote on his forehead. "*How* far up the motorway? Was it in the direction of Helsingør or Hillerød? *Think*, man!"

"You can't drive this fast," said Assad. "This isn't a patrol car."

"No, but it's functioning as one today," said Carl.

"That's what you think, but the police up here won't agree. They'll stop us for going 175 kilometers an hour in an Alpha Romeo without a siren on the roof. They'll arrest you, Carl, so slow down."

Rose patted Carl's shoulder from the back seat. "Just step on it, Carl. Assad is right, but . . ."

Carl was sweating. They had a rough idea about where the building was located and what it had looked like five years ago. But what if it had been finished in the meantime? Jurek Jasinski had described a single white concrete building opposite the one they were looking for and where he and his partner had used the toilet a few times. Unfortunately, that building had no distinguishing features.

"You can see it from the motorway—you can't miss it," he had said, and he got his thousand kroner.

"I still can't grasp how lucky it was that Assad already knew the man. What are the odds?" said Rose.

"When there are outside workers involved, anything can happen," said Assad. "Don't you know the story about the herd of camels that wanted to adopt a donkey because they thought it would make them more interesting? Oh, you don't? Well, they found the—"

"LOOK, CARL!" shouted Rose. "In there. Look at the building. It almost looks like ground zero. Look! It's built up higher on one side than the other."

"Was that how he described it?" Carl was unsure. He could not recognize the description.

"What else could it be? It's the first one like that on this whole stretch of the motorway. Turn off, Carl. Hurry up, you can make it."

"I'll tell you the donkey story some other time, Carl," said Assad. "I agree with Rose. It looks like the one Jurek described."

Carl took the exit with screeching tires and drove back into the industrial park.

"Can you see it? I can't!" said Carl, almost in a panic. There were at least twenty buildings in front of him that although different looked more or less the same to him. And various roads meandered in and out between the buildings without any apparent planning. It was the type of industrial park that had spread since the sixties and finally become a victim of its own ugliness.

"Can you tell me why a building would be left unfinished in this area?" asked Carl while trying one side road after another.

"Bad building materials can stop any building project," answered Assad.

"Just like that newly built high-rise out on Amager where the concrete foundations apparently can't bear all the floors," added Rose.

"Yes, that or the money just ran out," suggested Assad.

"What about your list of Sisle's properties, Assad? Does she have any vested interests in any properties out here?" asked Carl.

Assad shook his head. "I've already checked that, Carl, and she doesn't. But she could have rented it."

Carl shuddered. "Who apart from a psychopath like Sisle Park would rent a place like that with the sole purpose of killing?"

"Over there to the right, Carl" said Rose, pointing.

He could see it now. A concrete building where the ground floor appeared to be fully finished with doors and windows but otherwise seemed totally abandoned. It was surrounded by a large parking lot, where a sign advertised that you could rent a parking spot here on an annual basis. The price for standard parking was five thousand kroner a year. Because it was the holidays, there were no cars. But being in the middle of the industrial park, there was no doubt that it would be packed on workdays. Carl calculated that if all the spaces were rented out, it would bring in at least three quarters of a million. Not a bad business.

"Oh, noooo!" exclaimed Assad despairingly. "Now I get it. This *is* owned by Sisle. It's just that it was sold to her as a parking lot. It didn't dawn on me that there could be a building like this in the middle of a parking lot. If only I'd checked it."

No wonder he looked so despondent.

Carl stopped in front of the main entrance. If it had not been for the ten steps up, he would have crashed the car straight through the door.

Rose ran up the steps and tried the door, but of course it was locked.

"There might be an alarm," shouted Carl. "If we break into the building, she'll know about it."

"Yes, *if* she's inside the building. We don't know that for sure."

"No. If only we could see where the elevator is at the moment, we'd know. If it's still down there, it's likely that she is too," said Carl.

Assad pointed upward. "Look up there!"

They all looked at the southern wall rising up above the flat concrete roof. It was the only indication that the building had originally been intended to have more floors. The building would appear one floor higher from the south side, but from where they were standing it was plainly an illusion, much like a Hollywood movie set.

"What are we looking at, Assad?"

"We can't tell from down here why that wall was constructed, but don't you think the elevator tower was built at the same time?"

They all had the same thought and ran around to the other side of the building.

"How do you get up there?" asked Rose. The south wall certainly did not offer any solution to that problem, so they continued running around the building and ended up in something resembling a scrap-yard.

The entire area between the building and the perimeter fence ten meters away was covered in concrete blocks, moldy insulation material, rotten Euro-pallets, rusty T-irons, and barbed wire mixed in with random junk in a heap almost two meters high. A true testimony to the sloppy developer who had been in charge of the project.

"We won't get through this way, Assad!" shouted Carl. But like a hound on the scent, Assad was already gone.

Carl stopped for a moment and scanned around.

"Where did he go? Can you see him, Rose?" he asked.

She shook her head and looked at her watch with a worried expression. "Can we please call for reinforcements now, Carl? We *have* to get in there!"

Carl nodded and took out his phone. So this was the end of the line for him. *My last moment of freedom*, he thought when he was about to dial. But then he heard Assad shouting at them from above that he had made it up onto the roof.

"You have to pull the two pallets aside that are leaning up against each other. You're only four or five meters away from them, Carl."

Carl looked up and saw Assad peeking over the edge of the roof.

"Yes, that way," said Assad, pointing. "The elevator down on the ground floor is bolted shut. But you can just take the stairs up to the roof. The door to this floor is open, and from up here it looks like the elevator is in use. The problem is that it's locked."

All three of them were standing on the roof looking at the lock on the elevator. It was an ordinary lock that would probably just have to be turned to call the elevator and then the door would open automatically. But how would they open it without the key?

They looked intently around the concrete roof. There were at least twenty pallets strewn around with bags of hardened concrete and a lot of steel reinforcements. The building project must have been abandoned from one day to the next. A typical consequence for a developer who had bitten off more than they could chew and gone bankrupt.

"There has to be something up here we can jam into the lock," said Assad. But Rose looked doubtful.

"If we managed to do that, Assad, which I doubt we can, the elevator would start moving up and Sisle would be alerted."

Carl agreed with her, but what other choice did they have?

"If Maurits and Gordon are still alive, we'll have to take that risk. Maybe she won't do anything drastic when she knows that she's about to be caught."

"Maybe," huffed Rose. "Now I just wish that at least one of us was armed. What do we have to stop her with if we do make it down there and she's waiting for us?"

"These," said Assad, who was standing a couple of meters from them, holding a small bundle of sharp steel rebar cutoffs.

"Have you found anything we can wrench the lock open with, Assad? Otherwise those poles won't be of much help."

"Yes, here," he said, triumphantly holding up a tool belt.

He threw the belt to Carl, who fumbled in the different pockets without finding much except an empty packet of candy and a cigarette packet with one cigarette left in it.

"There's nothing in here, Assad."

Assad handed the steel poles to Carl and took the belt. "You can't see the wood for the treetops, Carl. Look at this!"

He held the belt buckle in front of Carl's face and pointed at the prong designed to go through the holes in the belt.

"Stainless steel, good quality," he said, pointing at the brand. Then he picked up a concrete block from the floor and hammered the point of the prong into the lock. "Sometimes it works and sometimes it doesn't," he said nervously. He waited for a moment, looking up at the elevator's motor, which was not reacting. Then he took a deep breath, grabbed the belt buckle, and twisted it. A few seconds later it was clear that this also did not work, so Carl took out his phone again to call for reinforcements.

"Wait! I'm not finished," said Assad, wondering if Carl had really expected that the simple sound of metal against metal was all it took to set the motor going with a gentle hum.

"I think it's ready now," said Assad, slightly surprised, putting his hand in his pocket. The bunch of keys he pulled out was nothing special to the untrained eye, but Assad took off one particular key and showed it to Rose and Carl.

"This is not a bump key, but it's close enough. You know the principle. A key with regular small teeth that you stick in the lock and gently tap before quickly turning it to the right so that the pins move to the side."

They nodded tentatively.

"But since I don't have one of those, I'll give this a try instead. Look, the teeth are not very long. It was for a mailbox in one of the places I lived before my family came back."

He gently stuck it in the lock.

"I was just checking before to see if the pins were loose, and they are now."

Carl held his breath as Assad gently tapped it a couple of times and tried to twist it immediately after.

When he had tried quite a few times without luck and was beginning to sweat, Carl turned on his phone and called Marcus Jacobsen.

"What's up, Carl?" came the immediate answer. "Are you ready to turn yourself in?"

"Yes, I don't have any choice," he answered.

"YES!" shouted Rose as Assad in that moment managed to turn the key, and the motor above them started humming.

"But it won't be just now, Marcus, so take care." And while the relays clicked from deep down and the elevator worked its way up, he turned off the phone and threw it out over the edge into the scrap heap down below.

65

SISLE/CARL

Boxing Day, Saturday, December 26, 2020

Sisle gave a start when she heard the relay click and the elevator going up.

Equal measure of confusion and doubt made her freeze momentarily. Was there a fault with the elevator—and if there was, how could she stop it? She leaped away from the table and kept pressing the elevator button. It *had* to be a fault, but if it went all the way to the top before stopping, would she be able to call it back down?

She pushed and pushed but to no avail.

She took a step back. If this was not a fault on the elevator control, it meant there was someone up there waiting for it. But who?

I set the house on fire, and I closed Debora's eyes. But did I check if Adam still had a pulse? she tried to recall. She was unsure.

Was it really possible that Adam had survived the blow? And was it possible that he had woken up in time before the flames consumed all the oxygen in the room?

Sisle put her ear to the elevator door. Adam was the only other person in the world who knew about this place and that she would be here just now. They had found the place together and no one—not even Debora—was told where it was. When Sisle drove out here, she *never* parked in her own parking lot. Better to walk five hundred meters and keep an eye out before running to the back of the building through the scrap heap and into the ground floor.

But despite her precautions, could it still be someone from one of the neighboring buildings? No, that was impossible. And calling the elevator also required a key, and who had that apart from her? Only Adam.

He'll kill me if he gets the chance, she thought. He had so much to avenge and was so good at taking lives. She was sure it must be him.

Sisle turned to the two men. Gordon Taylor was closest to her and she noticed the smirk on his face. He must have grasped what was about to happen.

"They're coming now," said Gordon, turning halfway around toward his fellow hostage. "Maurits, listen! They're coming to save us now. I knew it." He began laughing hysterically, and Sisle was disgusted. She had always loathed when people facing their fate made a scene. Why not just accept your fate with dignity?

"Shut up, Gordon Taylor, or I'll make you."

Maybe he did not understand that a battle is not won until your opponent has given up. It certainly wiped the smile off his face when she succeeded in pushing the heavy table in front of the elevator door.

"I'll deal with you two first, and then I can give Adam a shot with one of the used syringes. Thankfully, there's enough in them for the three of you. I'll stick the syringe in him the very moment he manages to push the table aside. Don't doubt that. So, dear friends, all in all you'll be an entire team on your way to hell."

The syringes were ready to use. She checked them quickly and then went over to place one on the floor in front of each man. Now all she needed to do was read the sentence and complete the ritual. Due to the circumstances, it would have to be quick. But as the clicks from the relays reminded her that Adam would be on this floor in less than a minute, this was a case of force majeure.

She stepped over to Maurits van Bierbek and looked him in the eye. There was no doubt he knew what was about to happen, but he had already given up.

"Maurits van Bierbek, you have lived a life of sin. You have in every imaginable way violated the rules and order that God in Heaven created for us humans to live by. Again and again, you have embodied the fall that since the Garden of Eden has tainted humanity. And now it is time for you to die, Maurits van Bierbek."

"WE'RE IN HERE! HELP!" shouted Gordon behind her at the top of his lungs. She had also heard the metallic sound from the elevator when it reached the bottom of the shaft, and the elevator automatically tried to open with a couple of bumps against the table.

Keep trying, Adam. I'll come to you when you manage to force it open, she thought.

"GORDON!" shouted an unexpected female voice, which made him scream with excitement and shout back for them to hurry up.

Sisle was shocked. Not because of the surprise, not because she had been caught red-handed. She was shocked because she had no idea what to do. What was her emergency plan?

She turned back to Maurits van Bierbek, who had tilted his head with an expression of nothing but sorrow.

"Maurits van Bierbek, do you repent your life and actions?" she asked, bringing the syringe closer to his heart.

"STOP IT, SISLE!" shouted Gordon behind her. "In the name of God, stop it!"

"In the name of God?" She smiled while Gordon kept shouting behind her. "In the name of God, I will follow my calling." She leaned forward and plunged the syringe into van Bierbek's chest with the full force of her weight.

"NOOOOO!" shouted Gordon.

Van Bierbek spasmed and opened his eyes wide. The pain of the thick needle plunged into the heart had a tendency to dumbfound her victims momentarily. Sisle recognized it from the two previous times.

"Maurits van Bierbek, thank your creator for the years he gave you to live on this earth," she said and injected the liquid.

The following seconds were chaotic. Van Bierbek cramped up and fell sideways from the chair with the chains rattling over him. Gordon screamed hysterically, and there were sounds of people shouting and knocking on the elevator door, which increased as the table slowly inched away.

And as Maurits van Bierbek's life slowly ebbed, his mouth frothing and his body convulsing, she turned to Gordon Taylor and bent down to pick up the syringe by his feet.

"WHY?" he screamed.

She spun around to face the elevator door and the table that suddenly tilted and fell over with a bang, sending the container of saline solution smashing against the floor, the liquid splashing everywhere.

The three devils from Department Q pushed their way out as one, each holding a steel pole, which they clearly intended to fight her with. The Middle Eastern one was closest and held the pole above his head, evidently intent on using it.

She breathed deeply and pointed the syringe at Gordon Taylor's heart. She was overcome by a strange feeling of peace. Was she not still the one with the upper hand?

"If you throw those poles at me, I'll plunge this in your friend's heart. Look what it'll do to him," she said with a nod to Maurits van Bierbek's final gasps for air.

"Put down the poles and stand against the far wall. If you stay calm, I'll cut Gordon loose and take him with me up in the elevator. But if you make even a single move, I'll inject him. And if he puts up a fight, I'll also inject him. You know I'm serious."

She gave them a threatening look, but they did not move. Then she pressed the needle a little into Gordon directly below his breastbone, and Gordon's scream made Carl and the woman drop their poles. But the third did not.

The woman in the group tried to talk him around, but he remained steadfast.

"Don't, Assad," moaned Gordon.

"No, she'll kill you in the elevator, Gordon. Believe me," said the man who must be Assad.

Sisle laughed. "You don't have much faith in me, do you, little man?"

Carl Mørck took a step forward.

"You won't kill him—and that's because he's innocent. Isn't that right, Sisle?"

She did not react.

"But you are an angel of justice, aren't you?"

"I'm an angel of vengeance and justice. Chosen by God."

"Then prove it, because I don't believe you," he said. "You killed a small boy and his name was Max. Today he would've been around Gordon's age, and, like Gordon, he was completely innocent. You also indirectly killed his mother, Maja. And she wasn't guilty either. Finally, you killed Pauline Rasmussen and, just like the other two, she was also innocent. So prove to me that you have God on your side and I'll listen to your demands."

"I'm not accountable to you, only to God, and He's marked me for all eternity," she said, pressing the needle a little deeper into Gordon.

Gordon's screams made the Department Q woman react. "Can we see your mark, Sisle? Then we'll leave you alone."

Sisle smiled. Since she had been discharged from the burns unit, only that bastard Palle Rasmussen had seen it. They had met each other and she had flirted with him to gain his trust. And without any warning or hesitation, he had ripped her blouse clean open.

He had gasped when he saw the scars, and Sisle had punched him hard. To her surprise, he had enjoyed both the scars and the punch.

"The mark that God has given me is here," she said, unbuttoning her blouse. The three of them were fixated on her body, and she enjoyed how their eyes caressed it. She always reacted the same when she saw herself naked in the mirror.

The rough white and red scars that dug their way into the flesh of most of her upper body were the suffering, and the middle of the scar that formed an unharmed cross was God's mercy. Could they not see that? Yes, she had been burned by lightning, but it had been sent directly from God's outstretched finger of justice. A holy symbol of her invincibility and mission.

She did not notice Assad tossing the pole, but she felt it penetrating through her lower back, throwing her to the ground. She immediately tried to get up but sensed it was futile.

Sisle looked down at herself and saw the pole protruding from her at one end, while the other end had penetrated Maurits van Bierbek's dead body as she fell. In other words, she was nailed to her own victim.

She watched as Assad rushed over and then squatted next to her while the woman cut her exhausted colleague loose.

"For the rest of your life you'll feel the punishment dealt by God to his false prophets," said Carl Mørck. "You'll be incarcerated in a place where you can't influence others with your sick ideas. You'll be isolated from the world until you can't remember it anymore. And every day you will pray for God's forgiveness for your madness, but he will never grant it, Sisle Park. You can count on that."

Sisle smiled. How wrong they were, these ignorant, stupid people. How pathetic and small. No mission, no aim. No fear of God and no hope of the salvation that was hers. The time had come for her to reap; finally, with peace of mind, she would be free from this unbearable and godless world. She raised her arm with a firm grip on the syringe. The needle had broken, and most of it was probably lodged under Gordon Taylor's breastbone, but it was still long enough for its intended purpose.

"Drop it," said Assad, quick-witted enough to take a step backward so she could not plunge it into his leg.

"None of your prophesies will come true, Carl Mørck. God is awaiting me, and he will take care of me for all eternity."

Then she closed her eyes, lifted her arm as high as she could, and plunged the syringe directly into the exposed skin above her heart where the white cross was visible.

When she pressed the shaft down to the bottom, everything inside her opened.

EPILOGUE

CARL

Boxing Day, Saturday, December 26, 2020

"**You need to** get going, Carl," said Rose. "Assad and I will call for a cab and go to the hospital to get Gordon checked out."

Carl looked at their pale colleague sitting there with his head between his knees, trying to overcome the shock and all the torment. It would take time before he was himself again. If ever.

Carl tentatively laid a hand on his back. "You did well, Gordon. It's over now. After all this, you deserve a few weeks' leave."

Apart from being exhausted, there was no sign of weakness in his eyes when he lifted his head toward Carl.

"Hell no," he said. "With monsters like Sisle Park in the world, you won't get rid of me so easily."

"That's it, get back on the camel," said Assad.

Rose tried to smile, but it was hard. What was awaiting them now as members of Department Q?

"Get a few hours alone with Mona, Carl," she said. "We'll wait until we've gone over the crime scene with Marcus and his team before we say where you are. And make sure it isn't at your place. It's bound to still be under surveillance."

———

He turned off onto the motorway and continued away from the city with all sorts of feelings rushing through his mind.

It had been hard, and it still was. Missing his family, corona, Gordon's suffering, all the sad people, and now the man they had tried to save was lying dead on a concrete floor.

A few years back, he had had a panic attack brought on by the old case of the nail gun murders, and now that case was part of his reality again. He was being hunted. Would he never be free of it?

He scoffed at himself. *Part of his reality again*—what an understatement. What was his reality? That he was going to jail? That he was currently on his way to the van Bierbek family home in Gammel Holte to give them the worst news anyone could ever receive?

He had done it before. Breaking a heart with the news that a loved one was dead. Traffic accidents, disasters, suicide, and now murder.

His steps up to the house felt heavy and depressing, and the situation was not improved when it was Laura and her little sister who opened the door.

He did not manage to say a word.

They knew straightaway.

Mona arrived a little later in the evening, and she helped Victoria and the children to calm down.

"You need to fight with all you've got, Carl," said Mona when they were finally alone. "I'll contact Hardy and we'll find out what he's got to say about it all. I'll let you know."

"What about Lucia, Mona? When will I see her?"

She smiled and looked at his red hair. "You're married to me now, and I'm no stranger to visiting prisons, so no doubt I'll be able to work it out, don't you think? But you'll have to wear a hat so you don't frighten her."

"Okay, and only *if* I have to go to prison."

"Yeah, if."

"Assad and Rose are still at the crime scene, so we can expect some-one here to arrest me anytime now," said Carl.

She nodded and held him.

After a few minutes, the walls around them were lit up with flashing blue lights and a sea of plainclothes colleagues came rushing toward the front door.

They did not wait to be invited in, and Marcus Jacobsen stepped forward toward him with Sniffer Dog and a multitude of faces Carl did not recognize behind him.

Marcus nodded to Mona and then briefly and reservedly to Carl.

"You solved the case and put an end to it all."

Carl nodded. "Yeah. We didn't manage to save van Bierbek's life, but we tried."

"Rose and Assad have explained everything to me, and we'll get back to it. In the meantime, we'd better get the formalities out of the way."

Carl nodded, and two men grabbed him and handcuffed his hands behind his back.

"Carl's innocent, Marcus. You ought to know that," said Mona.

Marcus Jacobsen smiled sarcastically, and at that moment Carl could have spat in his face. But he did not.

"Many things are possible, but hardly that," he said coldly, looking Carl straight in the eye.

"Carl Mørck. The time is nine seventeen a.m., and you're under arrest."

ACKNOWLEDGMENTS

Thank you to my wife and soulmate, Hanne, for her loving support and indispensable comments on the first draft. Thanks to Henning Kure for the big pat on the back. Thanks to Elisabeth Ahlefeldt-Laurvig for daily support, research, multitasking, and resourcefulness. Thanks also to Elsebeth Wæhrens, Eddie Kiran, Hanne Petersen, Micha Schmalstieg, Kes Adler-Olsen, Jesper Helbo, Sigrid Engeler, and Karlo Andersen for insightful early proofreading and suggestions. Thanks to my extremely thorough and versatile editor Lene Wissing at Politikens Forlag for her integrity and professionalism and ability to find solutions. Thanks to Lene Juul and Charlotte Weiss at Politikens Forlag for all manner of support and encouragement. Thanks to Charlotte Fournais for all her coordination efforts. Thanks to Tomas Henriksen for keeping a sensitive finger on the pulse of production and to Mogens Larsen at Nørhaven for opening doors. Thanks to Helle Skov Wacher for her PR work with the novel. Thanks to Louise Kønig for keeping us on track. Thanks to marketing director Pernille Weil and head of sales Pernille Hjorth for sending the novel out into the world. Thanks to proofreaders Jette Thillemann Wuff, Ane Horslund, and Louise Urth Olsen for their careful reading. Huge thanks to the rest of the team at Politikens Forlag for their invaluable work and for keeping the various processes running smoothly.

Thanks to Police Superintendent Leif Christensen for police-related corrections. Thanks to Rudi Urban Rasmussen and Sigrid Stavnem for important observations and for keeping the whole world turning. Thanks to Bobo Madsen, via Danmarks Insamlingen, for lending his name to one of the characters in the novel. Thanks to Olaf Slott-Petersen for once more creating a new and even better environment for writing in Barcelona. Thanks to the Danish National Police publicity manager Thomas Kristensen for coordination behind the scenes. Thanks to Superintendent Dannie Rise from Copenhagen Police for welcoming me to Teglholmen and updating my knowledge about police-related information. Thanks to Jesper Deis, Nicklas Josephsen, and Steffen Falch Larsen for ensuring that our writing workshop was ready in time. Thanks to Stine Bolther for a fantastic course in autumn 2020. Thanks to Tine Harden for once again creating a very special and evocative photographic starting point for the campaign, and thanks to Rie Kamp for allowing us the use of their great car-repair shop.

And finally, thanks to Ellie, who gave me the energy to write, and to whom the book is dedicated.

ABOUT THE AUTHOR

Jussi Adler-Olsen is Denmark's #1 crime writer and a *New York Times* bestselling author. His books routinely top the bestseller lists in Europe and have sold more than twenty-seven million copies around the world. His many prestigious worldwide crime-writing awards include the Barry Award and the Glass Key Award, also won by Henning Mankell, Jo Nesbø, and Stieg Larsson.